THE FLYING SORCERERS

Also edited by Peter Haining

THE WIZARDS OF ODD
TIMESCAPES

THE FLYING SORCERERS

More Comic Tales of Fantasy

Edited by
Peter Haining

SOUVENIR PRESS

First published 1997 by
Souvenir Press Ltd,
43 Great Russell Street, London WC1B 3PA
and simultaneously in Canada

ISBN 0 285 63388 0

Photoset by Rowland Phototypesetting Ltd,
Bury St Edmunds, Suffolk.
Printed in Great Britain by
Creative Print and Design Group (Wales), Ebbw Vale

So full of shapes is fancy,
That it alone is high fantastical.

William Shakespeare, *Twelfth Night*

CONTENTS

INTRODUCTION

Thirty years ago I first saw a memorable cartoon by Gahan Wilson, the American fantasy artist, whose jokes give expression to his macabre and wicked sense of humour. It shows a NASA spacecraft which has just landed and is surrounded by a circle of dancing Munchkins, those curious little folk who feature in *The Wizard of Oz*. Two slightly bemused astronauts are peering out from the escape hatch at the little men and also at a pair of black-clad legs in pointed, buckled shoes that clearly belong to a body which has been crushed by the descending spacecraft. The caption explains that the Munchkins are singing joyously: 'Ding dong the witch is dead!'

The picture, by a man who has entertained readers of *Playboy* and the *Magazine of Fantasy and Science Fiction* since the mid-Sixties, as well as being one of the prime movers of the first World Fantasy Convention in 1975, seems to me perfectly to sum up the enormous variety of comic fantasy. For it features some purely imaginary characters—the Munchkins; a supernatural figure—the witch; while the astronauts represent science fiction. And that, in a nutshell, is what this collection is all about. It is also—at the request of my publisher—a sequel to my previous anthology of comic tales of fantasy, *The Wizards of Odd*, published in 1996.

In the intervening period, fantasy fiction has reached even greater heights of popularity. In Britain, each new volume in Terry Pratchett's Discworld series becomes an automatic number one bestseller, a position that is also enjoyed in the US by Stephen Donaldson and Piers Anthony, to name just two of the top writers in the fantasy genre. Furthermore, in a recent poll conducted in the UK among the book-buying public, J. R. R. Tolkien's epic fantasy, *The Lord of the Rings*, was voted 'Book of the Century', scoring higher among the 25,000 voters who took part than the works of T. S. Eliot, Ernest Hemingway, Samuel Beckett and all the other literary greats. George Orwell's *1984* and *Animal Farm*—both arguably fantasies—followed in second and third places, with C. S. Lewis's *The Lion, the Witch and the Wardrobe* in 21st place, *The Hitch Hiker's Guide to the Galaxy* by Douglas Adams (24th), *Charlie and the Chocolate Factory* by Roald Dahl (34th), and Mervyn Peake's remarkable saga, *The Gormenghast Trilogy*, at number 55.

The conclusion is inescapable. There are an awful lot of readers who like imaginative escapist fiction—especially fantasy—and fantasy that is also humorous comes highly rated, too. In this book the reader will discover some of the best of such material in short story form—and among my contributors are a number who scored notably in the poll, including Lewis, Dahl, Peake, Kurt Vonnegut Jr (his *Slaughterhouse 5* came in at number 67) and Arthur C. Clarke (with *2001—A Space Odyssey* at 87). Together—like Gahan Wilson's cartoon—they encompass the fantastic, the supernatural and science fiction.

The title of this book is derived from the fact that a number of the stories feature characters who can fly: either under their own power, or with the help of machines that propel them into the heavens, or else they just run into trouble with aerial objects of one sort or another. (I trust the UFO fraternity will forgive my pun!) I also hope that the stories will—in the words of Professor Tolkien, when he was speaking once about the object of fantasy—provoke 'awe and wonder', at the same time as providing a lot of entertainment and amusement.

There is little need for me to say any more, except perhaps to repeat by way of encouragement an incantation that—like the soaring interest in fantasy—has suddenly become part of the language of the young whenever they are discussing thoughts of escaping into new worlds of pleasing experience. The phrase came originally from the Walt Disney fantasy film *Toy Story* and is the cue to activate one of the clockwork amphibian creatures that set off the toys' complex escape plan at the climax of the film. So in the words of the movie, '*Wind the frog!*'

PETER HAINING,
Boxford, Suffolk.

1

HORDES OF THE THINGS

Comic Fantasies

TURNTABLES OF THE NIGHT

Terry Pratchett

*To countless fantasy readers, the single most popular character in
contemporary fiction is Terry Pratchett's DEATH—the skeletal figure
who wields a scythe, rides a horse called 'Binky', is constantly bemused
by the strangeness and inhumanity of mankind, and (perhaps because
of this) always speaks in CAPITAL LETTERS. In all of Pratchett's
bestselling 'Discworld' novels, set in a world that spins through space
on the back of four elephants and a 10,000-mile-long turtle, he appears
as a kind of time-travelling Valkyrie, often running into other favourite
characters from the series, including the wizard Rincewind, Granny
Weatherwax the witch, and The Luggage, a wooden chest mounted on
scores of legs. In* Hogfather *(1996), DEATH, as unpredictably eccentric
as ever, decides to stand in for Discworld's equivalent of Father
Christmas in order to outwit some alien creatures plotting to destroy
the festive season. There is much that people have to be thankful for
in this particular incarnation of DEATH!*

According to The Times, *Terry Pratchett (1948–) 'must be the most
credible pretender to the long-vacant throne of P. G. Wodehouse'—a
tribute echoed by* The Mail on Sunday, *which described the 'Discworld'
books as 'now the longest series of comedies of any merit since
Wodehouse's death in 1975 closed the gates on Blandings Castle'. To
many this former newspaper reporter and press officer for the Central
Electricity Generating Board is simply the most popular living author.
Pratchett's first comic novel,* The Colour of Magic, *published in 1983,
represented a landmark in the comic fantasy genre and has since helped
to turn him into an international cult figure. With his greying beard,
trademark black fedora, and engaging sense of humour, he is every
inch the sophisticated jester of letters. In 'Turntables of the Night', we
find DEATH on yet another of his curious missions—collecting rock*

stars—but to give anything else away would spoil the comic situations and surprises that lie in store ...

*   *   *

Look, constable, what I don't understand is, surely *he* wouldn't be into blues? Because that was Wayne's life for you. A blues single. I mean, if people were music, Wayne would be like one of those scratchy old numbers, you know, re-recorded about a hundred times from the original phonograph cylinder or whatever, with some old guy with a name like Deaf Orange Robinson standing knee-deep in the Mississippi and moaning through his nose.

You'd think *he'd* be more into Heavy Metal or Meatloaf or someone. But I suppose he's into everyone. Eventually.

What? Yeah. That's my van, with Hellfire Disco painted on it. Wayne can't drive, you see. He's just not interested in anything like that. I remember when I got my first car and we went on holiday, and I did the driving and, okay, also the repairing, and Wayne worked the radio, trying to keep the pirate stations tuned in. He didn't really care where we went as long as it was on high ground and he could get Caroline or London or whatever. I didn't care where we went so long as we went.

I was always more into cars than music. Until now, I think. I don't think I want to drive a car again. I'd keep wondering who'd suddenly turn up in the passenger seat ...

Sorry. So. Yeah. The disco. Well, the deal was that I supplied the van, we split the cost of the gear, and Wayne supplied the records. It was really my idea. I mean, it seemed a pretty good bet. Wayne lives with his mum but they're down to two rooms now because of his record collection. Lots of people collect records, but I reckon Wayne really wants—wanted—to own every one that was ever made. His idea of a fun outing was going to some old store in some old town and rummaging through the stock and coming out with something by someone with a name like Sid Sputnik and the Spacemen, but the thing was, the funny thing was, you'd get back to his room and he'd go to a shelf and push all the records aside and there'd be this neat brown envelope with the name and date on it and everything—waiting.

Or he'd get me to drive him all the way to Preston or somewhere to find some guy who's a self-employed plumber now but maybe back in 1961 called Himself Ronnie Sequin and made it to number 152 in the charts, just to see if he'd got a spare copy of his one record which was really so naff you couldn't even find it in the specialist stores.

Wayne was the kind of collector who couldn't bear a hole in his collection. It was almost religious, really. He could out-talk John Peel in any case, but the records he really knew about were the ones he hadn't got. He'd wait years to get some practically demo disc from a punk group who probably died of safety-pin tetanus, but by the time he got his hands on it he'd be able to recite everything down to the name of the cleaning lady who scrubbed out the studio afterwards. Like I said, a collector.

So I thought, what more do you need to run a disco?

Well, basically just about everything which Wayne hadn't got—looks, clothes, common sense, some kind of idea about electric wiring and the ability to rabbit on like a prat. But at the time we didn't look at it like that, so I flogged the Capri and bought the van and got it nearly professionally re-sprayed. You can only see the words Midland Electricity Board on it if you know where to look. I wanted it to look like the van in the 'A-Team', except where theirs can jump four cars and still hare off down the road mine has trouble with drain covers.

Yes, I've talked to the other officer about the tax and insurance and MOT. Sorry, sergeant. Don't worry about it, I won't be driving a car ever again. Never.

We bought a load of amplifiers and stuff off Ian Curtis over in Wyrecliff because he was getting married and Tracey wanted him at home of a night, bunged some cards in news-agents' windows, and waited.

Well, people didn't exactly fall over themselves to give us gigs on account of people not really catching on to Wayne's style. You don't have to be a verbal genius to be a jock, people just expect you to say, 'Hey!' and 'Wow!' and 'Get down and boogie' and stuff. It doesn't actually matter if you sound like a pillock, it helps them feel superior. What they don't want, when they're all getting drunk after the wedding or whatever, is for someone to stand there with his eyes flashing worse than the lights saying things like, 'There's a rather interesting story attached to this record.'

Funny thing, though, is that after a while we started to get popular in a weird word-of-mouth kind of way. What started it, I reckon, was my sister Beryl's wedding anniversary. She's older than me, you understand. It turned out that Wayne had brought along just about every record ever pressed for about a year before they got married. Not just the top ten, either. The guests were all around the same age and pretty soon the room was so full of nostalgia you could hardly move. Wayne just hot-wired all their ignitions and took them for a joyride down Memory Motorway.

After that we started getting dates from what you might call the more older types, you know, not exactly kids but bits haven't started falling off yet. We were a sort of speciality disco. At the breaks people would come up to him to chat about this great number they recalled from way back or whenever and it would turn out that Wayne would always have it in the van. If they'd heard of it, he'd have it. Chances are he'd have it even if they hadn't heard of it. Because you could say this about Wayne, he was a true collector—he didn't worry whether the stuff was actually good or not. It just had to exist.

He didn't put it like that, of course. He'd say there was always something unique about every record. You might think that this is a lot of crap, but here was a man who'd got just about everything ever made over the last forty years and he really believed there was something special about each one. He loved them. He sat up there all through the night, in his room lined with brown envelopes, and played them one by one. Records that had been forgotten even by the people who made them. I'll swear he loved them all.

Yes, all right. But you've got to know about him to understand what happened next.

We were booked for this Hallowe'en Dance. You could tell it was Hallowe'en because of all the little bastards running around the streets shouting, 'Trickle treat,' and threatening you with milk bottles.

He'd sorted out lots of 'Monster Mash' type records. He looked pretty awful, but I didn't think much of it at the time. I mean, he always looked awful. It was his normal look. It came from spending years indoors listening to records, plus he had this bad heart and asthma and everything.

The dance was at . . . okay, you know all that. A Hallowe'en dance to raise money for a church hall. Wayne said that was a big joke, but he didn't say why. I expect it was some clever reason. He was always good at that sort of thing, you know, knowing little details that other people didn't know; it used to get him hit a lot at school, except when I was around. He was the kind of skinny boy who had his glasses held together with Elastoplast. I don't think I ever saw him raise a finger to anybody, only that time when Greebo Greaves broke a record Wayne had brought to some school disco and four of us had to pull Wayne off him and prise the iron bar out of his fingers and there was the police and an ambulance and everything.

Anyway.

I let Wayne set everything up, which was one big mistake but he wanted to do it, and I went and sat down by what they called the bar, ie, a couple of trestle tables with a cloth on it.

No, I didn't drink anything. Well, maybe one cup of the punch, and that was all fruit juice. All right, two cups.

But I know what I heard, and I'm absolutely certain about what I saw.

I think.

You get the same old bunch at these kind of gigs. There's the organiser, and a few members of the committee, some lads from the village who'd sort of drifted in because there wasn't much on the box except snooker. Everyone wore a mask but hadn't made an effort with the rest of the clothes so it looked as though Frankenstein and Co had all gone shopping in Marks and Sparks. There were Scouts' posters on the wall and those special kind of village hall radiators that suck the heat *in*. It smelled of tennis shoes. Just to sort of set the seal on it as one of the hotspots of the world there was a little mirror ball spinning up the rafters. Half the little mirrors had fallen off.

All right, maybe three cups. But it had bits of apple floating in it. Nothing serious has bits of apple floating in it.

Wayne started with a few hot numbers to get them stomping. I'm speaking metaphorically here, you understand. None of this boogie on down stuff, all you could hear was people not being as young as they used to be.

Now, I've already said Wayne wasn't exactly cut out for the business, and that night—last night—he was worse than usual. He kept mumbling, and staring at the dancers. He mixed the records up. He even scratched one. Accidentally, I mean—the only time I've ever seen Wayne really angry, apart from the Greebo business, was when scratch music came in.

It would have been very bad manners to cut in, so at the first break I went up to him and, let me tell you, he was sweating so much it was dropping on to the mixer.

'It's that bloke on the floor,' he said, 'the one in the flares.'

'Methuselah?' I said.

'Don't muck about. The black silk suit with the rhinestones. He's been doing John Travolta impersonations all night. Come on, you must have noticed. Platform soles. Got a silver medallion as big as a plate. Skull mask. He was over by the door.'

I hadn't seen anyone like that. Well, you'd remember, wouldn't you?

Wayne's face was frozen with fear. 'You must have!'

'So what, anyway?'

'He keeps staring at me!'

I patted his arm. 'Impressed by your technique, old son,' I said.

I took a look around the hall. Most people were milling around the punch now, the rascals. Wayne grabbed my arm.

'Don't go away!'

'I was just going out for some fresh air.'

'Don't . . .' he pulled himself together. 'Don't go. Hang around. Please.'

'What's up with you?'

'Please, John! He keeps looking at me in a funny way!'

He looked really frightened. I gave in. 'Okay. But point him out next time.'

I let him get on with things while I tried to neaten up the towering mess of plugs and adapters that was Wayne's usual contribution to electrical safety. If you've got the kind of gear we've got—okay, *had*— you can spend hours working on it. I mean, do you know how many different kinds of connectors . . . all right.

In the middle of the next number Wayne hauled me back to the decks.

'There! See him? Right in the middle!'

Well, there wasn't. There were a couple of girls dancing with each other, and everyone else were just couples who were trying to pretend the Seventies hadn't happened. Any rhinestone cowboys in that lot would have stood out like a strawberry in an Irish stew. I could see that some tact and diplomacy were called for at this point.

'Wayne,' I said, 'I reckon you're several coupons short of a toaster.'

'You can't see him, can you?'

Well, no. But . . .

. . . since he mentioned it . . .

. . . I could see the space.

There was this patch of floor around the middle of the hall which everyone was keeping clear of. Except that they weren't avoiding it, you see, they just didn't happen to be moving into it. It was just sort of accidentally there. And it stayed there. It moved around a bit, but it never disappeared.

All right, I know a patch of floor can't move around. Just take my word for it, this one did.

The record was ending but Wayne was still in control enough to have another one spinning. He faded it up, a bit of an oldie that they'd all know.

'Is it still there?' he said, staring down at the desk.

'It's a bit closer,' I said. 'Perhaps it's after a spot prize.'

. . . I wanna live forever . . .

'That's right, be a great help.'

. . . people will see me and cry . . .

There were quite a few more people down there now, but the empty patch was still moving around, all right, was being avoided, among the dancers.

I went and stood in it.

It was cold. It said: GOOD EVENING.

The voice came from all around me, and everything seemed to slow down. The dancers were just statues in a kind of black fog, the music a low rumble.

'Where are you?'

BEHIND YOU.

Now, at a time like this the impulse is to turn around, but you'd be amazed at how good I was at resisting it.

'You've been frightening my friend,' I said.

I DID NOT INTEND TO.

'Push off.'

THAT DOESN'T WORK, I AM AFRAID.

I did turn around then. He was about seven feet tall in his, yes, his platform soles. And, yes, he wore flares, but somehow you'd expect that. Wayne had said they were black but that wasn't true. They weren't any colour at all, they were simply clothes-shaped holes into Somewhere Else. Black would have looked blinding white by comparison. He did look a bit like John Travolta from the waist down, but only if you buried John Travolta for about three months.

It really was a skull mask. You could see the string.

'Come here often, do you?'

I AM ALWAYS AROUND.

'Can't say I've noticed you.' And I would have done. You don't meet many seven-foot, seven-stone people every day, especially ones that walked as though they had to think about every muscle movement in advance and acted as though they were alive and dead at the same time, like Cliff Richard.

YOUR FRIEND HAS AN INTERESTING CHOICE OF MUSIC.

'Yes. He's a collector, you know.'

I KNOW. COULD YOU PLEASE INTRODUCE ME TO HIM?

'Could I stop you?'

I DOUBT IT.

All right, perhaps four cups. But the lady serving said there was hardly anything in it at all except orange squash and home-made wine, and she looked a dear old soul. Apart from the Wolfman mask, that is.

But I know all the dancers were standing like statues and the music was just a faint buzz and there were these, all these blue and purple shadows around everything. I mean, drink doesn't do that.

Wayne wasn't affected. He stood with his mouth open, watching us.

'Wayne,' I said, 'this is—'

A FRIEND.

'Whose?' I said, and you could tell I didn't take to the person, because his flares were *huge* and he wore one of those silver identity bracelets on his wrist, the sort you could moor a battleship with, and they look so posey; the fact that his wrist was solid bone wasn't doing anything to help, either. I kept thinking there was a conclusion I ought to be jumping to, but I couldn't quite get a running start. My head seemed to be full of wool.

EVERYONE'S, he said, SOONER OR LATER. I UNDERSTAND YOU'RE SOMETHING OF A COLLECTOR.

'Well, in a small—' said Wayne.

I GATHER YOU'RE ALMOST AS KEEN AS I AM, WAYNE.

Wayne's face lit up. That was Wayne, all right. I'll swear if you shot him he'd come alive again if it meant a chance to talk about his hobby, sorry, his lifetime's work.

'Gosh,' he said. 'Are you a collector?'

ABSOLUTELY.

Wayne peered at him. 'We haven't met before, have we?' he said. 'I go to most of the collectors' meetings. Were you at the Blenheim Record Fest and Auction?'

I DON'T RECALL. I GO TO SO MANY THINGS.

'That was the one where the auctioneer had a heart attack.'

OH. YES. I SEEM TO REMEMBER POPPING IN, JUST FOR A FEW MINUTES.

'Very few bargains there, I thought.'

OH. I DON'T KNOW. HE WAS ONLY FORTY-THREE.

All right, inspector. Maybe six drinks. Or maybe it wasn't the drinks at all. But sometimes you get the feeling, don't you, that you can see a little way into the future? Oh, you don't. Well, anyway. I might not have been entirely in my right mind but I was beginning to feel pretty uncomfortable about all this. Well, anyone would. Even you.

'Wayne,' I said. 'Stop right now. If you concentrate, he'll go away. Settle down a bit. Please. Take a deep breath. This is all wrong.'

The brick wall on the other side of me paid more attention. I know Wayne when he meets fellow collectors. They have these weekend rallies. You see them in shops. Strange people. But none of them as strange as this one. He was *dead* strange.

'Wayne!'

They both ignored me. And inside my mind bits of my brain were jumping up and down, shouting and pointing, and I couldn't let myself believe what they were saying.

OH, I'VE GOT THEM ALL, he said, turning back to Wayne, ELVIS PRESLEY, BUDDY HOLLY, JIM MORRISON, JIMI HENDRIX, JOHN LENNON . . .

'Fairly wide spread, musically,' said Wayne. 'Have you got the complete Beatles?'

NOT YET.

And I swear they started to talk records. I remember Mr Friend saying he'd got the complete seventeenth, eighteenth and nineteenth century composers. Well, he would, wouldn't he?

I've always had to do Wayne's fighting for him, ever since we were at primary school, and this had gone far enough and I grabbed Mr Friend's shoulder and went to lay a punch right in the middle of that grinning mask.

And he raised his hand and I felt my fist hit an invisible wall which yielded like treacle, and he took off his mask and he said two words to me and then he reached across and took Wayne's hand, very gently . . .

And then the power amp exploded because, like I said, Wayne wasn't very good with connectors and the church hall had electrical wiring that dated back practically to 1800 or something, and then what with the decorations catching fire and everyone screaming and rushing about I didn't really know much about anything until they brought me round in the car park with half my hair burned off and the hall going up like a firework.

No. I don't know why they haven't found him either. Not so much as a tooth?

No. I don't know where he is. No, I don't think he owed anyone any money.

(But I think he's got a new job. There's a collector who's got them all—Presley, Hendrix, Lennon, Holly—and he's the only collector who'll ever get a complete collection, anywhere. And Wayne wouldn't pass up a chance like that. Wherever he is now, he's taking them out of their jackets with incredible care and spinning them with love on the turntables of the night ...)

Sorry. Talking to myself, there.

I'm just puzzled about one thing. Well, millions of things, actually, but just one thing right at the moment.

I can't imagine why Mr Friend bothered to wear a mask.

Because he looked just the same underneath, idio—officer.

What did he say? Well, I daresay he comes to everyone in some sort of familiar way. Perhaps he just wanted to give me a hint. He said DRIVE SAFELY.

No. No, really. I'll walk home, thanks.

Yes. I'll mind how I go.

A SLICE OF LIFE

P. G. Wodehouse

The comparison made in the previous introduction between Terry Pratchett and P. G. Wodehouse is well deserved: not only are both undoubted masters of comic fiction, but—surprising as it may seem— Wodehouse also wrote a number of fantasy short stories and a novel, The Swoop! Or How Clarence Saved England: A Tale of the Great Invasion, *published in 1909, which is now one of the rarest of his books, and much sought after by collectors of his works and lovers of fantasy fiction. The novel is a spoof of the Future-War genre which predicted the invasion of Britain in the decade until it almost happened with the outbreak of the First World War. It features one Clarence Chugwater, a young Englishman who manages to outsmart the might of invading Russian and German armies when he reveals to both that one force is paying its soldiers more than the other, and in the resulting upheaval the invasion plans collapse into farce. Wodehouse also introduced elements of comic fantasy in* Laughing Gas *(1936), in which an earl and an obnoxious child star change identities, and in the short stories 'Honeysuckle Cottage' (1928), about a haunted house; 'Mulliner's Buck-U-Uppo' (1933), concerning the curious inventions of a 'middling-Mad Scientist'; and especially 'A Slice of Life' (1926), reprinted here.*

Pelham Grenville Wodehouse (1881–1975), as big a bestseller in his day as Terry Pratchett, worked for two years in the Hong Kong and Shanghai Bank, before becoming a columnist on the London Globe *and starting to write the novels and short stories—especially those about the immortal Jeeves and Wooster—that made him world-famous. In all he wrote over ninety books which were translated into many languages and earned him the accolade from* The Times *of being 'a comic genius'. Although he lived for much of his life in America—and became a US citizen in 1956—he was knighted in the British New Year's Honours List at the age of ninety-three, just six weeks before his death. 'A Slice of Life' is one of the inimitable stories told by a popular Wodehouse character, Mr Mulliner, in which we encounter an evil baronet, Sir Jasper ffinch-ffarrowmere, a love-sick young man, and some tampering with the Secrets of Nature. The result is a farce as only the old master could write it!*

*   *   *

The conversation in the bar-parlour of the Anglers' Rest had drifted round to the subject of the Arts: and somebody asked if that film-serial, 'The Vicissitudes of Vera', which they were showing down at the Bijou Dream, was worth seeing.

'It's very good,' said Miss Postlethwaite, our courteous and efficient barmaid, who is a prominent first-nighter. 'It's about this mad professor who gets this girl into his toils and tries to turn her into a lobster.'

'Tries to turn her into a lobster?' echoed we, surprised.

'Yes, sir. Into *a* lobster. It seems he collected thousands and thousands of lobsters and mashed them up and boiled down the juice from their glands and was just going to inject it into this Vera Dalrymple's spinal column when Jack Frobisher broke into the house and stopped him.'

'Why did he do that?'

'Because he didn't want the girl he loved to be turned into a lobster.'

'What we mean,' said we, 'is why did the professor want to turn the girl into a lobster?'

'He had a grudge against her.'

This seemed plausible, and we thought it over for a while. Then one of the company shook his head disapprovingly.

'I don't like stories like that,' he said. 'They aren't true to life.'

'Pardon me, sir,' said a voice. And we were aware of Mr Mulliner in our midst.

'Excuse me interrupting what may be a private discussion,' said Mr Mulliner, 'but I chanced to overhear the recent remarks, and you, sir, have opened up a subject on which I happen to hold strong views—to wit, the question of what is and what is not true to life. How can we, with our limited experience, answer that question? For all we know, at this very moment hundreds of young women all over the country may be in the process of being turned into lobsters. Forgive my warmth, but I have suffered a good deal from this sceptical attitude of mind which is so prevalent nowadays. I have even met people who refused to believe my story about my brother Wilfred, purely because it was a little out of the ordinary run of the average man's experience.'

Considerably moved, Mr Mulliner ordered a hot Scotch with a slice of lemon.

'What happened to your brother Wilfred? Was he turned into a lobster?'

'No,' said Mr Mulliner, fixing his honest blue eyes on the speaker, 'he was not. It would be perfectly easy for me to pretend that he was turned into a lobster; but I have always made it a practice—and I always shall make it a practice—to speak nothing but the bare truth. My brother Wilfred simply had rather a curious adventure.'

My brother Wilfred (said Mr Mulliner) is the clever one of the family. Even as a boy he was always messing about with chemicals, and at the University he devoted his time entirely to research. The result was that while still quite a young man he had won an established reputation as the inventor of what are known to the trade as Mulliner's Magic Marvels—a general term embracing the Raven Gipsy Face-Cream, the Snow of the Mountains Lotion, and many other preparations, some designed exclusively for the toilet, others of a curative nature, intended to alleviate the many ills to which the flesh is heir.

Naturally, he was a very busy man: and it is to this absorption in his work that I attribute the fact that, though—like all the Mulliners—a man of striking personal charm, he had reached his thirty-first year without ever having been involved in an affair of the heart. I remember him telling me once that he simply had no time for girls.

But we all fall sooner or later, and these strong concentrated men harder than any. While taking a brief holiday one year at Cannes, he met a Miss Angela Purdue, who was staying at his hotel, and she bowled him over completely.

She was one of these jolly, outdoor girls; and Wilfred had told me that what attracted him first about her was her wholesome, sunburned complexion. In fact, he told Miss Purdue the same thing when, shortly after he had proposed and been accepted, she asked him in her girlish way what it was that had first made him begin to love her.

'It's such a pity,' said Miss Purdue, 'that the sunburn fades so soon. I do wish I knew some way of keeping it.'

Even in his moments of holiest emotion Wilfred never forgot that he was a business man.

'You should try Mulliner's Raven Gipsy Face-Cream,' he said. 'It comes in two sizes—the small (or half-crown) jar and the large jar at seven shillings and sixpence. The large jar contains three and a half times as much as the small jar. It is applied nightly with a small sponge before retiring to rest. Testimonials have been received from numerous members of the aristocracy and may be examined at the office by any bona-fide inquirer.'

'Is it really good?'

'I invented it,' said Wilfred, simply.

She looked at him adoringly.

'How clever you are! Any girl ought to be proud to marry you.'

'Oh, well,' said Wilfred, with a modest wave of his hand.

'All the same, my guardian is going to be terribly angry when I tell him we're engaged.'

'Why?'

'I inherited the Purdue millions when my uncle died, you see, and my guardian has always wanted me to marry his son, Percy.'

Wilfred kissed her fondly, and laughed a defiant laugh.

'Jer mong feesh der selar,' he said lightly.

But, some days after his return to London, whither the girl had preceded him, he had occasion to recall her words. As he sat in his study, musing on a preparation to cure the pip in canaries, a card was brought to him.

'Sir Jasper ffinch-ffarrowmere, Bart.,' he read. The name was strange to him.

'Show the gentleman in,' he said. And presently there entered a very stout man with a broad, pink face. It was a face whose natural expression should, Wilfred felt, have been jovial, but at the moment it was grave.

'Sir Jasper Finch-Farrowmere?' said Wilfred.

'ffinch - ffarrowmere,' corrected the visitor, his sensitive ear detecting the capital letters.

'Ah yes. You spell it with two small f's.'

'Four small f's.'

'And to what do I owe the honour—'

'I am Angela Purdue's guardian.'

'How do you do? A whisky-and-soda?'

'I thank you, no. I am a total abstainer. I found that alcohol had a tendency to increase my weight, so I gave it up. I have also given up butter, potatoes, soups of all kinds and — However,' he broke off, the fanatic gleam which comes into the eyes of all fat men who are describing their system of diet fading away, 'this is not a social call, and I must not take up your time with idle talk. I have a message for you, Mr Mulliner. From Angela.'

'Bless her!' said Wilfred. 'Sir Jasper, I love that girl with a fervour which increases daily.'

'Is that so?' said the baronet. 'Well, what I came to say was, it's all off.'

'What?'

'All off. She sent me to say that she had thought it over and wanted to break the engagement.'

Wilfred's eyes narrowed. He had not forgotten what Angela had said about this man wanting her to marry his son. He gazed piercingly at his visitor, no longer deceived by the superficial geniality of his appearance. He had read too many detective stories where the fat, jolly, red-faced man turns out a fiend in human shape to be a ready victim to appearances.

'Indeed?' he said, coldly. 'I should prefer to have this information from Miss Purdue's own lips.'

'She won't see you. But, anticipating this attitude on your part, I brought a letter from her. You recognise the writing?'

Wilfred took the letter. Certainly, the hand was Angela's, and the meaning of the words he read unmistakable. Nevertheless, as he handed the missive back, there was a hard smile on his face.

'There is such a thing as writing a letter under compulsion,' he said.

The baronet's pink face turned mauve.

'What do you mean, sir?'

'What I say.'

'Are you insinuating—'

'Yes, I am.'

'Pooh, sir!'

'Pooh to you!' said Wilfred. 'And, if you want to know what I think, you poor ffish, I believe your name is spelled with a capital F, like anybody else's.'

Stung to the quick, the baronet turned on his heel and left the room without another word.

Although he had given up his life to chemical research, Wilfred Mulliner was no mere dreamer. He could be the man of action when necessity demanded. Scarcely had his visitor left when he was on his way to the Senior Test-Tubes, the famous chemists' club in St James's. There, consulting Kelly's 'County Families', he learnt that Sir Jasper's address was ffinch Hall in Yorkshire. He had found out all he wanted to know. It was at ffinch Hall, he decided, that Angela must now be immured.

For that she was being immured somewhere he had no doubt. That letter, he was positive, had been written by her under stress of threats. The writing was Angela's, but he declined to believe that she was responsible for the phraseology and sentiments. He remembered reading a story where the heroine was forced into courses which she would not otherwise have contemplated by the fact that somebody was standing over her with a flask of vitriol. Possibly this was what that bounder of a baronet had done to Angela.

Considering this possibility, he did not blame her for what she had said about him, Wilfred, in the second paragraph of her note. Nor did he reproach her for signing herself 'Yrs truly, A. Purdue.' Naturally, when baronets are threatening to pour vitriol down her neck, a refined and sensitive young girl cannot pick her words. This sort of thing must of necessity interfere with the selection of the *mot juste*.

That afternoon, Wilfred was in a train on his way to Yorkshire. That evening, he was in the ffinch Arms in the village of which Sir Jasper was the squire. That night, he was in the gardens of ffinch Hall, prowling softly round the house, listening.

And presently, as he prowled, there came to his ears from an upper window a sound that made him stiffen like a statue and clench his hands till the knuckles stood out white under the strain.

It was the sound of a woman sobbing.

Wilfred spent a sleepless night, but by morning he had formed his plan of action. I will not weary you with a description of the slow and tedious steps by which he first made the acquaintance of Sir Jasper's valet, who was an habitué of the village inn, and then by careful stages won the man's confidence with friendly words and beer. Suffice it to say that, about a week later, Wilfred had induced this man with bribes to leave suddenly on the plea of an aunt's illness, supplying—so as to cause his employer no inconvenience—a cousin to take his place.

This cousin, as you will have guessed, was Wilfred himself. But a very different Wilfred from the dark-haired, clean-cut young scientist who had revolutionised the world of chemistry a few months before by proving that $H_2O+b3g4z7-m9z8=g6f5p3x$. Before leaving London on what he knew would be a dark and dangerous enterprise, Wilfred had taken the precaution of calling in at a well-known costumier's and buying a red wig. He had also purchased a pair of blue spectacles: but for the role which he had now undertaken these were, of course, useless. A blue-spectacled valet could not but have aroused suspicion in the most guileless baronet. All that Wilfred did, therefore, in the way of preparation, was to don the wig, shave off his moustache, and treat his face to a light coating of the Raven Gipsy Face-Cream. This done, he set out for ffinch Hall.

Externally, ffinch Hall was one of those gloomy, sombre country-houses which seem to exist only for the purpose of having horrid crimes committed in them. Even in his brief visit to the grounds, Wilfred had noticed fully half a dozen places which seemed incomplete without a cross indicating spot where body was found by the police. It was the sort of house where ravens croak in the front garden just before the death of the heir, and shrieks ring out from behind barred windows in the night.

Nor was its interior more cheerful. And, as for the personnel of the domestic staff, that was less exhilarating than anything else about the place. It consisted of an aged cook who, as she bent over her cauldrons, looked like something out of a travelling company of *Macbeth*, touring the smaller towns of the North, and Murgatroyd, the butler, a huge, sinister man with a cast in one eye and an evil light in the other.

Many men, under these conditions, would have been daunted. But not Wilfred Mulliner. Apart from the fact that, like all the Mulliners, he was as brave as a lion, he had come expecting something of this nature. He settled down to his duties and kept his eyes open, and before long his vigilance was rewarded.

One day, as he lurked about the dim-lit passage-ways, he saw Sir Jasper coming up the stairs with a laden tray in his hands. It contained a toast-rack, a half bot. of white wine, pepper, salt, veg., and in a covered dish something which Wilfred, sniffing cautiously, decided was a cutlet.

Lurking in the shadows, he followed the baronet to the top of the house. Sir Jasper paused at a door on the second floor. He knocked. The door opened, a hand was stretched forth, the tray vanished, the door closed, and the baronet moved away.

So did Wilfred. He had seen what he had wanted to see, discovered what he had wanted to discover. He returned to the servants' hall, and under the gloomy eyes of Murgatroyd began to shape his plans.

'Where you been?' demanded the butler, suspiciously.

'Oh, hither and thither,' said Wilfred, with a well-assumed airiness.

Murgatroyd directed a menacing glance at him.

'You'd better stay where you belong,' he said, in his thick, growling voice. 'There's things in this house that don't want seeing.'

'Ah!' agreed the cook, dropping an onion in the cauldron.

Wilfred could not repress a shudder.

But, even as he shuddered, he was conscious of a certain relief. At least, he reflected, they were not starving his darling. That cutlet had smelt uncommonly good: and, if the bill of fare was always maintained at this level, she had nothing to complain of in the catering.

But his relief was short-lived. What, after all, he asked himself, are cutlets to a girl who is imprisoned in a locked room of a sinister country-house and is being forced to marry a man she does not love? Practically nothing. When the heart is sick, cutlets merely alleviate, they do not cure. Fiercely Wilfred told himself that, come what might, few days should pass before he found the key to that locked door and bore away his love to freedom and happiness.

The only obstacle in the way of this scheme was that it was plainly going to be a matter of the greatest difficulty to find the key. That night, when his employer dined, Wilfred searched his room thoroughly. He found nothing. The key, he was forced to conclude, was kept on the baronet's person.

Then how to secure it?

It is not too much to say that Wilfred Mulliner was nonplussed. The brain which had electrified the world of Science by discovering that if you mixed a stiffish oxygen and potassium and added a splash of trinitrotoluol and a spot of old brandy you got something that could be sold in America as champagne at a hundred and fifty dollars the case, had to confess itself baffled.

To attempt to analyse the young man's emotions, as the next week dragged itself by, would be merely morbid. Life cannot, of course, be all sunshine: and in relating a story like this, which is a slice of life, one must pay as much attention to shade as to light: nevertheless, it would be tedious were I to describe to you in detail the soul-torments which afflicted Wilfred Mulliner as day followed day and no solution to the problem presented itself. You are all intelligent men, and you can picture to yourselves how a high-spirited young fellow, deeply in love, must have felt; knowing that the girl he loved was languishing in what practically amounted to a dungeon, though situated on an upper floor, and chaffing at his inability to set her free.

His eyes became sunken. His cheekbones stood out. He lost weight. And so noticeable was this change in his physique that Sir Jasper ffinch-ffarrowmere commented on it one evening in tones of uncon- cealed envy.

'How the devil, Straker,' he said—for this was the pseudonym under which Wilfred was passing, 'do you manage to keep so thin? Judging by the weekly books, you eat like a starving Esquimaux, and yet you don't put on weight. Now I, in addition to knocking off butter and potatoes, have started drinking hot unsweetened lemon-juice each night before retiring: and yet, damme,' he said—for, like all baronets, he was careless in his language, 'I weighed myself this morning, and I was up another six ounces. What's the explanation?'

'Yes, Sir Jasper,' said Wilfred, mechanically.

'What the devil do you mean, Yes, Sir Jasper?'

'No, Sir Jasper.'

The baronet wheezed plaintively.

'I've been studying this matter closely,' he said, 'and it's one of the seven wonders of the world. Have you ever seen a fat valet? Of course not. Nor has anybody else. There is no such thing as a fat valet. And yet there is scarcely a moment during the day when a valet is not eating. He rises at six-thirty, and at seven is having coffee and buttered toast. At eight, he breakfasts off porridge, cream, eggs, bacon, jam, bread, butter, more eggs, more bacon, more jam, more tea, and more butter, finishing up with a slice of cold ham and a sardine. At eleven o'clock he has his ''elevenses'', consisting of coffee, cream, more bread and more butter. At one, luncheon—a hearty meal, replete with every form of starchy food and lots of beer. If he can get at the port, he has port. At three, a snack. At four, another snack. At five, tea and buttered toast. At seven—dinner, probably with floury potatoes, and certainly with lots more beer. At nine, another snack. And at ten-thirty he retires to bed, taking with him a glass of milk and a plate of biscuits to keep himself from getting hungry in the night. And yet he remains as slender as a string-bean, while I, who have been dieting for years, tip the beam at two hundred and seventeen pounds, and am growing a third and supplementary chin. These are mysteries, Straker.'

'Yes, Sir Jasper.'

'Well, I'll tell you one thing,' said the baronet, 'I'm getting down one of those indoor Turkish Bath cabinet-affairs from London; and if that doesn't do the trick, I give up the struggle.'

The indoor Turkish Bath duly arrived and was unpacked; and it was some three nights later that Wilfred, brooding in the servants' hall, was aroused from his reverie by Murgatroyd.

'Here,' said Murgatroyd, 'wake up. Sir Jasper's calling you.'

'Calling me what?' asked Wilfred, coming to himself with a start.

'Calling you very loud,' growled the butler.

It was indeed so. From the upper regions of the house there was proceeding a series of sharp yelps, evidently those of a man in mortal stress. Wilfred was reluctant to interfere in any way if, as seemed probable, his employer was dying in agony; but he was a conscientious man, and it was his duty, while in this sinister house, to perform the work for which he was paid. He hurried up the stairs; and, entering Sir Jasper's bedroom, perceived the baronet's crimson face protruding from the top of the indoor Turkish Bath.

'So you've come at last!' cried Sir Jasper. 'Look here, when you put me into this infernal contrivance just now, what did you do to the dashed thing?'

'Nothing beyond what was indicated in the printed pamphlet accompanying the machine, Sir Jasper. Following the instructions, I slid Rod A into Groove B, fastening with Catch C—'

'Well, you must have made a mess of it, somehow. The thing's stuck. I can't get out.'

'You can't?' cried Wilfred.

'No. And the bally apparatus is getting considerably hotter than the hinges of the Inferno.' I must apologise for Sir Jasper's language, but you know what baronets are. 'I'm being cooked to a crisp.'

A sudden flash of light seemed to blaze upon Wilfred Mulliner.

'I will release you, Sir Jasper—'

'Well, hurry up, then.'

'On one condition.' Wilfred fixed him with a piercing gaze. 'First, I must have the key.'

'There isn't a key, you idiot. It doesn't lock. It just clicks when you slide Gadget D into Thingummybob E.'

'The key I require is that of the room in which you are holding Angela Purdue a prisoner.'

'What the devil do you mean? Ouch!'

'I will tell you what I mean, Sir Jasper ffinch-ffarrowmere. I am Wilfred Mulliner!'

'Don't be an ass. Wilfred Mulliner has black hair. Yours is red. You must be thinking of someone else.'

'This is a wig,' said Wilfred. 'By Clarkson.' He shook a menacing finger at the baronet. 'You little thought, Sir Jasper ffinch-ffarrowmere, when you embarked on this dastardly scheme, that Wilfred Mulliner was watching your every move. I guessed your plans from the start. And now is the moment when I checkmate them. Give me that key, you Fiend.'

'ffiend,' corrected Sir Jasper, automatically.

'I am going to release my darling, to take her away from this dreadful house, to marry her by special licence as soon as it can legally be done.'

In spite of his sufferings, a ghastly laugh escaped Sir Jasper's lips.

'You are, are you?'

'I am.'

'Yes, you are!'

'Give me the key.'

'I haven't got it, you chump. It's in the door.'

'Ha, ha!'

'It's no good saying "Ha, ha!" It is in the door. On Angela's side of the door.'

'A likely story! But I cannot stay here wasting time. If you will not give me the key, I shall go up and break in the door.'

'Do!' Once more the baronet laughed like a tortured soul. 'And see what she'll say.'

Wilfred could make nothing of this last remark. He could, he thought, imagine very clearly what Angela would say. He could picture her sobbing on his chest, murmuring that she knew he would come, that she had never doubted him for an instant. He leapt for the door.

'Here! Hi! Aren't you going to let me out?'

'Presently,' said Wilfred. 'Keep cool.' He raced up the stairs.

'Angela,' he cried, pressing his lips against the panel. 'Angela!'

'Who's that?' answered a well-remembered voice from within.

'It is I—Wilfred. I am going to burst open the door. Stand clear of the gates.'

He drew back a few paces, and hurled himself at the woodwork. There was a grinding crash, as the lock gave. And Wilfred, staggering on, found himself in a room so dark that he could see nothing.

'Angela, where are you?'

'I'm here. And I'd like to know why you are, after that letter I wrote you. Some men,' continued the strangely cold voice, 'do not seem to know how to take a hint.'

Wilfred staggered, and would have fallen had he not clutched at his forehead.

'That letter?' he stammered. 'You surely didn't mean what you wrote in that letter?'

'I meant every word and wish I had put in more.'

'But—but—but— But don't you love me, Angela?'

A hard, mocking laugh rang through the room.

'Love you? Love the man who recommended me to try Mulliner's Raven Gipsy Face-Cream!'

'What do you mean?'

'I will tell you what I mean. Wilfred Mulliner, look on your handiwork!'

The room became suddenly flooded with light. And there, standing with her hand on the switch, stood Angela—a queenly, lovely figure, in whose radiant beauty the sternest critic would have noted but one flaw—the fact that she was piebald.

Wilfred gazed at her with adoring eyes. Her face was partly brown and partly white, and on her snowy neck were patches of sepia that looked like the thumb-prints you find on the pages of books in the Free Library: but he thought her the most beautiful creature he had ever seen. He longed to fold her in his arms: and but for the fact that her eyes told him that she would undoubtedly land an upper-cut on him if he tried it he would have done so.

'Yes,' she went on, 'this is what you have made of me, Wilfred Mulliner—you and that awful stuff you call the Raven Gipsy Face-Cream. This is the skin you loved to touch! I took your advice and bought one of the large jars at seven and six, and see the result! Barely twenty-four hours after the first application, I could have walked into any circus and named my own terms as the Spotted Princess of the Fiji Islands. I fled here to my childhood home, to hide myself. And the first thing that happened'—her voice broke—'was that my favourite hunter shied at me and tried to bite pieces out of his manger: while Ponto, my little dog, whom I have reared from a puppy, caught one sight of my face and is now in the hands of the vet, and unlikely to recover. And it was you, Wilfred Mulliner, who brought this curse upon me!'

Many men would have wilted beneath these searing words, but Wilfred Mulliner merely smiled with infinite compassion and understanding.

'It is quite all right,' he said. 'I should have warned you, sweetheart, that this occasionally happens in cases where the skin is exceptionally delicate and finely-textured. It can be speedily remedied by an application of the Mulliner Snow of the Mountains Lotion, four shillings the medium-sized bottle.'

'Wilfred! Is this true?'

'Perfectly true, dearest. And is this all that stands between us?'

'No!' shouted a voice of thunder.

Wilfred wheeled sharply. In the doorway stood Sir Jasper ffinch-ffarrowmere. He was swathed in a bath-towel, what was visible of his person being a bright crimson. Behind him, toying with a horse-whip, stood Murgatroyd, the butler.

'You didn't expect to see me, did you?'

'I certainly,' replied Wilfred, severely, 'did not expect to see you in a lady's presence in a costume like that.'

'Never mind my costume.' Sir Jasper turned.

'Murgatroyd, do your duty!'

The butler, scowling horribly, advanced into the room.

'Stop!' screamed Angela.

'I haven't begun yet, miss,' said the butler, deferentially.

'You shan't touch Wilfred. I love him.'

'What!' cried Sir Jasper. 'After all that has happened?'

'Yes. He has explained everything.'

A grim frown appeared on the baronet's vermilion face.

'I'll bet he hasn't explained why he left me to be cooked in that infernal Turkish Bath. I was beginning to throw out clouds of smoke when Murgatroyd, faithful fellow, heard my cries and came and released me.'

'Though not my work,' added the butler.

Wilfred eyed him steadily.

'If,' he said, 'you used Mulliner's Reduc-o, the recognised specific for obesity, whether in the tabloid form at three shillings the tin, or as a liquid at five and six the flask, you would have no need to stew in Turkish Baths. Mulliner's Reduc-o, which contains no injurious chemicals, but is compounded purely of health-giving herbs, is guaranteed to remove excess weight, steadily and without weakening after-effects, at the rate of two pounds a week. As used by the nobility.'

The glare of hatred faded from the baronet's eyes.

'Is that a fact?' he whispered.

'It is.'

'You guarantee it?'

'All the Mulliner preparations are fully guaranteed.'

'My boy!' cried the baronet. He shook Wilfred by the hand. 'Take her,' he said, brokenly. 'And with her my b-blessing.'

A discreet cough sounded in the background.

'You haven't anything, by any chance, sir,' asked Murgatroyd, 'that's good for lumbago?'

'Mulliner's Ease-o will cure the most stubborn case in six days.'

'Bless you, sir, bless you,' sobbed Murgatroyd. 'Where can I get it?'

'At all chemists.'

'It catches me in the small of the back principally, sir.'

'It need catch you no longer,' said Wilfred.

There is little to add. Murgatroyd is now the most lissom butler in Yorkshire. Sir Jasper's weight is down under the fifteen stone and he is thinking of taking up hunting again. Wilfred and Angela are man and wife; and never, I am informed, have the wedding-bells of the old church at ffinch village rung out a blither peal than they did on that June morning when Angela, raising to her love a face on which the brown was as evenly distributed as on an antique walnut table, replied to the clergyman's question, 'Wilt thou, Angela, take this Wilfred?' with a shy, 'I will.' They now have two bonny bairns—the small, or Percival, at a preparatory school in Sussex, and the large, or Ferdinand, at Eton.

Here Mr Mulliner, having finished his hot Scotch, bade us farewell and took his departure.

A silence followed his exit. The company seemed plunged in deep thought. Then somebody rose.

'Well, good night all,' he said.

It seemed to sum up the situation.

THE BETTER MOUSETRAP

L. Sprague De Camp & Fletcher Pratt

Another famous series of 'bar-room tales'—perhaps not quite as widely known as Wodehouse's Mulliner yarns, but more specifically comic fantasies—are the Gavagan's Bar stories of which Anthony Boucher once wrote, 'It takes all kinds of people to make a bar—and you'll find them at Gavagan's.' With customers propping up the bar such as Professor Thott, Mr Gross and Mr Witherwax (a relative of Terry Pratchett's Granny Weatherwax, perhaps?), and a bartender who insists on everyone calling him Mr Cohan (emphasis on the last syllable, if you please), this is certainly no understatement. Like their counterparts in the Anglers' Rest, these jolly imbibers are never too surprised by anything they hear: even if it is the story of a young man who has fallen in love with a dryad, a building haunted by a poltergeist that smells, or—in the case of 'The Better Mousetrap'—an unfortunate soul who has recruited a dragon to get rid of a plague of mice.

Lyon Sprague De Camp (1907–) and Murray Fletcher Pratt (1897–1956) were for years probably the most versatile partnership in American comic fantasy fiction. De Camp, who had studied to be an aeronautical engineer, and Pratt, a historian and German translator, met through their joint love of legends, languages and humour, and rapidly became popular with readers of sf magazines for their hilarious sagas featuring Harold Shea, who was forever being whisked off to misadventures in lands of Norse mythology or the world of Spenser's Faerie Queene. *The two friends began the series of tall tales recounted by the frequenters of Gavagan's Bar in 1940: both plotting the story, De Camp writing the first draft, and Pratt polishing the final text. The bar sadly closed down after Fletcher Pratt's death, but De Camp has continued as a major force in fantasy fiction, writing tales of heroic fantasy and continuing the exploits of Robert E. Howard's mighty barbarian hero, Conan. There are dragons galore to be found in these tales—but certainly not one quite like the specimen which Mr Murdoch describes to the assembled company in Gavagan's . . .*

*   *   *

The taxidermist had imparted a drunken wink to the stuffed owl over the bar. Mr Witherwax returned the wink and kept his gaze fixed resolutely aloft, well aware that if he lowered it, Mr Gross would burst into anecdote. Considering the quality of the anecdotes, this was something to be avoided at any cost; but there must come the moment when the glass was empty, and Mr Witherwax must look down to have it refilled. Beside him Mr Gross cleared his throat ominously. Mr Witherwax deliberately turned his back to the sound, looked along the mahogany terrain toward the door, and beckoned to the bartender.

'Who's that, drinking by himself down there?' he asked. 'Maybe he'd like to join us; a man shouldn't be a solitary drinker. You can leave the cherry out of mine this time, Mr *Co*han.'

'Co-*han*, by God!' the bartender corrected. 'Him? His name is Murdoch, or maybe it's Mud, and I'm thinking he's not a lucky man for you to know. He may be having murder done on him . . . What'll you be having, Mr Gross?'

'The usual—a boilermaker. That reminds me, I knew a man once—'

'What is he, a gangster?' said Mr Witherwax. 'I don't want to get mixed up in nothing, only do him a favour. Bring him down here and give him a drink on me. Tell him the Devil died on Tuesday night, and we're holding the wake.'

Mr Cohan smiled a smile of sly superiority through his folds of fat as he set out the ingredients of the boilermaker. 'No, he would not be a gangster. It's worse even than that. He lost his dragon.'

'A friend of my uncle Pincus was kicked in the belly by a kangaroo once,' said Mr Gross. 'He—'

'I don't care whether he lost a dragon or found a mermaid,' said Mr Witherwax, desperately. 'Bring him down here and give him a drink.'

The bartender, with the shrug of a man who has done his duty and will not be responsible for the consequences, stepped to the end of the bar. As he spoke to Murdoch, the latter turned a thin and melancholy face toward the first comers, then nodded. There was no trace of previous potations in his gait, but he would have a double zombie, thanks. As he lifted his glass in salute, Mr Gross gazed at him with fatherly interest.

'Is it true,' he asked, 'that you lost your dragon?'

Murdoch choked on the last mouthful, set down his glass and looked at Mr Gross with pain. 'If it was only my dragon I wouldn't care,' he said, 'but it was borrowed.'

'That's right, and I misspoke meself,' said Mr Cohan, heartily. 'I remember it was right here at this bar that you loaned it off that magician felly, and him drinking his own special drink.'

Murdoch reached for another swallow. He drizzled some of it on his chin as the door opened, then gave a sigh of relief at the sight of a stranger.

Witherwax returned his gaze to the drunken owl, which stared back glassily. 'I haven't never seen a dragon, and I don't expect to,' he said. 'Didn't St George or somebody get rid of the last one?'

'He did not,' said Mr Cohan, having supplied the new arrival with beer. 'This here, now, animal we're talking about I seen it with my own eyes, and it was as dragon as could be, and it belonged to that magician felly Abaris.'

'Still does,' said Murdoch in a rueful tone. 'That is—well, I don't know why I let myself get mixed up—I didn't *like* him—oh, what the hell!' He took a long pull at his double zombie.

Witherwax turned his gaze to Mr Cohan. 'Who is this chap that owns a dragon? One of them scientists?'

'A magician I'm telling you,' said the bartender. 'He gave me his card once; maybe I got it here. Theophrastus V. Abaris (he lined the syllables out slowly); you would have seen him yourself, Mr Gross, he used to come in on Thursday nights when you did. A big, greasy tub of lard, not honest fat from the wife's cooking like myself. Pale as a corp' he was, with his hair hanging down over his coat-collar and a little squeaky voice like a choir-boy. It's not easy you could miss him if you seen him once.'

One of them real solitary drinkers he was, (Cohan continued) that never buy one for the bartender nor get one on the house, neither. Not that he wasn't friendly; he could and would talk down a Phillydelphia lawyer, only you couldn't understand half of what he said. I ast him once what he done for a living, and all he said was something that sounded like some kind of religion—I misremember the name. ('Pythagorean,' said Murdoch, gloomily, and took another drink.) That would be it, and thanks, Mr Murdoch. I never heard of it before, but I ast my brother Julius that's on the force about it, and he said it didn't look good, but there's no law against it as long as they don't tell fortunes. It has something to do with books. There's some of them old books that are worth all kinds of money.

That's what he went away for, he said, since the last time I seen him, to get some book, he said, a book by somebody named Nebulous or something like that. ('Zebulon,' said Murdoch.) You should of heard him talk about it. He says it's hundreds of years he's been after the book, which is always the way he talks, so that when you can understand what he's saying, you can't believe a word of it. It seems he had the book once; he says he found it on an island in the pink Arabian Sea, just as though I didn't know sea-water ain't pink.

Then he says the Holy Saint Peter stole the book off him, and besides being a lot of Malarkey, he shouldn't be putting his tongue to the names of the holy saints that way, and I told him so. But now he's going to get it back, he says, because there's going to be a convention of fellies in the same line of business over in Brooklyn, I think he said. ('Brocken,' corrected Murdoch.) Okay, in Brocken. I remember on account of the date being the first of May, and I thought maybe it was some gang of Commies or something like that, but my brother Julius, that's on the force, says no.

Still and all it's good for business having him in here once in a while, with the tricks he plays, moving his fingers all the time like he's playing a piano that ain't there. Did I ever show you the bottle of private stock he drinks out of, Mr Gross?

(Cohan ducked down to product it. '*Vin sable*,' read Witherwax from the label. 'I know what that means; that's French, and it means "sand wine". Have something yourself on this round, will you Mr Co*han?*')

Don't mind if I do; the first today but not the last, and thank you. Well, I guess they must use black sand with it or something, because you can see for yourself how dark it is, like it was mixed with ink. Gavagan gets it for him from Costello's, the importer. No, I wouldn't be selling you a drink of it, Mr Gross; it would be as much as my job was worth. This here Abaris is that particular, and he is a man I wouldn't want to have to take a dislike to me, because of the funny things he can do.

(A sound vaguely imitating a rusty hinge emanated from Murdoch.)

Why you wouldn't believe it yourself sometimes, and I wouldn't either, only I seen them with my own two eyes. You know Mr Jeffers, don't you, Mr Witherwax? Well, it's a different man he is today than he was, and all because of this Abaris. A fine young man and a fine young felly he always was, except that in the old days, before you began coming in here, Mr Witherwax, he maybe had too much money and spent too much of it on girls. Take them alone, either one; the money without the women, or a good girl without the money that can be a help to a young felly, and he's fixed for life. But put them together, and often as not, the young felly goes on the booze.

No, you needn't laugh, Mr Gross. I'm not the man to say anything against good liquor, but I wouldn't want anyone to walk out this door that couldn't go on home on his own two feet. Good liquor helps a man to see that after all it's a small thing that disturbs him, but when you take liquor without the trouble, then the liquor becomes the trouble itself, and that's bad.

This was the way it used to be with Mr Jeffers. He got to taking the liquor with the women, and then without them, and he could be a nasty drunk, too. When I would try to hold him back, he'd go around the corner there to that Italian place where they don't care what they sell you, and get himself a skinful. Many's the time my brother Julius had to take him home, blind drunk. This evening I'm telling you about Mr Jeffers was in here, and so was this Abaris—he used to call himself Dr Abaris, did I tell you? But when I ast him could he take a wart off her finger for the wife, he said no, so I'll not be giving him the name.

So I said to Abaris, was there any trick he could do to make Mr Jeffers stop drinking, like maybe the time he borrowed a bottle and poured three different things out of it. So he says: 'Yes, my dear Cohan; of course, my dear Cohan. Fill up his glass,' in that nancy voice of his, and he begins to make those motions like playing the piano.

I filled up Mr Jeffers' glass with brandy like he ordered and he puts his hand to it, but before he can get the glass to his lips, the brandy is back in the bottle, by God. So after we tried it three times, Mr Jeffers lets the glass alone, and a funny look comes over his face and he walks out. I thought maybe at the time he was headed for the Italian place again, but he comes back the next night, and you can call me an Orangeman if the same thing don't happen with the first drink Mr Jeffers orders, while he is cold sober. I don't know how it would be if he come in tonight, but Mr Jeffers hasn't touched a drop of anything stronger than beer since the day, and you all know it as well as I do. Abaris himself says the trick is simple; it's nothing but a continuing appropriation, he says. ('Apportation,' said Murdoch.)

I thank you, Mr Murdoch. Excuse it, I must see what this gentleman will be having.

'A cousin of mine in Milwaukee once—' began Gross, but Witherwax hastily addressed Murdoch: 'What's this business about a dragon? Did he make you think you'd seen one coming out of your drink?'

The young man sipped his zombie.

No, nothing like that, (he said reflectively). In fact, I thought it was all part of a stock joke, you know, like kidding someone over his luck with the dice or his long ears. I've seen plenty of magicians, like everybody else, at clubs and on the stage, and this Abaris didn't strike me as a particularly prepossessing specimen. In fact, I used to wonder how he made a go of it, because just as Mr Cohan says, he looked rather greasy and was never well dressed. People like to be fooled, but they want to have it done in the grand manner, by a man with a waxed moustache, wearing a white tie and tails.

So I was just joking myself when I asked him if he were really a magician. (Murdoch shuddered slightly and took another sip.) He has black eyes, with pupils that have a kind of vertical look that I can't describe; he looked at me out of them and said yes, he was, did I have any objections, and from the way he said it, I knew right off that I'd made a mistake. But there didn't seem anything to do but pretend that I hadn't noticed, so I laughed and said he was just the man I wanted; I needed a magician or a Pied Piper at least, to get the mice out of my apartment.

(Witherwax laid a bill on the counter and made a circular motion over the glasses; Mr Cohan bent to the task of making refills.)

I have an apartment on Fifth Street (continued Murdoch) on the third floor over one of those Fairfield restaurants. The only thing wrong with it is that it is—or was—simply overrun with mice. I had to keep all my food in metal or glass containers; they chewed the bindings of my books—really an affliction. You haven't any idea of what pests they can be when they get out of hand.

Now, wait a minute. (He held up a hand toward Witherwax, whose attitude indicated speech.) I know what you're going to say. You're going to ask why I didn't get an exterminator or a cat. Well, I live alone and do a good deal of travelling, so it would be no use trying to keep a cat. As for the exterminator, I did get one; I got half a dozen, in relays. They came around once a week with traps and mouse-seed which they scattered over the floor until it crunched underfoot, and I suppose they did kill a lot of mice. At least the place smelt like it. But the mice kept coming back.

The trouble was that Fairfield restaurant; it was a regular breeding-ground for them. You know the chain is owned by an old girl named Conybeare—Miss Gwen Conybeare. Like a good many other maiden ladies who have all the money they need and more time than they know what to do with, she fell for one of those Indian sects. You know, with meetings in dimly-lighted rooms and a prophet with a towel around his head. I suppose it's her business how she wants to spend her time and money, but this particular religion had a feature that made it my business, too. Her teacher convinced her that it was wrong to take life—not human life, but life of any kind, just as in India, where a man will get rid of a louse by picking it off himself and putting it on someone else.

She gave absolute orders that no death was to occur in a Fairfield restaurant, and wouldn't allow an exterminator on the premises. So you see that as fast as I got rid of the mice in my apartment, a new supply came up from below, and I had a real problem.

This Abaris person naturally couldn't know that. When I said I needed a magician to get the mice out of my place, he looked at me with those vertical-appearing pupils and made a kind of noise in his throat that I swear gave me the shivers all through. (Murdoch shivered again and gulped from his zombie.) I felt as though he were going to hypnotise me, or make my drink jump back into the bottle, like Jeffers', and so before anything like that could happen, I began to explain that it wasn't a joke. As soon as I got to the part about Miss Conybeare, he smiled all across his face.

'My dear young man,' he said, 'if it is a matter of a psychosophist, I should ask nothing better than the opportunity to assist you. They are the most repulsive of existing beings. Let me see—ha, I will provide you with the king of all the cats, and mouse corpses will litter the doorstep of Fairfield's.'

I explained that the king of the cats wouldn't do me much more good than the crown prince, because of my travelling.

He put a hand up to his mouth and spoke from underneath it. 'Hm, hm,' he said. 'That makes it more difficult, but the project is a worthy one and I will not willingly abandon it. I will lend you my dragon.'

I laughed, thinking that Abaris was a much cleverer man than he looked, to have turned a mild joke around on me in that fashion. But he didn't laugh back.

'It is a very young dragon,' he said, 'hatched from an egg presented to me by my old friend, Mr Sylvester. As nearly as I can determine, I am the first person to raise one from the egg, so I must ask you to take particularly good care of it, as I wish to present a report at the next meeting of the Imperial Society.'

I thought he was carrying the joke so far that it strained a bit, so I said of course I would take the best of care of his dragon, and if it wearied of a diet of mice, I'd be glad to see that it was provided with a beautiful young maiden tied to a tree, though I wouldn't guarantee the results, which I understood to be usually unfortunate for dragons in such cases.

He gave a giggle at that, but it trailed off in a nasty kind of way and he tapped his fingers two or three times on the bar. 'It appears that you treat this with a spirit of levity,' he said. 'These are high matters. Therefore, and purely as a preventative, I shall accompany the loan of the dragon with an engagement. I shall require you to permit me to put a curse on you when I return from the Brocken if my dragon is not returned in good order.' He produced a knife with a sharp scalpel blade. 'Prick your thumb,' he said.

Well, things had gone too far for me to pull out at this point without being ridiculous, and besides I was curious about what kind of charlatanry he was going to produce by a way of a dragon, so I stuck myself in the thumb and a drop of blood came out on the bar. Abaris leaned over it and made a little sort of humming song, all in minors, twiddling his fingers in the way Mr Cohan described. The drop of blood vanished.

(Mr Cohan had been leaning against the back of the bar with his arms akimbo. Now he came to life. 'Vanished, did it?' he said. 'The devil of a time I had trying to get the mark of that drop of blood out, and the best part of it's there yet. If you get the right angle and look close now—see—there it is, like it worked right through the varnish into the wood. Isn't that queer, now?')

There was nothing queer about the dragon, though (said Murdoch, and for the first time Witherwax noticed that the zombies were beginning to have some effect on his speech). It was a real dragon, I knew it was as soon as Abaris brought it to my place in a metal box, and that was when I really began to worry a little. It hooked its feef—I mean, it cooked its food on the hoof. Wouldn't touch a dead mouse at all, not at all. But when it got near a live one it would go *whooof* and shoot out a flame, and there was mouse, all cooked.

(Witherwax said: 'I never thought of that. They must have the flame for something, though. That is, if it was a real dragon.')

(Murdoch stuck out a finger. 'Look here, ol' man, don't you believe me?')

'Now, now,' Mr Cohan intervened heavily. 'There will be no arguments of the kind in Gavagan's Bar. Mr Murdoch, I am surprised at you. Not a word has Mr Witherwax said to show he doesn't believe you. And as for the dragon I seen it with my own two eyes, right here on this bar.'

He brought it in here in a big tomato-juice can (the bartender went on), to show it to me, because it was here he heard about it first, and because of the wonderful way it would be cleaning the mice out of his place, so there was hardly a one left. I will say it wasn't much to look at, being like one of them alligators about a foot and a half long, with a couple of little stubby wings sticking out of its back.

Maybe it didn't like being out on the bar or something, because before Mr Murdoch could get it back into the can, it run down to the end there, and there was a felly sitting drinking a Tom Collins and minding his own business. This dragon let off a puff of flame about a foot long that burned all the hair off the back of the felly's hand, and would you believe it? It boiled the Tom Collins right over the side of the glass so it made a mark on Gavagan's varnish. This felly jumped up and run out of here, and as that sort of thing is bad for business, I told Mr Murdoch he'd have to keep the dragon out of the place, and that was the beginning of all his troubles.

Now, Mr Murdoch, it's all right. I was just going to tell them that the reason you brung the dragon in here was thinking it would maybe help with the rats we have in the cellar, bad luck to them, and also because it was getting hungry. The mice were clean eaten out, and Mr Murdoch had no luck at all when he brought it home a piece of beefsteak or a pork chop, for beef or pork it would not have, but must catch its food for itself. The dragon was getting thin, he used to say, and would be saying something like 'Kwark, kwark,' and even trying to catch flies, that was so burned to pieces with the flame that it had nothing to eat from them at all.

So what does Mr Murdoch do? He does what any man of good sense would do, and tries to take it to the zoo until Mr Abaris gets home from Brooklyn or wherever it is. He puts it in the tomato-juice can with a cardboard top, but the dragon did not like the trip here to the bar at all, and it burns a hole in the cardboard, and out it comes. Then he puts it in a wooden box and the same thing happens, only it nearly burned up the apartment that time. Then he tries to call the zoo to come get it, but devil a bit would the zoo have to do with that.

('Why not?' asked Witherwax. 'Oh, it's a long story, a long, long story,' said Murdoch. 'They said they couldn't take it unless I gave it to them, and I said I couldn't do that, and they said I should take it to a pet shop—I mean, pet shop, and I told them it burned a hole in the box. That was bad, because the zoo, it said, what did it say? It said, oh yes, they'd send a wagon right around for the dragon, in charge of a keeper named Napoleon Bonaparte. So I hung up. Maybe the whole thing didn't happen.')

It happened as I'm the living witness (said Mr Cohan stoutly). When Mr Murdoch gave me the word on this, I says to him, if you can't take the dragon to his food, then do the next best thing. Doc Brenner now, he tells me there's places where you can buy rats and mice and things like that for experiments, and if this isn't an experiment, what is it? So when I got the address of one of those places from Doc Brenner, Mr Murdoch goes there right away, and then he remembers he has ordered some wood to make bookshelves out of. So what does he do but leave the key to his place downstairs in the restaurant.

Well, this boy that brought the boards in—he was in here afterwards, and young as he was, I wouldn't refuse him a drink, because he was needing it—this lad puts the boards down, when all of a sudden a mouse runs out of the corner by the pipes, with the dragon after it. It must of been a new mouse. The dragon was not stalking like a cat, the way it usually did, but hopping across the floor, with its claws scratching the boards and its wings trying to fly, and every third hop it would let out a flame a foot long.

The mouse made a dive for that pile of lumber, with the dragon after him. The lad that brought the boards was hit by a tongue of flame— he had a hole in his pants-leg you could shove your fist through— before he got out of there, thinking maybe Gavagan's would be a better place for him. What happened next I cannot tell you, but the nearest a man can come to it, the mouse crawled in among them boards and the dragon set them afire while trying to cook the mouse.

However that may be, when Mr Murdoch got back with a box under his arm and live mice in it, his apartment was in a fine grand blaze, and firemen spraying water through the window and chopping things up with their axes and having themselves a rare old time. That part was all right, because Mr Murdoch had insurance. But there was no insurance on the dragon, and when he got in afterward, by God, not a trace of the beast could he find. Whether it got burned up, or flushed down with the hoses or run away to the Fairfield Restaurant, he has no idea at all. And now here's this Abaris coming back from Brooklyn and Mr Murdoch with no dragon for him, nothing but the box of mice he has been keeping, hoping the dragon would show up.

So now this Abaris will put the curse on him, and what it will be I don't know and neither does he. No, Mr Murdoch, you will excuse me from giving you another double zombie this night.

SAM SMALL'S BETTER HALF

Eric Knight

A character who enjoyed cult status among lovers of fantasy in the 1940s was Sam Small, a tiny, grizzled Yorkshireman, part mortal and part god, who likes to lend a hand in upholding law and order, can fly under his own power (shades of a rural Superman here), and can even turn animals into young girls! His exploits first appeared in a series of short stories in the US periodical, Harper's Magazine, *beginning in 1938, and for some years the author, Eric Knight, who lived in the San Fernando Valley, California, was assumed to be an American. In fact, he was as much a Yorkshireman as his character, Sam Small, who lives in a mythical little spot known as Polkingthorpe Brig, 'not all that far from Huddersfield'. In fact, Knight drew on memories of his own childhood in that part of the country to write his fantasies about the feisty little mill-worker who becomes rich by inventing a 'self-doffing spindle', and freed from drudgery by his new-found wealth, is soon stumbling into one hilarious adventure after another.*

Eric Mowbray Knight (1897–1943) was born in poverty near Leeds, and would probably have become a mill-worker like Sam if his spirit of adventure had not inspired him to emigrate to Boston in the USA shortly before the outbreak of the First World War. Initially, he tried to make a career as an artist and illustrator, but tests showed that he was colour-blind. Instead he became a journalist on the Philadelphia Public Ledger *and there made a name for himself with his acerbic and often outspoken film reviews. These notices brought him to the attention of one of the Hollywood studio bosses who, in a typical act of self-interest, lured Knight to the film capital as a scriptwriter. It did not take him long to become disillusioned with movies, and he turned his hand to writing novels. In 1935 he made his debut with a pastiche of the then-popular hardboiled genre,* You Play the Red and the Black Comes Up, *and followed this with two rather more traditional novels,* The Happy Land *(1940) and* This Above All *(1941). A year later came a children's story,* Lassie Come Home *(1942), about a resourceful collie dog (based on Knight's own collie, 'Toots'), which was filmed starring a beautiful eleven-year-old newcomer, Elizabeth Taylor. The extraordinary success of this movie inspired a number of sequels and a long-running television serial which turned the faithful Lassie into a household name. Tragically, Eric Knight died in a plane crash before Lassie's fame could be added to the cult which already surrounded Sam Small. In 'Sam Small's Better Half', the little Yorkshireman suddenly finds himself divided into two—a state of being which offers great possibilities until his other half moves in with his wife ...*

*   *   *

'If there's one thing I'd like to do,' Mully Small said, as she sat before the hearth, 'it's travel. Now we're wealthy and retired, as tha maught say, I'd like to go round the world.'

Sam ignored the gambit altogether as he put down the evening paper.

'What,' he asked, rhetorically and pugnaciously, 'would the British working man be without his pint of ale at the day's end?'

'That's something the world'll never know till one of 'em tries it,' Mully snapped. 'And as I don't suppose tha's in the mood for noble experiments, for goodness' sake away ye go down to the pub, for I see I'll get no peace until tha does. Although I did think, since I'm poorly, that tha might have spent one evening at home.'

Sam got up and stood undecided. Truly Mully didn't look so well, and he wanted to stay. But he wanted his evening mug of ale, too. A sort of short, but bitter, tug-of-war took place inside him—and the ale won.

'Now I'll not be long,' he said, in a tone of hopeful appeasement.

Mully refused the scant olive branch.

'Ah'll gamble,' she said sarcastically, in her broadest Yorkshire dialect. 'Chucking out time!'

'Now isn't that just like a woman's dirty suspicions, for thee?' Sam asked the vacant air. 'I'll be back long before chucking out.'

At the time Sam really meant what he said—if only to prove to Mully how grossly she wronged him with her accusations. But when he got to the pub, unfortunately there was an argument going on. Moreover, it was just the sort of argument that needed the sagacity, erudition and forensic abilities of Sam Small—and Sam Small was the best man in all Yorkshire for giving his opinion in an argument.

'It's this way, Sam,' explained Rowlie Helliker. 'It says here as how a doctor thinks this Hitler chap has got—'

He peered at the newspaper.

'—anyway, the word means a split personality, it says.'

'Oh, aye,' responded Sam nonchalantly. 'Schizoperennial.'

'What's coming off here?' asked Huckle, the publican.

'That's just the technicological name o' the disease,' Sam said. 'It means a chap splits into two personalities—that's what.'

'Ah've seen two personalities,' offered Annie, the barmaid. 'It were in t'cinema once. One were—'

'Ah've come to a decision,' interrupted Gaffer Sitherthwick. 'If ye mean to stand theer and tell me that a chap can divide into two, then what Ah say is—it ain't human, it's just dirty propaganda.'

'Hold on, Gaffer,' Sam said. 'Ye see, science has discovered that every one of us is a couple of people, really. And ye can't beat science when it comes to—to—to science, can ye?'

'Science is off to get itself into a hole some day, if it goes on discovering things,' warned Capper Wambley darkly.

'Well, ye've heard o' twins, haven't ye?' Rowlie Helliker offered. 'Happen this here schizoperennia's like that, only a chap becomes twins after he's born instead of before.'

'Nonsense,' the Capper said. 'Ah would have heard of it before this. Ah'm the oldest chap here, and I never heard of that happening.'

'But it's only just come out, like,' Sam explained.

'Ah still don't believe a chap can split in two,' roared the Gaffer.

'Nor me, nawther,' agreed Capper Wambley.

'Hold on, British fair play every time,' Rowlie Helliker shouted. 'Two against one. Now what I say is this . . .'

And so the argument rumbled, with words flowing ponderously and sagely in the Yorkshire way, and the white arms of Annie, the barmaid, flashing up and down as she gave the long pull on the mild and bitter pumps. Until, in no time whatsoever, as you might say, there rose the voice of Huckle above the din, his voice sounding the well-known British curfew, 'Time gentlemen, please! Time!'

Sam Small stood, like Cinderella hearing the stroke of midnight.

'Eigh, by gum,' he muttered, aghast. 'And I promised Mully faithful I'd be home afore chucking out . . .'

Off Sam went, through the door as fast as his stubby legs would carry him. As he skeltered up along the Green, the thought seeped into his mind that if he got home quickly he might be able to say he left before closing time, but had strolled home lazily.

He began to feel guilty—not because he was preparing the evidence for another lie, but because he had left Mully alone all evening. He wished he hadn't done that.

He was feeling angry at himself, and then . . .

It happened!

There was a flash, a sort of silent explosion, a whirling of planets and comets in an endless purple void, and Sam found himself sitting on the pavement half-dazed.

'By gum,' he muttered thickly. 'I must have bumped into the lamp-post.'

But then, as he collected his senses, he saw another man, similarly situated on the pavement.

'So—it was thee bumped into me,' Sam began pugnaciously. 'Why doesn't tha look where tha's going?'

'It's six o' one and half a dozen o' t'other, lad.'

'Now, don't argue wi' me,' Sam groaned. 'Gie us a hand up.'

'How about thee gi'ing me a hand up?' the other said.

'Why, I never met such a nasty, unobliging chap,' Sam said. 'But I've no time to argue wi' thee. My wife's poorly and I promised to be home afore chucking out time, and here I am . . .'

'Beer-swiller!' accused the other. 'If thy wife's poorly, why doesn't tha sit with her? That's what I've been doing at ma home over the Green.'

'Thy home?' breathed Sam.

His voice rose in suspicion, and a chilly vibration ran up his spine. For he had an eerie feeling that the voice of the other man was familiar— too familiar, somehow.

'Who are ye?' Sam cried.

They both rose from the pavement, and Sam dragged the other under the street light. Then he gasped. For Sam Small found that he was looking at none other than himself!

For a second only was Sam nonplussed, and then his brain functioned. He grabbed the other tightly.

'A blooming impostor!' he said. 'I've got thee!'

'Impostor thysen,' the other said. 'I'm Sam Small.'

'Oooo, you liar. I'm Sam Small.'

'Now, now, don't contradict. Look at me and see if I don't look like Sam Small.'

'By gum, so tha does,' Sam admitted. Then he moaned, 'Eigh, don't go mixing me all up, or ye'll have me so conflummoxed I won't know what to think. How can ye prove ye're Sam Small?'

'Well,' the other began, glaring suspiciously. 'I have a wife whose name is Mully. And I have a daughter rising seventeen whose name's Vinnie, and . . .'

'I'll be jiggered,' Sam said. 'I see tha's a very clever impostor indeed. At least, tha's looked up all ma background. But tha's slipped up, my lad, for I know where I have thee!'

As he spoke Sam tugged at the heavy gold chain on his waistcoat and drew out a great turnip of a gold watch, and snapped open the back with a gesture.

'There,' he said. 'Read that. For I know it by heart. It says on it, "To Sam Small, from his loyal wife, Millicent, on their wedding day."'

'Well, I'll be jiggered,' said the other. 'For it says exactly the same—here!'

And, with a similar gesture, tugging at a similar chain, he snapped open the back of a similar watch.

'Oooo, by gum,' Sam moaned. 'I *am* in trouble. I must have done summat wrong. And here I stand, not knowing whether I'm me, or tha's me—or I'm thee—or whether us is both we.'

He stood a second.

'Why, that's it,' he yelped.

'What's it?'

'We're both me—both of us. It's schizoperennial. My personality's split wide open, just like we've been arguing about down the pub—and I've become two on us.'

'Well, by gum. Think o' that, now,' said the other. 'But—but what can us do about it?'

'Look, this is a very important happening, lad,' Sam said. 'And we've got to go careful about it. I think, before anyone sees us and spoils it all, we'd better take a walk out on the moor and discuss it proper. For the sake of getting it straight a bit, suppose I call thee Sammywell, and call mysen Sam? That'll get us separated for purposes o' discussion, as ye might say.'

And off they went over the moor, with Sam explaining his view of what had happened.

'If we handle it carefully,' said Sam, 'there's a fortune in it. For instance, doctors and such wi' scientific curiosity—why they'd pay a right lot o' brass to meet a couple of chaps like us.'

'I don't care for doctors, Sam. Happen they'd want to operate on us,' Sammywell ventured.

'Aye, I don't care for 'em, either. But happen we could get a tent and travel round wi' the feasts—we'd be champion curiosities, and people'd pay a shilling to see us.'

'I'd object to being a freak, like,' Sammywell droned.

'Nay, there's nowt wrong wi' making a little honest brass, lad, and I've not got it all worked out yet, but there's brass in the general idea. Just look at t'brass Ah've just made off ma self-doffing spindle.'

'Aye,' said Sammywell, 'but an invention's a fact.'

'So is this a fact,' Sam said. 'Think on it! The Government might take an interest in us, as tha might say. Why, if they could multiply every man by two they could double the manpower o' t'army!'

'Aye, but us can't sit out here all night, lad, while tha works it out. There's Mully waiting up for me at home.'

'Well, we can't go home,' Sam expostulated, 'not the two on us.'

'That's so,' Sammywell agreed. 'But one on us could stay out here tonight and puzzle out what's best to do. T'other can go home and say nowt to Mully. It won't be cold sleeping out here for thee, Sam—and in the morning I can slip out and bring thee a few licks to eat, like.'

'Hold on a bit. I don't like that idea—thee going home to my wife. It—it ain't moral!'

'But since tha explained it to me that we're both one, when I go home it's really thee, too, tha knows,' Sammywell said. 'Now be sensible; one of us has got to take a back seat for a while until we get this all figgered out. Why don't you go away for a few days and we'll both put our thinking caps on?'

'Me go away?' echoed Sam.

Then he thought a while. He began to see possibilities in the suggestion. If he went away he could have a right good beano.

Sam glowed inwardly. But he put on a sad face.

'Eigh, it's sad and all to think of a man giving up the rightful comfort of his own hearth and home, and going forth, an uncherished wanderer on the face o' t'earth, as ye might say. But for the sake of Mully and her peace o' mind, I make the great sacrifice. Goodbye.'

'Where are ye going?'

'Why—I'll cut over the moor and be in Bradley by morning. Then I'll drop in the bank and get a little cash—'

'Hey. Thee be careful wi' my savings account,' Sammywell wavered.

'*Our* savings account, Sammywell, lad. So long.'

And then Sammywell was alone.

'Sam,' he shouted into the darkness. 'When'll ye be back?'

'Expect me when ye see me,' floated back the voice of Sam. 'Keep the home fires burning, Sammywell. Keep the home fires burning!'

'Do you want a railway ticket, lad?' asked the man behind the little bars at the station, helpfully.

'Aye, that's it exactly,' Sam said. 'But Mully generally tends to all this part of it, and I'm at a bit of a loss wi'out her. What sort o' tickets have ye got?'

'Oh, first, third, excursion, return.'

'I'll have a return.'

'One return. Good. Where to?'

'Why back here, of course, gormless.'

The chap, thinking Sam was kidding him, got quite upset. So the argument began. Sam got his Yorkshire up and wouldn't be pinned down as to where he was going.

'Now any fool can let people buy what they want,' Sam pointed out. 'But I've read it takes a real salesman to sell a doubtful customer.'

'But *where* do you want to go?'

'How would I know afore I hear what expense I'm off to run into? No sensible man runs ahead of his brass. So cite me a few bargains.'

The man blew out his breath and picked up a printed list.

'Llandudno, very special, twenty-six and six?' he offered.

'Couldn't spell it,' Sam said. 'I wouldn't live in a town I couldn't spell. I'd feel all defeated, like.'

'Scarborough, fifteen and—'

'Dearie, no. I had a chum went there once, broke his leg, he did. I'd be that sad thinking on him. He was putting his trowsis on, he was, and just toppled over and broke his leg.'

'They could set it, couldn't they?'

'Aye, but his wife were that upset, 'cause his leg didn't look the same. She were always after him to break the other. They never had a peaceful day together after that. A plumber, he were. Name o' Billy Sandyson. Ever meet him?'

'No! Blackpool, twelve and six, ten-day excursion?'

'Blackpool? Now that's getting me interested.'

'Shall it be Blackpool, then?'

'Don't rush me. I were there once. I ate so many whelks wi' vinegar I were sick on the train coming home. Eigh, I had a champion time.'

'Then it'll be Blackpool?'

'Hold on a minute. If I don't use the return part in ten days, can I cash it in on a full fare coming back?'

'Yes,' sighed the man. 'Yes.'

'Then sold!' said Sam.

And off he went to Blackpool.

Sam did have a rare old time at Blackpool. There was so much to do that he'd sally out each morning and never even go back to his boarding-house for meals. But this didn't matter as there were any number of places where a chap could buy winkles and cockles and fried fish and pease pudding and ices. And since it was a holiday without Mully, Sam didn't feel so bad about flinging his money about.

And Sam winked at all the lasses there on their holidays—for though a bit snowy in the pow, Sam was feeling quite a dog.

One day, by the bandstand, a big, fine-looking woman smiled at him. Sam brought himself a walking cane on the strength of it. The next day she smiled again, so he got himself a straw hat for one-and-tuppence.

Then one day it got warm, and everyone went wading on the sands. The sands were a big squoggy at Blackpool, but San, full of holiday freedom, didn't mind. With his trousers rolled up, he paddled and splashed to his heart's content—all through the day, until the sun began to go down, blood-red, and a chill wind came in suddenly from the sea.

Sam Small shivered.

'Happen I got ma trowsis wet,' he said to himself. 'Wouldn't Mully give me a talking-to?'

He went up higher on the sands, intending to put on his stockings and boots, and then go by the bandstand to see what the fine-looking woman thought of his straw hat. But somehow, when he was dressed, he didn't feel like strolling. And yet—he wanted something.

'Now what can it be?' Sam said to himself. 'Happen I want summat to eat.'

So he thought of pork pies and saveloys and sausage rolls and oysters, and all the things sold at the shops; but it wasn't any of those he wanted.

He tried to puzzle it out, considering a walk on the promenade as against a stroll on the pier, a look at the zoo or a go at the merry-go-round, or perhaps the ferris wheel. But it wasn't any of these things he wanted.

As he sat the sun sank, the wet sands glowed in the dusk, and a sort of cosmic sadness washed in from the dying day and seeped over him. The lights in the shops behind him popped on, one by one, and the electric signs came on to spangle the holiday front of the town, and people laughed and screamed. And over the ocean the day ebbed away to other lands and there was nothing left of the sea but its hushing.

Finally Sam gave up trying to puzzle it out and went back to his boarding-house. He was in a strange bad temper.

'I think I've copped a cold,' he told his landlady.

'More like some o' the stuff tha's been eating,' she said. 'Tripe and cowheel and chitterlins and eel-pies and poloney and trunnel-pies and hokeypokey and blood pudding . . .'

'Are ye selling summat?' Sam said. 'If I weren't upset when I come home, I am now.'

'Then I'll gie thee some lickerish powder. I allus used to give ma husband lickerish powder. A fine chap he were . . .'

'Thy husband? Where's he now?'

'Eigh, he's deead.'

'I tell ye, it's nowt I ate. What's more, if it were I wouldn't take lickerish powder. I tell ye I've copped a cold.'

'Then I'll fix thee a mustard footbath.'

'I don't want a footbath. Mully gi's me hot rum and treacle.'

'Well, I've no rum. I'll gie ye the treacle now and ye can take the rum tomorrow.'

'By gum, there's no help from women. Tha sounds like Mully hersen.'

'Heaven pity her, if she has to put up wi' thee.'

'By gow, I should ha' known better than to expect either sense or sympathy i' Lancashire!'

'Huh!' snorted the landlady. 'Yorkshire!'

'That's done it!' roared Sam. 'That's the final insult. First thing in the morn I'm off home to Mully.'

And home he went.

As Sam Small swung along by the Green in the twilight, suddenly his happiness fled. For, as if for the first time, he remembered Sammywell.

'By gum,' he breathed, 'if I walk in and he's there, Mully'll find out the whole thing, and want to know where I've been—then I'll cop Halifax. I'd better go sly.'

So Sam crept up to his cottage and looked in the window. And there he saw Mully, knitting as she rocked in the chair before the fire, with Sammywell reading aloud to her.

Sam felt queer and hopeless and unwanted, seeing another man before his fire, with himself outside and tired—and badly in need of a good cup of tea.

He retreated into the garden and began slipping bits of stone at the window. After a long time the door opened and a beam of light poured out. With it, from far back in the room, came Mully's voice. Sam heard it pouring over him, like a rush of warm blood in his chest.

'If that's them Kidderley bairns again, Sam, shout out to them not to be naughty.'

'Psst,' Sam hissed. 'Sammywell! I want a word wi' thee. Meet me up the Green corner.'

'What is it, Sam, love?' came Mully's voice.

'Nowt,' called back Sammywell. 'I think I'll get ma jacket and take a stroll, Mully—and a smoke. Then I won't choke the house up wi' baccy smoke.'

'Aye, do. A breath of air'll do thee good, Sam,' said Mully's voice.

Then the door closed. Sam stalked up to the corner of the Green. Over and over again he heard Mully's words—and the tones. Her voice had been soft and warm. And she had called Sammywell 'Sam, love.' That wasn't like Mully. She never called *him* 'love'.

By the time he saw Sammywell approaching, Sam was fair hopping with anger and jealousy.

'Tha's off to take a walk wi' me, lad,' Sam growled.

'Why, what's wrong, Sam?'

'Never heed what's wrong, I've just decided that it's high time I came home and took ma rightful and proper place beside my wife— ye—ye—Judas!'

'But, Sam, I thought ye wanted to go away and have a fling.'

'Well, I've flung—and now it's thy turn to go away.'

'Oh, no, Sam,' said Sammywell self-righteously. 'I'm that comfortable. I stay home evenings wi' Mully and—'

'Aye. I heard her gi'ing thee the soft-soap voice. An' her ma wife?'

'*Our* wife, Sam.'

'Now don't conflummox me,' Sam groaned. 'Tha's had a comfortable week—now it's ma turn. Go away for a visit.'

'But Sam, tha's the one who likes to go away. I'm the one who likes to stay home.'

'Ooah, ba gum,' moaned Sam. 'Do I have to argue wi' thee? Look, I'm hungry—I haven't had ma tea yet—and I've been poorly. Now hop it like a good chap.'

'Not me,' said Sammywell. 'My place is in the home, and there's where I'm off right now.'

'Well I'm off wi' thee, then.'

'And have her find out? Nay, I'm not bahn to have her upset.'

'Now look here, Sammywell. If I know Mully, she's off to find out sooner or later—so it might as well be sooner, and then I can have ma tea!'

'And I say ye'll not . . .'

But away darted Sam, full tilt. For he realised that if he got home first, then the whole problem would be shifted onto the shoulders of Sammywell.

Down the Green went Sam with Sammywell legging it after him. They were both, of course, evenly matched. But unfortunately Sam had to open the gate and the door. He managed the first all right, but before he reached the door Sammywell grabbed him, and down they went, wrestling and struggling. They were so intent that they hardly realised the door had opened until they heard Mully's voice.

'What's up now?'

They stopped wrestling and blinked into the light. So the three stood!

'Ooah, ma dear,' moaned Mully. 'Get in this house, here—afore anyone sees us.'

Shamefacedly the two men went into the cottage and stood on the hearth. Mully looked at them, and then flopped into the rocking chair and began to cry.

'Now what tricks are ye playing on me, Sam Small?' she cried. 'Whichever one of ye is Sam?'

'We're both Sam,' Sammywell said.

'To think ye never told me ye had a twin brother,' sobbed Mully. 'But one of ye's Sam—and when I find out which one it is—he's off to wish he'd never been born.'

'Now hold on, Mully,' Sam said. 'We're both us—that is, we're both me.'

Then he explained as best he could how his personality had split the week before.

'Well, which one's been here this past week?' Mully asked.

'Me,' said Sammywell quickly. 'He's been on a trip to Blackpool!'

'Ha, ye scallywag,' said Mully triumphantly. 'Now I know which one's Sam Small. It's thee! So tha would go gallivanting away and leave thy true wife wi' a stranger...'

She advanced on Sam, but Sammywell interposed a hand.

'Nay, Mully,' he said. 'Don't be angry. Hasn't it been better with him away? Haven't I stayed by thy side this week and nursed thee through a cold?'

'Aye,' she said. 'Tha's been that considerate and kind—I knew there must be summat wrong. I were too happy for it to be true.'

She sat down and wept, and Sam stood, head hanging, and shuffled his feet. For a while he thought, and then went to his wife.

'Mully Small,' he said. 'Do ye mean that? Have ye really been so happy wi'—wi' yon, while I've been away?'

Now Mully was, after all, a woman. And she couldn't help being a bit spiteful in her answer.

'Sam Small,' she said. 'I've never been so cherished in all ma born days. It's been the best week of ma married life.'

Sam stared into the fire and drew his breath.

'I see,' he said softly. 'Well, somehow there ain't much for a chap to say when he finds out he's failed, is there? What I mean is—well, t'would be a poor man who'd stand in the way of his wife's happiness so—goodbye—and good luck, lass.'

Sam turned on his heel and made for the door, while Mully watched as in a trance. Perhaps she would have let him go, but Sammywell's voice wakened her.

'Ye see, Sam,' cried Sammywell triumphantly. 'I told ye I were the man to make her happy.'

That started Mully.

'Now hold on,' she cried. 'I've got summat to say about all this. Come back, lad, and sit here by the hearth. If this is true about this here split personality, what us has got to do is think it out.'

'Aye, but us has done all the thinking us can. Why couldn't we all stay here?' Sammywell suggested.

'What, me live wi' two husbands?' breathed Mully. 'That's bigamy.'

'But me and Sam is both the same husband,' Sammywell pointed out.

'Aye,' said Mully. 'We know that, because we're open-minded, but I'm afraid the British law hasn't caught up wi' such modern things, and'll come to the conclusion that two husbands is two.'

'Hold on,' said Sam. 'Tha's nobbut had one marriage.'

'Then one on ye's churched, and the other's unchurched, and that's still against the law.'

'Aye,' Sam said.

'Don't interrupt,' said Mully. 'Now all keep quiet till I think this out.'

For a long time she sat, and then she sighed and rose.

'Well, I've decided,' she said. 'Ma mother allus used to say to me, "When in doubt, go to sleep." '

'So,' crooned Sammywell, smiling.

'So,' she said. 'I'm off to bed and go to sleep—and ye two are off outside.'

'But look here, Mully,' Sammywell groaned. 'I don't like—'

'Neither do I,' she chipped in. 'But ye doubled yoursen wi'out ma help. Happen ye can best sort it out the same road.'

And firmly she chivvied the two of them to the door and pushed them out. Only as Sam went past, she said, quietly, 'Don't come home till there's nobbut one of ye.'

Then the door closed, the bolt clicked, and the two were out in the night.

'Now, we'd better take a walk and think some more,' Sam said. 'And thee stick close to me if ye know what's good. We'll take a turn on the moor.'

As the two reached the Green, they still wore the same thoughtful expressions.

'Have ye thought of owt?' Sammywell asked.

'Look, I'm fair sick to deeath o' thee,' Sam warned. 'Now be quiet.'

He paused and looked about. They were by the lamp-post.

'Here's where we first met,' Sam mused.

'If tha'd nobbut stayed away,' Sammywell began.

'Now look here, ma lad,' Sam burst out. 'One more peep out o' thee, and tha'll get a thick lip. Why, for two pins . . .'

Then, as Sam lifted his hand, he seemed to hear the words of Mully, whispered as if for him alone, 'Don't come back till there's nobbut one of ye.'

The idea raced through his brain.

'Sam Small,' cried Sammywell, in terror. 'Tha has murder in thy heart.'

Sam smiled gently.

'Tha's ruddy right, I have,' he said. 'Come on, Sammywell, put up thy dukes and stand up like a Yorkshireman.'

'But I don't like brawling, Sam.'

'Well, I'll sweeten ye up to it, then, Sammywell, ma lad. There!'

And Sam popped a left on one side of Sammywell's nose.

'And there!'

And he popped a right on the other side.

'Well,' Sammywell said, outraged. 'The Good Book says if ye're slapped on one cheek, turn the other. But it gives no instructions what to do if that gets slapped. However, I suppose that mean's a chap's got to use his own judgement. So—there!'

And he banged a beautiful and righteous left smack in the middle of Sam's nose.

'Ow,' said Sam. 'Here I come!'

Then, with fists flailing, the two went at each other in as strange a fight as you could wish to see. For, both being Sam Small, they were evenly matched as never were any two men before in prize-ring history. Each had the same strength and each mind worked exactly alike. If Sam swung with the right, Sammywell blocked with his left. It was like boxing before a mirror. So on and on it went, with neither gaining an advantage, and both becoming more and more tired.

Then Sam got an inspiration.

'The thing to do next time he leads,' he said to himself, 'is not to block, but to take it and just let him have one with everything I've got.'

And at exactly that second, Sammywell was thinking exactly the same thing.

The result was, they both swung, neither blocked, and then for each there was nothing but a blinding flash, a crack, and an interstellar polka-dot display.

Suddenly Sam felt his spirit lifting. Below him he could see the two bodies lying, unconscious. And beside him was another soaring spirit.

'Ooah, ma gum,' Sam moaned. 'So now there's four on us.'

'No, Sam,' said Sammywell, gently. 'Look.'

As they watched, the two bodies below slowly drifted together and begun to merge.

'Now,' Sammywell said. 'Come, Sam. We've both got to fit in there.'

So they floated down and began to squeeze and wriggle themselves into the body. And then Sam heard voices.

'Poor owd Sam,' said someone. 'He must ha' bumped into the lamp-post.'

Sam wanted to tell them that it had been a fight, but the words wouldn't come out. And in what seemed to be a sort of flash-past of time, he was in the cottage and Mully was bending over him.

'Eigh, Sam,' she moaned. 'I' trouble again.'

'Nay, Mully,' he said thickly. 'I'm not drunk.'

She bent near him.

'Neither tha is,' she agreed.

Sam looked into her eyes.

'I killed him,' he said.

'Who?'

'Sammywell!'

'Sammywell? Sammywell who?'

Sam thought this over and began to smile.

Women—they were the wonderful ones. They knew what part of a man's life to pretend to forget.

Sam felt a rush of warmth and love for Mully—plump Mully who was now bathing his head with a cool damp towel.

'Dosta forgive me, Mully?'

'Eigh, Sam Small,' she sighed. 'I been forgiving thee so many years I wouldn't know how to get out o' the habit now.'

'Mully,' said Sam. 'I'm off to treat thee nicer. For one thing, I weren't happy away at Blackpool, and for another, well—after I killed Sammywell tonight, we sort of amalgamated. A merger, as ye might say. So now I've got him inside me, too, and he's the good side of me—and from now on I'm off to let my good side come to the front.'

'Hush,' Mully said. 'If ye do ye'll be sort of anatomically twisted.'

'And I'm never going down The Spread Eagle any more. I'm bahn to stay home every evening and read to thee while tha knits.'

'Heaven forbid,' Mully said. 'I'd never have a moment's peace then. Eigh, I like ye just as ye are, Sam, ye old scallywag.'

'Dosta, Mully? But I'm determined—fro' now on I'm off to be more like Sammywell; he's really ma better half.'

'Nay, tha's got nobbut one better half,' Mully said. 'And that's me. Upsydaisy. Up ye come to bed.'

DANSE MACABRE

Mervyn Peake

There are critics who claim that Mervyn Peake's Gormenghast *trilogy about a crumbling, far-future world is an even greater work of fantasy than Tolkien's* Lord of the Rings. *Certainly, the adventures of Titus, 77th Earl of Gormenghast and heir to the House of Groan, told with a mixture of wit and dazzling imagination, rate among the great works of the genre, and thoroughly deserve John Clute's accolade in* The Encyclopedia of Science Fiction *(1995) when he calls* Gormenghast *'one of the most richly realised alternate worlds in all the literature of fantasy or sf'. Fans of the trilogy include the musicians Nigel Kennedy, Sting and Phil Collins; chef Keith Floyd, who claims to have found some kitchens in Spain which instantly reminded him of the ancestral kitchens in the book; and the writers Michael Moorock and Anthony Burgess, who once referred to the work as 'a rich wine of fancy chilled by the intellect to just the right temperature'. A stage version of* Gormenghast *has already been produced, and Walt Disney studios own the film rights.*

Mervyn Laurence Peake (1911–1968) was born in Kuling in southern China, where his father was a medical missionary, and the memories of those 'rich, alien years' shaped much of his later career when he returned to England and began working as an artist and writer. His love of fantasy was demonstrated in his first book, Captain Slaughterboard Drops Anchor, *published in 1939; and during the subsequent war years while he was serving in the Royal Engineers he started work on what would ultimately become the* Gormenghast *trilogy. At the end of the hostilities, Peake was the first artist to be sent to the Belsen concentration camp, another profoundly affecting experience. Shortly after completing the three comic masterpieces about Titus Groan, he was found to be suffering from a form of Parkinson's disease which tragically shortened his life. 'Danse Macabre', originally published in* Science Fantasy *in 1963, is one of Mervyn Peake's few short stories,*

*and a tale as curious as anything he wrote. It is also about the ability
to fly—not human beings, though, but* people's clothes . . .

*   *   *

Whether it was the full moon that woke me, I do not know. It may
have been. Or it may be that the melancholy which had settled on my
spirit and which coloured my dreams, had become too strong for me
to bear and had broken through my sleep and left me, of a sudden,
aware and trembling.

It is no part of my story to tell you of the unhappy circumstances
which had driven my dear wife away from me. I cannot tell you of that
dreadful separation. It is sufficient to say that in spite of, or it may be
because of our ill omen'd love, we were driven apart, although, as you
shall hear, this desperate act brought nothing but horror in the end.

I had drawn wide the curtains when I had gone to bed, for the night
was close, and now, with my eyes wide open, I found that my bedroom
was filled with the light of the moon.

Facing me, as I lay upon my side was my wardrobe, a tall piece of
furniture, and my gaze wandered across the panels until they came to
rest upon one of the metal door knobs.

Uneasy as I was, I had as yet no concrete cause for alarm; and would
have closed my eyes had it not been that all at once my heart stopped
beating. For the metal knob on which my gaze was fixed had begun,
very slowly, very surely, to revolve, without a sound.

I cannot recall with any exactness what thoughts possessed me during
the interminable turning of that brass knob. All I know is that what febrile
thoughts I had were soaked in fear, so that my brain began to sweat no
less than my body. But I could not turn my eyes away, nor close them. I
could only watch as the cupboard door itself began to sway slowly open
with hideous deliberation until it lay wide to the moon-filled room.

And then it happened . . . happened in the stillness when not so much
as the call of a little owl from the nearby woods or a sigh in the leaves,
disturbed the small hours of that summer night, when my dress clothes
on their hanger sailed slowly out of the depths of the wardrobe and with
infinite smoothness came to a rest in mid-air immediately before my dressing table.

So unexpected, so ludicrous was this, that it was a wonder I did not
lose my nerve and scream. But the terror was caught in my throat and
I made no sound but continued to watch as the trousers slid from the

cross-bar of the hanger until their extremities were no more than a couple of inches from the floor, in which position they remained, loose and empty. No sooner had this happened than an agitation at the shoulders made it plain that the white waistcoat and the long black tailcoat were trying to dislodge themselves from the hanger and then, all at once they were free, and the hanger, leaving behind it in the room a headless, handless, footless spectre, floated into the depths of the cupboard and the door closed upon it.

By now the limp arms, for all their lack of hands, appeared in dumb-show to be knotting a white tie about a white collar, and then, most strange of all, the empty figure at the next moment was leaning forward in mid-air at an angle of thirty degrees from the floor flinging the limp sleeves forwards as though about to dive and with a whisk of the 'tails' it floated across the room and out of the window.

Before I knew what I was doing I had reached the window and was just in time to see far away beyond the lawn, my dress clothes skimming their way towards the oak wood where they disappeared into the darkness beneath the trees.

How long I stood staring down across the lawn to the long dense margin of the oak wood I do not know, nor yet, when at last I returned across the room, how long I stared at the knob on the wardrobe door, before I had the courage to grip it and turn it and fling it open. I only know that at last I did so and saw the naked wooden hanger suspended there.

At last I slammed the door upon them and turned my back upon the cupboard. I began to pace the room in a fever of fearful foreboding. At last I fell exhausted upon my bed. It was only when dawn broke that I fell into a clammy sleep.

When I awoke it was past mid-day. The countryside was alive with familiar sounds; the squabbling of sparrows in the ivy outside the window; a dog barking and the drone of a tractor several fields across and listening half-asleep, it was a full minute before I recollected the nightmare I had suffered. Of course it was a nightmare! What else could it have been? With a short laugh I flung the bedclothes from me and got to my feet and began to dress. It was only when I was about to open the wardrobe door that I paused for a moment. The dream had been too vivid to be entirely disregarded even in the same light of a summer day but again I laughed, and the sound of my own laughter chilled me. It was like a child I once heard shouting out in his terror, 'I'm not afraid of *you*. I'm not afraid of *you*.'

*   *   *

Opening the door of the cupboard I sighed with relief for there, hanging demurely in the semi-darkness, were my evening clothes. Taking a tweed jacket from its hanger, I was about to close the door when I saw, clinging to the knee of my evening trousers, a wisp of grass.

It had always been a habit of mine, almost a fixation you might say, to keep my clothes in good condition. It seemed odd to me this being so, that, having brushed my suit a night or two previously, there should be any kind of blemish. Why had the wisp of grass not caught my attention? However, strange as it seemed, I told myself there must, of course, be some simple explanation, and I dismissed the little problem from my mind.

Why I do not quite know, but I told no one of the dream, perhaps because anything strange or bizarre is distasteful to me and I presumed, perhaps wrongly, that such things are distasteful to others also. The memory of that horrible night lingered all day with me. Had it not been that I hate to be thought peculiar I think I would have found release in confiding the silly dream to someone or other. You see it was not simply frightening; it was ludicrous too. Something more to smile about than to be afraid of. But I found I could not smile.

The next six days passed uneventfully enough. On the seventh evening, which was a Friday, I went to bed much later than is my usual practice, for some friends who had come to dinner with me had stayed talking until well after midnight and when they had gone I began to read, so that it was close upon two o'clock before I climbed to my bedroom where I sank upon the bed still fully clothed and continued for at least twenty minutes more to read my book.

By now I was drowsy but before I got to my feet in order to undress, I found that against my will I was directing my gaze at the cupboard. Fully believing that the dream had indeed been a dream, and nothing but a dream, the hideous habit had taken hold of me, so that the last thing I saw before I fell asleep was always, the doorknob.

And again it moved, and again as terrible to me as ever before, it went on turning with the deliberate rotation and my heart seemed to be stuck between my ribs, hammering for release in the silence of the second ghastly night. The sweat poured out of my skin and the avid taste of terror filled my mouth.

The fact that it was happening all over again; that it was a *repetition* in no way helped me, for it appeared that what was once *unbelievable* was now an unarguable fact.

Slowly, inexorably, the knob turned and the cupboard door swung open and my evening clothes floated out as before and the trousers slid until they touched the ground, the hanger dislodged itself from the shoulders and it seemed there was no change in the absurd, yet ghastly ritual, until it came to that moment when the apparition was about to turn to the window. This time it turned to me, and, though it had no face, I knew it *was* looking at me.

Then, as its entire body began to shake violently, I closed my eyes for no more than a second but during that instant the clothes had disappeared through the open window.

I leapt to my feet and rushed to the window. At first I could see nothing for I was directing my gaze at the lawn that stretched away for about sixty yards to the outskirts of the woods. No creature, ghost or mortal could have covered that distance in the few seconds it took me to reach the window. But then, some movement in the semi-darkness caused me to look down, and there it was, standing on the narrow gravel path immediately below me. Its back was to the house and its sleeves were raised a little on either side, empty though they were.

Being exactly above the headless creature I found that I was forced to see down into the horrible darkness of that circular pit whose outward rim was formed by the stiff, white collar. As I started, nauseated, it began to skim, or glide—towards the lawn; it is hard to find a word that can adequately suggest the way it propelled itself across the ground, the tailcoat unnaturally upright, and the trouser-ends appearing almost to trail the grass, although they did not really touch the ground.

That I was dressed, I think, gave me courage, for, in spite of my inner terror, I ran down the stairs and out of the house and was just in time to see the apparition about to disappear into the woods beyond the lawn. I noted, as I ran, the spot at which it entered the forest, and fearing that I might lose the unholy thing, I raced feverishly across the widespread lawn.

It was well that I did this for on reaching the margin of the oak wood, I caught a glimpse of the high white collar and the gleam of cuffs away ahead and to the right.

Of course I knew the forest well enough by daylight but by night it seemed a very different place, yet I followed as best I could, stumbling at times and all but losing sight of the floating thing as it flitted through the trees ahead of me. There seemed to be no hesitancy in its progress and it occurred to me that, judging by the direction it was taking, it must very soon be coming upon the first of those long rides that ran from east to west across the forest.

And this was so, for it was only a few moments later that the foliage cleared above my head and I found myself standing on the verge of the long grassy avenue of oaks and not a hundred paces to my left I saw my bodiless vesture.

Bodiless it may have been, but it did not appear so in spite of the lack of feet or hands or head. For it became obvious that the garments were in a high state of agitation, turning this way and that, sometimes circling an oak tree on the far side of the avenue, sometimes floating an inch above the ground with the shoulders stooping forwards, almost as though in spite of its headlessness it peered down the long dwindling perspective of the forest ride.

Then, of a sudden, my heart leapt to my mouth; for my evening dress (its cuffs and collar gleaming in the dim light) had begun to tremble violently, and turning my eyes in the direction in which the suit was facing, I saw, gliding towards us from a great way off, an ice-blue evening dress.

Nearer and nearer it came, nearer and nearer, floating with an effortless beauty, the long skirt trailing the ground. But there were no feet, and there were no arms or hands. And there was no head and yet there was something *familiar* about it as at last it reached my black attire and as I saw the sleeve of my coat pass itself around the ice-blue silken waist of the hollow lady and a dance began which chilled my blood, for although the movements were slow, almost leisurely, yet the headless thing was vibrating like the plucked string of a fiddle.

In contrast to this horrible vacillation, the evening dress of the other dancer moved in a strangely frozen manner made all the more horrible by its lack of arms. As I watched I began to feel a horrible sickness in my body and my knees began to give. In reaching for support I gripped a branch at my side and to my horror it snapped off in my hands, with a report, which in the silence of the night sounded like a gun-shot. I lost my balance and fell upon my knees, but recovering at once I turned my gaze to the dancers. They were gone—gone as though they had never been. The avenue of tall trees stretched away in solemn, moonlit silence.

And then I saw what seemed to be a little heap of material jumbled untidily together on the sward. Steeling myself I stepped out into the moonlight and made my way, step by step towards the lifeless heap, and on reaching to within twelve feet of it I saw that it was composed of black material intertwined with a lovelier fabric the colour of blue ice.

I began to sweat where I stood, and I cannot tell how long I must have remained there, the sickness mounting in my stomach and my brain, when a movement in the untidy heap led at once to a further movement, and then before my eyes the parts began to disentangle themselves and to rise one by one from the ground and to reassemble in the air, and in another instant they were gone; the lovely dress skimming the grass in the direction from which it had come until it dwindled to an ice-blue speck in the distance of the ride. My suit, no less swiftly, fled in the opposite direction and was gone and I was left alone.

How I reached my home I shall never know—more I think by instinct than by reason, for I was feverish and deadly tired.

When at last I stumbled up the stairs and into my room I fell upon my knees and could not rise again for several minutes. When I did regain my feet I turned my gaze to the wardrobe, and stared at the brass knob until a gust of courage filled me and I turned the handle and the door swung open.

And there, hanging as primly as ever, were my tails and trousers.

During the week that followed I lived in a state of nervous excitement; an excitement most beastly. I was frightened, but I was also fascinated. I found myself thinking of nothing else but what would happen on the following Friday. The few friends I saw in the vicinity of my house were shocked at my appearance for my face, which was naturally a fresh and ruddy colour, had turned grey. My hands trembled and my eyes kept darting here and there as though I were at bay.

I told no one of what had happened. It was not that I was brave. It was more that I was cowardly. I have always had a distaste for the unearthly or anything remotely smacking of the supernatural and I would never have lifted my head again in public if I knew myself to be regarded as some kind of metaphysical crank. I knew that I would rather go through this business alone, frightened as I was, than risk the raised eyebrows—the sidelong glance. When possible over the next seven days I avoided my friends. But there was one particular engagement which I could not avoid, nor wished to avoid.

I had promised, faithfully promised, to join some friends who were giving a small dinner party on the following Friday. But it was not just that—for if that had been all I would have invented some plausible excuse. No, it was for a very different reason. It was because my wife was to be there—our mutual friends, in their ignorance, were eager to re-unite us. They had seen our illness mounting. For myself, my whole system was sick, for in truth I was but half a creature without her. And *she*? She who left me, seeing no hope for us but only strengthening of that perverse and hideous *thing* that drives men to their own destruction, the more the love, the more the wish to hurt. What of her? Like me, they told me, those friends of mine, she also was sickening fast.

We were too proud to meet of our own will. Too proud, or too selfish. And so this dinner had been cunningly arranged and the time came when I arrived and was greeted by my hostess and my host and began to mix with the guests.

There was dinner and there was a little dancing, and, were I not to have been possessed, I might have enjoyed the evening, but my face kept turning to a little gold clock on the mantelpiece and from the clock to the door beyond the curtains that led to the hall.

As the evening wore on I began to suffer an absolute darkness of the spirit when suddenly she appeared and my heart gave a great bound and I trembled desperately, for though she was completely beautiful, it was not her face I noticed first but the ice-blue of her dress.

We came together as though we had never parted and though we knew that our meeting had been engineered, yet there was suddenly too much joy in us for any thought of resentment to darken our thoughts.

But underneath our mounting joy was terror, for we could see in one another's eyes that we had suffered the same nightmare. We knew that, as we danced, our clothes were only waiting for the moment, two hours ahead, when some kind of dreaded thing could arrive and invest them with another life.

What were we to do? One thing we knew at once and that was that we must get away from the music and the gathering—a gathering which felt pleased with itself no doubt, for we must have looked like lovers as we left the room trembling and hand in hand.

We knew we must keep together. But I also knew, as she knew, that if we were to break the spell at all we must attack; and end our role. But how? What could we do? Firstly, we must stay together, secondly we must remain in our evening clothes.

The last hours before three o'clock were as long as all the days of our lives. I had driven her back to my house, or *our* house again, and we had rested there for the most part in silence. At first we talked of what it could mean but it was beyond us. We had been chosen, so it seemed, to be the play-things of some demon.

We had all but fallen asleep when the first tremor swarmed my spine. Her head had been on my shoulder and she awoke in an instant to find me rising to my feet, my body quaking and the material of my back and across my shoulders beginning to flap gently like a sail. Even in my horror I turned to her and she was rising also from the divan, rising as though drawn upwards with no effort and most horrible of all, there was a kind of blur across her lovely face, as though her features were less real than before.

'Oh Harry,' she cried, 'Harry, where are you?' and she flung out her hand to me, and, oh, how precious was the touch of one another's fingers, for they had seemed to be no longer *there*, and by now our faces had *fled* also and our feet and our hands, yet we could *feel* the ground with our feet and the pressure of our cold palms.

Then there came to us the long shudder and the beginning of the *malevolence*. All I could see of her now was her ice-blue dress but an evil of some kind, a malevolent evil, seemed to be entering our clothes— a vile restlessness, and we were torn apart and from that moment I was never able to touch her again, or receive the blessing of her fingertips. And then, against our wills, we began to move, and as we moved together towards the windows I heard her voice again, 'Harry! Harry,' very faint and far away, although we were quite close to one another, 'Harry! Harry, don't leave me.'

I could do nothing for we were swept together out of the wide windows and without touching the lawn with our feet were flung to and fro in the air as though our clothes had but one object—to shake themselves free of us. There was no way of knowing how long this silent tumult went on. I only knew it was fraught with evil.

But, as the moments passed there seemed to come a slackening in the violence, and though the sense of evil was in essence as vile as ever, yet it seemed that the clothes were tiring. By the time they entered the wood, they appeared to rest themselves on our bodies and though we heard nothing, it was as though they were gasping for breath, or gasping for strength. It was as though there was the *will* to kill us, but the means of doing so eluded them. By the time we reached the ride we were moving laboriously and a little later we collapsed together beneath the oak tree.

It was almost dawn when I recovered my consciousness. I was drenched with an icy dew.

For a moment I had no idea where I was but then the whole thing rose in my mind, and turning my head to right and left I found I was alone. My wife had gone.

In an agony of mind I stumbled home and up the stairs and into my bedroom. It was dark and I struck a match. I hardly knew which way I was facing as I struck it but I was not long left in doubt for before me was the long mirror of the wardrobe. There facing me by the light of the match was a headless man, his shirt front, his cuffs and his collar were gleaming.

Turning away in horror, not only at the sight, but at the idea that the apparition was even now at large and that our struggle with the demons had been of no avail, I struck another match and turned to the bed.

Two people were lying there side by side, and peering closer I could see that they were smiling peacefully. My wife lay nearest to the window and I lay in my accustomed place, in the shadow of the wardrobe.

We were both dead.

THE SHODDY LANDS

C. S. Lewis

The group of Oxford academics who called themselves 'The Inklings' and numbered in their ranks J. R. R. Tolkien, Charles Williams and C. S. Lewis have had a profound effect upon modern fantasy fiction via their respective works. To Tolkien's stories of Middle Earth and Williams's fantasies about the Holy Grail, Lewis added his Narnia series for children and the Cosmic trilogy about the interplanetary traveller, Dr Ransom. The books about Narnia, a kingdom ruled by a lion named Aslan, which Lewis wrote in the Fifties, are still among the most popular fantasies with younger readers, while his planetary romances with their mixture of science, mythology and fantasy still attract an older audience and have been compared to those of H. G. Wells, who the author readily admitted was an influence. The meetings of 'The Inklings', at which they read extracts of their work in progress to one another, have become legendary and generated intriguing rumours about the extent of the input of the writers on each other's classic fantasies.

Clive Staples Lewis (1898–1963) was born in Belfast and climaxed a brilliant university career by being appointed Professor of Medieval and Renaissance English at Cambridge. It was, however, while he was a Fellow at Magdalen College, Oxford, that he began to develop his talent for fantasy fiction. The first of his Cosmic trilogy, Out of the Silent Planet, *published in 1938, made an immediate impact, but it was not until he had completed the other two novels in the series that he produced the first Narnia story,* The Lion, the Witch and the Wardrobe, *in 1950, and thereafter became a household name. Among Lewis's other notable fantasies for adults which are leavened with a clever use of comedy are* Dymer *(1926), a narrative fantastic poem;* The Great Divorce *(1945), an allegory about Heaven and Hell; and* Till We Have Faces *(1956), based on the myth of Cupid and Psyche. During his lifetime, Lewis also wrote a number of short stories, including the following, which was originally published in* The Magazine of Fantasy and Science Fiction *in February 1956. 'The Shoddy Lands' are certainly a most peculiar place where trees have no branches, grass has no blades, and the people are 'Walking Things'. Take care!*

*   *   *

Being, as I believe, of sound mind and in normal health, I am sitting down at 11 p.m. to record, while the memory of it is still fresh, the curious experience I had this morning.

It happened in my rooms in college, where I am now writing, and began in the most ordinary way with a call on the telephone. 'This is Durward,' the voice said. 'I'm speaking from the porter's lodge. I'm in Oxford for a few hours. Can I come across and see you?' I said yes, of course. Durward is a former pupil and a decent enough fellow; I would be glad to see him again. When he turned up at my door a few moments later I was rather annoyed to find that he had a young woman in tow. I loathe either men or women who speak as if they were coming to see you alone and then spring a husband or a wife, or fiancé or a fiancée on you. One ought to be warned.

The girl was neither very pretty nor very plain, and of course she ruined my conversation. We couldn't talk about any of the things Durward and I had in common because that would have meant leaving her out in the cold. And she and Durward couldn't talk about the things they (presumably) had in common because that would have left me out. He introduced her as 'Peggy' and said they were engaged. After that, the three of us just sat and did social patter about the weather and the news.

I tend to stare when I am bored, and I am afraid I must have stared at that girl, without the least interest, a good deal. At any rate I was certainly doing so at the moment when the strange experience began. Quite suddenly, without any faintness or nausea or anything of that sort, I found myself in a wholly different place. The familiar room vanished; Durward and Peggy vanished. I was alone. And I was standing up.

My first idea was that something had gone wrong with my eyes. I was not in darkness, nor even in twilight, but everything seemed curiously blurred. There was a sort of daylight, but when I looked up I didn't see anything that I could very confidently call a sky. It might, just possibly, be the sky of a very featureless, dull, grey day, but it lacked any suggestion of distance. 'Nondescript' was the word I would have used to describe it. Lower down and closer to me, there were

upright shapes, vaguely green in colour, but of a very dingy green. I
peered at them for quite a long time before it occurred to me that they
might be trees. I went nearer and examined them; and the impression
they made on me is not easy to put into words. 'Trees of a sort,' or,
'Well, trees, if you call *that* a tree,' or, 'An attempt at trees,' would
come near it. They were the crudest, shabbiest apology for trees you
could imagine. They had no real anatomy, no real branches even; they
were more like lamp-posts with great, shapeless blobs of green stuck
on top of them. Most children could draw better trees from memory.

It was while I was inspecting them that I first noticed the light: a
steady, silvery gleam some distance away in the Shoddy Wood. I turned
my steps towards it at once, and then first noticed what I was walking
on. It was comfortable stuff, soft and cool and springy to the feet; but
when you looked down it was horribly disappointing to the eye. It was,
in a very rough way, the colour of grass; the colour grass has on a very
dull day when you look at it while thinking pretty hard about something
else. But there were no separate blades in it. I stooped down and tried
to find them; the closer one looked, the vaguer it seemed to become.
It had in fact just the same smudged, unfinished quality as the trees:
shoddy.

The full astonishment of my adventure was now beginning to descend
on me. With it came fear, but, even more, a sort of disgust. I doubt if
it can be fully conveyed to anyone who has not had a similar experience.
I felt as if I had suddenly been banished from the real, bright, concrete,
and prodigally complex world into some sort of second-rate universe
that had all been put together on the cheap; by an imitator. But I kept
on walking towards the silvery light.

Here and there in the shoddy grass there were patches of what looked,
from a distance, like flowers. But each patch, when you came close to
it, was as bad as the trees and the grass. You couldn't make out what
species they were supposed to be. And they had no real stems or petals;
they were mere blobs. As for the colours, I could do better myself with
a shilling paint-box.

I should have liked very much to believe that I was dreaming, but
somehow I knew I wasn't. My real conviction was that I had died. I
wished—with a fervour that no other wish of mine has ever achieved—
that I had lived a better life.

A disquieting hypothesis, as you see, was forming in my mind. But
next moment it was gloriously blown to bits. Amidst all that shoddiness
I came suddenly upon daffodils. Real daffodils, trim and cool and
perfect. I bent down and touched them; I straightened my back again

and gorged my eyes on their beauty. And not only their beauty but—
what mattered to me even more at the moment—their, so to speak,
honesty; real, honest, finished daffodils, live things that would bear
examination.

But where, then, could I be? 'Let's get on to that light. Perhaps
everything will be made clear there. Perhaps it is at the centre of this
queer place.'

I reached the light sooner than I expected, but when I reached it I
had something else to think about. For now I met the Walking Things.
I have to call them that, for 'people' is just what they weren't. They
were of human size and they walked on two legs; but they were, for
the most part, no more like true men than the Shoddy Trees had been
like trees. They were indistinct. Though they were certainly not naked,
you couldn't make out what sort of clothes they were wearing, and
though there was a pale blob at the top of each, you couldn't say they
had faces. At least that was my first impression. Then I began to notice
curious exceptions. Every now and then one of them became partially
distinct; a face, a hat, or a dress would stand out in full detail. The odd
thing was that the distinct clothes were always women's clothes, but the
distinct faces were always those of men. Both facts made the crowd—at
least, to a man of my type—about as uninteresting as it could possibly
be. The male faces were not the sort I cared about; a flashy-looking
crew—gigolos, fripons. But they seemed pleased enough with themselves. Indeed they all wore the same look of fatuous admiration.

I now saw where the light was coming from. I was in a sort of street.
At least, behind the crowd of Walking Things on each side, there
appeared to be shop-windows, and from these the light came. I thrust
my way through the crowd on my left—but my thrusting seemed to
yield no physical contacts—and had a look at one of the shops.

Here I had a new surprise. It was a jeweller's, and after the vagueness
and general rottenness of most things in that queer place, the sight fairly
took my breath away. Everything in that window was perfect; every
facet on every diamond distinct, every brooch and tiara finished down
to the last perfection of intricate detail. It was good stuff too, as even
I could see; there must have been hundreds of thousands of pounds'
worth of it. 'Thank Heaven!' I gasped. 'But will it keep on?' Hastily
I looked at the next shop. It *was* keeping on. This window contained
women's frocks. I'm no judge, so I can't say how good they were. The
shop beyond this one sold women's shoes. And it was still keeping on.
They were real shoes; the toe-pinching and very high-heeled sort which,
to my mind, ruins even the prettiest foot, but at any rate real.

I was just thinking to myself that some people would not find this place half as dull as I did, when the queerness of the whole thing came over me afresh. 'Where the hell,' I began, but immediately changed it to 'Where on earth'—for the other word seemed, in all the circumstances, singularly unfortunate—'Where on earth have I got to? Trees no good; grass no good; sky no good; flowers no good, except the daffodils; people no good; shops first-class. What can that possibly mean?'

The shops, by the way, were all women's shops, so I soon lost interest in them. I walked the whole length of that street, and then, a little way ahead, I saw sunlight.

Not that it was proper sunlight, of course. There was no break in the dull sky to account for it, no beam slanting down. All that, like so many other things in that world, had not been attended to. There was simply a patch of sunlight on the ground, unexplained, impossible (except that it was there), and therefore not at all cheering; hideous, rather, and disquieting. But I had little time to think about it; for something in the centre of that lighted patch—something I had taken for a small building—suddenly moved, and with a sickening shock I realised that I was looking at a gigantic human shape. It turned round. Its eyes looked straight into mine.

It was not only gigantic, but it was the only complete human shape I had seen since I entered the world. It was female. It was lying on sunlit sand, on a beach apparently, though there was no trace of any sea. It was very nearly naked, but it had a wisp of some brightly coloured stuff round its hips and another round its breasts; like what a modern girl wears on a real beach. The general effect was repulsive, but I saw in a moment or two that this was due to the appalling size. Considered abstractly, the giantess had a good figure; almost a perfect figure, if you like the modern type. The face—but as soon as I had really taken in the face, I shouted out.

'Oh, I say! There you are. Where's Durward? And where's this? What's happened to us?'

But the eyes went on looking straight at me and through me. I was obviously invisible and inaudible to her. But there was no doubt who she was. She was Peggy. That is, she was recognisable; but she was Peggy changed. I don't mean only the size. As regards the figure, it was Peggy improved. I don't think anyone could have denied that. As to the face, opinions might differ. I would hardly have called the change an improvement myself. There was no more—I doubt if there was as much—sense or kindness or honesty in this face than in the original Peggy's. But it was certainly more regular. The teeth in particular, which I had noticed as a weak point in the old Peggy, were perfect, as in a good denture. The lips were fuller. The complexion was so perfect that it suggested a very expensive doll. The expression I can best describe by saying that Peggy now looked exactly like the girl in all the advertisements.

If I had to marry either, I should prefer the old, unimproved Peggy. But even in hell I hoped it wouldn't come to that.

And, as I watched, the background—the absurd little bit of sea-beach—began to change. The giantess stood up. She was on a carpet. Walls and windows and furniture grew up around her. She was in a bedroom. Even I could tell it was a very expensive bedroom, though not at all my idea of good taste. There were plenty of flowers, mostly orchids and roses, and these were even better finished than the daffodils had been. One great bouquet (with a card attached to it) was as good as any I have ever seen. A door which stood open behind her gave me a view into a bathroom which I should rather like to own, a bathroom with a sunk bath. In it there was a French maid fussing about with towels and bath salts and things. The maid was not nearly so finished as the roses, or even the towels, but what face she had looked more French than any real Frenchwoman's could.

The gigantic Peggy now removed her beach equipment and stood up naked in front of a full-length mirror. Apparently she enjoyed what she saw there; I can hardly express how much I didn't. Partly the size (it's only fair to remember that) but, still more, something that came as a terrible shock to me, though I suppose modern lovers and husbands must be hardened to it. Her body was (of course) brown, like the bodies in the sun-bathing advertisements. But round her hips, and again round her breasts, where the coverings had been, there were two bands of dead white which looked, by contrast, like leprosy. It made me for the moment almost physically sick. What staggered me was that she could stand and admire it. Had she no idea how it would affect ordinary male eyes? A very disagreeable conviction grew in me that this was a subject of no interest to her; that all her clothes and bath salts and two-piece swimsuits, and indeed the voluptuousness of her every look and gesture, had not, and never had had, the meaning which every man would read, and was intended to read, into them. They were a huge overture to an opera in which she had no interest at all; a coronation procession with no queen at the centre of it; gestures, gestures about nothing.

And now I became aware that two noises had been going for a long time; the only noises I ever heard in that world. But they were coming from outside, from somewhere beyond that low, grey covering which

served the Shoddy Lands instead of a sky. Both the noises were knockings—patient knockings, infinitely remote, as if two outsiders, two
excluded people, were knocking on the walls of that world. The one
was faint, but hard; and with it came a voice saying, 'Peggy, Peggy,
let me in.' Durward's voice, I thought. But how shall I describe the
other knocking? It was, in some curious way, soft; 'soft as wool and
sharp as death', soft but unendurably heavy, as if at each blow some
enormous hand fell on the outside of the Shoddy Sky and covered it
completely. And with that knocking came a voice at whose sound my
bones turned to water: 'Child, child, child, let me in before the night
comes.'

'*Before the night comes*'—instantly common daylight rushed back
upon me. I was in my own rooms again and my two visitors were
before me. They did not appear to notice that anything unusual had
happened to me, though, for the rest of that conversation, they might
well have supposed I was drunk. I was so happy. Indeed, in a way I
was drunk—drunk with the sheer delight of being back in the real
world, free, outside the horrible little prison of that land. There were
birds singing close to a window; there was real sunlight falling on a
panel. That panel needed repainting; but I could have gone down on
my knees and kissed its very shabbiness—the precious real, solid, thing
it was. I noticed a tiny cut on Durward's cheek where he must have
cut himself shaving that morning; and I felt the same about it. Indeed
anything was enough to make me happy: I mean, any Thing, as long
as it really was a Thing.

Well, those are the facts; everyone may make what he pleases of
them. My own hypothesis is the obvious one which will have occurred
to most readers. It may be too obvious; I am quite ready to consider
rival theories. My view is that by the operation of some unknown
psychological—or pathological law, I was, for a second or so, let into
Peggy's mind; at least to the extent of seeing her world, the world as
it exists for her. At the centre of that world is a swollen image of
herself, remodelled to be as like the girls in the advertisements as
possible. Round this are grouped clear and distinct images of the things
she really cares about. Beyond that, the whole earth and sky are a vague
blur. The daffodils and roses are especially instructive. Flowers only
exist for her if they are the sort that can be cut and put in vases or sent
as bouquets; flowers in themselves, flowers as you see them in the
woods, are negligible.

As I say, this is probably not the only hypothesis which will fit the
facts. But it has been a most disquieting experience. Not only because

I am sorry for poor Durward. Suppose this sort of thing were to become common? And how if, some other time, I were not the explorer but the explored?

HARRISON BERGERON

Kurt Vonnegut Jr

Kurt Vonnegut Jr is fantasy's master of black humour, and his inter-
fering aliens, the Tralfamadorians, and bizarre religion, the Church of
God the Utterly Indifferent, are two of the genre's classic inventions.
The aliens, who appear in both The Sirens of Titan *(1959) and* Slaugh-
terhouse-Five *(1969), underline their creator's philosophy that the*
secret of life is to live only in its happy moments. As he said in a recent
interview in Inc. Technology, *discussing his feelings about living in an*
increasingly computerised world, 'I tell you, we are here on Earth to
fart around and don't let anybody tell you any different!'
    Vonnegut (1922–) was born in Indianapolis and served in the US
Army in Europe during the Second World War. Taken prisoner, he was
held in Dresden during the firebombing of the city by Allied planes
which had a traumatic effect on him and was to exert a considerable
influence on his later highly idiosyncratic writing. For a time he worked
as a public relations officer for the General Electric Company until he
was able to earn a living from his fiction. Following the success of
early short stories for magazines as disparate as Collier's Weekly *and*
Galaxy, *plus his novels including* Player Piano *(1952), about the*
takeover by machines, Cat's Cradle *(1963), featuring the invention of*
'ice-nine', which threatens the end of the world, and Breakfast of Cham-
pions *(1973), which introduced the hapless sf author, Kilgore Trout,*
Kurt Vonnegut is now recognised as one of the major contemporary
American writers. He also has a certain notoriety for having been the
first writer to use the word 'fuck' in the title of a commercially published
story, 'The Big Space Fuck', which appeared in Again, Dangerous
Visions, *edited by Harlan Ellison, in 1972. 'Harrison Bergeron' was*
written ten years earlier for The Magazine of Fantasy and Science
Fiction *and records life in a not-too-distant future America where every-*
one is equal and anyone who tries to break the law risks punishment

at the hands of the awesome Handicapper General, Diana Moon Glampers, and her agents . . .

*   *   *

The year was 2081, and everybody was finally equal. They weren't only equal before God and the law. They were equal every which way. Nobody was smarter than anybody else. Nobody was better looking than anybody else. Nobody was stronger or quicker than anybody else. All this equality was due to the 211th, 212th, and 213th Amendments to the Constitution, and to the increasing vigilance of agents of the United States Handicapper General.

Some things about living still weren't quite right, though. April, for instance, still drove people crazy by not being springtime. And it was in that clammy month that the H-G men took George and Hazel Bergeron's fourteen-year-old son, Harrison, away.

It was tragic, all right, but George and Hazel couldn't think about it very hard. Hazel had a perfectly average intelligence, which meant she couldn't think about anything except in short bursts. And George, while his intelligence was way above normal, had a little mental handicap radio in his ear. He was required by law to wear it at all times. It was turned to a government transmitter. Every twenty seconds or so, the transmitter would send out some sharp noise to keep people like George from taking unfair advantage of their brains.

George and Hazel were watching television. There were tears on Hazel's cheeks, but she'd forgotten for the moment what they were about.

On the television screen were ballerinas.

A buzzer sounded in George's head. His thoughts fled in panic, like bandits from a burglar alarm.

'That was a real pretty dance, that dance they just did,' said Hazel.

'Huh?' said George.

'That dance—it was nice,' said Hazel.

'Yup,' said George. He tried to think a little about the ballerinas. They weren't really very good—no better than anybody else would have been, anyway. They were burdened with sash-weights and bags of birdshot, and their faces were masked, so that no one, seeing a free and graceful gesture or a pretty face, would feel like something the cat dragged in. George was toying with the vague notion that maybe dancers shouldn't be handicapped. But he didn't get very far with it before another noise in his ear radio scattered his thoughts.

George winced. So did two out of the eight ballerinas.

Hazel saw him wince. Having no mental handicap herself, she had to ask George what the latest sound had been.

'Sounded like somebody hitting a milk bottle with a ball-peen hammer,' said George.

'I'd think it would be real interesting, hearing all the different sounds,' said Hazel, a little envious. 'All the things they think up.'

'Um,' said George.

'Only, if I was Handicapper General, you know what I would do?' said Hazel. Hazel, as a matter of fact, bore a strong resemblance to the Handicapper General, a woman named Diana Moon Glampers. 'If I was Diana Moon Glampers,' said Hazel, 'I'd have chimes on Sunday— just chimes. Kind of in honour of religion.'

'I could think, if it was just chimes,' said George.

'Well—maybe make 'em real loud,' said Hazel. 'I think I'd make a good Handicapper General.'

'Good as anybody else,' said George.

'Who knows better'n I do what normal is?' said Hazel.

'Right,' said George. He began to think glimmeringly about his abnormal son who was now in jail, about Harrison, but a twenty-one-gun salute in his head stopped that.

'Boy!' said Hazel, 'that was a doozy, wasn't it?'

It was such a doozy that George was white and trembling, and tears stood on the rims of his red eyes. Two of the eight ballerinas had collapsed to the studio floor, were holding their temples.

'All of a sudden you look so tired,' said Hazel. 'Why don't you stretch out on the sofa, so's you can rest your handicap bag on the pillows, honeybunch.' She was referring to the forty-seven pounds of birdshot in a canvas bag, which was padlocked around George's neck. 'Go on and rest the bag for a little while,' she said. 'I don't care if you're not equal to me for a while.'

George weighed the bag with his hands. 'I don't mind,' he said. 'I don't notice it any more. It's just a part of me.'

'You been so tired lately—kind of wore out,' said Hazel. 'If there was just some way we could make a little hole in the bottom of the bag, and just take out a few of them lead balls. Just a few.'

'Two years in prison and two thousand dollars fine for every ball I took out,' said George. 'I don't call that a bargain.'

'If you could just take a few out when you came home from work,' said Hazel. 'I mean—you don't compete with anybody around here. You just set around.'

'If I tried to get away with it,' said George, 'then other people'd get away with it—and pretty soon we'd be right back to the dark ages again, with everybody competing against everybody else. You wouldn't like that, would you?'

'I'd hate it,' said Hazel.

'There you are,' said George. 'The minute people start cheating on laws, what do you think happens to society?'

If Hazel hadn't been able to come up with an answer to this question, George couldn't have supplied one. A siren was going off in his head.

'Reckon it'd fall all apart,' said Hazel.

'What would?' said George blankly.

'Society,' said Hazel uncertainly. 'Wasn't that what you just said?'

'Who knows?' said George.

The television programme was suddenly interrupted for a news bulletin. It wasn't clear at first as to what the bulletin was about, since the announcer, like all announcers, had a serious speech impediment. For about half a minute, and in a state of high excitement, the announcer tried to say, 'Ladies and gentlemen—'

He finally gave up, handed the bulletin to a ballerina to read.

'That's all right—' Hazel said of the announcer, 'he tried. That's the big thing. He tried to do the best he could with what God gave him. He should get a nice raise for trying so hard.'

'Ladies and gentlemen—' said the ballerina, reading the bulletin. She must have been extraordinarily beautiful, because the mask she wore was hideous. And it was easy to see that she was the strongest and most graceful of all the dancers, for her handicap bags were as big as those worn by two-hundred-pound men.

And she had to apologise at once for her voice, which was a very unfair voice for a woman to use. Her voice was a warm, luminous, timeless melody. 'Excuse me—' she said, and she began again, making her voice absolutely uncompetitive.

'Harrison Bergeron, age fourteen,' she said in a grackle squawk, 'has just escaped from jail, where he was held on suspicion of plotting to overthrow the government. He is a genius and an athlete, is under-handicapped, and should be regarded as extremely dangerous.'

A police photograph of Harrison Bergeron was flashed on the screen—upside down, then sideways, upside down again, then right side up. The picture showed the full length of Harrison against a background calibrated in feet and inches. He was exactly seven feet tall.

The rest of Harrison's appearance was Halloween and hardware. Nobody had ever borne heavier handicaps. He had outgrown hindrances faster than the H-G men could think them up. Instead of a little ear radio for a mental handicap, he wore a tremendous pair of earphones, and spectacles with thick wavy lenses. The spectacles were intended to make him not only half blind, but to give him whanging headaches besides.

Scrap metal was hung all over him. Ordinarily, there was a certain symmetry, a military neatness to the handicaps issued to strong people, but Harrison looked like a walking junkyard. In the race of life, Harrison carried three hundred pounds.

And to offset his good looks, the H-G men required that he wear at all times a red rubber ball for a nose, keep his eyebrows shaved off, and cover his even white teeth with black caps at snaggle-tooth random.

'If you see this boy,' said the ballerina, 'do not—I repeat, do not— try to reason with him.'

There was the shriek of a door being torn from its hinges.

Screams and barking cries of consternation came from the television set. The photograph of Harrison Bergeron on the screen jumped again and again, as though dancing to the tune of an earthquake.

George Bergeron correctly identified the earthquake, and well he might have—for many was the time his own home had danced to the same crashing tune. 'My God—' said George, 'that must be Harrison!'

The realisation was blasted from his mind instantly by the sound of an automobile collision in his head.

When George could open his eyes again, the photograph of Harrison was gone. A living, breathing Harrison filled the screen.

Clanking, clownish and huge, Harrison stood in the centre of the studio. The knob of the uprooted studio door was still in his hand. Ballerinas, technicians, musicians and announcers cowered on their knees before him, expecting to die.

'I am the Emperor!' cried Harrison. 'Do you hear? I am the Emperor! Everybody must do what I say at once!' He stamped his foot and the studio shook.

'Even as I stand here—' he bellowed, 'crippled, hobbled, sickened— I am a greater ruler than any man who ever lived! Now watch me become what I *can* become!'

Harrison tore the straps off his handicap harness like wet tissue paper, tore straps guaranteed to support five thousand pounds.

Harrison's scrap-iron handicaps crashed to the floor.

Harrison thrust his thumbs under the bar of the padlock that secured his head harness. The bar snapped like celery. Harrison smashed his headphones and spectacles against the wall.

He flung away his rubber-ball nose, revealed a man that would have awed Thor, the god of thunder.

'I shall now select my Empress!' he said, looking down on the cowering people. 'Let the first woman who dares rise to her feet claim her mate and her throne!'

A moment passed, and then a ballerina arose, swaying like a willow.

Harrison plucked the mental handicap from her ear, snapped off her physical handicaps with marvellous delicacy. Last of all, he removed her mask.

She was blindingly beautiful.

'Now—' said Harrison, taking her hand, 'shall we show the people the meaning of the word dance? Music!' he commanded.

The musicians scrambled back into their chairs, and Harrison stripped them of their handicaps, too. 'Play your best,' he told them, 'and I'll make you barons and dukes and earls.'

The music began. It was normal at first—cheap, silly, false. But Harrison snatched two musicians from their chairs, waved them like batons as he sang the music as he wanted it played. He slammed them back into their chairs.

The music began again and was much improved.

Harrison and his Empress merely listened to the music for a while— listened gravely, as though synchronising their heartbeats with it.

They shifted their weights to their toes.

Harrison placed his big hands on the girl's tiny waist, letting her sense the weightlessness that would soon be hers.

And then, in an explosion of joy and grace, into the air they sprang!

Not only were the laws of the land abandoned, but the law of gravity and the laws of motion as well.

They reeled, whirled, swivelled, flounced, capered, gambolled and spun.

They leaped like deer on the moon.

The studio ceiling was thirty feet high, but each leap brought the dancers nearer to it.

It became their obvious intention to kiss the ceiling.

They kissed it.

And then, neutralising gravity with love and pure will, they remained suspended in air inches below the ceiling, and they kissed each other for a long, long time.

It was then that Diana Moon Glampers, the Handicapper General, came into the studio with a double-barrelled ten-gauge shotgun. She fired twice, and the Emperor and the Empress were dead before they hit the floor.

Diana Moon Glampers loaded the gun again. She aimed it at the musicians and told them they had ten seconds to get their handicaps back on.

It was then that the Bergerons' television tube burned out.

Hazel turned to comment about the blackout to George. But George had gone out into the kitchen for a can of beer.

George came back in with the beer, paused while a handicap signal shook him up. And then he sat down again. 'You been crying?' he said to Hazel.

'Yup,' she said.

'What about?' he said.

'I forget,' she said. 'Something real sad on television.'

'What was it?' he said.

'It's all kind of mixed up in my mind,' said Hazel.

'Forget sad things,' said George.

'I always do,' said Hazel.

'That's my girl,' said George. He winced. There was the sound of a riveting gun in his head.

'Gee—I could tell that one was a doozy,' said Hazel.

'You can say that again,' said George.

'Gee—' said Hazel, 'I could tell that one was a doozy.'

POSSIBLE TO RUE

Piers Anthony

With larger-than-life characters who rejoice in the names of Sos, Neq and Veg, and stories that range from Prostho Plus *(1971), about a twentieth-century Earth dentist kidnapped by extraterrestrials who force him to practise on a gruesome variety of alien teeth, to the pornographic fantasy,* Pornucopia *(1989), Piers Anthony enjoys a similar status among American fans of comic fantasy to that of Terry Pratchett in the UK. Curiously, Piers was also born in England, but took out US citizenship in 1958 and has lived there ever since. A prolific and imaginative writer with a sense of humour that varies from the alarming to the poetic, he has produced a number of series including the 'Incarnations of Immortality', 'Apprentice Adept' and, most famously of all, the 'Xanth' series. These latter books, with titles such as* Centaur Aisle *(1982),* Dragon on a Pedestal *(1983) and* Vale of the Vole *(1987), have won a worldwide audience of admirers, and like the Discworld series inspired a number of spin-offs including* Piers Anthony's Visual Guide to Xanth *(1989). Similarly, each new volume in the series has topped the US bestseller lists on publication, helping to make humorous fantasy one of the most popular literary forms in the nation, as well as spurring a whole new generation of writers to turn to the genre. Thankfully, Anthony's own rich vein of humour shows no sign of wearing out.*

Born Piers Anthony Dillingham Jacob (1934–) in Oxford, he was educated in America and for some years worked as a technical writer for a communications company before a period teaching English at the Admiral Farragut Academy. His novel, Sos the Rope *(1968), won the $5,000 Pyramid Award and this plus encouragement from Arthur C. Clarke inspired him to become a full-time writer. In recent years, Anthony has written almost solely at novel length, but 'Possible to Rue', which originally appeared in* Fantastic *magazine in April 1963, is typical of his style of comic fantasy, and in its story of a little boy* *who wants to own that most prized of all flying creatures, a Pegasus, neatly rounds off this opening section.*

*   *   *

'I want a Pegasus, Daddy,' Junior greeted him at the door, his curly blond head bobbling with excitement. 'A small one, with white fluttery wings and an aerodynamic tail and—'

'You shall have it, son,' Daddy said warmly, absent-mindedly stripping off jacket and tie. Next week was Bradley Newton Jr's sixth birthday, and Bradley Senior had promised a copy of *Now We Are Six* and a pet for his very own. Newton was a man of means, so that this was no empty pledge. He felt he owed it to the boy, to make up in some token the sorrow of Mrs N's untimely departure.

He eased himself into the upholstered chair, vaguely pleased that his son showed such imagination. Another child would have demanded something commonplace, like a mongrel or a Shetland pony. But a pegasus now—

'Do you mean the winged horse, son?' Newton inquired, a thin needle of doubt poking into his complacency.

'That's right, Daddy,' Junior said brightly. 'But it will have to be a very small one, because I want a pegasus that can really fly. A full-grown animal's wings are non-functional because the proportionate wing span is insufficient to get it off the ground.'

'I understand, son,' Newton said quickly. 'A small one.' People had laughed when he had insisted that Junior's nurse have a graduate degree in general science. Fortunately he had been able to obtain one inexpensively by hiring her away from the school board. At this moment he regretted that it was her day off; Junior could be very single-minded.

'Look, son,' he temporised, 'I'm not sure I know where to buy a horse like that. And you'll have to know how to feed it and care for it, otherwise it would get sick and die. You wouldn't want that to happen, would you?'

The boy pondered. 'You're right, Daddy,' he said at last. 'We would be well advised to look it up.'

'Look it up?'

'In the encyclopedia, Daddy. Haven't you always told me that it was an authoritative factual reference?'

The light dawned. Junior believed in the encyclopedia. 'My very words, Son. Let's look it up and see what it says about . . . let's see . . . here's *Opinion to Possibility* . . . should be in this volume. Yes.'

He found the place and read aloud: ' ''Pegasus—horse with wings which sprang from the blood of the Gorgon Medusa after Perseus cut off her head.'' '

Junior's little mouth dropped open. 'That has got to be figurative,' he pronounced. 'Horses are not created from—'

' ''. . . a creature of Greek mythology'',' Newton finished victoriously.

Junior digested that. 'You mean, it doesn't exist,' he said dispiritedly. Then he brightened. 'Daddy, if I ask for something that does exist, then can I have it for a pet?'

'Certainly, Son. We'll just look it up here, and if the book says it's real, we'll go out and get one. I think that's a fair bargain.'

'A unicorn,' Junior said.

Newton restrained a smile. He reached for the volume marked *Trust to Wary* and flipped the pages. ' ''Unicorn—a mythological creature resembling a horse—'' ' he began.

Junior looked at him suspiciously. 'Next year I'm going to school and learn to read for myself,' he muttered. 'You are alleging that there is no such animal?'

'That's what the book says, Son—honest.'

The boy looked dubious, but decided not to make an issue of it. 'All right—let's try a zebra.' He watched while Newton pulled out *Watchful to Indices*. 'It's only fair to warn you, Daddy,' he said ominously, 'that there is a picture of one on the last page of my alphabet book.'

'I'll read you just exactly what it says, Son,' Newton said defensively. 'Here it is: ''Zebra—A striped horse-like animal reputed to have lived in Africa. Common in European and American legend, although entirely mythical—'' '

'Now you're making that up,' Junior accused angrily. 'I've got a picture.'

'But Son—I thought it was real myself. I've never seen a zebra, but I thought—look. You have a picture of a ghost too, don't you? But you know that's not real.'

There was a hard set to Junior's jaw. 'The examples are not analogous. Spirits are preternatural—'

'Why don't we try another animal?' Newton cut in. 'We can come back to the zebra later.'

'Mule,' Junior said sullenly.

Newton reddened, then realised that the boy was not being personal. He withdrew the volume covering *Morphine to Opiate* silently. He was somewhat shaken up by the turn events had taken. Imagine spending all his life believing in an animal that didn't exist. Yet of course it was stupid to swear by a horse with prison stripes . . .

' "Mule", ' he read. ' "The offspring of the mare and the male ass. A very large, strong hybrid, sure-footed with remarkable sagacity. A creature of folklore, although, like the unicorn and zebra, widely accepted by the credulous . . ." '

His son looked at him. 'Horse,' he said.

Newton somewhat warily opened *Hoax to Imaginary*. He was glad he wasn't credulous himself. 'Right you are, son. "Horse—A fabled hoofed creature prevalent in mythology. A very fleet four-footed animal complete with flowing mane, hairy tail and benevolent disposition. Metallic shoes supposedly worn by the animal are valued as good luck charms, in much the same manner as the unicorn's horn—" '

Junior clouded up dangerously. 'Now wait a minute, Son,' Newton spluttered. 'I know that's wrong. I've seen horses myself. Why, they use them in TV westerns—'

'The reasoning is specious,' Junior muttered but his heart wasn't in it.

'Look, Son—I'll prove it. I'll call the race track. I used to place— I mean, I used to go there to see the horses. Maybe they'll let us visit the stables.' Newton dialled with a quivering finger; spoke into the phone. A brief frustrated interchange later he slammed the receiver down again. 'They race dogs now,' he said.

He fumbled through the yellow pages, refusing to let himself think. The book skipped rebelliously from *Homes* to *Hospital*. He rattled the bar for the operator to demand the number of the nearest horse farm, then angrily dialled 'O'; after some confusion he ended up talking to 'Horsepower, Inc.', a tractor dealer.

Junior surveyed the proceedings with profound disgust. 'Methinks the queen protests too much,' he quoted sweetly.

In desperation, Newton called a neighbour. 'Listen, Sam—do you know anybody around here who owns a horse? I promised my boy I'd show him one today . . .'

Sam's laughter echoed back over the wire. 'You're a card, Brad. Horses, yet. Do you teach him to believe in fairies too?'

Newton reluctantly accepted defeat. 'I guess I was wrong about the horse, Son,' he said awkwardly. 'I could have sworn—but never mind. Just proves a man is never too old to make a mistake. Why don't you pick something else for your pet? Tell you—whatever you choose, I'll give you a matched pair.'

Junior cheered up somewhat. He was quick to recognise a net gain. 'How about a bird?'

Newton smiled in heartfelt relief. 'That would be fine, Son, just fine. What kind did you have in mind?'

'Well,' Junior said thoughtfully. 'I think I'd like a big bird. A real big bird, like a roc, or maybe a harpy—'

Newton reached for *Possible to Rue*.

2

DEADLY NIGHTSHAPES

Tales of the Supernatural

THE RIGHT SIDE

John Collier

Once described by The Saturday Review of Literature *as 'a collector of demons, connoisseur of jinns, and an old acquaintance of the devil himself', John Collier is the ideal writer to introduce a section of comic fantasy stories devoted to the supernatural. His novels and short stories are famous for featuring all manner of extraordinary characters, from a fiend with a cold in the head to a supernatural parrot, from an angel who falls in love with a young student of architecture to a colony of department-store ghosts. The leading American critic Clifton Fadiman has referred to him as the master of 'perverse nonsense that's preciously perfect'.*

Although John Collier (1901–1980) was born in England, he spent much of his working life in America and for a time was a leading Hollywood scriptwriter, putting his talents behind such landmark movies as The African Queen *(1952), which starred Humphrey Bogart and Katharine Hepburn, and* I Am a Camera *(1955), based on Christopher Isherwood's famous book. Collier was a great admirer of P. G. Wodehouse and acknowledged the fact in a classic Wodehousian tale, 'Squirrels Have Bright Eyes', which features a villain called 'the abominable Fenshawe-Fanshawe', an Amazonian heroine given to outbursts such as, 'the world cannot utter its gross libidinous sneers at a girl who lives chastely with her Lee-Enfield, her Ballard and her light Winchester', and an ineffectual young man who remains immobile for a whole day while pretending to be stuffed and mounted! Collier's novel,* His Monkey Wife, or Married to a Chimp *(1930), is acknowledged as a fantasy classic, but it is for his short stories that he is most admired—and imitated. 'The Right Side' is ostensibly a tale on the timeless theme of a deal with the devil—an idea that has, of course, been popular in folklore for centuries—but in John Collier's witty imagination becomes something both unique and very amusing . . .*

*   *   *

A young man, who was looking extremely pale, walked to the middle of Westminster Bridge and clambered onto the parapet. A swarthy gentleman, some years his senior, in evening dress, with dark red carnation, Inverness cape, monocle, and short imperial, appeared as if from nowhere, and had him by the ankle.

'Let me go, damn you!' muttered the would-be suicide, with a tug and a kick.

'Get down, and walk beside me,' said the stranger, 'or that policeman, who has already taken a step or two in our direction, will most certainly run you in. Let us pretend to be two friends, one of whom wished for a thrill, while the other was anxious that he should not tumble over.'

The young man, who was so eager to be in the Thames, had a great aversion to being in prison. Accordingly he fell into step with the stranger, and, smiling (for now they were just passing the bobby), 'Damn and blast you!' he said. 'Why can't you mind your own silly business?'

'But, my dear Philip Westwick,' replied the other, 'I regard you as very much my business.'

'Who may you be?' cried the young man impatiently. 'I don't know you. How did you get hold of my name?'

'It came into my mind,' said his companion, 'just half an hour ago, when first you formed your rash resolution.'

'I don't know how that can be,' said Philip. 'Nor do I care.'

'You lovers,' said his companion, 'are surprised by nothing, except first that your mistresses should fancy you, and next, that they should fancy someone else.'

'How do you know,' cried our poor Philip, 'that it was over that sort of thing?'

'I know that, and much more, equally ridiculous,' replied the other. 'What would you say if I reminded you that no less than a month ago, when you considered yourself in Heaven, and were, in point of fact, in your Millicent's arms, you discerned something of the essence of ennui in the nape of her neck, and actually wished her transformed into the little brunette who serves in a tea-shop in Bond Street? And now you are on the brink of suicide because your Millicent has left you, though the little brunette is, for all you know, in Bond Street still. What do you say to that?'

'You seem to be unaware,' said Philip, 'that what a man wishes when he is in his girl's arms, and what he wishes when someone else is probably there, are two very different things. Otherwise, I admit your knowledge is devilish uncanny.'

'That is only natural,' replied the other with a complacent smile, from which Philip immediately realised that he was in the company of none other than the Devil himself.

'What are you up to?' he demanded, drawing back a little.

The Devil, with a look of great benevolence, offered him a cigarette.

'I suppose it's not doped?' inquired Philip, sniffing at it suspiciously.

'Oh, come!' said the Devil with a sneer. 'Do you think I need resort to such measures as that, to overcome you? I have *reason* on my side. Will you have a light?' Without pausing for a reply, he extended his middle finger, the tip of which immediately ignited the cigarette.

'You have a reputation for reasoning to some effect,' said Philip. 'I have very little desire to be eternally damned.'

'What did you expect, then,' said the Devil, 'when you contemplated suicide?'

'I see nothing wrong in that,' said our hero.

'Nor does a puppy that destroys his master's slipper,' retorted the Devil. 'However, he is punished for it.'

'I can't believe it,' said Philip obstinately.

'Come with me, then,' said the Devil, and took him to a Fun Fair in the neighbourhood of the Tottenham Court Road. Here a number of the ugliest wretches on earth were amusing themselves with gambling games; others were peering into stereoscopes which showed scenes of Parisian night life. The rest of them were picking pockets, making overtures to certain female habituées of the place, swearing, and indulging in all manner of filthy conversation.

The Devil looked on all these much as one who has been walking among the poppies and the wild cornflowers of the fields looks upon the cultivated plants in the garden about his back door. The commissionaire touched his cap much as gardeners do; the Devil acknowledged the salute and, taking out a latch-key, led Philip to a little door in the wall which, being opened, discovered a small private elevator.

They got in, and descended for several minutes at an incredible speed.

'My dear Devil,' said Philip, puffing at his cigarette, which was, in fact, doped, and gave him the impression of being a man of affairs, 'my dear Devil, if we go on at this rate, we shall soon be in Hell itself.'

Nothing could have been more true. The lift stopped and they got out. They were in a vast hall which resembled nothing so much as the foyer of some gargantuan theatre or picture palace. There were two or three box offices, in front of which the prices of admission were displayed: Stalls—gluttony; Private Boxes—lechery; Dress Circle—vanity; Gallery—sloth; and so forth. There was also a bar, at which one or two uniformed fiends were chatting with the barmaids, among whom our friend was astonished to see the little brunette from Bond Street.

Now and then a door opened upon the vast auditorium, and it was apparent that the play or movie in progress was a lively one.

'There's a dance lounge through here,' said the Devil, 'to which I particularly wanted to take you.'

A door was opened for them. They found themselves in a reasonably large apartment got up in the grotto style, with ferns and imitation rock-work, and a damp and chilly air. A band was playing a travesty of Scarlatti. Several people were dancing rather listlessly. Philip observed that many of them were disgustingly fat.

The Devil led him up to a slim and pale girl, murmured a few words, and Philip, seeing nothing else to do, bowed, offered her his arm, and they began to circle the room.

She danced very languidly, and kept her heavy lids dropped low over her eyes. Philip uttered one or two trifling remarks. 'Do you come here often?' he said. She smiled faintly, but did not reply.

He was a little piqued at her remaining so listless (besides, he had smoked one of the Devil's cigarettes). 'How very cold your hand is!' he said, giving it a slight squeeze. It certainly was. He manoeuvred this unresponsive partner into a corner, where he clutched her waist rather more tightly than was necessary for dancing. He felt a chilly moisture penetrate the sleeve of his jacket, and a faint but unmistakable smell of river-mud become perceptible. He looked at her closely, and observed something extremely pearly about her eyes.

'I did not catch your name,' said Philip.

His partner scarcely moved her colourless lips. 'Ophelia,' she said.

'Excuse me,' said Philip.

He lost no time in rejoining the Devil.

'Now,' said that worthy, 'are you still unable to believe that those who drown themselves are eternally damned?'

Philip was forced to admit the point.

'You have no idea how bored that poor girl is,' said the Devil compassionately. 'And she has only been here a few hundred years. What is that, in comparison to Eternity?'

'Very little. Very little, indeed,' said Philip.

'You see what sort of partners she gets,' continued the arch-fiend. 'During every dance they reveal to her, and she to them, some little unpleasantness of the sort that so disquieted you.'

'But why should they be in a dance lounge?' asked Philip.

'Why not?' said the Devil with a shrug. 'Have another cigarette.'

He then proposed that they should adjourn to his office, to talk matters over.

'Now, my dear Westwick,' said he, when they were comfortably ensconced in armchairs, 'what shall our little arrangement be? I can, of course, annihilate all that has occurred. In that case you will find yourself back on the parapet, in the very act of jumping, just as you were when I caught you by the ankle. Shortly afterwards you will arrive in the little dance lounge you saw; whether fat or thin depends upon the caprice of the waters.'

'It is night,' said Philip. 'The river flows at four miles an hour. I should probably get out to sea unobserved. Yes, I should almost certainly be one of the fat ones. They appeared to me remarkably deficient in *it* or S.A., if those terms are familiar to you.'

'I have heard of them,' said the Devil, with a smile. 'Have a cigar.'

'No, thanks,' said Philip. 'What alternative do you suggest?'

'Here is our standard contract,' said the Devil. 'Do have a cigar. You see—unlimited wealth, fifty years, Helen of Troy—well, that's obsolete. Say Miss——,' and he mentioned the name of a delightful film star.

'Of course,' said Philip, 'there's this little clause about possession of my soul. Is that essential?'

'Well, it's the usual thing,' said the Devil. 'Better let it stand. This is where you sign.'

'Well, I don't know,' said Philip. 'I don't think I'll sign.'

'What?' cried the Devil.

Our hero pursed his lips.

'I don't want to influence you, my dear Westwick,' said the Devil, 'but have you considered the difference between coming in tomorrow as a drowned suicide, and coming in—fifty glorious years hence, mind—as a member of staff? Those were members of the staff you saw talking to the little brunette at the bar. Nice girl!'

'All the same,' said Philip, 'I don't think I'll sign. Many thanks, though.'

'All right,' said the Devil. 'Back you go, then!'

Philip was aware of a rushing sensation: he seemed to be shooting upwards like a rocket. However, he kept his presence of mind, kept his weight on his heels, and, when he got to the parapet, jumped down, but on the right side.

NASTY

Fredric Brown

If men and women tend to get the better of the denizens of the supernatural world in John Collier's tales, the reverse is true with Fredric Brown, whose short-short stories full of punning gags with a sting in the tail are among the gems of comic fantasy. For example, a small-time crook in one tale who is given the power to make everything he says come true becomes a victim of his favourite catch-phrase, 'Drop dead!', while a man who falls in love with a mermaid and is offered a transformation by a Triton discovers that a vital part of his anatomy is now missing. During the Fifties and Sixties, Brown was the undisputed master of the form, and his word, 'Geezenstacks', used to refer to kinds of demonic life form, is now part of the terminology of comic fantasy.

Fredric Brown (1906–1972) was a newspaperman in Milwaukee and New York before beginning to write his sf and fantasy shorts with 'Placet is a Crazy Place' (1946), an early example of the comically improbable kind of world that has now been made so popular by Terry Pratchett and his contemporaries. When the best of Brown's short fictions were collected together in 1961 as Nightmares and Geezenstacks, *they highlighted his ability to write genuinely original fantasy stories—some only a few hundred words long—in which he managed to withhold vital information until the twist ending left readers surprised and amused. Brown was also one of the first fantasists to introduce erotica into his tales, as you will discover in 'Nasty', whose ageing Lothario, Walter Beauregard, uses black magic to call up a demon to restore his flagging lust. As ever, our author has an unexpected twist in store for the old lecher.*

*   *   *

Walter Beauregard had been an accomplished and enthusiastic lecher for almost fifty years. Now, at the age of sixty-five, he was in danger of losing his qualifications for membership in the lechers' union. In danger of losing? Nay, let us be honest; he had *lost*. For three years now he had been to doctor after doctor, quack after quack, had tried nostrum after nostrum. All utterly to no avail.

Finally he remembered his books on magic and necromancy. They were books he had enjoyed collecting and reading as part of his extensive library, but he had never taken them seriously. Until now. What did he have to lose?

In a musty, evil-smelling but rare volume he found what he wanted. As it instructed, he drew the pentagram, copied the cabbalistic markings, lighted the candles and read aloud the incantation.

There was a flash of light and a puff of smoke. And the demon. I won't describe the demon except to assure you that you wouldn't have liked him.

'What is your name?' Beauregard asked. He tried to make his voice steady but it trembled a little.

The demon made a sound somewhere between a shriek and a whistle, with overtones of a bull fiddle being played with a crosscut saw. Then he said, 'But you won't be able to pronounce that. In your dull language it would translate as Nasty. Just call me Nasty. I suppose you want the usual thing.'

'What's the usual thing?' Beauregard wanted to know.

'A wish, of course. All right, you can have it. But not three wishes; that business about three wishes is sheer superstition. One is all you get. And you won't like it.'

'One is all I want. And I can't imagine not liking it.'

'You'll find out. All right, I know what your wish is. And here is the answer to it.' Nasty reached into thin air and his hand vanished and came back holding a pair of silvery-looking swimming trunks. He held them out to Beauregard. 'Wear them in good health,' he said.

'What are they?'

'What do they look like? Swimming trunks. But they're special. The material is out of the future, a few millenniums from now. It's indestructible; they'll never wear out or tear or snag. Nice stuff. But the spell on them is a plenty old one. Try them on and find out.'

The demon vanished.

Walter Beauregard quickly stripped and put on the beautiful silvery swimming trunks. Immediately he felt wonderful. Virility coursed through him. He felt as though he were a young man again, just starting his lecherous career.

Quickly he put on a robe and slippers. (Have I mentioned that he was a rich man? And that his home was a penthouse atop the swankiest hotel in Atlantic City? He was, and it was.) He went downstairs in his private elevator and outside to the hotel's luxurious swimming pool. It was, as usual, surrounded by gorgeous Bikini-clad beauties showing off their wares under the pretence of acquiring sun tans, while they waited for propositions from wealthy men like Beauregard.

He took time choosing. But not too much time.

Two hours later, still clad in the wonderful magic trunks, he sat on the edge of his bed and stared at and sighed for the beautiful blonde who lay stretched out on the bed beside him, Bikiniless—and sound asleep.

Nasty had been so right. And so well named. The miraculous trunks, the indestructible, untearable trunks worked perfectly. But if he took them off, or even let them down . . .

THE GRIPES OF WRAITH

Nelson Bond

Ghosts and haunted houses have been a popular theme in humorous supernatural fiction since the early years of the Victorian era—especially as practised by writers like Richard Barham ('The Spectre of Tappington Hall', 1840), Frank Stockton ('The Transferred Ghost', 1884) and Oscar Wilde, whose much-anthologised classic, 'The Canterville Ghost' (1891), has been filmed several times for the cinema and television. So rich in fact is this particular seam of comedy that there have even been a number of anthologies devoted to it, including Dorothy Scarborough's fine collection, Humorous Ghosts, *published in 1921. Among more recent authors who have excelled at this kind of tale have been Thorne Smith, James Thurber and Nelson Bond, whose comic inventions were greatly admired by James Branch Cabell, creator of the legendary Poictesme fantasy series.*

Nelson Slade Bond (1908–), a former public relations officer and rare book dealer, has been described as one of the pre-eminent writers of 'nutty' fiction, and among his various popular series must be listed the stories of Pat Pending, maker of extraordinary inventions; Lancelot Briggs, an odd-ball space traveller; Hank Horse-Sense, a teller of tall tales; and Squaredeal Sam McGhee, who features in the following story. Bond started writing comic fantasy stories in 1937, and that same year produced a classic, 'Mr Mergenthwirker's Lobbies', which has since been turned into a radio series, successful play and TV adaptation. His love of trick endings has earned him comparison with O. Henry, while much of his fiction displays the same wit and love of the fantastic as his more famous contemporaries, Fredric Brown and Robert Bloch. Nelson Bond created the Squaredeal Sam McGhee stories for Bluebook *magazine during the Forties and Fifties, and 'The Gripes of Wraith', with its punning title and account of a ghost that is afraid of human beings and takes to drink, is one of the very best . . .*

* * *

> *Ghosts have just as good a right,*
> *In every way, to fear the light,*
> *As Men to fear the dark.*

'Do you,' queried Squaredeal Sam McGhee abruptly, 'believe in ghosts?'

The old gambler, con and carny man had been sitting quietly and patiently in my office for the past hour, waiting for me to finish my latest masterpiece. Now, as I patted the sheets into a tidy oblong he opened his attack, coincidentally bending forward to help himself to one of my cigars.

I grinned, recognising the gambit as one of the old rascal's inimitable preludes to a touch, a sort of narrative hook calculated to pique my curiosity and collar my dollars. Denial being his obvious objective, I countered with a nod.

'But of course,' I replied. 'I'm an ardent believer in spirits. Maybe I'm ghoulish that way, but I can't help it; it runs in the family. My dad's triplet cousins died three sheets in the wind. My great-uncle, Eerie McSlug, was a phantomweight boxer. And my sister's house has spooks in the kitchen.'

'Spooks in the kitchen?'

'That's right. She's got h'ants in her pantry.'

'Funny man!' frowned Sam reprovingly. 'Life o' the party! I'm sorry I tooken up so much of your time. I'll run along so's you can get back to readin' your Joe Miller.'

He rose, reaching for his weatherbeaten derby, but I chuckled and shoved him back in his chair.

'Calm down, chum. I was only gagging.'

'On them jokes,' said Sam, 'I would too.'

'But since we seem to be on the subject of spirits, I've got *proof* of their existence here,' I said, rummaging in my desk drawer. '*100 proof.* Sure you have to leave?'

'Well, now,' McGhee settled back, appraising my peace offering with a competently appreciative eye, 'come to think of it, I got nothin' to do which can't wait a couple o' fingers . . . I mean hours. Easy on that there seltzer water. It gives a guy awful headaches.'

I poured and passed.

'You were saying something about ghosts?'

Sam shrugged. 'It don't matter. Skip it.'

'But,' I said, 'I'm interested. You've had some sort of unnerving experience with the supernatural?'

'Yes,' said Sam, 'an' no. That is, I had a sort of experience, an' it got on my nerves . . . only not in the way you might think. If you can spare another drop of that snake-bite remedy—?'

I poured.

'When!' said Sam as the liquor ran over the edge of his glass. He sighed contentedly and lifted his high-topped shoes to the surface of my desk. 'Well, it was like this. I guess you know there's a housing shortage—'

I guess you know (said Squaredeal Sam), there's a housing shortage these days. Houses for sale is as rare as boogie beats in a Salvation Army concert; rental properties has all been rented at terrific rates by smart alecks who rented their *own* rental properties at terrific rates. An' as for apartments . . . well, a friend o' mine that works for the telephone company told me that one o' their public phones was reported out of order, an' before he could get into the booth to repair it he had to dispossess a guy who was livin' there with his wife, three kids an' a maiden aunt.

Of course (allowed Sam), he might o' been exaggeratin' a trifle. I don't see how there was room enough in that booth for a maiden aunt.

Anyhow, the sitchyation looked pretty hopeless when I blew back into town atter a winter of greasin' palms in the beach of the same name. Florida's a great place for folks in their old age . . . an' it helps them get there faster, too. You go down for a change and a rest; the bellboy gets the change, an' the hotel gets the rest. The day I checked out they give me a bill which looked like the distance to the farthest star computed in inches, an' if I hadn't been able to leave behind me a suitcase containin' ten thousand shares in a copper mine which may be discovered in Colorado some day, I would o' felt mighty guilty slidin' down that rainspout.

Imagine my surprise, then, when the day after I hit town I was strollin' through a nice residential district an' *bingo!* there's a fine-lookin' house with a placard hangin' on the front door: *Room To Let.*

My first thought was that the Health Department had run short of smallpox quarantines, but sure enough, it turned out to be the real McCoy. A wizened-up little old guy with a nose like a mildewed gherkin said yes, he had a room to rent, an' no, it hadn't been spoken for, an' if I didn't mind that would be two weeks in advance, please.

I said, 'Now, wait a minute, Mr—'

'Snead,' he admitted. 'Ephraim Snead.'

'Leave us not be im*pee*tuous about this,' I said. 'How do I know I'm goin' to like this room? I ain't even seen it.'

'Oh, you'll like it,' he guaranteed eagerly. 'It's the finest room in the house; large, sunny and cheerful.'

'An' as far as rent's concerned,' I continued, 'I'll have to ask you to wait a few days till I get myself lined up. I just got back from a long vacation, an' I'm temporarily what the economists call financially astringent.

'However,' I told him, 'as anybody in show business can tell you, Sam McGhee is as square as the sum of the hypothesis. So if you don't mind puttin' me on the cuff for a short time—?'

Old Picklepuss frowned, an' for a couple o' seconds I thought I was goin' to continue collectin' my bills in care of General Delivery. But finally he shrugged an' puckered up in what he used for a smile. 'Very well,' he said. 'I guess that will be all right. This way, please.' An' he showed me up a flight of stairs to the front room on the second floor.

Right then an' there I ought to have knew there was somethin' smelly in Sweden. In the first place, this Ephraim Snead character wasn't the type to dole out somethin' for nothin'. He wore suspenders an' a belt, both . . . the sure sign of a canny joe. Also, he had them calluses between the pointin' finger an' thumb which is the sign of either a pro gambler or a miser, an' from personal acquaintance I knew he wasn't the former. Finally, the room itself was just what he had claimed . . . large an' sunny an' cheerful. Things bein' how they are, the only good reason for it bein' vacant has to be a bad one.

But I didn't stop to think of them things. I grabbed one gander at the environs an' told Uncle Eph to take down the *To Let* sign. When he'd disappeared I took off my coat, flopped myself acrost a huge, old-fashioned feather bed . . . an' in two shakes of a cocktail I was lost in the arms of Murphy.

All I meant to do was take a short nap before dinner. But you know how them things is. Like the poet says, 'The best laid plans o' mice an' men oft gang up on a guy.' I was poohed an' the bed was soft. One wink led to another till when I finally woke up it was past midnight an' the room was as black as a bride's biscuits.

That is, it *should* have been black. But it wasn't; not completely. Over in the lounge chair that set beside the fireplace there was a funny, wriggly, greyish sort of a *glow*. Not a light, exactly. More like the reflection of a wore-out lightnin'-bug's tail light seen in a steamed mirror through a pair of dark glasses. Kind of fuzzy an' uncertain.

I sat bolt upright in bed. 'Hey!' I said. 'What goes on here?'

The minute I spoke, the glow brightened an' become a shape . . . the

shape of a man. It turned its head, stared at me for a split second . . .
then screamed bloody murder.

Sam sighed reflectively as he scrubbed a pyramid of cigar ash into the
nap of my carpet. I frowned at him.

'*It* screamed bloody murder?' I repeated. 'You mean *you* did, don't
you?'

'I mean *it* did,' said Sam. 'Or rather, *he* did.'

'But if it was really a ghost you saw—'

'He was a ghost,' Sam asseverated, 'an' it was him that hollered.
You see, he was scared of humans.'

I stared at him. 'He was which?'

'Nothin' of the sort,' said my friend. 'Witches is wenches. Edgar
was a plain old-fashioned he-male spook.'

'Edgar?'

'That was his name. Of course, I didn't learn that till later. First I
had to quiet him down. He was a nervous wrench.'

This Edgar (continued Squaredeal Sam McGhee) was a nervous wrench
if ever I seen one. He not only screamed when he seen me, he also
leaped out o' that chair an' started runnin' around the room in circles
like a will-o'-the-wisp bein' chased by a merry-go-round.

The exercise apparently charged his generator, too, because he kept
gettin' brighter an' solider and solider, until when at last I got him
cornered between the highboy an' the washstand he was emittin' enough
candle-power to read fine print by. Also, in case you ever write a ghost
story, you might want to know what he felt like. Well, like a cobweb,
only transparenter an' resilienter. You could poke a finger right through
him an' it didn't bother him. He popped right back together again when
you pulled out your pinky.

An' he was cold, too . . . colder than that brass monkey people keep
talkin' about. A funny kind of cold that when you touched him crawled
through your veins like frosted caterpillars.

I darn near got chilblains doin' it, but eventually I made him stand
still an' stop his God-awful bleatin'. When his wails had subsided to a
whimper, I give him what for.

'You're a fine one!' I scolded. 'Such a commotion. What are you
trying' to do . . . raise the dead?'

He said sulkily, 'You snuck up on me. You ought to be ashamed of
yourself, picking on a poor bodiless spirit.'

'You're the one,' I said, 'who ought to be ashamed. The idea of a great big spook like you jumpin' out of his ectoplasm just because somebody speaks to him. You're supposed to scare people, not vicey-versy.'

Edgar said, 'Yes, but—' an' brooded for a minute. Then he nodded. 'Okay. Maybe you got something there. *Boo!*'

An' he pulled an awful face at me, or what was supposed to be an awful face. But on him, with his big sad eyes an' mournful mouth, it just looked ridiculous. I pulled one right back at him, an' squiggled my fingers in his face.

'Boo yourself,' I chuckled, 'an' see how— Hey! Come down offen there.'

Because the minute I booed at him he skinned up the wall like a startled chemise, whisked acrost the ceiling, an' perched on the chandelier tremblin' like he had the egg.

'Don't *do* that!' he wailed. 'I can't stand it. It hurts my astral spirit!'

'An' you give *me* a pain, too,' I snorted. 'What's the matter with you? Ain't you got *any* courage at all?'

'Don't be ridiculous,' he snapped pettishly. 'If I had any guts, I wouldn't be a ghost, would I?'

He groaned, an' two big tears rolled down his cheeks. 'You don't know how horrible it is to be a wraith,' he said. 'Up all night . . . nothing but a nasty old winding-sheet to wear . . . no friends to talk to. And cold, horribly cold, all the time.' He sneezed to prove his point. I stared at him thoughtfully.

'What you need,' I decided, 'is a good stiff drink. Come down here an' I'll treat you to a snort of bottled anti-freeze. Stop frownin'. It's good stuff. Guaranteed to make you see pink elephants . . . an' other beasts of bourbon.'

But Edgar shook his head.

'It's no use,' he said dolefully. 'I can't drink. I'm a ghost. Liquor would go right through me.'

'That,' I frowned, 'complicates things. But then, I always heard you shouldn't mix your spirits—' A flash of inspiration hit me. 'Wait a minute. You could drink the *ghost* of a drink, couldn't you?'

He looked dubious. 'I suppose so. I never tried.'

'So atter I've tooken a drink,' I told him, 'it's a gone goose, no? You've heard of "dead soldiers", ain't you?'

His eyes brightened. 'Empty bottles, you mean? Of course! Do you really think it will work?'

'There's no harm in tryin',' I said. 'Here's how!' I got out a bottle of my favourite lumbago lotion, poured four fingers into a glass, an' drained it in one gulp. Then I handed him the empty glass, which he held onto with an effort ... but it wasn't an *empty* glass no longer. Because, you see, I had *killed* that drink! When he lifted the glass to his lips I seen a pale, shimmery, yellowish mist sloshin' around in it; the identical twin to the drink I'd just swallowed, only ghostlier. An' it had an identical effect, too, only in technicolor. As it run down Edgar's eerie canal he started gettin' brighter, warmer, an' cheerfuller, till when he'd assimilated it all he looked exactly like a lemon soufflé with a cherry in its middle.'

Sam paused and glanced at me sidewise. 'I reckon,' he ventured, 'you find this a mite hard to believe?'

'Oh no!' I assured him sanguinely. 'I can believe anything. I'm the original Wide-Eyed William ... the *naïf* soul Dean Swift had in mind when he wrote *Gullible's Travels.* I believe radio commercials, the campaign speeches of politicians and the daily weather forecasts. I believe in deodorants, telepathy and the sanctity of womanhood. I believe that time heals all wounds, honesty is the best policy, and many a mickle makes a muckle. I believe—'

'You're a cynic,' said McGhee reproachfully, 'an' I don't mean the kind where you wash the dishes. You've got a mean, suspicious mind, an' I bet you look under the crust of pies before you taste 'em.

'Just the same, you'd believe this story if you had seen that room. It *looked* like a room in a haunted house. I studied it carefully while me an' Edgar polished off the contents of that bottle. It had old-timey horsehair furnishings an' block-linen wallpaper with a design that almost drove you nuts tryin' to folly it with your eyes. Between slugs, Edgar pointed out how the old woodwork was carved, an' how the windows was deep-set between long, upright columns—'

'Pilastered?' I asked.

'Edgar?' replied McGhee. 'I'll say! To the gills! As a matter of fact, we both was.'

Despite the fact (continued Squaredeal Sam McGhee) that he was lookin' at the windows, neither of us was feelin' any pain. Ordinarily, I'm a pretty fair hand at punishin' demon rum, but I hadn't had anything to eat since breakfast, which left me a pushover for a hangover.

Furthermore, Edgar had a thirst that was absolutely out of this world ... which same is understandable considerin' the fact that he hadn't had a drink since the day he shovelled off this mortal coil. An' of course he couldn't take a drink until I'd already tooken its material predecessor, so you can see where that put *me*. Right under the table.

In fifteen minutes we had swapped names, addresses, an' telephone numbers; a half bottle later he was harmonisin' on such old spirituals as '*A-haunting We Will Go*', an' '*Genie With the Light Brown Hair*', not to mention '*Semper Apparition*', which is the Ghost Guard marchin' song. An' by the time we'd knocked off the quart, Edgar an' me was such bosom companions that he was settin' on my lap, sobbin' out to me the story of his brief, unhappy existence as a human.

It seemed Edgar had been dead a long time. In life he had been a junior clerk at a bank. In his work he handled large amounts o' money. 'Thousands of dollars, every day,' he told me. 'And the sum was my undoing.'

He told how one day he come home from work to discover that completely by accident he had walked off with several hundred dollars' worth of the bank's beans in his jeans.

'The funny part of it was,' he said miserably, 'the accounts had balanced perfectly at the end of the day. Not a penny out, one way or the other. Yet there I was, stuck with $450.00 that didn't belong to me!'

'*I* should be stuck like that some time,' I grunted. 'If you ever meet anybody that's looking for a volunteer pin-cushion—'

'I worried about it all that night,' he said. 'The next day I went over the books with a fine-tooth comb ... but I couldn't find the error. It took me four solid days of study to locate it, and as it turned out, I was the only person who could possibly have done so. Unintentionally, I had stumbled across an absolutely foolproof way of defrauding double-entry bookkeeping.'

He sighed, an' to take his mind off his woes I give him the butt of a cigarette I'd just crushed out. He dragged on a fresh new ghost-tube comfortably an' continued, 'To make things worse, there was no possible way of putting that money back into the accounts. To do so, I would have had to juggle the entries in so obvious a fashion that I would have been caught in jig-time. And for the life of me I couldn't think of any reasonable explanation why I should *put* what appeared to be my personal money into the vaults.

'You've got to believe I didn't want that money. I was ashamed of it, and of myself for embezzling it. That is, at first. But then the war came along and brought inflation with it. Shortages set in, prices rose, and my salary wasn't adequate for my needs. Before I realised it, I had used that $450.00 ... and my expenses were so high that I needed more.

'And that—' Edgar turned his mournful eyes on me as if pleadin' for understanding—'was the beginning of my downfall. I borrowed a few more hundreds from the bank . . . then a few more . . . and still more . . . till at last one day I discovered to my horror that I had stolen twenty thousand dollars!'

I whistled, noddin' gravely.

'An' then,' I guessed, 'they caught you?'

'No,' said Edgar hollowly, 'then, at the nadir of my infamy, I ran away. Not through any dread of being caught. As I've told you, my method was foolproof. My flight was an effort to escape my own conscience. I ran away from my home town and worked my way north, after unbelievable difficulties, to New York.

'Even then my intentions were good. Although I had spent most of the money, I somehow hoped to pay it back. But the week after I rented this room I contracted a severe cold. The cold developed into pneumonia, and—' Edgar groaned dismally—'and here I am. Earthbound to this room for the rest of my immortal existence, because in it I died with a crime on my conscience.'

There was a long, awkward silence punctuated only by the sound of his sobbin'. Then I asked, 'Isn't there any way you can stop bein' a ghost, Eddie?'

'Only one,' he said. 'I must atone for my crime.'

'You mean pay back the money you borrowed?'

'That's the only way.' He looked at me with sudden hope. 'Sam,' he said, 'maybe *you* can help me?'

'Me? How?'

'You're alive. You can get the money I need to pay my debt of honour . . . send it to the Richmond bank I stole it from. Then my soul will be freed. I can go to—'

'Check!' I said. 'You can go to! I believe in the good neighbour policy an' all o' that there, but if you think I got twenty grand to toss around like it was a sack of nuts, you got hair *in* your head as well as on it. Anyhow, where do you think *I* can raise all that money?'

'You could borrow it from Snead, maybe?' Edgar suggested. 'The old miser's got ten times that much hidden away in this house.'

'An' what would I give him for an I.O.U.? My right arm?'

'Well, you could—' Edgar coughed delicately—'I thought you might be able to borrow the money like I borrowed it from the bank—'

'An' join you in spookland when I cash in my chips? No, thanks! Squaredeal Sam McGhee's conscience is clear as restaurant soup, an' he means to keep it that way.'

'Well, you don't have to be so snide about it,' said Edgar sulkily. 'It was just a suggestion. And, after all, he *owes* me the money . . . in a way. It was tightwads like him that got rich off people like me during the war.'

'What do you mean?' I asked him.

Edgar explained. He explained in some detail, an' with considerable vehemence, considerin' the facts. But what he said give me a start, an' then set me to cogitatin'.

When he had finished explainin' I done a rightabout face on my original decision.

'See here, chum,' I said, 'maybe me an' you *can* do business, after all. Suppose I clear up this debt of yours . . . will you do me a favour in return?'

'Anything you say, old pal,' swore Edgar earnestly. 'Just name it, old pal, old pal.'

'I will when I get back,' I told him, '—which should be not long from now. Just sit tight an' wait for me. I got an idea you'll be out of the shroud by dawning.'

So I left him. I went downtown an' got the twenty thousand dollars, slipped it in an envelope an' mailed it to the bank, then hurried home again, burnin' with eagerness. But I got damped off quick an' complete. Because when I got to my room, Edgar was gone. He'd vanished like a gob's pay on shore leave. An' I ain't never seen him since.'

Sam sighed and relapsed into a brooding silence. I waited patiently for a moment, then prodded him.

'Well, Sam?'

He shrugged ruefully. 'Well . . . that's all. Where I made my mistake was in not claimin' my favour in advance. The way I figger it, Edgar didn't sneak out on me. He was a victim of circumstances. Bein' an honourable spook like he was, he would have *liked* to stick around, but the instant his crime was atoned he stopped bein' earthbound. He's probably strummin' a harp right now. Or if not that, at any rate he's warm enough in his new home.'

Sam glanced at me thoughtfully. 'So now you see my reason for comin' here to see you. It's not as if I was askin' you to *give* me the money. All I want is a loan on an investment that can't miss—'

'You mean,' I exclaimed, 'you expect me to lend you *twenty thousand dollars*! Are you crazy?'

'Hell, no!' snorted Sam. 'Are you? Did I say anything about twenty gees? All I want is the temporary loan of a five spot so I can trot down to a good spiritualist an' call Edgar on the Ouija board. He still owes me a return favour . . . an' I want to know how that trick double-entry bookkeeping he dreamed up works. I already got myself lined up for a job as junior clerk at the First National Bank, beginnin' next week. An' bein' conscientious like I am, I wouldn't want to work for a new employer without knowin' the fine points of the rack . . . I mean, the business.'

'But the twenty grand you sent Edgar's bank?' I expostulated. 'How are you going to repay that? And where did you get it? You said that you were broke when you hit New York.'

'*Almost* broke,' corrected Sam. 'I still had one or two bucks in my pocket. Enough to buy a barrelful or two of what it took to pay off Edgar's debt of honour.

'I told you he'd been dead a long time. An' I told you it was wartime inflation that turned him into a criminal. What I maybe forgot to mention is that he lived an' done his thievin' durin' the Civil War. The minute I learned that, I seen the way to pay off his debt for him. I sent the Bank of Richmond as full restitution . . . twenty thousand dollars in Confederate money!'

THE ROACHES

Thomas M. Disch

In the long tradition of witchcraft stories, the vast majority of witches have appeared as malevolent old crones of uncertain supernatural powers dwelling amidst hatred and mistrust in isolated communities across Britain, Europe and America. In comic fantasy, however, the modern witch tends to turn up in a variety of disguises from a jolly, harmless old biddy in a rural community to a rather more sardonic and sophisticated woman living in the town or city. In this genre, at least, witchcraft has moved with the times, and witches often appear as figures of remarkable powers blessed—rather than cursed—with a sense of humour. 'The Roaches' is one of the most original examples of this kind of tale, and has been described by Jack Sullivan in The Encyclopedia of Horror and the Supernatural *(1986) as 'one of the most horrible and hilarious stories in the literature'.*

Thomas Michael Disch (1940–) has been praised as 'one of the most formidable of sf's wits and stylists'. Formerly employed in advertising and a bank in New York, Disch has subsequently lived in several countries including Italy, Turkey, Mexico and the UK since he served notice of his special blend of wry comedy in his collections, One Hundred and Two H Bombs *(1966) and* White Fang Goes Dingo and Other Funny SF Stories, *published in 1971. His novel* The Puppies of Terra *(1966) pictures an Earth taken over by aliens who make pets of mankind, and this has been followed by a number of other idiosyncratic works including* Highway Sandwiches *(1970),* The Tale of Dan de Lion *(1986),* The Brave Little Toaster Goes to Mars *(1988) and* The Silver Pillow: A Tale of Witchcraft *(1988). In 'The Roaches' we are introduced to what Jack Sullivan calls 'the ultimate urban witch'—a woman who can make cockroaches answer her commands. But be warned: this is a gruesome as well as a comic story . . .*

*   *   *

Miss Marcia Kenwell had a perfect horror of cockroaches. It was an altogether different horror than the one which she felt, for instance, toward the colour puce. Marcia Kenwell loathed the little things. She couldn't see one without wanting to scream. Her revulsion was so extreme that she could not bear to crush them under the soles of her shoes. No, that would be too awful. She would run, instead, for the spray can of Black Flag and inundate the little beast with poison until it ceased to move or got out of reach into one of the cracks where they all seemed to live. It was horrible, unspeakably horrible, to think of them nestling in the walls, under the linoleum, only waiting for the lights to be turned off, and then . . . No, it was best not to think about it.

Every week she looked through the *Times* hoping to find another apartment, but either the rents were prohibitive (this *was* Manhattan, and Marcia's wage was a mere $62.50 a week, gross) or the building was obviously infested. She could always tell: there would be husks of dead roaches scattered about in the dust beneath the sink, stuck to the greasy backside of the stove, lining the out-of-reach cupboard shelves like the rice on the church steps after a wedding. She left such rooms in a passion of disgust, unable even to think till she reached her own apartment, where the air would be thick with the wholesome odours of Black Flag, Roach-It, and the toxic pastes that were spread on slices of potato and hidden in a hundred cracks which only she and the roaches knew about.

At least, she thought, *I keep my apartment clean.* And truly, the linoleum under the sink, the backside and underside of the stove, and the white contact paper lining her cupboards were immaculate. She could not understand how other people could let these matters get so entirely out-of-hand. *They must be Puerto Ricans*, she decided—and shivered again with horror, remembering that litter of empty husks, the filth and the disease.

Such extreme antipathy toward insects—toward one particular insect—may seem excessive; but Marcia Kenwell was not really exceptional in this. There are many women, bachelor women like Marcia chiefly, who share this feeling, though one may hope, for sweet charity's sake, that they escape Marcia's peculiar fate.

Marcia's phobia was, as in most such cases, hereditary in origin. That is to say, she inherited it from her mother, who had a morbid fear of anything that crawled or skittered or lived in tiny holes. Mice, frogs, snakes, worms, bugs—all could send Mrs Kenwell into hysterics, and it would indeed have been a wonder if little Marcia had not taken after her. It was rather strange, though, that her fear had become so particular, and stranger still that it should particularly be cockroaches that captured her fancy, for Marcia had never seen a single cockroach, didn't know what they were. (The Kenwells were a Minnesota family, and Minnesota families simply don't have cockroaches.) In fact, the subject did not arise until Marcia was nineteen and setting out (armed with nothing but a high school diploma and pluck, for she was not, you see, a very attractive girl) to conquer New York.

On the day of her departure, her favourite and only surviving aunt came with her to the Greyhound Terminal (her parents being deceased) and gave her this parting advice: 'Watch out for the roaches, Marcia darling. New York City is full of cockroaches.' At that time (at almost any time really) Marcia hardly paid attention to her aunt, who had opposed the trip from the start and given a hundred or more reasons why Marcia had better not go, not till she was older at least.

Her aunt had been proven right on all counts: Marcia, after five years and fifteen employment agency fees, could find nothing in New York but dull jobs at mediocre wages; she had no more friends than when she lived on West 16th; and, except for its view (the Chock Full O'Nuts warehouse and a patch of sky), her present apartment on lower Thompson Street was not a great improvement on its predecessor.

The city was full of promises, but they had all been pledged to other people. The city Marcia knew was sinful, indifferent, dirty, and dangerous. Every day she read accounts of women attacked in subway stations, raped in the streets, knifed in their own beds. A hundred people looked on curiously all the while and offered no assistance. And on top of everything else there were the roaches!

There were roaches everywhere, but Marcia didn't see them until she'd been in New York a month. They came to her—or she to them— at Silversmith's on Nassau Street, a stationery shop where she had been working for three days. It was the first job she'd been able to find. Alone or helped by a pimply stockboy (in all fairness it must be noted that Marcia was not without an acne problem of her own), she wandered down rows of rasp-edged metal shelves in the musty basement, making an inventory of the sheaves and piles and boxes of bond paper, leatherette-bound diaries, pins and clips, and carbon paper. The basement was dirty and so dim that she needed a flashlight for the lowest shelves. In the obscurest corner, a faucet leaked perpetually into a grey sink: she had been resting near this sink, sipping a cup of tepid coffee (saturated, in the New York manner, with sugar and drowned in milk), thinking, probably, of how she could afford several things she simply couldn't afford, when she noticed the dark spots moving on the side of the sink. At first she thought they might be no more than motes floating in the jelly of her eyes, or the giddy dots that one sees after over-exertion on a hot day. But they persisted too long to be illusory, and Marcia drew nearer, feeling compelled to bear witness. *How do I know they are insects?* she thought.

How are we to explain the fact that what repels us most can be at times—at the same time—inordinately attractive? Why is the cobra poised to strike so beautiful? The fascination of the abomination is something that . . . Something which we would rather not account for. The subject borders on the obscene, and there is no need to deal with it here, except to note the breathless wonder with which Marcia observed these first roaches of hers. Her chair was drawn so close to the sink that she could see the mottling of their oval, unsegmented bodies, the quick scuttering of their thin legs, and the quicker flutter of their antennae. They moved randomly, proceeding nowhere, centred nowhere. They seemed greatly disturbed over nothing. *Perhaps*, Marcia thought, *my presence has a morbid effect on them?*

Only then did she become aware, aware fully, that these were the cockroaches of which she had been warned. Repulsion took hold; her flesh curdled on her bones. She screamed and fell back in her chair, almost upsetting a shelf of odd-lots. Simultaneously the roaches disappeared over the edge of the sink and into the drain.

Mr Silversmith, coming downstairs to inquire the source of Marcia's alarm, found her supine and unconscious. He sprinkled her face with tapwater, and she awoke with a shudder of nausea. She refused to explain why she had screamed and insisted that she must leave Mr Silversmith's employ immediately. He, supposing that the pimply stockboy (who was his son) had made a pass at Marcia, paid her for the three days she had worked and let her go without regrets. From that moment on, cockroaches were to be a regular feature of Marcia's existence.

On Thompson Street Marcia was able to reach a sort of stalemate with the cockroaches. She settled into a comfortable routine of pastes and powders, scrubbing and waxing, prevention (she never had even a cup of coffee without washing and drying cup and coffeepot immediately afterward) and ruthless extermination. The only roaches who trespassed upon her two cosy rooms came up from the apartment below, and they did not stay long, you may be sure. Marcia would have complained to the landlady, except that it was the landlady's apartment and her roaches.

She had been inside, for a glass of wine on Christmas Eve, and she had to admit that it wasn't exceptionally dirty. It was, in fact, more than commonly clean—but *that* was not enough in New York. If *everyone*, Marcia thought, *took as much care as I, there would soon be no cockroaches in New York City.*

Then (it was March and Marcia was halfway through her sixth year in the city) the Shchapalovs moved in next door. There were three of them—two men and a woman—and they were old, though exactly how old it was hard to say: they had been aged by more than time. Perhaps they weren't more than forty. The woman, for instance, though she still had brown hair, had a face wrinkly as a prune and was missing several teeth. She would stop Marcia in the hallway or on the street, grabbing hold of her coatsleeve, and talk to her—always a simple lament about the weather, which was too hot or too cold or too wet or too dry. Marcia never knew half of what the old woman was saying, she mumbled so. Then she'd totter off to the grocery with her bagful of empties.

The Shchapalovs, you see, drank. Marcia, who had a rather exaggerated idea of the cost of alcohol (the cheapest thing she could imagine was vodka), wondered where they got the money for all the drinking they did. She knew they didn't work, for on days when Marcia was home with the flu she could hear the three Shchapalovs through the thin wall between their kitchen and hers screaming at each other to exercise their adrenal glands. *They're on welfare*, Marcia decided. Or perhaps the man with only one eye was a veteran on pension.

She didn't so much mind the noise of their arguments (she was seldom home in the afternoon), but she couldn't stand their singing. Early in the evening they'd start in, singing along with the radio stations. Everything they listened to sounded like Guy Lombardo. Later, about eight o'clock they sang *a cappella*. Strange, soulless noises rose and fell like Civil Defence sirens; there were bellowings, bayings, and cries. Marcia had heard something like it once on a Folkways record of Czechoslovakian wedding chants. She was quite beside herself whenever the awful noise started up and had to leave the house till they were done. A complaint would do no good: the Shchapalovs had a right to sing at that hour.

Besides, one of the men was said to be related by marriage to the landlady. That's how they got the apartment, which had been used as a storage space until they'd moved in. Marcia couldn't understand how the three of them could fit into such a little space—just a room-and-a-half with a narrow window opening onto the air shaft. (Marcia had discovered that she could see their entire living space through a hole that had been broken through the wall when the plumbers had installed a sink for the Shchapalovs.)

But if their singing distressed her, *what* was she to do about the roaches? The Shchapalov woman, who was the sister of one man and married to the other—or else the men were brothers and she was the wife to one of them (sometimes, it seemed to Marcia, from the words that came through the walls, that she was married to neither of them—or to both), was a bad housekeeper, and the Shchapalov apartment was soon swarming with roaches. Since Marcia's sink and the Shchapalovs' were fed by the same pipes and emptied into a common drain, a steady overflow of roaches was disgorged into Marcia's immaculate kitchen. She could spray and lay out more poisoned potatoes; she could scrub and dust and stuff Kleenex tissues into holes where the pipes passed through the wall: it was all to no avail. The Shchapalov roaches could always lay another million eggs in the garbage bags rotting beneath the Shchapalov sink. In a few days they would be swarming through the pipes and cracks and into Marcia's cupboards. She would lie in bed and watch them (this was possible because Marcia kept a nightlight burning in each room) advancing across the floor and up the walls, trailing the Shchapalovs' filth and disease everywhere they went.

One such evening the roaches were especially bad, and Marcia was trying to muster the resolution to get out of her warm bed and attack them with Roach-It. She had left the windows open from the conviction that cockroaches do not like the cold, but she found that she liked it much less. When she swallowed, it hurt, and she knew she was coming down with a cold. And all because of *them!*

'*Oh go away!*' she begged. '*Go away! Go away! Get out of my apartment.*'

She addressed the roaches with the same desperate intensity with which she sometimes (though not often in recent years) addressed prayers to the Almighty. Once she had prayed all night long to get rid of her acne, but in the morning it was worse than ever. People in intolerable circumstances will pray to anything. Truly, there are no atheists in foxholes: the men there pray to the bombs that they may land somewhere else.

The only strange thing in Marcia's case is that her prayers were answered. The cockroaches fled from her apartment as quickly as their little legs could carry them—and in straight lines, too. Had they heard her? Had they understood?

Marcia could still see one cockroach coming down from the cupboard. *'Stop!'* she commanded. And it stopped.

At Marcia's spoken command, the cockroach would march up and down, to the left and to the right. Suspecting that her phobia had matured into madness, Marcia left her warm bed, turned on the light, and cautiously approached the roach, which remained motionless, as she had bidden it. *'Wiggle your antennas,'* she commanded. The cockroach wiggled its antennae.

She wondered if they would *all* obey her and found, within the next few days, that they all would. They would do anything she told them to. They would eat poison out of her hand. Well, not exactly out of her hand, but it amounted to the same thing. They were devoted to her. Slavishly.

It is the end, she thought, *of my roach problem*. But of course it was only the beginning.

Marcia did not question too closely the *reason* the roaches obeyed her. She had never much troubled herself with abstract problems. After expending so much time and attention on them, it seemed only natural that she should exercise a certain power over them. However she was wise enough never to speak of this power to anyone else—even to Miss Bismuth at the insurance office. Miss Bismuth read the horoscope magazines and claimed to be able to communicate with her mother, aged sixty-eight, telepathically. Her mother lived in Ohio. But what would Marcia have said: that *she* could communicate telepathically with cockroaches? Impossible.

Nor did Marcia use her power for any other purpose than keeping the cockroaches out of her own apartment. Whenever she saw one, she simply commanded it to go to the Shchapalov apartment and stay there. It was surprising, then, that there were always more roaches coming back through the pipes. Marcia assumed that they were younger generations. Cockroaches are known to breed fast. But it was easy enough to send them back to the Shchapalovs.

'Into their beds,' she added as an afterthought. 'Go *into their beds*.' Disgusting as it was, the idea gave her a queer thrill of pleasure.

The next morning, the Shchapalov woman, smelling a little worse than usual (Whatever was it, Marcia wondered, that they drank?), was waiting at the open door of her apartment. She wanted to speak to Marcia before she left for work. Her housedress was mired from an attempt at scrubbing the floor, and while she sat there talking, she tried to wring out the scrubwater.

'No idea!' she exclaimed. 'You ain't got no idea how bad! 'S terrible!'

'What?' Marcia asked, knowing perfectly well what.

'The boogs! Oh, the boogs are just everywhere. Don't you have em, sweetheart? I don't know what to do. I try to keep a decent house, God knows—' She lifted her rheumy eyes to heaven, testifying. '—but I don't know what to do.' She leaned forward, confidingly. 'You won't believe this, sweetheart, but last night . . .' A cockroach began to climb out of the limp strands of hair straggling down into the woman's eyes. '. . . they got into bed with us! Would you believe it? There must have been a hundred of 'em. I said to Osip, I said—What's wrong, sweetheart?'

Marcia, speechless with horror, pointed at the roach, which had almost reached the bridge of the woman's nose. 'Yech!' the woman agreed, smashing it and wiping her dirtied thumb on her dirtied dress. 'Goddam boogs! I hate em, I swear to God. But what's a person gonna do? Now, what I wanted to ask, sweetheart, is do you have a problem with the boogs? Being as how you're right next door, I thought—' She smiled a confidential smile, as though to say this is just between us ladies. Marcia almost expected a roach to skitter out between her gapped teeth.

'No,' she said. 'No, I use Black Flag.' She backed away from the doorway toward the safety of the stairwell. 'Black Flag,' she said again, louder. 'Black Flag,' she shouted from the foot of the stairs. Her knees trembled so, that she had to hold onto the metal banister for support.

At the insurance office that day, Marcia couldn't keep her mind on her work five minutes at a time. (Her work in the Actuarial Dividends department consisted of adding up long rows of two-digit numbers on a Burroughs adding machine and checking the similar additions of her co-workers for errors.) She kept thinking of the cockroaches in the tangled hair of the Shchapalov woman, of her bed teeming with roaches, and of other, less concrete horrors on the periphery of consciousness. The numbers swam and swarmed before her eyes, and twice she had to go to the Ladies' Room, but each time it was a false alarm. Nevertheless, lunchtime found her with no appetite. Instead of going down to the employee cafeteria she went out into the fresh April air and strolled along 23rd Street. Despite the spring, it all seemed to bespeak a sordidness, a festering corruption. The stones of the Flatiron Building oozed damp blackness; the gutters were heaped with soft decay; the smell of burning grease hung in the air outside the cheap restaurants like cigarette smoke in a close room.

The afternoon was worse. Her fingers would not touch the correct numbers on the machine unless she looked at them. One silly phrase kept running through her head: 'Something must be done. Something must be done.' She had quite forgotten that she had sent the roaches into the Shchapalovs' bed in the first place.

That night, instead of going home immediately, she went to a double feature on 42nd Street. She couldn't afford the better movies. Susan Hayward's little boy almost drowned in quicksand. That was the only thing she remembered afterward.

She did something then that she had never done before. She had a drink in a bar. She had two drinks. Nobody bothered her; nobody even looked in her direction. She took a taxi to Thompson Street (the subways weren't safe at that hour) and arrived at her door by eleven o'clock. She didn't have anything left for a tip. The taxi driver said he understood.

There was a light on under the Shchapalovs' door, and they were singing. It was eleven o'clock. 'Something must be done,' Marcia whispered to herself earnestly. 'Something must be *done*.'

Without turning on her own light, without even taking off her new spring jacket from Ohrbach's, Marcia got down on her knees and crawled under the sink. She tore out the Kleenexes she had stuffed into the cracks around the pipes.

There they were, the three of them, the Shchapalovs, drinking, the woman plumped on the lap of the one-eyed man, and the other man, in a dirty undershirt, stamping his foot on the floor to accompany the loud discords of their song. Horrible. They were drinking of course, she might have known it, and now the woman pressed her roachy mouth against the mouth of the one-eyed man—kiss, kiss. Horrible, horrible. Marcia's hands knotted into her mouse-coloured hair, and she thought: *The filth, the disease!* Why, they hadn't learned a thing from last night!

Some time later (Marcia had lost track of time) the overhead light in the Shchapalovs' apartment was turned off. Marcia waited till they made no more noise. 'Now,' Marcia said, 'all of you.

'All of you in this building, all of you that can hear me, gather round the bed, but wait a little while yet. Patience. All of you . . .' The words of her command fell apart into little fragments, which she told like the beads of a rosary—little brown ovoid wooden beads. '. . . gather round . . . wait a little while yet . . . all of you . . . patience . . . gather round . . .' Her hand stroked the cold water pipes rhythmically, and it seemed that she could hear them—gathering, scuttering up through the walls, coming out of the cupboards, the garbage bags—a host, an army, and she was their absolute queen.

'Now!' she said. 'Mount them! Cover them! Devour them!'

There was no doubt that she could hear them now. She heard them quite palpably. Their sound was like grass in the wind, like the first stirrings of gravel dumped from a truck. Then there was the Shchapalov woman's scream, and curses from the men, such terrible curses that Marcia could hardly bear to listen.

A light went on, and Marcia could see them, the roaches, everywhere. Every surface, the walls, the floors, the shabby sticks of furniture, was mottly thick with *Blattellae Germanicae*. There was more than a single thickness.

The Shchapalov woman, standing up on her bed, screamed monotonously. Her pink rayon nightgown was speckled with brown-black dots. Her knobbly fingers tried to brush bugs out of her hair, off her face. The man in the undershirt who a few minutes before had been stomping his feet to the music stomped now more urgently, one hand still holding onto the lightcord. Soon the floor was slimy with crushed roaches, and he slipped. The light went out. The woman's scream took on a rather choked quality, as though . . .

But Marcia wouldn't think of that. 'Enough,' she whispered. 'No more. Stop.'

She crawled away from the sink, across the room on to her bed, which tried, with a few tawdry cushions, to dissemble itself as a couch for the daytime. Her breathing came hard, and there was a curious constriction in her throat. She was sweating incontinently.

From the Shchapalovs' room came scuffling sounds, a door banged, running feet, and then a louder, muffled noise, perhaps a body falling downstairs. The landlady's voice: 'What the hell do you think you're—' Other voices overriding hers. Incoherences, and footsteps returning up the stairs. Once more, the landlady: 'There ain't no *boogs* here, for heaven's sake. The boogs is in your heads. You've got the d.t.'s, that's what. And it wouldn't be any wonder, if there were boogs. The place is filthy. Look at that crap on the floor. Filth! I've stood just about enough from you. Tomorrow you move out, hear? This *used* to be a decent building.'

The Shchapalovs did not protest their eviction. Indeed, they did not wait for the morrow to leave. They quitted their apartment with only a suitcase, a laundry bag, and an electric toaster. Marcia watched them go down the steps through her half-open door. *It's done*, she thought. It's all *over*.

With a sigh of almost sensual pleasure, she turned on the lamp beside the bed, then the other lamps. The room gleamed immaculately. Deciding to celebrate her victory, she went to the cupboard, where she kept a bottle of *crème de menthe*.

The cupboard was full of roaches.

She had not told them where to go, where *not* to go, when they left the Shchapalov apartment. It was her own fault.

The great silent mass of roaches regarded Marcia calmly, and it seemed to the distracted girl that she could read *their* thoughts, their thought rather, for they had but a single thought. She could read it as clearly as she could read the illuminated billboard for Chock Full O'Nuts outside her window. It was delicate as music issuing from a thousand tiny pipes. It was an ancient music box open after centuries of silence: 'We love you we love you we love you we love you.'

Something strange happened inside Marcia then, something unprecedented: she responded.

'I love you too,' she replied. 'Oh, I love you. Come to me, all of you. Come to me. I love you. Come to me. I love you. Come to me.'

From every corner of Manhattan, from the crumbling walls of Harlem, from restaurants on 56th Street, from warehouses along the river, from sewers and from orange peels mouldering in garbage cans, the loving roaches came forth and began to crawl toward their mistress.

THE LADY OF THE HOUSE
OF LOVE

Angela Carter

The vampire, too, generally appears in fiction as a blood-thirsty prowler of the night, continuing the tradition that Bram Stoker popularised a century ago in his classic novel, Dracula *(1897). The exceptions to this rule have been few and far between, either in print or on film. David Niven starred in the comedy* Vampira *(1974), and humorous fantasy stories by Anthony Boucher ('They Bite', 1943), Robert Bloch ('The Bat Is My Brother', 1944), Philip K. Dick ('The Cookie Lady', 1953) also venture in a different direction. Together with Angela Carter's tale here, these are arguably the best examples. In 'The Lady of the House of Love' we meet a reluctant female vampire who dresses in a white négligé, wears green glasses, loves playing patience and would much rather keep rabbits as pets than eat them when no human nourishment is available.*

Angela Carter (1940–1992) has been described by The Times *as 'a fabulist of demonic energy' who drew on myths and legends in the creation of her witty baroque novels and short stories. Born in Sussex, she was a teacher of creative writing in England and America for some years while developing the unique style that characterises such highly acclaimed fantasy novels as* The Magic Toyshop *(which won the John Llewellyn Rhys prize in 1967),* The Infernal Desire Machines of Doctor Hoffman *(1972) and* Nights at the Circus *(1984, winner of the James Tait Black Memorial Prize). Carter's werewolf story, 'The Company of Wolves', which parodied the story of Little Red Riding Hood, was filmed in 1984 by Neil Jordan. 'The Lady of the House of Love' is something of a parody of* Dracula, *too, although our 'queen of the vampires' really wants to be human and her handsome young visitor is not a lawyer's clerk arriving by coach at dead of night, but a tweedy young tourist who innocently appears on a hot summer's day outside her Carpathian mansion* riding a bicycle . . .

*   *   *

At last the revenants became so troublesome the peasants abandoned the village and it fell solely into the possession of subtle and vindictive inhabitants who manifest their presences by shadows that fall almost imperceptibly awry, too many shadows, even at midday, shadows that have no source in anything visible; by the sound, sometimes, of sobbing in a derelict bedroom where a cracked mirror suspended from a wall does not reflect a presence; by a sense of unease that will afflict the traveller unwise enough to pause to drink from the fountain in the square that still gushes spring water from a faucet stuck in a stone lion's mouth. A cat prowls in a weedy garden; he grins and spits, arches his back, bounces away from an intangible on four fear-stiffened legs. Now all shun the village below the château in which the beautiful somnambulist helplessly perpetuates her ancestral crimes.

Wearing an antique bridal gown, the beautiful queen of the vampires sits all alone in her dark, high house under the eyes of the portraits of her demented and atrocious ancestors, each one of whom, through her, projects a baleful posthumous existence; she counts out the Tarot cards, ceaselessly construing a constellation of possibilities as if the random fall of the cards on the red plush tablecloth before her could precipitate her from her chill, shuttered room into a country of perpetual summer and obliterate the perennial sadness of a girl who is both death and the maiden.

Her voice is filled with distant sonorities, like reverberations in a cave: now you are at the place of annihilation, now you are at the place of annihilation. And she is herself a cave full of echoes, she is a system of repetitions, she is a closed circuit. 'Can a bird sing only the song it knows or can it learn a new song?' She draws her long, sharp fingernail across the bars of the cage in which her pet lark sings, striking a plangent twang like that of the plucked heartstrings of a woman of metal. Her hair falls down like tears.

The castle is mostly given over to ghostly occupants but she herself has her own suite of drawing room and bedroom. Closely barred shutters and heavy velvet curtains keep out every leak of natural light. There is a round table on a single leg covered with a red plush cloth on which she lays out her inevitable Tarot; this room is never more than faintly illuminated by a heavily shaded lamp on the mantelpiece and the dark red figured wallpaper is obscurely, distressingly patterned by the rain that drives in through the neglected roof and leaves behind it random areas of staining, ominous marks like those left on the sheets by dead lovers. Depredations of rot and fungus everywhere. The unlit chandelier is so heavy with dust the individual prisms no longer show any shapes; industrious spiders have woven canopies in the corners of this ornate and rotting place, have trapped the porcelain vases on the mantelpiece in soft grey nets. But the mistress of all this disintegration notices nothing.

She sits in a chair covered in moth-ravaged burgundy velvet at the low, round table and distributes the cards; sometimes the lark sings, but more often remains a sullen mound of drab feathers. Sometimes the Countess will wake it for a brief cadenza by strumming the bars of its cage; she likes to hear it announce how it cannot escape.

She rises when the sun sets and goes immediately to her table where she plays her game of patience until she grows hungry, until she becomes ravenous. She is so beautiful she is unnatural; her beauty is an abnormality, a deformity, for none of her features exhibit any of those touching imperfections that reconcile us to the imperfection of the human condition. Her beauty is a symptom of her disorder, of her soullessness.

The white hands of the tenebrous belle deal the hand of destiny. Her fingernails are longer than those of the mandarins of ancient China and each is pared to a fine point. These and teeth as fine and white as spikes of spun sugar are the visible signs of the destiny she wistfully attempts to evade via the arcana; her claws and teeth have been sharpened on centuries of corpses, she is the last bud of the poison tree that sprang from the loins of Vlad the Impaler who picnicked on corpses in the forests of Transylvania.

The walls of her bedroom are hung with black satin, embroidered with tears of pearl. At the room's four corners are funerary urns and bowls which emit slumbrous, pungent fumes of incense. In the centre is an elaborate catafalque, in ebony, surrounded by long candles in enormous silver candlesticks. In a white lace négligé stained a little with blood, the Countess climbs up on her catafalque at dawn each morning and lies down in an open coffin.

A chignoned priest of the Orthodox faith staked out her wicked father at a Carpathian crossroad before her milk teeth grew. Just as they staked him out, the fatal Count cried: 'Nosferatu is dead; long live Nosferatu!' Now she possesses all the haunted forests and mysterious habitations of his vast domain; she is the hereditary commandant of the army of shadows who camp in the village below her château, who penetrate the woods in the form of owls, bats and foxes, who make the milk curdle and the butter refuse to come, who ride the horses all night on a wild hunt so they are sacks of skin and bone in the morning, who milk the cows dry and, especially, torment pubescent girls with fainting fits, disorders of the blood, diseases of the imagination.

But the Countess herself is indifferent to her own weird authority, as if she were dreaming it. In her dream, she would like to be human; but she does not know if that is possible. The Tarot always shows the same configuration: always she turns up La Papesse, La Mort, La Tour Abolie, wisdom, death, dissolution.

On moonless nights, her keeper lets her out into the garden. This garden, an exceedingly sombre place, bears a strong resemblance to a burial ground and all the roses her dead mother planted have grown up into a huge, spiked wall that incarcerates her in the castle of her inheritance. When the back door opens, the Countess will sniff the air and howl. She drops, now, on all fours. Crouching, quivering, she catches the scent of her prey. Delicious crunch of the fragile bones of rabbits and small, furry things she pursues with fleet, four-footed speed; she will creep home, whimpering, with blood smeared on her cheeks. She pours water from the ewer in her bedroom into the bowl, she washes her face with the wincing, fastidious gestures of a cat.

The voracious margin of huntress's nights in the gloomy garden, crouch and pounce, surrounds her habitual tormented somnambulism, her life or imitation of life. The eyes of this nocturnal creature enlarge and glow. All claws and teeth, she strikes, she gorges; but nothing can console her for the ghastliness of her condition, nothing. She resorts to the magic comfort of the Tarot pack and shuffles the cards, lays them out, reads them, gathers them up with a sigh, shuffles them again, constantly constructing hypotheses about a future which is irreversible.

An old mute looks after her, to make sure she never sees the sun, that all day she stays in her coffin, to keep mirrors and all reflective surfaces away from her—in short, to perform all the functions of the servants of vampires. Everything about this beautiful and ghastly lady is as it should be, queen of night, queen of terror—except her horrible reluctance for the role.

Nevertheless, if an unwise adventurer pauses in the square of the deserted village to refresh himself at the fountain, a crone in a black dress and white apron presently emerges from a house. She will invite you with smiles and gestures; you will follow her. The Countess wants fresh meat. When she was a little girl, she was like a fox and contented herself entirely with baby rabbits that squeaked piteously as she bit into their necks with a nauseated voluptuousness, with voles and field-mice that palpitated for a bare moment between her embroidress's fingers. But now she is a woman, she must have men. If you stop too long beside the giggling fountain, you will be led by the hand to the Countess's larder.

All day, she lies in her coffin in her négligé of blood-stained lace. When the sun drops behind the mountain, she yawns and stirs and puts on the only dress she has, her mother's wedding dress, to sit and read her cards until she grows hungry. She loathes the food she eats; she would have liked to take the rabbits home with her, feed them on lettuce, pet them and make them a nest in her red-and-black chinoiserie escritoire, but hunger always overcomes her. She sinks her teeth into the neck where an artery throbs with fear; she will drop the deflated skin from which she has extracted all the nourishment with a small cry of both pain and disgust. And it is the same with the shepherd boys and gipsy lads who, ignorant or foolhardy, come to wash the dust from their feet in the water of the fountain; the Countess's governess brings them into the drawing room where the cards on the table always show the Grim Reaper. The Countess herself will serve them coffee in tiny cracked, precious cups, and little sugar cakes. The hobbledehoys sit with a spilling cup in one hand and a biscuit in the other, gaping at the Countess in her satin finery as she pours from a silver pot and chatters distractedly to put them at their fatal ease. A certain desolate stillness of her eyes indicates she is inconsolable. She would like to caress their lean brown cheeks and stroke their ragged hair. When she takes them by the hand and leads them to her bedroom, they can scarcely believe their luck.

Afterwards, her governess will tidy the remains into a neat pile and wrap it in its own discarded clothes. This mortal parcel she then discreetly buries in the garden. The blood on the Countess's cheeks will be mixed with tears; her keeper probes her fingernails for her with a little silver toothpick, to get rid of the fragments of skin and bone that have lodged there

> Fee fie fo fum
> I smell the blood of an Englishman.

One hot, ripe summer in the pubescent years of the present century, a young officer in the British army, blond, blue-eyed, heavy-muscled, visiting friends in Vienna, decided to spend the remainder of his fur-

lough exploring the little-known uplands of Romania. When he quixotic-
ally decided to travel the rutted cart-tracks by bicycle, he saw all the
humour of it: 'on two wheels in the land of the vampires'. So, laughing,
he sets out on his adventure.

He has the special quality of virginity, most and least ambiguous of
states: ignorance, yet at the same time, power in potentia, and furthermore, unknowingness, which is not the same as ignorance. He is more
than he knows—and has about him, besides, the special glamour of
that generation for whom history has already prepared a special, exemp-
lary fate in the trenches of France. This being, rooted in change and time,
is about to collide with the timeless Gothic eternity of the vampires, for
whom all is as it has always been and will be, whose cards always fall
in the same pattern.

Although so young, he is also rational. He has chosen the most
rational mode of transport in the world for his trip round the Carpathians.
To ride a bicycle is in itself some protection against superstitious fears,
since the bicycle is the product of pure reason applied to motion. Geom-
etry at the service of man! Give me two spheres and a straight line and
I will show you how far I can take them. Voltaire himself might have
invented the bicycle, since it contributes so much to man's welfare and
nothing at all to his bane. Beneficial to the health, it emits no harmful
fumes and permits only the most decorous speeds. How can a bicycle
ever be an implement of harm?

A single kiss woke up the Sleeping Beauty in the Wood.

The waxen fingers of the Countess, fingers of a holy image, turn up
the card called Les Amoureux. Never, never before . . . never before
has the Countess cast herself a fate involving love. She shakes, she
trembles, her great eyes close beneath her finely veined, nervously
fluttering eyelids; the lovely cartomancer has, this time, the first time,
dealt herself a hand of love and death.

> Be he alive or be he dead
> I'll grind his bones to make my bread.

At the mauvish beginnings of evening, the English m'sieu toils up
the hill to the village he glimpsed from a great way off; he must
dismount and push his bicycle before him, the path too steep to ride.
He hopes to find a friendly inn to rest the night; he's hot, hungry,
thirsty, weary, dusty . . . At first, such disappointment, to discover the
roofs of all the cottages caved in and tall weeds thrusting through the
piles of fallen tiles, shutters hanging disconsolately from their hinges,

an entirely uninhabited place. And the rank vegetation whispers, as if foul secrets, here, where, if one were sufficiently imaginative, one could almost imagine twisted faces appearing momentarily beneath the crumbling eaves ... but the adventure of it all, and the consolation of the poignant brightness of the hollyhocks still bravely blooming in the shaggy gardens, and the beauty of the flaming sunset, all these considerations soon overcame his disappointment, even assuaged the faint unease he'd felt. And the fountain where the village women used to wash their clothes still gushed out bright, clear water; he gratefully washed his feet and hands, applied his mouth to the faucet, then let the icy stream run over his face.

When he raised his dripping, gratified head from the lion's mouth, he saw, silently arrived beside him in the square, an old woman who smiled eagerly, almost conciliatorily at him. She wore a black dress and a white apron, with a housekeeper's key ring at the waist; her grey hair was neatly coiled in a chignon beneath the white linen headdress worn by elderly women of that region. She bobbed a curtsy at the young man and beckoned him to follow her. When he hesitated, she pointed towards the great bulk of the mansion above them, whose façade loured over the village, rubbed her stomach, pointed to her mouth, rubbed her stomach again, clearly miming an invitation to supper. Then she beckoned him again, this time turning determinedly upon her heel as though she would brook no opposition.

A great, intoxicated surge of the heavy scent of red roses blew into his face as soon as they left the village, inducing a sensuous vertigo; a blast of rich, faintly corrupt sweetness strong enough almost, to fell him. Too many roses. Too many roses bloomed on enormous thickets that lined the path, thickets bristling with thorns, and the flowers themselves were almost too luxuriant, their huge congregations of plush petals somehow obscene in their excess, their whorled, tightly budded cores outrageous in their implications. The mansion emerged grudgingly out of this jungle.

In the subtle and haunting light of the setting sun, that golden light rich with nostalgia for the day that is just past, the sombre visage of the place, part manor house, part fortified farmhouse, immense, rambling, a dilapidated eagle's nest atop the crag down which its attendant village meandered, reminded him of childhood tales on winter evenings, when he and his brothers and sisters scared themselves half out of their wits with ghost stories set in just such places and then had to have candles to light them up newly terrifying stairs to bed. He could almost have regretted accepting the crone's unspoken invitation; but now, standing before the door of time-eroded oak while she selected a huge iron key from the clanking ringful at her waist, he knew it was too late to turn back and brusquely reminded himself he was no child, now, to be frightened of his own fancies.

The old lady unlocked the door, which swung back on melodramatically creaking hinges, and fussily took charge of his bicycle, in spite of his protests. He felt a certain involuntary sinking of the heart to see his beautiful two-wheeled symbol of rationality vanish into the dark entrails of the mansion, to, no doubt, some damp outhouse where they would not oil it or check its tyres. But, in for a penny, in for a pound— in his youth and strength and blond beauty, in the invisible, even unacknowledged pentacle of his virginity, the young man stepped over the threshold of Nosferatu's castle and did not shiver in the blast of cold air, as from the mouth of a grave, that emanated from the lightless, cavernous interior.

The crone took him to a little chamber where there was a black oak table spread with a clean white cloth and this cloth was carefully laid with heavy silverware, a little tarnished, as if someone with foul breath had breathed on it, but laid with one place only. Curiouser and curiouser; invited to the castle for dinner, now he must dine alone. All the same, he sat down as she had bid him. Although it was not yet dark outside, the curtains were closely drawn and only the sparing light trickling from a single oil lamp showed him how dismal his surroundings were. The crone bustled about to get him a bottle of wine and a glass from an ancient cabinet of wormy oak; while he bemusedly drank his wine, she disappeared but soon returned bearing a steaming platter of the local spiced meat stew with dumplings, and a shank of black bread. He was hungry after his long day's ride, he ate heartily and polished his plate with the crust, but this coarse food was hardly the entertainment he'd expected from the gentry and he was puzzled by the assessing glint in the dumb woman's eyes as she watched him eating.

But she darted off to get him a second helping as soon as he'd finished the first one and she seemed so friendly and helpful, besides, that he knew he could count on a bed for the night in the castle, as well as his supper, so he sharply reprimanded himself for his own childish lack of enthusiasm for the eerie silence, the clammy chill of the place.

When he'd put away the second plateful, the old woman came and gestured he should leave the table and follow her once again. She made a pantomime of drinking; he deduced he was now invited to take after-dinner coffee in another room with some more elevated member of the household who had not wished to dine with him but, all the same, wanted to make his acquaintance. An honour, no doubt; in deference to his host's opinion of himself, he straightened his tie, brushed the crumbs from his tweed jacket.

He was surprised to find how ruinous the interior of the house was—cobwebs, worm-eaten beams, crumbling plaster; but the mute crone resolutely wound him on the reel of her lantern down endless corridors, up winding staircases, through the galleries where the painted eyes of family portraits briefly flickered as they passed, eyes that belonged, he noticed, to faces, one and all, of a quite memorable beastliness. At last she paused and, behind the door where they'd halted, he heard a faint, metallic twang as of, perhaps, a chord struck on a harpsichord. And then, wonderfully, the liquid cascade of the song of a lark, bringing to him, in the heart—had he but known it—of Juliet's tomb, all the freshness of morning.

The crone rapped with her knuckles on the panels; the most seductively caressing voice he had ever heard in his life softly called out, in heavily accented French, the adopted language of the Romanian aristocracy: 'Entrez.'

First of all, he saw only a shape, a shape imbued with a faint luminosity since it caught and reflected in its yellowed surfaces what little light there was in the ill-lit room; this shape resolved itself into that of, of all things, a hoop-skirted dress of white satin draped here and there with lace, a dress fifty or sixty years out of fashion but once, obviously, intended for a wedding. And then he saw the girl who wore the dress, a girl with the fragility of the skeleton of a moth, so thin, so frail that her dress seemed to him to hang suspended, as if untenanted in the dank air, a fabulous lending, a self-articulated garment in which she lived like a ghost in a machine. All the light in the room came from a low-burning lamp with a thick greenish shade on a distant mantelpiece; the crone who accompanied him shielded her lantern with her hand, as if to protect her mistress from too suddenly seeing, or their guest from too suddenly seeing her.

So that it was little by little, as his eyes grew accustomed to the half-dark, that he saw how beautiful and how very young the bedizened scarecrow was, and he thought of a child dressing up in her mother's clothes, perhaps a child putting on the clothes of a dead mother in order to bring her, however briefly, to life again.

The Countess stood behind a low table, beside a pretty, silly, gilt-and-wire birdcage, hands outstretched in a distracted attitude that was almost one of flight; she looked as startled by their entry as if she had not requested it. With her stark white face, her lovely death's head surrounded by long dark hair that fell down as straight as if it were soaking wet, she looked like a shipwrecked bride. Her huge dark eyes almost broke his heart with their waiflike, lost look; yet he was disturbed, almost repelled, by her extraordinary fleshy mouth, a mouth with wide, full prominent lips of a vibrant purplish-crimson, a morbid mouth. Even—but he put the thought away from him immediately—a whore's mouth. She shivered all the time, a starveling chill, a malarial agitation of the bones. He thought she must be only sixteen or seventeen years old, no more, with the hectic, unhealthy beauty of a consumptive. She was the châtelaine of all this decay.

With many tender precautions, the crone now raised the light she held to show his hostess her guest's face. At that, the Countess let out a faint, mewing cry and made a blind, appalled gesture with her hands, as if pushing him away, so that she knocked against the table and a butterfly dazzle of painted cards fell to the floor. Her mouth formed a round 'o' of woe, she swayed a little and then sank into her chair, where she lay as if now scarcely capable of moving. A bewildering reception. Tsk'ing under her breath, the crone busily poked about on the table until she found an enormous pair of dark green glasses, such as blind beggars wear, and perched them on the Countess's nose.

He went forward to pick up her cards for her from a carpet that, he saw to his surprise, was part rotted away, partly encroached upon by all kinds of virulent-looking fungi. He retrieved the cards and shuffled them carelessly together, for they meant nothing to him, though they seemed strange playthings for a young girl. What a grisly picture of a capering skeleton! He covered it up with a happier one—of two young lovers, smiling at one another, and put her toys back into a hand so slender you could almost see the frail net of bone beneath the translucent skin, a hand with fingernails as long, as finely pointed, as banjo picks.

At this touch, she seemed to revive a little and almost smiled, raising herself upright.

'Coffee,' she said. 'You must have coffee.' And scooped up her cards into a pile so that the crone could set before her a silver spirit kettle, a silver coffee pot, cream jug, sugar basin, cups ready on a silver tray, a strange touch of elegance, even if discoloured, in this devastated interior whose mistress ethereally shone as if with her own blighted, submarine radiance.

The crone found him a chair and, tittering noiselessly, departed, leaving the room a little darker.

While the young lady attended to the coffee-making, he had time to contemplate with some distaste a further series of family portraits which decorated the stained and peeling walls of the room; these livid faces all seemed contorted with a febrile madness and the blubber lips, the huge, demented eyes that all had in common bore a disquieting resemblance to those of the hapless victim of inbreeding now patiently filtering her fragrant brew, even if some rare grace has so finely transformed those features when it came to her case. The lark, its chorus done, had long ago fallen silent; no sound but the chink of silver on china. Soon, she held out to him a tiny cup of rose-painted china.

'Welcome,' she said in her voice with the rushing sonorities of the ocean in it, a voice that seemed to come elsewhere than from her white, still throat. 'Welcome to my château. I rarely receive visitors and that's a misfortune since nothing animates me half as much as the presence of a stranger . . . This place is so lonely, now the village is deserted, and my one companion, alas, she cannot speak. Often I am so silent that I think I, too, will soon forget how to do so and nobody here will ever talk any more.'

She offered him a sugar biscuit from a Limoges plate; her fingernails struck carillons from the antique china. Her voice, issuing from those red lips like the obese roses in her garden, lips that do not move— her voice is curiously disembodied; she is like a doll, he thought, a ventriloquist's doll, or, more, like a great, ingenious piece of clockwork. For she seemed inadequately powered by some slow energy of which she was not in control; as if she had been wound up years ago, when she was born, and now the mechanism was inexorably running down and would leave her lifeless. This idea that she might be an automaton, made of white velvet and black fur, that could not move of its own accord, never quite deserted him; indeed, it deeply moved his heart. The carnival air of her white dress emphasised her unreality, like a sad Columbine who lost her way in the wood a long time ago and never reached the fair.

'And the light. I must apologise for the lack of light . . . a hereditary affliction of the eyes . . .'

Her blind spectacles gave him his handsome face back to himself twice over; if he presented himself to her naked face, he would dazzle her like the sun she is forbidden to look at because it would shrivel her up at once, poor night bird, poor butcher bird.

Vous serez ma proie.

You have such a fine throat, m'sieu, like a column of marble. When you came through the door retaining about you all the golden light of the summer's day of which I know nothing, nothing, the card called 'Les Amoureux' had just emerged from the tumbling chaos of imagery before me; it seemed to me you had stepped off the card into my darkness and, for a moment, I thought, perhaps, you might irradiate it.

I do not mean to hurt you. I shall wait for you in my bride's dress in the dark.

The bridegroom is come, he will go into the chamber which has been prepared for him.

I am condemned to solitude and dark; I do not mean to hurt you.

I will be very gentle.

(And could love free me from the shadows? Can a bird sing only the song it knows, or can it learn a new song?)

See, how I'm ready for you. I've always been ready for you; I've been waiting for you in my wedding dress, why have you delayed for so long ... it will all be over very quickly.

You will feel no pain, my darling.

She herself is a haunted house. She does not possess herself; her ancestors sometimes come and peer out of the windows of her eyes and that is very frightening. She has the mysterious solitude of ambiguous states; she hovers in a no-man's-land and between life and death, sleeping and waking, behind the hedge of spiked flowers, Nosferatu's sanguinary rosebud. The beastly forebears on the walls condemn her to a perpetual repetition of their passions.

(One kiss, however, and only one, woke up the Sleeping Beauty in the Wood.)

Nervously, to conceal her inner voices, she keeps up a front of inconsequential chatter in French while her ancestors leer and grimace on the walls; however hard she tries to think of any other, she only knows of one kind of consummation.

He was struck, once again, by the birdlike, predatory claws which tipped her marvellous hands; the sense of strangeness that had been growing on him since he buried his head under the streaming water in the village, since he entered the dark portals of the fatal castle, now fully overcame him. Had he been a cat, he would have bounced backwards from her hands on four fear-stiffened legs, but he is not a cat: he is a hero.

A fundamental disbelief in what he sees before him sustains him, even in the boudoir of Countess Nosferatu herself; he would have said, perhaps, that there are some things which, even if they *are* true, we should not believe possible. He might have said: it is folly to believe one's eyes. Not so much that he does not believe in her; he can see her, she is real. If she takes off her dark glasses, from her eyes will stream all the images that populate this vampire-haunted land, but, since he himself is immune to shadow, due to his virginity—he does not yet know what there is to be afraid of—and due to his heroism, which makes him like the sun, he sees before him, first and foremost, an inbred, highly strung girl child, fatherless, motherless, kept in the dark too long and pale as a plant that never sees the light, half-blinded by some hereditary condition of the eyes. And though he feels unease, he cannot feel terror; so he is like the boy in the fairy tale, who does not know how to shudder, and not spooks, ghouls, beasties, the Devil himself and all his retinue could do the trick.

This lack of imagination gives his heroism to the hero.

He will learn to shudder in the trenches. But this girl cannot make him shudder.

Now it is dark. Bats swoop and squeak outside the tightly shuttered windows. The coffee is all drunk, the sugar biscuits eaten. Her chatter comes trickling and diminishing to a stop; she twists her fingers together, picks at the lace of her dress, shifts nervously in her chair. Owls shriek; the impedimenta of her condition squeak and gibber all around us. Now you are at the place of annihilation, now you are at the place of annihilation. She turns her head away from the blue beams of his eyes; she knows no other consummation than the only one she can offer him. She has not eaten for three days. It is dinner-time. It is bed-time.

> Suivez-moi.
> Je vous attendais.
> Vous serez ma proie.

The raven caws on the accursed roof. 'Dinnertime, dinnertime,' clang the portraits on the walls. A ghastly hunger gnaws her entrails; she has waited for him all her life without knowing it.

The handsome bicyclist, scarcely believing his luck, will follow her into her bedroom; the candles around her sacrificial altar burn with a low, clear flame, light catches on the silver tears stitched to the wall. She will assure him, in the very voice of temptation: 'My clothes have but to fall and you will see before you a succession of mysteries.'

She has no mouth with which to kiss, no hands with which to caress, only the fangs and talons of a beast of prey. To touch the mineral sheen of the flesh revealed in the cool candle gleam is to invite her fatal embrace; in her low, sweet voice, she will croon the lullaby of the House of Nosferatu.

Embraces, kisses; your golden head, of a lion, although I have never seen a lion, only imagined one, of the sun, even if I've only seen the picture of the sun on the Tarot card, your golden head of the lover who I dreamed would one day free me, this head will fall back, its eyes roll upwards in a spasm you will mistake for that of love and not of death. The bridegroom bleeds on my inverted marriage bed. Stark and dead, poor bicyclist; he has paid the price of a night with the Countess and some think it too high a fee while some do not.

Tomorrow, her keeper will bury his bones under her roses. The food her roses feed on gives them their rich colour, their swooning odour, that breathes lasciviously of forbidden pleasures.

Suivez-moi.

'Suivez-moi!'

The handsome bicyclist, fearful for his hostess's health, her sanity, gingerly follows her hysterical imperiousness into the other room; he would like to take her into his arms and protect her from the ancestors who leer down from the walls.

What a macabre bedroom!

His colonel, an old goat with jaded appetites, had given him the visiting card of a brothel in Paris where, the satyr assured him, ten louis would buy just such a lugubrious bedroom, with a naked girl upon a coffin; offstage, the brothel pianist played the *Dies Irae* on a harmonium and, amidst all the perfumes of the embalming parlour, the customer took his necrophiliac pleasure of a pretended corpse. He had good-naturedly refused the old man's offer of such an initiation; how can he now take criminal advantage of the disordered girl with fever-hot, bone-dry, taloned hands and eyes that deny all the erotic promises of her body with their terror, their sadness, their dreadful, balked tenderness?

So delicate and damned, poor thing. Quite damned.

Yet I do believe she scarcely knows what she is doing.

She is shaking as if her limbs were not efficiently joined together, as if she might shake into pieces. She raises her hands to unfasten the neck of her dress and her eyes well with tears, they trickle down beneath the rim of her dark glasses. She can't take off her mother's wedding dress unless she takes off her dark glasses; she has fumbled the ritual, it is no longer inexorable. The mechanism within her fails her, now, when she needs it most. When she takes off the dark glasses, they slip from her fingers and smash to pieces on the tiled floor. There is no room in her drama for improvisation; and this unexpected, mundane noise of breaking glass breaks the wicked spell in the room, entirely. She gapes blindly down at the splinters and ineffectively smears the tears across her face with her fist. What is she to do now?

When she kneels to try to gather the fragments of glass together, a sharp sliver pierces deeply into the pad of her thumb; she cries out, sharp, real. She kneels among the broken glass and watches the bright bead of blood form a drop. She has never seen her own blood before, not her *own* blood. It exercises upon her an awed fascination.

Into this vile and murderous room, the handsome bicyclist brings the innocent remedies of the nursery; in himself, by his presence, he is an exorcism. He gently takes her hand away from her and dabs the blood with his own handkerchief, but still it spurts out. And so he puts his mouth to the wound. He will kiss it better for her, as her mother, had she lived, would have done.

All the silver tears fall from the wall with a flimsy tinkle. Her painted ancestors turn away their eyes and grind their fangs.

How can she bear the pain of becoming human?

The end of exile is the end of being.

He was awakened by larksong. The shutters, the curtains, even the long-sealed windows of the horrid bedroom were all opened and light and air streamed in; now you could see how tawdry it all was, how thin and cheap the stain, the catafalque not ebony at all but black-painted paper stretched on struts of wood, as in the theatre. The wind had blown droves of petals from the roses outside into the room and this crimson residue swirled fragrantly about the floor. The candles had burnt out and she must have set her pet lark free because it perched on the edge of the silly coffin to sing him its ecstatic morning song. His bones were stiff and aching, he'd slept on the floor with his bundled-up jacket for a pillow, after he'd put her to bed.

But now there was no trace of her to be seen, except, lightly tossed across the crumpled black satin bedcover, a lace négligé lightly soiled with blood, as it might be from a woman's menses, and a rose that must have come from the fierce bushes nodding through the window. The air was heavy with incense and roses and made him cough. The Countess must have got up early to enjoy the sunshine, slipped outside to gather him a rose. He got to his feet, coaxed the lark on to his wrist and took it to the window. At first, it exhibited the reluctance for the sky of a long-caged thing, but, when he tossed it up on to the currents of the air, it spread its wings and was up and away into the clear blue bowl of the heavens; he watched its trajectory with a lift of joy in his heart.

Then he padded into the boudoir, his mind busy with plans. We shall take her to Zurich, to a clinic; she will be treated for nervous hysteria. Then to an eye specialist, for her photophobia, and to a dentist to put her teeth into better shape. Any competent manicurist will deal with her claws. We shall turn her into the lovely girl she is; I shall cure her of all these nightmares.

The heavy curtains are pulled back, to let in brilliant fusillades of early morning light; in the desolation of the boudoir, she sits at her round table in her white dress, with the cards laid out before her. She has dropped off to sleep over the cards of destiny that are so fingered, so soiled, so worn by constant shuffling that you can no longer make the image out on any single one of them.

She is not sleeping.

In death, she looked far older, less beautiful and so, for the first time, fully human.

I will vanish in the morning light; I was only an invention of darkness.

And I leave you as a souvenir the dark, fanged rose I plucked from between my thighs, like a flower laid on a grave. On a grave.

My keeper will attend to everything.

Nosferatu always attends his own obsequies; she will not go to the graveyard unattended. And now the crone materialised, weeping, and roughly gestured him to begone. After a search in some foul-smelling outhouses, he discovered his bicycle and, abandoning his holiday, rode directly to Bucharest where, at the poste restante, he found a telegram summoning him to rejoin his regiment at once. Much later, when he changed back into uniform in his quarters, he discovered he still had the Countess's rose, he must have tucked it into the breast pocket of his cycling jacket after he had found her body. Curiously enough, although he had brought it so far away from Romania, the flower did not seem to be quite dead and, on impulse, because the girl had been so lovely and her death so unexpected and pathetic, he decided to try and resurrect her rose. He filled his tooth glass with water from the carafe on his locker and popped the rose into it, so that its withered head floated on the surface.

When he returned from the mess that evening, the heavy fragrance of Count Nosferatu's roses drifted down the stone corridor of the barracks to greet him, and his spartan quarters brimmed with the reeling odour of a glowing, velvet, monstrous flower whose petals had regained all their former bloom and elasticity, their corrupt, brilliant, baleful splendour.

Next day, his regiment embarked for France.

THE STONE THING
A Tale of Strange Parts

Michael Moorcock

*Supernatural forces of evil have for a long time been an important
ingredient in tales of heroic fantasy—stories of conflict and magic—
as well as in its more recent subgenre, sword and sorcery, a term said
to have been invented by the American fantasist Fritz Leiber. Among
the heroes of these stories are the brutal, amorous swordsman, Conan,
created by Robert E. Howard; C. L. Moore's mighty warrior Northwest
Smith; Fritz Leiber's pair of resourceful, light-hearted adventurers,
Fafhrd and Gray Mouser; and the protagonist of the bestselling 'Chron-
icles of Thomas Covenant the Unbeliever', written by Stephen Donaldson. Neither heroic fantasy nor sword and sorcery lend themselves
particularly well to humour, with their unending accounts of bloody
battles and violent death, but there are always exceptions to the rule,
as Michael Moorcock proves in this next study, a parody, which he
wrote for the fanzine* Triode *specifically devoted to sword and sorcery.*

Michael Moorcock (1939–), who was born in London and wrote for
Tarzan Adventures *and* Sexton Blake Library *before establishing himself among the foremost contemporary writers of sf and fantasy, has
also contributed his own sword and sorcery hero to the pantheon of
these superheroes—Elric of Melniboné who, with his supernatural
sword, Stormbringer, has rampaged through dozens of adventures for
over thirty years. Among Moorcock's other heroic figures are the Eter-
nal Champion, the Warrior of Mars, Hawkmoon, Corum and Von Bek,
who all operate in imaginary lands where magic works and the forces
of law and chaos struggle for supremacy. He is also the author of one
of the few serious studies of the genre,* Wizardry and Wild Romance:
A Study of Epic Fantasy *(1987). 'The Stone Thing' requires no more
introduction than to say it introduces the same kind of mighty swordsman and beautiful maiden that are to be found in so many sword and*

sorcery tales—but here the pair are plunged into a hilarious situation that I feel sure none of their kind have ever faced before!

*   *   *

Out of the dark places; out of the howling mists; out of the lands without sun; out of Ghonorea came tall Catharz, with the moody sword Oakslayer in his right hand, the cursed spear Bloodlicker in his left hand, the evil bow Deathsinger on his back together with his quiver of fearful rune-fletched arrows, Heartseeker, Goregreedy, Soulsnatcher, Orphanmaker, Eyeblinder, Sorrowsower, Beanslicer, and several others.

Where his right eye should have been there was a jewel of slumbering scarlet whose colour sometimes shifted to smouldering blue, and in the place of his left eye was a many-faceted crystal, which pulsed as if possessed of independent life. Where Catharz had once had a right hand, now a thing of iron, wood and carved amethyst sat upon his stump; nine-fingered, alien, cut by Catharz from the creature who had sliced off his own hand. Catharz' left hand was at first merely gauntleted, but when one looked further it could be observed that the gauntlet was in fact a many-jointed limb of silver, gold and lapis lazuli, but as Catharz rode by, those who saw him pass remarked not on the murmuring sword in his right hand, not on the whispering spear in his left hand, not on the whining bow upon his back or the grumbling arrows in the quiver; neither did they remark on his right eye of slumbering scarlet, his left eye of pulsing crystal, his nine-fingered right hand, his shining metallic left hand; they saw only the fearful foot of Cwlwwymwn which throbbed in the stirrup at his mount's right flank.

The foot of the Aching God, Cwlwwymwn Rootripper, whose ambition upon the old and weary Earth had been to make widows of all wives; Cwlwwymwn the Striker, whose awful feet had trampled whole cities when men had first made cities; Cwlwwymwn of the Last Ones, Last of the Last Ones, who had been driven back to his island domain on the edge of the world, beyond the Western Ice, and who now came limping after Catharz screaming out for vengeance, demanding the return of his foot, sliced from his leg by Oakslayer so that Catharz might walk again and continue upon his doom-laden quest, bearing weapons which were not his protection but his burden, seeking consolation for the guilt which ate at his soul since it was he who had been responsible for the death of his younger brother, Forax the Golden, for the death of his niece, Libia Gentleknee, for the living death of his cousin, Wertigo the Unbalanced, seeking the whereabouts of his lost love, Cyphila the Fair, who had been stolen from him by his arch-enemy, the wizard To'me'ko'op'r, most powerful, most evil, most lustful of all the great sorcerers of this magic-clouded world.

And there were no friends here to give aid to Catharz God-foot. He must go alone, with shuddering terror before him and groaning guilt behind him, and Cwlwwymwn, screaming, vengeful, limping Cwlwwymwn, following always.

And Catharz rode on, rarely stopping, scarcely ever dismounting, anxious to claim his own vengeance on the sorcerer, and the foot of Cwlwwymwn, Last of the Last Ones, was heavy on him, as well it might be for it was at least eighteen inches longer than his left foot and naked, for he had had to abandon his boot when he had found that it did not fit. Now Cwlwwymwn possessed the boot; it was how he had known that Catharz was the mortal who had stolen his green, seventeen-clawed limb, attaching it by fearful sorcery to the flesh of his leg. Catharz' left leg was not of flesh at all, but of lacquered cork, made for him by the People of the World Beneath the Reefs, when he had aided them in their great fight against the Gods of the Lowest Sea.

The sun had stained the sky a livid crimson and had sunk below the horizon before Catharz would allow himself a brief rest and it was just before dark that he came in sight of a small stone cottage, sheltered beneath terraces of glistening limestone, where he hoped he might find food, for he was very hungry.

Knocking upon the door he called out:

'Greetings, I come in friendship, seeking hospitality, for I am called Catharz the Melancholy, who carries the curse of Cwlwwymwn Rootripper upon him, who has many enemies and no friends, who slew his brother, Forax the Golden, and caused the death of Libia Gentleknee, famous for her beauty, and who seeks his lost love Cyphila the Fair, prisoner of the wizard To'me'ko'op'r, and who has a great and terrible doom upon him.'

The door opened and a woman stood there. Her hair was the silver of a spiderweb in the moonlight, her eyes were the deep gold found at the centre of a beehive, her skin had the pale, blushing beauty of the tea-rose. 'Welcome, stranger,' she said. 'Welcome to all that is left of the home of Lanoli, whose father was once the mightiest in these parts.'

And, upon beholding her, Catharz forgot Cyphila the Fair, forgot that he had slain his brother, his niece, and betrayed his cousin, Wertigo the Unbalanced.

'You are very beautiful, Lanoli,' he said.

'Ah,' said she, 'that is what I have learned. But beauty such as mine

can only thrive if it is seen and it has been so long since anyone came
to these lands.'

'Let me help your beauty thrive,' he said.

Food was forgotten, guilt was forgotten, fear was forgotten as Catharz
divested himself of his sword, his spear, his bow and his arrows and
walked slowly into the cottage. His gait was a rolling one, for he still
bore the burden that was the foot of the Last of the Last Ones, and it
took him some time to pull it through the door, but at length he stood
inside and had closed the door behind him and had taken her in his
arms and had pressed his lips to hers.

'Oh, Catharz,' she breathed. 'Catharz!'

It was not long until they stood naked before one another. Her eyes
travelled over his body and it was plain that the eyes of scarlet and
crystal were lovely to her, that she admired his silver hand and his
nine-fingered hand, that even the great foot of Cwlwwymwn was beautiful in her sight. But then her eyes, shy until now, fell upon that which
lay between his legs, and those eyes widened a little, and she blushed.
Her lovely lips framed a question, but he moved forward as swiftly as
he could and embraced her again.

'How?' she murmured. 'How, Catharz?'

'It is a long tale and a bloody one,' he whispered, 'of rivalry and
revenge, but suffice to say that it ended in my father, Xympwell the
Cruel, taking a terrible vengeance upon me. I fled from his court into
the wastes of Grxiwynn, raving mad, and it was there that the tribesmen
of Velox found me and took me to the Wise Man of Oorps in the
mountains beyond Katatonia. He nursed me and carved that for me. It
took him two years, and all through those two years I remained raving,
living off dust and dew and roots, as he lived. The engravings had
mystical significance, the runes contain the sum of his great wisdom,
the tiny pictures show all that there is to show of physical love. Is it
not beautiful? More beautiful than that which it has replaced?'

Her glance was modest; she nodded slowly.

'It is indeed, very beautiful,' she agreed. And then she looked up at
him and he saw that tears glistened in her eyes. 'But did it *have* to be
made of Sandstone?'

'There is little else,' he explained sadly, 'in the mountains beyond
Katatonia.'

(From *The Outcast of Kitzoprenia*
Volume 67 in *The History of the
Purple Poignard*)

THE SHRINK AND THE MINK

Robert Bloch

*The manifestation of supernatural evil in the modern world has been
a theme in a number of the works by Robert Bloch, a writer well known
for his black comedies, and dubbed 'the master of ghoulish humour'.
Among the memorable dabblers in the occult he created are Karl Jorla,
a horror-movie star who owes his devilishly authentic performances
to membership of certain secret cults; racketeer Solly Vincent, who
ill-advisedly falls in love with a beautiful vampire; and Leo Winston,
a concert pianist whose studies of 'Solar Science' have endowed his
grand piano with a vengeful life all of its own! Like Fredric Brown,
Bloch was fond of using grisly jokes in his fiction, and once told me
that he wrote many of his stories after thinking up 'a nasty last line'.
Despite accusations from certain quarters that his work 'sometimes
reads like a series of sick jokes', he remained at the forefront of the
American fantasy genre for almost half a century.*

*Robert Bloch (1917–1994) was born in Chicago, but after winning
a national following for his stories in* Weird Tales *and creating the
scripts for a popular US radio programme,* Stay Tuned for Terror, *he
gained worldwide celebrity when Alfred Hitchcock filmed his novel*
Psycho *in 1960. Moving to Los Angeles, he scripted numerous movies
and TV series as well as continuing to produce brilliant short stories.
The best of these appeared in collections such as* Bogey Man (1963),
Tales in a Jugular Vein (1965) *and* Out of My Head (1986). *In 1975,
Bloch was given a Lifetime Award at the first World Fantasy Convention, and his recent death has robbed comic fantasy of one of its most
original voices. 'The Shrink and the Mink', first published in the contro-
versial US magazine,* Hustler, *in 1983, is a typical Bloch 'black fantasy',
mixing horror with humour in a tale set in present-day California and
focusing on the activities of a most persistent incubus (a demon who
has carnal relations with women in their sleep). But* that *is only the
beginning of some truly hilarious events . . .*

*   *   *

Angela was adorable. Tall, blonde and twenty, she had more curves than a roller-coaster and much better seating-accommodations.

Young Dr Degradian was no fool. Five minutes after she entered the office he had her on the couch.

So much for the joys of psychiatry.

Now it was time to begin the process known as case-entry. And this was one case Dr Degradian felt sorely tempted to enter—until she began to talk.

Notebook in hand, he seated himself in a chair beside her, pencil poised. 'What's the first thing that comes into your mind?' he asked.

'Milton.'

'Who?'

'My husband.'

Dr Degradian frowned. 'You didn't tell me you were married.'

'I'm not. He died last Thursday.'

Dr Degradian made a note. 'How did it happen?'

'He fell off a ladder.'

'Was he a painter?'

'No—a voyeur. He was looking through this second-storey window at a motel when the ladder broke.'

'I see.'

'That's what he used to say all the time—"I see."' Angela shrugged. 'Our marriage was never consummated, you know. He died on our wedding night, and now I'm just a poor widow. All he left me was the broken ladder and a pair of binoculars.'

'Did you know he was a voyeur when you married him?'

'I should have guessed. He kept telling me I was a sight for sore eyes.' Angela smiled coquettishly. 'Do you find me attractive?'

Dr Degradian shook his head. 'This is a psychiatric examination, not a beauty contest. We are here to find the source of your mental disturbance—'

'Not mental. Physical.'

'You are physically disturbed?'

'Constantly,' Angela nodded. 'I'm no expert on the subject, but it doesn't seem possible that anyone could keep up such a pace—sometimes ten, even fifteen times a night.'

'You're sleeping with somebody?'

'Who sleeps?' Angela sighed.

Dr Degradian made another note. 'Tell me about this man.'

'He isn't a man. He's an incubus.'

'A *what*?'

'An incubus.' She blushed, tossing her golden curls. 'A demon who has carnal relations with women in their sleep. Look it up in your dictionary if you don't believe me.'

'I know what an incubus is,' Dr Degradian said. 'And I do believe you. You have these dreams—'

'It's not a dream!' Angela sat up, eyes flashing. 'I told you I don't sleep. The minute I turn out the light and climb into bed he shows up out of nowhere and starts fooling around. At first I tried to stall him— I said I had a headache, but he didn't listen, just ripped off my nightie and *bam*!'

'Bam? What does that mean?'

For the next fifteen minutes she explained what it meant; explained in such detail that Dr Degradian found himself trying to make notes long after there was no more lead in his pencil.

'Good Lord!' The young psychiatrist stared at her. 'I've never heard such graphic porno! And you say this is only the foreplay?'

'Two-play,' Angela murmured. 'I don't think I could stand it if there was another couple involved.'

'And this goes on every evening? He comes in and rips off your nightie—'

'Not any more. I ran out of nighties so now I just go to bed in the nude.' Angela gazed at him imploringly. 'That's why I'm here, Doctor. You've got to help me, before I catch my death of cold.'

'Of course.' Dr Degradian reached for a fresh pencil and scribbled out several prescriptions. 'Here, get these filled at the pharmacy downstairs.'

'What are they for?'

'Tranquillisers and a sedative.'

'It's no use. I'm sure he won't take them.'

'They're for you. To help you sleep.' Dr Degradian smiled reassuringly. 'I want to see you again on Wednesday, same time. I think I can promise you that by then your incubus will have disappeared.'

'Thank you, Doctor. I certainly hope so.'

And with a grateful smile and a farewell wiggle, she was gone.

Gone, but not forgotten. During the next two days Dr Degradian couldn't put the girl out of his mind. What a shame that so lovely a young lady should have these grotesque fantasies! And they were fantasies, he had no doubt of that—she was hallucinating about a mythical creature out of medieval legend. It was obviously a classic case of sexual frustration, but the dosage he'd prescribed would put an end to her nightmares. Once they disappeared he'd have no need to explain she'd been imagining things; it would all be self-evident. And as Wednesday neared he found himself happily anticipating her arrival.

Promptly at three she swept in, trailing a cloud of perfume, and settled herself on the couch.

'Well,' he said. 'How did everything work out?'

'Don't talk to me about work-outs!' Her full lips formed a provocative pout. 'Did you ever try doing it when you were half-asleep?'

Dr Degradian blinked. 'You mean you still have these dreams?'

Angela's eyes flashed blue fire. 'I told you it's not a dream! There really is an incubus. Please, Doctor, isn't there something you can do?'

'Certainly.' The psychiatrist nodded. 'There are several ways. Normally we might rid you of this obsession by using electro-shock therapy, but that's not practical, now that electricity-bills are so high. Perhaps we should opt for more orthodox methods. If you can arrange to come in five days a week for the next three years—'

'Three years?' She stared at him incredulously.

'You don't understand. A thorough analysis takes that much time to talk things out.'

'You're the one who doesn't understand,' Angela said. 'This thing isn't going to be talked out of it. No matter what I say he just keeps bamming away.' She rose, sighing. 'Obviously you can't help me. I should have gone to Father O'Flannery in the first place.'

'Father O'Flannery?'

'The priest at the church down the street. I'm going to ask him to perform an exorcism.'

Dr Degradian frowned. 'Surely you're not serious? Nobody believes in such nonsense nowadays.'

'Father O'Flannery does.' Angela nodded. 'Just last Sunday he preached a sermon about casting out demons. He even told us how it's done. First they open all the windows, then they start with the ceremony. Plenty of fresh air and exorcise, that's the cure.'

Dr Degradian bit his lip. No sense arguing; of course he had no faith in exorcism or in incubi either, but *she* did. And that was the point. If this superstitious ritual could rid her of her fixation, so be it.

'I wish you luck,' he said.

'Thank you, Doctor.'

Then she was gone, leaving a scent of perfume behind.

In the days that passed the scent vanished, but not the memories— memories of her perfume, and her behind. Dr Degradian lost a little sleep himself wondering about the girl. Could it be that he had more than a professional interest in her? Here he was, just thirty years old, a reputable psychiatrist with an established practice and already the owner of his first condominium. He should be thinking of his career, maybe buying a second couch, but instead he found himself mooning over a patient. He remembered the last words of his sainted mother on her deathbed.

'Promise me just one thing,' she whispered. 'Don't ever get mixed up with a Nutsy Fagan.'

Over the weekend Dr Degradian recalled her plea and made a firm resolution. But on Monday afternoon, when Angela came in, his resolution turned to flab. One look at her and he knew the truth—he had fallen in love with a flake.

'Surprised to see me?' she said.

'Yes, I am.' He ventured a wary smile. 'Changed your mind, did you?'

'What do you mean? Father O'Flannery performed the exorcism Friday night.'

'How did it go?'

'Very quickly. So quickly that Father never even had a chance to see it.'

'But you're sure the incubus was exorcised?'

'Positive.'

'Then what's wrong?'

'Father O'Flannery.' She fluttered her eyelashes nervously. 'You see, once the incubus was gone, that left just the two of us. There I was, lying naked on the bed, and there was Father O'Flannery standing over me with that big font in his hand, and—well, it just happened—'

Dr Degradian's eyes widened. 'You seduced a priest?'

'It wasn't a seduction.' She reddened. 'Like I told you, he had this perfectly enormous font, and the next thing you know—'

'Bam.'

'Several bams.' Angela sighed. 'It was then I realised I still had a problem.'

'And what about Father O'Flannery?'

'I'm afraid the poor man took it very hard, if you'll pardon the expression. When we talked afterwards he said he'd decided to leave the priesthood and enter a convent.'

'You mean a monastery.'

'No, a convent. He's not gay, you know.'

'These things happen.' Dr Degradian nodded. 'You mustn't burden yourself by feeling guilty.'

'That's just it,' Angela said. 'I don't feel guilty. I feel—neglected.'

'Neglected?'

'Well, I mean, all this happened on Friday night. Saturday and Sunday night I slept like a baby.'

'So?'

'I'm not a baby! I'm a woman, and I haven't had sex for two whole nights in a row.'

Dr Degradian took a deep breath. 'You really do need help.'

'Exactly.' Angela dropped onto the couch and lay back, smiling. 'I knew I could count on you. But would you mind locking the door first?'

Now it was Dr Degradian's turn to redden. 'None of that, young lady,' he said. 'If you really want help, just sit up and pay attention. Get into this chair and let me run a Rorschach on you.'

'In a chair? Oh, neat—'

'It's a test,' the psychiatrist told her. 'I want you to look at these ink-blots and tell me what you see.'

He held up the first card. 'What does this look like?'

'That's easy. It's a whale.'

'Are you sure?'

'Of course. It's a sperm whale.'

Dr Degradian gulped and reached for a second card. Angela stared at it, nodding. 'This one is a bird.'

'A bird?'

'Yes. A cockatoo.'

He held up a third card. 'And this?'

Angela studied the squiggles. 'A man and a woman, twisting each other's necks around.'

'And what does that mean?'

'They're screwing their heads off.'

The psychiatrist threw the rest of the cards in the wastebasket. 'Angela, let me speak frankly. You are suffering from a severe case of sexual fixation.'

'Is it contagious?'

'I certainly hope not. And there may be a remedy, if you'll permit me to suggest it.'

'Go ahead.' Angela smiled in happy anticipation. 'Be as suggestive as you like.'

Dr Degradian leaned forward. 'Last year I had a patient with a complaint very similar to your own. Her obsessions with sex reached the point where she was taking obscene phone-calls even when they were collect.'

'You cured her?'

'No, but a gynaecologist did.' He nodded. 'I came to the conclusion that her mental condition was linked to a physical disturbance. So I sent her to a gynaecologist and sure enough, he discovered she had a chronic inflammation of the uterus. A few days of medication and her troubles were over.'

'Do you think something like that is wrong with me?'

'Let's find out.' Dr Degradian buzzed his receptionist on the intercom. 'Miss Carriage? Get me Mount Sinus Hospital. I want to refer a patient to Dr Pruritis. That's right, the specialist—eye, ear, nose and vagina—'

Angela listened as he set up an appointment for her the following morning.

'Let me see you tomorrow afternoon when it's over,' he told her. 'With any luck, this could be the solution to your sexual problems.'

She rose and wiggled to the door. 'I'll keep my fingers crossed.'

'Good idea,' Dr Degradian said. 'Also your legs.'

It was already five o'clock next afternoon when Angela appeared at Dr Degradian's office.

'Sorry I'm late,' she said. 'I got waylaid.'

'I know.' The psychiatrist frowned. 'Dr Pruritis just called me.' He shook his head. 'It's unbelievable—an old man like that—how could you do such a thing?'

'It was easy. All I did was—'

'Spare me the details.' He sat back, sighing. 'Poor old Pruritis! You have just ruined one of the profession's finest and most upstanding members.'

'But I didn't ruin it,' the girl protested. 'As a matter of fact, he told me it had never felt better in years.'

'Incredible,' Dr Degradian shook his head. 'And here I thought we were making progress.'

'But we are. Didn't he tell you the results of the examination?'

'That's just it. He said you were in perfect physical condition. No inflammation, infection or abnormality whatsoever. Which means the trouble is all in your mind. If you'd just consent to analysis and put your trust in me and Medicare—'

'I can't wait three years.' The blue eyes clouded with tears. 'The way I feel now I can't wait three minutes. I need him now.'

'Who?'

'The incubus. I want him back.'

'But my dear young lady—'

'I'm not your dear young lady!' Angela began to sob quietly. 'And if you won't help me I won't be your patient, either.' She started for the door and Dr Degradian raised his hand hastily.

'Let's talk this over—'

'Talking doesn't work. I've had enough of that, Dr Degradian.' She paused abruptly. 'You're Armenian, aren't you?'

He nodded.

'And is it true most Armenian names end in "ian"?'

'Yes. That means "son of".'

'Then you ought to call yourself Dr Bitchian!'

'Now see here—'

'I'm sorry.' Angela's voice softened. 'It's just that I'm so uptight. I thought the incubus was bad, but now that he's gone this hangup is ten times worse. I don't want to go through the rest of my life coming on with every man I meet. If there was only some way to get the incubus back again—'

Once more her sobs began, and Dr Degradian's heart melted in her tears.

'Stop sniffling,' he told her. 'Perhaps there is a way.'

'You mean you could do it?'

'Give me a chance to think. This is Friday. Suppose you come in on Monday afternoon.'

Angela stared at him, new hope in her eyes. 'Can you really bring the incubus back for me?'

'I'll try,' said Dr Degradian.

Alone in his office, he pondered the problem. Removing a patient's hallucinations was part of his job, but restoring them would be quite another matter. Nothing in psychiatric procedure offered any precedent, and he'd have to start from square one.

Suppose Angela had been right and he'd been wrong? Suppose there actually was such a thing as an incubus? She thought so, and so did the priest who'd exorcised it. And since the exorcism had worked, maybe the incubus did exist.

But if so, how could he find it? You just don't look up an incubus in the Yellow Pages—

Stung by inspiration, he reached for the phone-book, then riffled through it as he searched for the proper heading.

Obstetricians, Ophthalmologists, Opticians—nothing there. He turned back a few pages and suddenly he found it.

Occultists.

The list was long and the accompanying display advertisements were of little help. He couldn't use a palmist, a spirit medium, or a team of fortune-tellers who promised to work their crystal balls off for you.

For a moment he was tempted by a necromancer who proclaimed 'You Raise the Cash—We Raise the Dead! Contact the corpse of your choice without paying a stiff price! All Major Credit Cards Accepted.'

It sounded good, but he wasn't looking for a chance to palaver with a cadaver. The incubus, if such a thing existed, was very much alive. He needed someone specialising in witchcraft or black magic.

Suddenly his eyes strayed to the bottom of the listings. 'Malcolm Hex, M.D. Practising witch-doctor. Call anytime—midnight till dawn.'

He reached for the phone.

Promptly at the stroke of twelve, Dr Degradian entered the witch-doctor's office in a rundown section of town and seated himself in the shabby little reception-room. He picked up a tattered copy of *Who's Who in Hoodoo* but before he could start reading it in the guttering candlelight Malcolm Hex appeared and ushered him into his private office.

The office looked encouraging; its walls were covered with magical spells scrawled in chicken-blood and there was a goat-skeleton hanging at one corner. Malcolm Hex was obviously a black magician, black as the ace of spades.

It seemed a little strange to see this tall man in a conventional business suit seated behind his desk while he stirred the contents of a bubbling cauldron, and Dr Degradian couldn't control his curiosity.

'What's in the pot?' he inquired.

'Just the usual voodoo goo.' Malcolm Hex smiled. 'Bat brains, human entrails, lizard eyes, that sort of thing.'

'Toadstools?'

'No. My toads are all constipated.'

Dr Degradian stared uneasily at a shrunken head dangling from the ceiling; it reminded him of his congressman. 'Your ad said you're an M.D.,' he said.

'And so I am.' Malcolm Hex nodded. 'Master of Demonology. Graduated from Miskatonic University back in '78.'

'Can you conjure up a demon?'

'Evocation is my vocation. Just say the word and I'll say the spell.'

'What about an incubus?'

'No problem.' The black man rose, stripping off his jacket and shirt. He stood there, naked to the waist, his body glistening in the candlelight as he rubbed a pungent ointment into his gleaming torso. 'I always scrub before an operation,' he said.

Reaching into a desk-drawer he pulled out a jar of newt's blood and smeared its contents over his face, then stuck a gleaming white object in his nose.

'What's that?' the psychiatrist asked.

'Just a baby's femur. I've got to bone up for the occasion.'

Malcolm Hex began to stir the cauldron again, using a rooster's claw, and a hiss of steam arose. 'Now about this incubus of yours,' he said. 'Are you quite sure that's what you want? Most of my male clients prefer a succubus.'

Dr Degradian reddened. 'This isn't for me. It's for a young lady I know.'

'I see. Suppose you tell me about her.'

'Well to begin with, she's a widow—'

Malcolm Hex frowned and stopped stirring. Then he took the bone out of his nose and dropped it into the pot.

'Sorry,' the black man said. 'I don't do widows.'

Sunday arrived, and with it came a call from Dr Degradian's answering-service. He dialled the number given to him and Angela's voice greeted him.

'Any luck?' she murmured.

'Not yet. But I'm still trying.'

'You'd better come up with something,' she told him. 'If not, I'm leaving town tomorrow.'

The psychiatrist's heart skipped a beat. 'Where on earth are you going?'

'Bangkok. I like the name.'

She hung up, leaving him speechless. Poor girl—he knew he couldn't bear to lose her now, but how could he prevent it?

Desperately, Dr Degradian wrestled with his problem and lost. If the witch-doctor wouldn't help, he'd have to do the job himself.

Way to go—and he went. The psychiatrist spent the entire morning racing from one bookstore to another. Most of them were closed, and the few remaining open couldn't supply him with what he needed.

It was late afternoon when he stumbled into a dingy second-hand shop and unearthed the proper volume from behind a dusty stack in the rear of the establishment, wedged beside an autographed copy of the Bible.

Back at home he spent the entire evening hours feverishly scanning the crumbling yellowed pages of the ancient iron-bound *grimoire*, translating the Latin text as he did so. Just before midnight he found the right incantation, and another hour passed before he finished drawing the pentagram on the kitchen floor, set the tall candles in place, and began to utter the spell aloud.

As he did so he was still conscious of his own doubts. Here he was, the member of an illustrious profession that included such historic figures as Sigmund Freud and Dr Joyce Brothers, resorting to sorcery! But he had no choice, and if it worked—

A rumbling sound arose. Suddenly his nostrils were assailed with the noxious odour of sulphur and brimstone, like rush-hour on the freeway.

Then, just beyond the chalk-drawn outline of the pentagram, a towering spiral of smoke whirled and coalesced into solid shape.

Dr Degradian stared at the incubus in horror as it squatted before him.

The naked body was manlike, but its skin was green and purple; no man ever wore such horns or looked so horny. It was an incubus, no doubt of that, for now its grinning countenance changed into the face of Burt Reynolds.

'Jesus Christ!' the psychiatrist muttered.

'Sorry—you must have the wrong spell,' the creature told him. 'I'm an incubus.' He gestured towards his thighs.

'I can see that, all right,' Dr Degradian said. 'You certainly are well-organised.'

'Flattery will get you nowhere,' the creature growled. 'Why did you summon me?'

'I have a task for you.'

The incubus blinked its scaly eyelids. 'What sort of task?'

'No big deal. Just the usual.'

The demon cringed. 'Please—' He sighed loudly, and the dishes in the kitchen cupboard began to shake. 'In case you don't know it, I happen to be the last of my line. Nobody else does this sort of thing any more, and I'm all booked up. Fed up, too.' He sighed again, breaking several glasses on the sink-top. 'If you only knew how sick I am of visiting all those little old ladies in the retirement homes—all those members of Women's Lib—'

'It's nothing like that,' Dr Degradian soothed.

But the incubus ignored him. 'You don't know what I've been through,' he croaked. 'In the good old days, before this damned permissiveness came in, everything was easy. I dated good-looking unmarried women, beautiful young wives with elderly husbands, even school-girls.

A little loving went a long way and giving them what they wanted was a piece of cake, in a manner of speaking. But today—' The incubus shuddered. 'Today they've all read those sex-manuals, they've watched too many X-rated movies.' He gestured towards his face. 'I even have to keep changing my appearance to satisfy them. First it was Paul Newman, then Robert Redford. Now it's this Burt Reynolds character, and next year I suppose I'll have to do an entire rock-group. Look at me—I'm worn out, nothing but skin and bones! It's getting so I'm not even good for a one-night stand any more. What I need is a leave of absence, a black sabbatical. And you expect me to take on a new job?'

Dr Degradian shrugged. 'Calm yourself. It's not a new job. All I want you to do is go back to an old one. There's a girl named Angela—'

'Angela?' The creature began to tremble. 'Oh no—not Angela!'

'You remember her?'

'Remember her?' the incubus wailed. 'Why do you think I'm in this condition? She's the one who really wore me out. Another go-round with her and I'll be wearing a truss!' He shook his head so emphatically that his horns rattled. 'No way! Angela is a nympholept. An incubus can't help her—what she needs is a psychiatrist.'

'But you're my last chance—'

'Sorry.' The thing rose from his crouching position and yawned wearily, blowing out several candles in the process. 'Now if you'll excuse me, I must be on my way. I'm calling it a night just as soon as I finish at the orphanage.'

'Orphanage?'

The incubus nodded. 'It's my duty,' he murmured. 'You know the old saying—spare the rod and spoil the child.'

Then, in a puff of smoke, he disappeared.

Monday dawned. Dr Degradian scrubbed the kitchen floor and aired the place out, then sank into bed and an uneasy slumber. He wouldn't have gone to the office at all if it wasn't for Angela's afternoon appointment.

He dragged himself in, carrying his load of guilt. He had failed the girl, failed himself, and now there was no hope to cling to.

Instead he clung to his desk as she breezed in, buoyant and lovely as ever, her eyes bright with expectation.

'How did you manage yourself?' Dr Degradian asked. 'Were you able to cope?'

Angela blushed prettily. 'There was no one to cope with,' she said. 'Finally I went for a walk to take my mind off you-know-what.'

'Did that help?'

'Yes, a little. I lucked out by finding a construction site where I could watch the erection of a tall building.'

Dr Degradian nodded, bracing himself for the inevitable question.

The blue eyes turned to him, alive with anticipation. 'And what about you, Doctor—did you get the incubus back?'

'I'm afraid not.'

The eyes began to brim with tears, and Dr Degradian agonised at the sight of her despair. 'He said you were a nympho, and no one could help you now but a psychiatrist.'

Angela stared at him. Then, surprisingly she smiled. 'You're a psychiatrist.'

Dr Degradian shrugged. 'But you refuse treatment. What can I do?'

'Marry me.'

'What—?'

'Marry me!' Angela rose. 'Don't you see I've had a thing about you all along?' She nodded eagerly. 'Who needs an incubus anyway—all those horns and that smelly sulphur and brimstone!'

'But—'

'No buts. I've made up my mind. We're going to get married!'

And then the nympho leapt.

The wedding took place the following week and Dr Degradian stiffened himself for the ordeal ahead. That night, after Angela retired to bed, he was still undressing in the bathroom when she called to him.

'Coming,' he said.

The prediction proved correct. And much to his astonishment his new bride was completely satisfied. Snuggling against the pillows she offered him a happy smile. 'So that's what an orgasm is,' she murmured. 'I always wondered.'

'You mean you never—?'

'Not until now.' Angela put her arms around him. 'Darling, do you think you could possibly—?'

'It seems highly probable,' Dr Degradian told her.

And so it turned out to be a happy marriage after all. As a matter of fact, she didn't really become frigid until almost three months later . . .

AH SWEET MYSTERY OF LIFE

Roald Dahl

Belief in superstition is often denied by people who always put their right shoe on before the left, avoid walking under a ladder, and touch wood for good luck—without a second thought that they are actually being superstitious. Yet, having said this, author James Turner declared in his Unlikely Ghosts *(1969) that 'satire has almost destroyed superstition', despite the evidence provided by comic fantasy writers like A. E. Coppard, H. Russell Wakefield and Henry Kuttner, who built careers with stories in which superstition plays a major role. To this list can be added Roald Dahl who, while he is known as one of the twentieth century's most popular children's authors, was also a very accomplished fantasy writer and based his first book on a Second World War superstition—gremlins. It was while he was serving as a pilot in the RAF that Dahl first heard tales about these sly little creatures who were supposed to be the cause of all aircraft mishaps and featured them in a children's story,* The Gremlins *(1943), and then later an sf novel,* Sometime Never *(1947). In this, the gremlins attempt to take over the world, but when mankind is plunged into a destructive nuclear war, they find themselves inheriting the planet anyway! Dahl also wrote a number of other sardonic little fantasies which can be found in three collections,* Someone Like You *(1953),* Kiss Kiss *(1960) and* Switch Bitch *(1974).*

Roald Dahl (1916–1990) was born in Wales of Norwegian parents and worked initially in the oil industry. After being invalided out of the RAF, he served as an air attaché in Washington, where he started to write. His macabre sense of humour made his stories suitable for television, and he hosted a series of adaptations, Way Out, *in America in 1961, which was followed by the worldwide success of the British-made* Tales of the Unexpected *(1979–1984). His fame as a unique voice in children's literature was launched with* Charlie and the Chocolate Factory *(1964) and confirmed with later bestsellers like* Danny the Champion of the World *(1975) and* The BFG *(1982). Dahl never altogether*

*abandoned his love of fantasy, however—nor his interest in super-
stition—as he reveals in 'Ah Sweet Mystery of Life', written for the*
Daily Telegraph Magazine *in 1974. It is a story based on a quaint
country superstition about bulls and cows and the direction of the sun.
Inimitable Dahl!*

*   *   *

The other day, when this Magazine invited me to write a short piece
on more or less any subject, I declined. I was struggling with a new
children's book, I said, and I find it difficult to switch over from one
thing to another. But I had no sooner replaced the receiver when I
began to have second thoughts.

'*The Daily Telegraph,*' I told myself, 'is read by almost everybody
of consequence in the country, including leaders of industry and trades
union bosses and even members of the Cabinet. So what a tremendous
opportunity this would be to say something of world-shaking importance
and to implant the message directly into the minds of powerful men.'

But did I have such a message? Nothing in the least bit trivial would
do. Nothing political or witty or smart-aleck. It must, in fact, be something of major benefit to mankind the world-over. Something along
the lines of Salk and his polio vaccine or Roentgen with his exposed
photographic plate or Fleming with that little bacteria-free circle on the
watch glass. Something like that.

Well now, I thought. And I went on thinking and thinking and nothing
much happened . . . until suddenly click went a little trigger somewhere
inside the head and I cried out, 'I've got it!' And indeed I had.

For the past twenty-seven years I have been stewing and brewing
about an incident that took place one misty autumn afternoon in a
farmyard on the outskirts of the village of Great Missenden, and I have
many times wondered where and when I should make the facts known
to the world. This surely was my chance. So here we go. The story is
a true one.

Back in 1947 when there was still a postwar shortage of milk in
England, we kept a cow in our orchard. The house I was then living
in with my mother and my youngest sister is presently owned by Mr
Harold Wilson, the Prime Minister. So is the orchard. I mention this
for a reason. When my story breaks upon the world, thousands of people
will flock to Great Missenden to stand and stare at the house where it
all started. And Mr Wilson, who is no less of an egomaniac than any
other politician, will almost certainly think they have come to look at

him. He will probably wave to them from an upstairs window and he may even try to make an electioneering speech. If he does, he will be jeered.

Anyway, on this misty autumn day in 1947, our cow started bulling. She was ready for the bull. So I tied a rope around her neck and I set off with her down the lane toward a farm across the valley. The owner of the farm, whom I shall call Rummins, was well known to me and he had previously agreed to make his bull available when the time came. He himself kept a fine herd of dairy cattle and he also had an enormous black and white Frisian bull, the pride of his farm.

We trotted briskly down the lane, the cow and I. It was one of those warm still September afternoons that Keats used to write about, and I could see clusters of big ripe hazelnuts in the hedgerows and once I saw a bush of crabapples the colour of lemons. At the bottom of the lane we crossed the main road and climbed up the hill on the other side of the valley and came at last to the farm.

Rummins, carrying a pail of milk across the yard, saw us coming. He set the pail down slowly and walked to meet us. 'She's ready, is she then?' he said.

'Been bulling all day,' I said. 'Yelling her head off.'

Rummins walked around my cow, examining her carefully. He was a short man, built squat and broad like a frog. He had a wide frog mouth and broken teeth and shifty eyes, but over the years I had grown to respect him for his wisdom and the sharpness of his mind.

'All right then' he said. 'What is it you want, a heifer calf or a bull calf?'

'Can I choose?'

'Of course you can choose.'

'Then I'll have a heifer,' I said, keeping a straight face. 'We want milk not beef.'

'Hey, Bert!' Rummins called out. 'Come and give us a hand!'

Bert emerged from the cowsheds. He was Rummins's youngest son, a tall boneless boy with a runny nose and something wrong with one eye. The eye was pale and misty-grey all over, like a boiled fish eye. And it moved quite independently from the other eye. 'Get a halter,' Rummins said.

Bert fetched a rope and looped it around my cow's neck so that she now had two ropes holding her, my own and Bert's. 'He wants a heifer,' Rummins said. 'Face her into the sun.'

'Into the sun?' I said. 'There isn't any sun.'

'There's always sun,' Rummins said. 'Them bloody clouds don't make no difference. Come on now. Get a jerk on, Bert. Bring her round. Sun's over there.'

With Bert on one side and me on the other, each holding a rope we pulled the cow around until her head was facing directly toward that place in the sky where the sun was hidden behind the clouds.

'Hold her steady now!' ordered Rummins. 'Don't let her jump round!' Then he hurried over to a separate shed in the far corner of the yard and brought out his enormous bull. He led it by a chain which was attached to a ring through the bull's nose.

The bull approached my cow slowly, staring at her with dangerous white eyes. He gave a couple of deep snorts and pawed the ground with a foreleg. Then with surprising agility he heaved himself up on to the cow's back. What happened next happened very fast.

It was all over in thirty seconds. Rummins led the bull back into the shed and tied him up. When he rejoined us I thanked him and then I asked him if he really believed that facing the cow into the sun during the mating would produce a female calf.

'Don't be so damn silly,' he said. 'Of course I believe it. Facts is facts.'

'What do you mean facts is facts?'

'I mean what I say, mister. It's a certainty. That's right, ain't it, Bert?'

Bert swivelled his misty eye around in its socket and said, 'Too bloody true it's right.'

'And if you face her away from the sun does it get you a male?'

'Every single time,' Rummins said. I smiled and he saw it. 'You don't believe me, do you?'

'Not really,' I said.

'Come with me,' he said. 'And when you see what I'm going to show you, you'll bloody well have to believe me. Tie the cow up to the gate, Bert.'

Rummins led me into the farmhouse. The room we went into was dark and small and somewhat dirty. From a drawer in the sideboard he produced a whole stack of thin exercise books. They were the kind children use at school. 'These is calving books,' he announced. 'And in here is a record of every mating that's ever been done on this farm since I first started thirty-two years ago.'

He opened a book at random and allowed me to look. There were four columns on each page: COW'S NAME, DATE OF MATING, DATE OF BIRTH, SEX OF CALF.

I glanced down the sex column. *Heifer*, it said. *Heifer, Heifer, Heifer, Heifer, Heifer.*

'We don't want no bull calves here,' Rummins said. 'Bull calves is a dead loss on a dairy farm.'

I turned over a page. Heifer, it said. Heifer, Heifer, Heifer, Heifer, Heifer.

'Hey,' I said. 'Here's a bull calf.'

'That's quite right,' Rummins said. 'Now take a look at what I wrote opposite that one at the time of mating.' I glanced at column two.

'COW JUMPED AROUND,' I said.

'Some of them gets fractious and you can't hold 'em steady,' Rummins said. 'So they finish up facing the other way. That's the only time I ever get a bull.'

'This is fantastic,' I said, leafing through the book.

'Of course it's fantastic,' Rummins said. 'It's one of the most fantastic things in the whole world. Do you actually know what I average on this farm? I average ninety-eight per cent heifers year in year out! Check it for yourself. Go on and check it, I'm not stopping you.'

'I'd like very much to check it,' I said. 'May I sit down?'

'Help yourself,' Rummins said. 'I've got work to do.' I found a pencil and paper and I proceeded to go through each one of the thirty-two little books with great care. There was one book for each year, from 1915 to 1946.

There were approximately eighty calves a year born on the farm, and my final results over the thirty-two-year period were as follows:

Heifer calves 2,516
Bull calves 56
Total calves born, including stillborn 2,572

I went outside to look for Rummins. He was in the dairy pouring milk into the separator. 'Haven't you ever told anyone about this?' I asked him.

'Never have,' he said.

'Why not?'

'I reckon it ain't nobody else's business.'

'But my dear man, this could transform the entire milk industry the world over.'

'It might,' he said. 'It might easily do that. It wouldn't do the beef business no harm either if they could get bulls every time.'

'How did you hear about it in the first place?'

'My old dad told me,' Rummins said. 'When I were about eighteen, my old dad said to me, ''I'll tell you a secret,'' he said, ''that'll make you rich.'' And he told me this.'

'Has it made you rich?'

'I ain't done too bad for myself, have I?' he said.

'But did your father offer any sort of explanation as to why it works?' I asked.

Rummins explored the inner rim of one nostril with the end of his thumb, holding the noseflap between thumb and forefinger as he did so. 'A very clever man, my old dad was,' he said. 'Very clever indeed. Of course he told me how it works.'

'How?'

'He explained to me that a cow don't have nothing to do with deciding the sex of the calf,' Rummins said. 'All a cow's got is an egg. It's the bull decides what the sex is going to be. The sperm of the bull.'

'Go on,' I said.

'According to my old dad, a bull has two different kinds of sperm, female sperm and male sperm. You follow me so far?'

'Yes,' I said. 'Keep going.'

'So when the old bull shoots off his sperm into the cow, a sort of swimming race takes place between the male and the female sperm to see which can reach the egg first. If the female sperm wins, you get a heifer.'

'But what's the sun got to do with it?' I asked.

'I'm coming to that,' he said, 'so listen carefully. When an animal is standing on all fours like a cow, and when you face her head into the sun, then the sperm has also got to travel directly into the sun to reach the egg. Switch the cow around and they'll be travelling away from the sun.'

'So what you're saying,' I said, 'is that the sun exerts a pull of some sort on the female sperm and makes them swim faster than the male sperm.'

'Exactly!' cried Rummins. 'That's exactly it! It exerts a pull. It drags them forward! That's why they always win! And if you turn the cow around the other way, it's pulling them backwards and the male sperm wins instead.'

'It's an interesting theory,' I said. 'But it hardly seems likely that the sun, which is millions of miles away, could exert a pull on a bunch of spermatozoa inside a cow.'

'You're talking rubbish!' cried Rummins. 'Absolute and utter rubbish! Don't the moon exert a pull on the bloody tides of the ocean to make 'em high and low? Of course it does! So why shouldn't the sun exert a pull on the female sperm?'

'I see your point.'

Suddenly Rummins seemed to have had enough.

'Better take your cow home now,' he said, turning away. 'You'll have a heifer calf for sure, don't you worry about that.'

'Mr Rummins,' I said.

'What?'

'Is there any reason why this shouldn't work with humans as well?'

'Of course it'll work with humans,' he said. 'Just so long as you remember everything's got to be pointed in the right direction. A cow ain't lying down you know. It's standing on all fours.'

'I see what you mean.'

'And it ain't no good doing it at night either,' he said, 'because at night the sun is shielded behind the earth and it can't influence anything.'

'That's true,' I said, 'but have you any sort of proof it works with humans?'

Rummins laid his head to one side and gave me another of his long sly broken-tooth grins. 'I've got four boys of my own, ain't I?' he said.

'So you have.'

'Ruddy girls ain't no use to me around here,' he said. 'Boys is what you want on a farm and I've got four of 'em, right?'

'Right,' I said, 'you're absolutely right.'

3

VACANT SPACE

Stories of Science Fiction

THE MAN IN ASBESTOS
An Allegory of the Future

Stephen Leacock

Science fiction has been the butt of comic fantasy for over a century: ever since, in fact, the genre was effectively launched in the public imagination by the works of H. G. Wells. Indeed, Wells himself was not averse to introducing a little humour into his work, and aside from classic sf novels like The Time Machine *(1895),* The Island of Dr Moreau *(1896),* The War of the Worlds *(1898) and* The First Men in the Moon *(1901), he also wrote several short stories that are full of amusing incidents, including 'The Inexperienced Ghost', 'The Truth About Pyecraft' and 'The Wild Asses of the Devil', one of his little-known comic fantasies which I reprinted in my previous anthology* The Wizards of Odd *(1996). However, among the comic writers who have parodied Wells's work, mention must be made of E. V. Lucas and his sexist epic,* The War of the Wenuses *(1898), Max Beerbohm's cynical* Perkins and Mankind *(1912), and Stephen Leacock's 'The Man in Asbestos', written in 1917 as part of a series entitled 'Nonsense Novels' in which he poked fun at the sf, fantasy and mystery genres.*

Stephen Leacock (1869–1944) was born in Canada and has been linked with James Thurber as the two finest North American humorists of the twentieth century. (Thurber, incidentally, also wrote a comic fantasy novel, The 13 Clocks *(1950), and several uproarious short stories, including 'The Night The Ghost Got In', which would easily fit into a collection such as this if space permitted.) Leacock was a master of the short story, and a considerable number of his tales are spoofs of sf themes, as indicated by the titles of collections such as* Moonbeams from the Larger Lunacy *(1917),* The Iron Man and the Tin Woman, with Other Such Futurities *(1929) and* Afternoons in Utopia: Tales of the New Time *(1932). My own favourite among his parodies of science fiction is 'The Man in Asbestos', which brilliantly sends up Wells's*

*story of the time traveller and makes a perfect opening for this last
section of the book.*

*   *   *

To begin with let me admit that I did it on purpose. Perhaps it was
partly from jealousy.

It seemed unfair that other writers should be able at will to drop into
a sleep of four or five hundred years, and to plunge head-first into a
distant future and be a witness of its marvels.

I wanted to do that too.

I always had been, I still am, a passionate student of social problems.
The world of today with its roaring machinery, the unceasing toil of
its working class, its strife, its poverty, its war, its cruelty, appals me
as I look at it. I love to think of the time that must come some day
when man will have conquered nature, and the toil-worn human race
enter upon an era of peace.

I loved to think of it, and I longed to see it.

So I set about the thing deliberately.

What I wanted to do was to fall asleep after the customary fashion,
for two or three hundred years at least, and wake and find myself in
the marvel world of the future.

I made my preparations for the sleep.

I bought all the comic papers that I could find, even the illustrated
ones. I carried them up to my room in my hotel: with them I brought
up a pork pie and dozens and dozens of doughnuts. I ate the pie and
the doughnuts, then sat back in the bed and read the comic papers one
after the other. Finally, as I felt the awful lethargy stealing upon me, I
reached out my hand for the *London Weekly Times*, and held up the
editorial page before my eye.

It was, in a way, clear, straight suicide, but I did it.

I could feel my senses leaving me. In the room across the hall there
was a man singing. His voice, that had been loud, came fainter and
fainter through the transom. I fell into a sleep, the deep immeasurable
sleep in which the very existence of the outer world was hushed. Dimly
I could feel the days go past, then the years, and then the long passage
of the centuries.

Then, not as it were gradually, but quite suddenly, I woke up, sat
up, and looked about me.

Where was I?

Well might I ask myself.

I found myself lying, or rather sitting up, on a broad couch. I was in a great room, dim, gloomy, and dilapidated in its general appearance, and apparently, from its glass cases and the stuffed figures that they contained, some kind of museum.

Beside me sat a man. His face was hairless, but neither old nor young. He wore clothes that looked like the grey ashes of paper that had burned and kept its shape. He was looking at me quietly, but with no particular surprise or interest.

'Quick,' I said, eager to begin; 'where am I? Who are you? What year is this; is it the year 3000, or what is it?'

He drew in his breath with a look of annoyance on his face.

'What a queer, excited way you have of speaking,' he said.

'Tell me,' I said again, 'is this the year 3000?'

'I think I know what you mean,' he said; 'but really I haven't the faintest idea. I should think it must be at least that, within a hundred years or so; but nobody has kept track of them for so long, it's hard to say.'

'Don't you keep track of them any more?' I gasped.

'We used to,' said the man. 'I myself can remember that a century or two ago there were still a number of people who used to try to keep track of the year, but it died out along with so many other faddish things of that kind. Why,' he continued, showing for the first time a sort of animation in his talk, 'what was the use of it? You see, after we eliminated death—'

'Eliminated death!' I cried, sitting upright. 'Good God!'

'What was that expression you used?' queried the man.

'Good God!' I repeated.

'Ah,' he said, 'never heard it before. But I was saying that after we had eliminated Death, and Food, and Change, we had practically got rid of Events, and—'

'Stop!' I said, my brain reeling. 'Tell me one thing at a time.'

'Humph!' he ejaculated. 'I see, you must have been asleep a long time. Go on then and ask questions. Only, if you don't mind, just as few as possible, and please don't get interested or excited.'

Oddly enough the first question that sprang to my lips was—

'What are those clothes made of?'

'Asbestos,' answered the man. 'They last hundreds of years. We have one suit each, and there are billions of them piled up, if anybody wants a new one.'

'Thank you,' I answered. 'Now tell me where I am?'

'You are in a museum. The figures in the cases are specimens like yourself. But here,' he said, 'if you want really to find out about what is evidently a new epoch to you, get off your platform and come out on Broadway and sit on a bench.'

I got down.

As we passed through the dim and dust-covered buildings I looked curiously at the figures in the cases.

'By Jove!' I said, looking at one figure in blue clothes with a belt and baton, 'that's a policeman!'

'Really,' said my new acquaintance, 'is *that* what a *policeman* was? I've often wondered. What used they to be used for?'

'Used for?' I repeated in perplexity. 'Why, they stood at the corner of the street.'

'Ah, yes, I see,' he said, 'so as to shoot at the people. You must excuse my ignorance,' he continued, 'as to some of your social customs in the past. When I took my education I was operated upon for social history, but the stuff they used was very inferior.'

I didn't in the least understand what the man meant, but had no time to question him, for at that moment we came out upon the street, and I stood riveted in astonishment.

Broadway! Was it possible? The change was absolutely appalling! In place of the roaring thoroughfare that I had known, this silent, moss-grown desolation. Great buildings fallen into ruin through the sheer stress of centuries of wind and weather, the sides of them coated over with a growth of fungus and moss! The place was soundless. Not a vehicle moved. There were no wires overhead—no sound of life or movement except, here and there, there passed slowly to and fro human figures dressed in the same asbestos clothes as my acquaintance, with the same hairless faces, and the same look of infinite age upon them.

Good heavens! And was this the era of the Conquest that I had hoped to see! I had always taken for granted, I do not know why, that humanity was destined to move forward. This picture of what seemed desolation on the ruins of our civilisation rendered me almost speechless.

There were little benches placed here and there on the street. We sat down.

'Improved, isn't it,' said the man in asbestos, 'since the days when you remember it?'

He seemed to speak quite proudly.

I gasped out a question.

'Where are the street cars and the motors?'

'Oh, done away with long ago,' he said; 'how awful they must have been. The noise of them!' and his asbestos clothes rustled with a shudder.

'But how do you get about?'

'We don't,' he answered. 'Why should we? It's just the same being here as being anywhere else.' He looked at me with an infinity of dreariness in his face.

A thousand questions surged into my mind at once. I asked one of the simplest.

'But how do you get back and forwards to your work?'

'Work!' he said. 'There isn't any work. It's finished. The last of it was all done centuries ago.'

I looked at him a moment open-mouthed. Then I turned and looked again at the grey desolation of the street with the asbestos figures moving here and there.

I tried to pull my senses together. I realised that if I was to unravel this new and undreamed-of future, I must go at it systematically and step by step.

'I see,' I said after a pause, 'that momentous things have happened since my time. I wish you would let me ask you about it all systematically, and would explain it to me bit by bit. First, what do you mean by saying that there is no work?'

'Why,' answered my strange acquaintance, 'it died out of itself. Machinery killed it. If I remember rightly, you had a certain amount of machinery even in your time. You had done very well with steam, made a good beginning with electricity, though I think radial energy had hardly as yet been put to use.'

I nodded assent.

'But you found it did you no good. The better your machines, the harder you worked. The more things you had the more you wanted. The pace of life grew swifter and swifter. You cried out, but it would not stop. You were all caught in the cogs of your own machine. None of you could see the end.'

'That is quite true,' I said. 'How do you know it all?'

'Oh,' answered the Man in Asbestos, 'that part of my education was very well operated—I see you do not know what I mean. Never mind, I can tell you that later. Well, then, there came, probably almost two hundred years after your time, the Era of the Great Conquest of Nature, the final victory of Man and Machinery.'

'They did conquer it?' I asked quickly, with a thrill of the old hope in my veins again.

'Conquered it,' he said, 'beat it out! Fought it to a standstill! Things came one by one, then faster and faster, in a hundred years it was all done. In fact, just as soon as mankind turned its energy to decreasing its needs instead of increasing its desires, the whole thing was easy. Chemical Food came first. Heavens! the simplicity of it. And in your time thousands of millions of people tilled and grubbed at the soil from morning till night. I've seen specimens of them—farmers, they called them. There's one in the museum. After the invention of Chemical Food we piled up enough in the emporiums in a year to last for centuries. Agriculture went overboard. Eating and all that goes with it, domestic labour, housework—all ended. Nowadays one takes a concentrated pill every year or so, that's all. The whole digestive apparatus, as you knew it, was a clumsy thing that had been bloated up like a set of bagpipes through the evolution of its use!'

I could not forbear to interrupt. 'Have you and these people,' I said, 'no stomachs—no apparatus?'

'Of course we have,' he answered, 'but we use it to some purpose. Mine is largely filled with my education—but there! I am anticipating again. Better let me go on as I was. Chemical Food came first: that cut off almost one-third of the work, and then came Asbestos Clothes. That was wonderful! In one year humanity made enough suits to last for ever and ever. That, of course, could never have been if it hadn't been connected with the revolt of women and the fall of Fashion.'

'Have the Fashions gone,' I asked, 'that insane, extravagant idea of—' I was able to launch into one of my old-time harangues about the sheer vanity of decorative dress, when my eye rested on the moving figures in asbestos, and I stopped.

'All gone,' said the Man in Asbestos. 'Then next to that we killed, or practically killed, the changes of climate. I don't think that in your day you properly understood how much of your work was due to the shifts of what you called the weather. It meant the need of all kinds of special clothes and houses and shelters, a wilderness of work. How dreadful it must have been in your day—wind and storms, great wet masses—what did you call them?—clouds—flying through the air, the ocean full of salt, was it not?—tossed and torn by the wind, snow thrown all over everything, hail, rain—how awful!'

'Sometimes,' I said, 'it was very beautiful. But how did you alter it?'

'Killed the weather!' answered the Man in Asbestos. 'Simple as anything—turned its forces loose one against the other, altered the composition of the sea so that the top became all more or less gelatinous. I really can't explain it, as it is an operation that I never took at school, but it made the sky grey, as you see it, and the sea gum-coloured, the weather all the same. It cut out fuel and houses and an infinity of work with them!'

He paused a moment. I began to realise something of the course of evolution that had happened.

'So,' I said, 'the conquest of nature meant that presently there was no more work to do?'

'Exactly,' he said, 'nothing left.'

'Food enough for all?'

'Too much,' he answered.

'Houses and clothes?'

'All you like,' said the Man in Asbestos, waving his hand. 'There they are. Go out and take them. Of course, they're falling down—slowly, very slowly. But they'll last for centuries yet, nobody need bother.'

Then I realised, I think for the first time, just what work had meant in the old life, and how much of the texture of life itself had been bound up in the keen effort of it.

Presently my eyes looked upward: dangling at the top of a moss-grown building I saw what seemed to be the remains of telephone wires.

'What became of all that,' I said, 'the telegraph and the telephone and all the system of communication?'

'Ah,' said the Man in Asbestos, 'that was what a telephone meant, was it? I knew that it had been suppressed centuries ago. Just what was it for?'

'Why,' I said with enthusiasm, 'by means of the telephone we could talk to anybody, call up anybody, and talk at any distance.'

'And anybody could call you up at any time and talk?' said the Man in Asbestos, with something like horror. 'How awful! What a dreadful age yours was, to be sure. No, the telephone and all the rest of it, all the transportation and intercommunication was cut out and forbidden. There was no sense in it. You see,' he added, 'what you don't realise is that people after your day became gradually more and more reason-able. Take the railroad, what good was that? It brought into every town a lot of people from every other town. Who wanted them? Nobody. When work stopped and commerce ended, and food was needless, and the weather killed, it was foolish to move about. So it was all terminated. Anyway,' he said, with a quick look of apprehension and a change in his voice, 'it was dangerous!'

'So!' I said. 'Dangerous! You still have danger?'

'Why, yes,' he said, 'there's always the danger of getting broken.'

'What do you mean,' I asked.

'Why,' said the Man in Asbestos, 'I suppose it's what you would call being dead. Of course, in one sense there's been no death for centuries past; we cut that out. Disease and death were simply a matter of germs. We found them one by one. I think that even in your day you had found one or two of the easier, the bigger ones?'

I nodded.

'Yes, you had found diphtheria and typhoid, and, if I am right, there were some outstanding, like scarlet fever and smallpox, that you called ultra-microscopic, and which you were still hunting for, and others that you didn't even suspect. Well, we hunted them down one by one and destroyed them. Strange that it never occurred to any of you that Old Age was only a germ! It turned out to be quite a simple one, but it was so distributed in its action that you never even thought of it.'

'And you mean to say,' I ejaculated in amazement, looking at the Man in Asbestos, 'that nowadays you live for ever?'

'I wish,' he said, 'that you hadn't that peculiar, excitable way of talking; you speak as if everything *mattered* so tremendously. Yes,' he continued, 'we live for ever, unless, of course, we get broken. That happens sometimes. I mean that we may fall over a high place or bump on something, and snap ourselves. You see, we're just a little brittle still—some remnant, I suppose, of the Old Age germ—and we have to be careful. In fact,' he continued, 'I don't mind saying that accidents of this sort were the most distressing feature of our civilisation till we took steps to cut out all accidents. We forbid all street cars, street traffic, aeroplanes, and so on. The risks of your time,' he said, with a shiver of his asbestos clothes, 'must have been awful.'

'They were,' I answered, with a new kind of pride in my generation that I had never felt before, 'but we thought it part of the duty of brave people to—'

'Yes, yes,' said the Man in Asbestos impatiently, 'please don't get excited. I know what you mean. It was quite irrational.'

We sat silent for a long time. I looked about me at the crumbling buildings, the monotone, unchanging sky, and the dreary, empty street. Here, then, was the fruit of the Conquest, here was the elimination of work, the end of hunger and of cold, the cessation of the hard struggle, the downfall of change and death—nay, the very millennium of happiness. And yet, somehow, there seemed something wrong with it all. I pondered, then I put two or three rapid questions, hardly waiting to reflect upon the answers.

'Is there any war now?'

'Done with centuries ago. They took to settling international disputes with a slot machine. After that all foreign dealings were given up. Why have them? Everybody thinks foreigners awful.'

'Are there any newspapers now?'

'Newspapers! What on earth would we want them for? If we should need them at any time there are thousands of old ones piled up. But what is in them, anyway; only things that *happen*, wars and accidents and work and death. When these went newspapers went too. Listen,' continued the Man in Asbestos, 'you seem to have been something of a social reformer, and yet you don't understand the new life at all. You don't understand how completely all our burdens have disappeared. Look at it this way. How used your people to spend all the early part of their lives?'

'Why,' I said, 'our first fifteen years or so were spent in getting education.'

'Exactly,' he answered; 'now notice how we improved on all that. Education in our day is done by surgery. Strange that in your time nobody realised that education was simply a surgical operation. You hadn't the sense to see that what you really did was to slowly remodel, curve and convolute the inside of the brain by a long and painful mental operation. Everything learned was reproduced in a physical difference to the brain. You knew that, but you didn't see the full consequences. Then came the invention of surgical education—the simple system of opening the side of the skull and engrafting into it a piece of prepared brain. At first, of course, they had to use, I suppose, the brains of dead people, and that was ghastly'—here the Man in Asbestos shuddered like a leaf—'but very soon they found how to make moulds that did just as well. After that it was a mere nothing; an operation of a few minutes would suffice to let in poetry or foreign languages or history or anything else that one cared to have. Here, for instance,' he added, pushing back the hair at the side of his head and showing a scar beneath it, 'is the mark where I had my spherical trigonometry let in. That was, I admit, rather painful, but other things, such as English poetry or history, can be inserted absolutely without the least suffering. When I think of your painful, barbarous methods of education through the ear, I shudder at it. Oddly enough, we have found lately that for a great many things there is no need to use the head. We lodge them—things like philosophy and metaphysics, and so on—in what used to be the digestive apparatus. They fill it admirably.'

He paused a moment. Then went on:

'Well, then, to continue, what used to occupy your time and effort after your education?'

'Why,' I said, 'one had, of course, to work, and then, to tell the truth, a great part of one's time and feeling was devoted toward the other sex, towards falling in love and finding some woman to share one's life.'

'Ah,' said the Man in Asbestos, with real interest. 'I've heard about your arrangements with the women, but never quite understood them. Tell me; you say you selected some woman?'

'Yes.'

'And she became what you called your wife?'

'Yes, of course.'

'And you worked for her?' asked the Man in Asbestos in astonishment.

'Yes.'

'And she did not work?'

'No,' I answered, 'of course not.'

'And half of what you had was hers?'

'Yes.'

'And she had the right to live in your house and use your things?'

'Of course,' I answered.

'How dreadful!' said the Man in Asbestos. 'I hadn't realised the horrors of your age till now.'

He sat shivering slightly, with the same timid look in his face as before.

Then it suddenly struck me that of the figures on the street, all had looked alike.

'Tell me,' I said, 'are there no women now? Are they gone too?'

'Oh, no,' answered the Man in Asbestos, 'they're here just the same. Some of those are women. Only, you see, everything has been changed now. It all came as part of their great revolt, their desire to be like the men. Had that begun in your time?'

'Only a little,' I answered; 'they were beginning to ask for votes and equality.'

'That's it,' said my acquaintance, 'I couldn't think of the word. Your women, I believe, were something awful, were they not? Covered with feathers and skins and dazzling colours made of dead things all over them? And they laughed, did they not, and had foolish teeth, and at any moment they could inveigle you into one of those contracts! Ugh!'

He shuddered.

'Asbestos,' I said (I knew no other name to call him), as I turned on him in wrath, 'Asbestos, do you think that those jelly-bag Equalities out on the street there, with their ash-barrel suits, can be compared for one moment with our unredeemed, unreformed, heaven-created, hobble-skirted women of the twentieth century?'

Then, suddenly, another thought flashed into my mind—

'The children,' I said, 'where are the children? Are there any?'

'Children,' he said, 'no! I have never heard of there being any such things for at least a century. Horrible little hobgoblins they must have been! Great big faces, and cried constantly! And *grew*, did they not? Like funguses! I believe they were longer each year than they had been the last, and—'

I rose.

'Asbestos!' I said, 'this, then, is your coming Civilisation, your millennium. This dull, dead thing, with the work and the burden gone out of life, and with them all the joy and the sweetness of it. For the old struggle—mere stagnation, and in place of danger and death, the dull monotony of security and the horror of an unending decay! Give me back,' I cried, and I flung wide my arms to the dull air, 'the old life of danger and stress, with its hard toil and its bitter chances, and its heart-breaks. I see its value! I know its worth! Give me no rest,' I cried aloud—

'Yes, but give a rest to the rest of the corridor!' cried an angered voice that broke in upon my exultation.

Suddenly my sleep had gone.

I was back again in the room of my hotel, with the hum of the wicked, busy old world all about me, and loud in my ears the voice of the indignant man across the corridor.

'Quit your blatting, you infernal blatherskite,' he was calling. 'Come down to earth.'

I came.

FEMALE OF THE SPECIES

John Wyndham

John Wyndham was another author who, like his avowed mentor, H. G. Wells, is today best remembered for his classic sf novels, The Day of the Triffids *(1951),* The Kraken Wakes *(1953) and* The Midwich Cuckoos *(1957), although he also possessed a mischievous sense of humour and was not above parodying the masters of the genre in his short stories. He was particularly amused by all the tales of 'mad scientists' which proliferated in the American sf pulp magazines of the Thirties to which he contributed his own early stories. Wells might, of course, be accused of having inspired this type of fiction with his gruesome novel,* The Island of Dr Moreau—*although Mary Shelley was probably the true pioneer with* Frankenstein, *published in 1818—but he could hardly be blamed for some of the outrages that his successors allowed their eccentric men of science to commit against animals and human beings. In 'Female of the Species', John Wyndham pays a tongue-in-cheek 'tribute' to Dr Moreau and his fellow experimenters!*

John Wyndham Parkes Lucas Beynon Harris (1903–1969) used all of his names in varying combinations for pseudonyms during his writing career, but remains best known by the first two. Born in Warwickshire, he tried unsuccessfully to be a farmer, lawyer, commercial artist and even advertising agent before finding his métier in the Thirties as a writer of fantasy and science fiction. It was not, however, until after his Army service in the Second World War that Wyndham became famous with his chilling account of the deadly, mobile plants, the Triffids, and his subsequent bestsellers which were mostly filmed and often televised. 'Female of the Species' was originally written in 1937 as 'The Perfect Creature' when, apparently, Doctor Dixon's creation was a male. By the time it appeared, retitled, in Argosy *magazine in October 1953, as John Wyndham wanted it, the 'he' had become a 'she'. The instinct which had driven the rampaging creature in both versions was, nevertheless, precisely the same*—to find a mate . . .

*   *   *

The first thing I knew of the Dixon affair was when a deputation came from the village of Membury to ask us if we would investigate the alleged curious goings-on there.

But before that, perhaps, I had better explain the word 'us'.

I happen to hold a post as Inspector for the S.S.M.A.—in full, the Society for the Suppression of the Maltreatment of Animals—in the district that includes Membury. Now, please don't assume that I am wobble-minded on the subject of animals. I needed a job. A friend of mine who has influence with the Society got it for me; and I do it, I think, conscientiously. As for the animals themselves, well, as with humans, I like some of them. In that, I differ from my co-Inspector, Alfred Weston; he likes—liked?—them all; on principle, and indiscriminately.

It could be that, at the salaries they pay, the S.S.M.A. has doubts of its personnel—though there is the point that where legal action is to be taken two witnesses are desirable; but, whatever the reason, there is a practice of appointing their inspectors as pairs to each district; one result of which was my daily and close association with Alfred.

Now, one might describe Alfred as the animal-lover *par excellence*. Between him and all animals there was complete affinity—at least, on Alfred's side. It wasn't his fault if the animals didn't quite understand it; he tried hard enough. The very thought of four feet or feathers seemed to do something to him. He cherished them one and all, and was apt to talk of them, and to them, as if they were his dear, dear friends temporarily embarrassed by a diminished I.Q.

Alfred himself was a well-built man, though not tall, who peered through heavily-rimmed glasses with an earnestness that seldom lightened. The difference between us was that while I was doing a job, he was following a vocation—pursuing it wholeheartedly, and with a powerful imagination to energise him.

It didn't make him a restful companion. Under the powerful magnifier of Alfred's imagination the commonplace became lurid. At a run-of-the-mill allegation of horse-thrashing, phrases about fiends, barbarians and brutes in human form would leap into his mind with such vividness that he would be bitterly disappointed when we discovered, as we invariably did, (*a*) that the thing had been much exaggerated, anyway, and (*b*) that the perpetrator had either had a drink too many, or briefly lost his temper.

It so happened that we were in the office together on the morning that the Membury deputation arrived. They were a more numerous body than we usually received, and as they filed in I could see Alfred's eyes begin to widen in anticipation of something really good—or horrific, depending on which way you were looking at it. Even I felt that this ought to produce something a cut above cans tied to cats' tails, and that kind of thing.

Our premonitions turned out rightly. There was a certain confusion in the telling, but when we had it sorted out, it seemed to amount to this:

Early the previous morning, one Tim Darrell, while engaged in his usual task of taking the milk to the station, had encountered a phenomenon in the village street. The sight had so surprised him that while stamping on his brakes he had let out a yell which brought the whole place to its windows or doors. The men had gaped, and most of the women had set up screaming when they, too, saw the pair of creatures that were standing in the middle of their street.

The best picture of these creatures that we would get out of our visitors suggested that they must have looked more like turtles than anything else—though a very improbable kind of turtle that walked upright upon its hind legs.

The overall height of the apparitions would seem to have been about five foot six. Their bodies were covered with oval carapaces, not only at the back, but in front, too. The heads were about the size of normal human heads, but without hair, and having a horny-looking surface. Their large, bright black eyes were set above a hard, shiny projection, debatably a beak or a nose.

But this description, while unlikely enough, did not cover the most troublesome characteristic—and the one upon which all were agreed despite other variations. This was that from the ridges at the sides, where the back and front carapaces joined, there protruded, some two-thirds of the way up, a pair of human arms and hands!

Well, about that point I suggested what anyone else would: that it was a hoax, a couple of fellows dressed up for a scare.

The deputation was indignant. For one thing, it convincingly said, no one was going to keep up that kind of hoax in the face of gunfire—which was what old Halliday who kept the saddler's had give them. He had let them have half a dozen rounds of twelve-bore; it hadn't worried them a bit, and the pellets had just bounced off.

But when people had got around to emerging cautiously from their doors to take a closer look, they had seemed upset. They had squawked harshly at one another, and then set off down the street at a kind of waddling run. Half the village, feeling braver now, had followed them. The creatures had not seemed to have an idea of where they were going, and had run out over Baker's Marsh. There they had soon struck one of the soft spots, and finally they had sunk out of sight into it, with a great deal of floundering and squawking.

The village, after talking it over, had decided to come to us rather than to the police. It was well meant, no doubt, but, as I said:

'I really don't see what you can expect us to do if the creatures have vanished without trace.'

'Moreover,' put in Alfred, never strong on tact, 'it sounds to me that we should have to report that the villagers of Membury simply hounded these unfortunate creatures—whatever they were—to their deaths, and made no attempt to save them.'

They looked somewhat offended at that, but it turned out that they had not finished. The tracks of the creatures had been followed back as far as possible, and the consensus was that they could not have had their source anywhere but in Membury Grange.

'Who lives there?' I asked.

It was a Doctor Dixon, they told me. He had been there these last three or four years.

And that led us on to Bill Parsons' contribution. He was a little hesitant about making it at first.

'This'll be confidential like?' he asked.

Everyone for miles around knows that Bill's chief concern is other people's rabbits. I reassured him.

'Well, it was this way,' he said. ''Bout three months ago it'd be—'

Pruned of its circumstantial detail, Bill's story amounted to this: finding himself, so to speak, in the grounds of the Grange one night, he had taken a fancy to investigate the nature of the new wing that Doctor Dixon had caused to be built on soon after he came. There had been considerable local speculation about it, and, seeing a chink of light between the curtains there, Bill had taken his opportunity.

'I'm telling you, there's things that's not right there,' he said. 'The very first thing I seen, back against the far wall, was a line of cages, with great thick bars to 'em—the way the light hung I couldn't see what was inside: but why'd anybody be wanting them in his house?

'And then when I shoved myself up higher to get a better view, there in the middle of the room I saw a horrible sight—a horrible sight it was!' He paused for a dramatic shudder.

'Well, what was it?' I asked, patiently.

'It was—well, it's kind of hard to tell. Lying on a table, it was, though. Lookin' more like a white bolster than anything—'cept that it was moving a bit. Kind of inching, with a sort of ripple in it—if you understand me.'

I didn't much. I said:

'Is that all?'

'That it's not,' Bill told me, approaching his climax with relish. 'Most of it didn't 'ave no real shape, but there was a part of it as did—a pair of hands, human hands, a-stickin' out from the sides of it . . .'

In the end I got rid of the deputation with the assurance we would look into the matter. When I turned back from closing the door behind the last of them I perceived that all was not well with Alfred. His eyes were gleaming widely behind his glasses, and he was trembling.

'Sit down,' I advised him. 'You don't want to go shaking parts of yourself off.'

I could see that there was a dissertation coming: probably something to beat what we had just heard. But, for once, he wanted my opinion first, while manfully contriving to hold his own down for a time. I obliged:

'It has to turn out simpler than it sounds,' I told him. 'Either somebody *was* playing a joke on the village—or there are some very unusual animals which they've distorted by talking it over too much.'

'They were unanimous about the carapaces and arms—two structures as thoroughly incompatible as can be,' Alfred said, tiresomely.

I had to grant that. And arms—or, at least, hands—had been the only describable feature of the bolster-like object that Bill had seen at the Grange . . .

Alfred gave me several other reasons why I was wrong, and then paused meaningly.

'I, too, have heard rumours about Membury Grange,' he told me.

'Such as?' I asked.

'Nothing very definite,' he admitted. 'But when one puts them all together . . . After all, there's no smoke without—'

'All right, let's have it,' I invited him.

'I think,' he said, with impressive earnestness, 'I think we are on the track of something *big* here. Very like something that will at last stir people's consciences to the iniquities which are practised under the cloak of scientific research. Do you know what I think is happening on our very doorstep?'

'I'll buy it,' I told him, patiently.

'I think we have to deal with a super-vivisectionist!' he said, wagging a dramatic finger at me.

I frowned. 'I don't get that,' I told him. 'A thing is either vivi- or it isn't. Super-vivi- just doesn't—'

'Tcha!' said Alfred. At least, it was that kind of noise. 'What I mean is that we are up against a man who is outraging nature, abusing God's creatures, wantonly distorting the forms of animals until they are no longer recognisable, or only in parts, as what they were before he started distorting them,' he announced, involvedly.

At this point I began to get a line on the truly Alfredian theory that was being propounded this time. His imagination had got its teeth well in, and, though later events were to show that it was not biting quite deeply enough, I laughed:

'I see it,' I said, 'I've read *The Island of Dr Moreau*, too. You expect to go up to the Grange and be greeted by a horse walking on its hind legs and discussing the weather; or perhaps you hope a super-dog will open the door to you, and inquire your name?

'A thrilling idea, Alfred. But this is real life, you know. Since there has been a complaint, we must try to investigate it, but I'm afraid you're going to be dreadfully disappointed, old man, if you're looking forward to going into a house filled with the sickly fumes of ether and hideous with the cries of tortured animals. Just come off it a bit, Alfred. Come down to earth.'

But Alfred was not to be deflated so easily. His fantasies were an important part of his life, and, while he was a little irritated by my discerning the source of his inspiration, he was not quenched. Instead, he went on turning the thing over in his mind, and adding a few extra touches to it here and there.

'Why turtles?' I heard him mutter. 'It only seems to make it more complicated, to choose reptiles.'

He contemplated that for some moments, then he added:

'Arms. Arms and hands! Now where on earth would he get a pair of arms from?'

His eyes grew still larger and more excited as he thought about that.

'Now, now! Keep a hold on it!' I advised him.

All the same, it was an awkward, uneasy kind of question . . .

The following afternoon Alfred and I presented ourselves at the lodge of Membury Grange, and gave our names to the suspicious-looking man who lived there to guard the entrance. He shook his head to indicate that we hadn't a hope of approaching more closely, but he did pick up the telephone.

I had a somewhat unworthy hope that his discouraging attitude might be confirmed. The thing ought, of course, to be followed up, if only to pacify the villagers, but I could have wished that Alfred had had longer to go off the boil. At present, his agitation and expectation were, if anything, increased. The fancies of Poe and Zola are mild compared with the products of Alfred's imagination powered by suitable fuel. All night long, it seemed, the most horrid nightmares had galloped through his sleep, and he was now in a vein where such phrases as the 'wanton torturing of our dumb friends' by 'the fiendish wielders of the knife', and 'the shuddering cries of a million quivering victims ascending to high heaven' came tripping off his tongue automatically. It was awkward. If I had not agreed to accompany him, he would certainly have gone alone, in which case he would be likely to come to some kind of harm on account of the generalised accusations of mayhem, mutilation and sadism with which he would undoubtedly open the conversation.

In the end I had persuaded him that his course would be to keep his eyes cunningly open for more evidence while I conducted the interview. Later, if he was not satisfied, he would be able to say his piece. I just had to hope that he would be able to withstand the internal pressure.

The guardian turned back to us from the telephone, wearing a surprised expression.

'He says as he'll see you!' he told us, as though not quite certain he had heard aright. 'You'll find him in the new wing—that red-brick part, there.'

The new wing, into which the poaching Bill had spied, turned out to be much bigger than I had expected. It covered a ground-area quite as large as that of the original house, but was only one storey high. A door in the end of it opened as we drove up, and a tall, loosely-clad figure with an untidy beard stood waiting for us there.

'Good Lord!' I said, as we approached. 'So that was why we got in so easily! I'd no idea you were *that* Dixon. Who'd have thought it?'

'Come to that,' he retorted, 'you seem to be in a surprising occupation for a man of intelligence, yourself.'

I remembered my companion.

'Alfred,' I said, 'I'd like to introduce you to Doctor Dixon—once a poor usher who tried to teach me something about biology at school, but later, by popular repute, the inheritor of millions, or thereabouts.'

Alfred looked suspicious. This was obviously wrong: a move towards fraternisation with the enemy at the very outset! He nodded ungraciously, and did not offer to shake hands.

'Come in!' Dixon invited.

He showed us into a comfortable study-cum-office which tended to confirm the rumours of his inheritance. I sat down in a magnificent easy-chair.

'You'll very likely have gathered from your watchman that we're here in an official way,' I said. 'So perhaps it would be better to get the business over before we celebrate the reunion. It'd be a kindness to relieve the strain on my friend Alfred.'

Doctor Dixon nodded, and cast a speculative glance at Alfred who had no intention of compromising himself by sitting down.

'I'll give you the report just as we had it,' I told him, and proceeded to do so. When I reached a description of the turtle-like creatures he looked somewhat relieved.

'Oh, so that's what happened to them,' he said.

'Ah!' cried Alfred, his voice going up into a squeak with excitement. 'So you admit it! You admit that you are responsible for those two unhappy creatures!'

Dixon looked at him, wonderingly.

'I *was* responsible for them—but I didn't know they were unhappy: how did you?'

Alfred disregarded the question.

'That's what we want,' he squeaked. 'He admits that he—'

'Alfred,' I told him coldly. 'Do be quiet, and stop dancing about. Let me get on with it.'

I got on with it for a few more sentences, but Alfred was building up too much pressure to hold. He cut right in:

'Where—where did you get the arms? Just tell me where *they* came from?' he demanded, with deadly meaning.

'Your friend seems a little over—er, a little dramatic,' remarked Doctor Dixon.

'Look, Alfred,' I said severely, 'just let me get finished, will you? You can introduce your note of ghoulery later on.'

When I ended, it was with an excuse that seemed necessary. I said to Dixon: 'I'm sorry to intrude on you with all this, but you see how we stand. When supported allegations are laid before us, we have no choice but to investigate. Obviously this is something quite out of the usual run, but I'm sure you'll be able to clear it up satisfactorily for us. And now, Alfred,' I added, turning to him, 'I believe you have a question or two to ask, but do try to remember that our host's name is Dixon, and not Moreau.'

Alfred leapt, as from a slipped leash.

'What I want to know is the meaning, the reason and the method of these outrages against nature. I demand to be told by what right this man considers himself justified in turning normal creatures into unnatural mockeries of natural forms.'

Doctor Dixon nodded gently.

'A comprehensive inquiry—though not too comprehensibly expressed,' he said. 'I deplore the loose, recurrent use of the word "nature"—and would point out that the word "unnatural" is a vulgarism which does not even make sense. Obviously, if a thing has been done at all it was in someone's nature to do it, and in the nature of the material to accept whatever was done. One can act only within the limits of one's nature: that is an axiom.'

'A lot of hairsplitting isn't going to—' began Alfred, but Dixon continued smoothly:

'Nevertheless, I think I understand you to mean that my nature has prompted me to use certain material in a manner which your prejudices do not approve. Would that be right?'

'There may be lots of ways of putting it, but I call it vivisection—*vivisection!*' said Alfred, relishing the word like a good curse. 'You may have a licence. But there have been things going on here that will require a very convincing explanation indeed to stop us taking the matter to the police.'

Doctor Dixon nodded.

'I rather thought you might have some such idea: and I'd prefer you did not. Before long, the whole thing will be announced by me, and become public knowledge. Meanwhile, I want at least two, possibly three, months to get my findings ready for publication. When I have explained, I think you will understand my position better.'

He paused, thoughtfully eyeing Alfred who did not look like a man intending to understand anything. He went on:

'The crux of this is that I have not, as you are suspecting, either grafted, or readjusted, nor in any way distorted living forms. I have *built* them.'

For a moment, neither of us grasped the significance of that—though Alfred thought he had it.

'Ha! You can quibble,' he said, 'but there had to be a basis. You must have had some kind of living animal to start with—and one which you wickedly mutilated to produce these horrors.'

But Dixon shook his head.

'No, I mean what I said. I have *built*—and then I have induced a kind of life into what I have built.'

We gaped. I said, uncertainly: 'Are you really claiming that you can create a living creature?'

'Pooh!' he said. 'Of course I can, so can you. Even Alfred here can do that, with the help of a female of the species. What I am telling you is that I can animate the inert because I have found how to induce the—or, at any rate, a—life-force.'

The lengthy pause that followed that was broken at last by Alfred.

'I don't believe it,' he said, loudly. 'It isn't possible that you, here in this one-eyed village, should have solved the mystery of life. You're just trying to hoax us because you're afraid of what we shall do.'

Dixon smiled calmly.

'I said that I had found *a* life-force. There may be dozens of other kinds for all I know. I can understand that it's difficult for you to believe; but, after all, why not? Someone was bound to find one of them somewhere sooner or later. What's more surprising to me is that this one wasn't discovered before.'

But Alfred was not to be soothed.

'I don't believe it,' he repeated. 'Nor will anybody else unless you produce proofs—if you can.'

'Of course,' agreed Dixon. 'Who would take it on trust? Though I'm afraid that when you examine my present specimens you may find the construction a little crude at first. Your friend, Nature, puts in such a lot of unnecessary work that can be simplified out.

'Of course, in the matter of arms, that seems to worry you so much, if I could have obtained real arms immediately after the death of the owner I might have been able to use them—I'm not sure whether it wouldn't have been more trouble though. However, such things are not usually handy, and the building of simplified parts is not really diffi-cult—a mixture of engineering, chemistry and common sense. Indeed, it has been quite possible for some time, but without the means of animating them it was scarcely worth doing. One day they may be made finely enough to replace a lost limb, but a very complicated technique will have to be evolved before that can be done.

'As for your suspicion that my specimens suffer, Mr Weston, I assure you that they are coddled—they have cost me a great deal of money and work. And, in any case, it would be difficult for you to prosecute me for cruelty to an animal hitherto unheard of, with habits unknown.'

'I am not convinced,' said Alfred, stoutly.

The poor fellow was, I think, too upset by the threat to his theory for the true magnitude of Dixon's claim to reach him.

'Then, perhaps a demonstration . . . ?' Dixon suggested. 'If you will follow me . . .'

*   *   *

Bill's peeping exploit had prepared us for the sight of the steel-barred cages in the laboratory, but not for many of the other things we found there—one of them was the smell.

Doctor Dixon apologised as we choked and gasped:

'I forgot to warn you about the preservatives.'

'It's reassuring to know that that's all they are,' I said, between coughs.

The room must have been getting on for a hundred feet in length, and about thirty high. Bill had certainly seen precious little through his chink in the curtain, and I stared in amazement at the quantities of apparatus gathered there. There was a rough division into sections: chemistry in one corner, bench and lathes in another, electrical apparatus grouped at one end and so on. In one of several bays stood an operating table, with cases of instruments to hand; Alfred's eyes widened at the sight of it, and an expression of triumph began to enliven his face. In another bay there was more the suggestion of a sculptor's studio, with moulds and casts lying about on tables. Farther on were large presses, and sizeable electric furnaces, but most of the gear other than the simplest conveyed little to me.

'No cyclotron, no electron-microscope; otherwise, a bit of everything,' I remarked.

'You're wrong there. There's the electron—Hullo! Your friend's off.'

Alfred had kind of homed at the operating-table. He was peering intently all around and under it, presumably in the hope of bloodstains. We walked after him.

'Here's one of the chief primers of that ghastly imagination of yours,' Dixon said. He opened a drawer, took out an arm and laid it on the operating table. 'Take a look at that.'

The thing was a waxy yellow, and without other colouring. In shape, it did have a close resemblance to a human arm, but when I looked closely at the hand, I saw that it was smooth, unmarked by whorls or lines: nor did it have fingernails.

'Not worth bothering about at this stage,' said Dixon, watching me.

Nor was it a whole arm: it was cut off short between the elbow and the shoulder.

'What's that?' Alfred inquired, pointing to a protruding metal rod.

'Stainless steel,' Dixon told him. 'Much quicker and less expensive than making matrices for pressing bone forms. When I get standardised I'll probably go to plastic bones: one ought to be able to save weight there.'

Alfred was looking worriedly disappointed again; that arm was convincingly non-vivisectional.

'But why an arm? Why any of this?' he demanded, with a wave that largely included the whole room.

'In the order of askings: an arm—or, rather, a hand—because it is the most useful tool ever evolved, and I certainly could not think of a better. And "any of this" because once I had hit upon the basic secret I took a fancy to build as my proof the perfect creature—or as near that as one's finite mind can reach.

'The turtle-like creatures were an early step. They had enough brain to live, and produce reflexes, but not enough for constructive thought. It wasn't necessary.'

'You mean that your "perfect creature" does have constructive thought?' I asked.

'She has a brain as good as ours, and slightly larger,' he said. 'Though, of course, she needs experience—education. Still, as the brain is already fully developed, it learns much more quickly than a child's would.'

'May we see it—her?' I asked.

He sighed regretfully.

'Everyone always wants to jump straight to the finished product. All right then. But first we will have a little demonstration—I'm afraid your friend is still unconvinced.'

He led across towards the surgical instrument cases and opened a preserving cupboard there. From it he took a shapeless white mass which he laid on the operating table. Then he wheeled it towards the electric apparatus farther up the room. Beneath the pallid, sagging object I saw a hand protruding.

'Good heavens!' I exclaimed. 'Bill's "bolster with hands"!'

'Yes—he wasn't entirely wrong, though from your account he laid it on a bit. This little fellow is really my chief assistant. He's got all the essential parts; alimentary, vascular, nervous, respiratory. He can, in fact, live. But it isn't a very exciting existence for him—he's a kind of testing motor for trying out newly-made appendages.'

While he busied himself with some electrical connections he added:

'If you, Mr Weston, would care to examine the specimen in any way, short of harming it, to convince yourself that it is not alive at present, please do.'

Alfred approached the white mass. He peered through his glasses at it closely, and with distaste. He prodded it with a tentative forefinger.

'So the basis is electrical?' I said to Dixon.

He picked up a bottle of some grey concoction and measured a little into a beaker.

'It may be. On the other hand, it may be chemical. You don't think I am going to let you into *all* my secrets, do you?'

When he had finished his preparations he said:

'Satisfied, Mr Weston? I'd rather not be accused later on of having shown you a conjuring trick.'

'It doesn't seem to be alive,' Alfred admitted, cautiously.

We watched Dixon attach several electrodes to it. Then he carefully chose three spots on its surface and injected at each from a syringe containing a pale-blue liquid. Next, he sprayed the whole form twice from different atomisers. Finally, he closed four or five switches in rapid succession.

'Now,' he said, with a slight smile, 'we wait for five minutes—which you may spend, if you like, in deciding which, or how many, of my actions were critical.'

After three minutes the flaccid mass began to pulsate feebly. Gradually the movement increased until gentle, rhythmic undulations were running through it. Presently it half-sagged or rolled to one side, exposing the hand that had been hidden beneath it. I saw the fingers of the hand tense, and try to clutch at the smooth table-top.

I think I cried out. Until it actually happened, I had been unable to believe that it would. Now some part of the meaning of the thing came flooding in on me. I grabbed Dixon's arm.

'Man!' I said. 'If you were to do that to a dead body . . .'

But he shook his head.

'No. It doesn't work. I've tried. One is justified in calling this life— I think . . . But in some way it's a different kind of life. I don't at all understand why . . .'

Different kind or not, I knew that I must be looking at the seed of a revolution, with potentialities beyond imagination . . .

And all the time that fool Alfred kept on poking around the thing as if it were a sideshow at a circus, and he was out to make sure that no one was putting anything across him with mirrors, or working it with bits of string.

It served him right when he got a couple of hundred volts through his fingers . . .

'And now,' said Alfred, when he had satisfied himself that at least the grosser forms of deception were ruled out, 'now we'd like to see this ''perfect creature'' you spoke about.'

He still seemed as far as ever from realising the marvel he had witnessed. He was convinced that an offence of some kind was being committed, and he intended to find the evidence that would assign it to its proper category.

'Very well,' agreed Dixon. 'By the way, I call her Una. No name I could think of seemed quite adequate, but she is certainly the first of her kind, so Una she is.'

He led us along the room to the last and largest of the row of cages. Standing a little back from the bars, he called the occupant forward.

I don't know what I expected to see—nor quite what Alfred was hoping for. But neither of us had breath for comment when we did see what lumbered towards us.

Dixon's 'Perfect Creature' was a more horrible grotesquerie than I had ever imagined in life or dreams.

Picture, if you can, a dark conical carapace of some slightly glossy material. The rounded-off peak of the cone stood well over six feet from the ground: the base was four foot six or more in diameter; and the whole thing supported on three short, cylindrical legs. There were four arms, parodies of human arms, projecting from joints about halfway up. Eyes, set some six inches below the apex, were regarding us steadily from beneath horny lids. For a moment I felt close to hysterics.

Dixon looked at the thing with pride.

'Visitors to see you, Una,' he told it.

The eyes turned to me, and then back to Alfred. One of them blinked, with a click from its lid as it closed. A deep, reverberant voice emerged from no obvious source.

'At last! I've been asking you long enough,' it said.

'Good God!' said Alfred. 'That appalling thing can talk?'

The steady gaze dwelt upon him.

'That one will do. I like his glass eyes,' rumbled the voice.

'Be quiet, Una. This isn't what you think,' Dixon interposed. 'I must ask you,' he added to us, but looking at Alfred, 'to be careful in your comments. Una naturally lacks the ordinary background of experience, but she is aware of her distinction—and of her several physical superiorities. She has a somewhat short temper, and nothing is going to be gained by offending her. It is natural that you should find her appearance a little surprising at first, but I will explain.'

A lecturing note crept into his voice.

'After I had discovered my method of animation, my first inclination was to construct an approximately anthropoid form as a convincing demonstration. On second thoughts, however, I decided against mere imitation. I resolved to proceed functionally and logically, remedying certain features which seemed to me poorly or weakly designed in man and other existing creatures. It also proved necessary later to make a few modifications for technical and constructional reasons. However, in general, Una is the result of my resolve.' He paused, looking fondly at the monstrosity.

'I—er—you did say "*logically*"?' I inquired.

Alfred paused for some time before making his comment. He went on staring at the creature which still kept its eyes fixed on him. One could almost see him causing what he likes to think of as his better nature to override mere prejudice. He now rose nobly above his earlier, unsympathetic remark.

'I do not consider it proper to confine so large an animal in such restricted quarters,' he announced.

One of the horny eyelids clicked again as it blinked.

'I like him. He means well. He will do,' the great voice rumbled.

Alfred wilted a little. After a long experience of patronising dumb friends, he found it disconcerting to be confronted by a creature that not only spoke, but patronised him as it did so. He returned its steady stare uneasily.

Dixon, disregarding the interruption, resumed:

'Probably the first thing that will strike you is that Una has no distinct head. That was one of my earliest rearrangements; the normal head is too exposed and vulnerable. The eyes should be carried high, of course, but there is no need whatever for a semi-detached head.

'But in eliminating the head, there was sight to be considered. I therefore gave her three eyes, two of which you can see now, and one which is round the back—though, properly speaking, she has no back. Thus she is easily able to look and focus in any direction without the complicated device of a semi-rotatory head.

'Her general shape almost ensures that any falling or projected object would glance off the reinforced plastic carapace, but it seemed wise to me to insulate the brain from shock as much as possible by putting it where you might expect the stomach, I was thus able to put the stomach higher and allow for a more convenient disposition of the intestines.'

'How does it eat?' I put in.

'Her mouth is round the other side,' he said shortly. 'Now, I have to admit that at first glance the provision of four arms might give an impression of frivolity. However, as I said before, the hand is the perfect tool—*if* it is the right size. So you will see that Una's upper pair are delicate and finely moulded, while the lower are heavily muscular.

'Her respiration may interest you, too. I have used a flow principle. She inhales here, exhales there. An improvement, you must admit, on our own rather disgusting system.

'As regards the general design, she unfortunately turned out to be considerably heavier than I had expected—slightly over one ton, in fact—and to support that I had to modify my original plan somewhat. I redesigned the legs and feet rather after the pattern of the elephant's so as to spread the weight, but I'm afraid it is not altogether satisfactory; something will have to be done in the later models to reduce the overall weight.

'The three-legged principle was adopted because it is obvious that the biped must waste quite a lot of muscular energy in merely keeping its balance, and a tripod is not only efficient, but more easily adaptable to uneven surfaces than a four-legged support.

'As regards the reproductory system—'

'Excuse me interrupting,' I said, 'but with a plastic carapace, and stainless steel bones I don't—er—quite see—'

'A matter of glandular balance: regulation of the personality. Something had to be done there, though I admit that I'm not quite satisfied that I have done it the best way. I suspect that an approach on parthenogenetic lines would have been ... However, there it is. And I have promised her a mate. I must say I find it a fascinating speculation ...'

'He will do,' interrupted the rumbling voice, while the creature continued to gaze fixedly at Alfred.

'Of course,' Dixon went on to us, a little hurriedly, 'Una has never seen herself to know what she looks like. She probably thinks she—'

'I know what I want,' said the deep voice, firmly and loudly, 'I want—'

'Yes, yes,' Dixon interposed, also loudly. 'I'll explain to you about that later.'

'But I want—' the voice repeated.

'Will you be quiet!' Dixon shouted fiercely.

The creature gave a slight rumbling protest, but desisted.

Alfred drew himself up with the air of one who after communing seriously with his principles is forced into speech.

'I cannot approve of this,' he announced. 'I will concede that this creature may be your own creation—nevertheless, once created it becomes, in my opinion, entitled to the same safeguards as any other dumb—er, as any other creature.

'I say nothing whatever about your application of your discovery—except to say that it seems to me that you have behaved like an irresponsible child let loose with modelling clay, and that you have produced an unholy—and I use that word advisedly—unholy mess; a monstrosity, a perversion. However, I say nothing about that.

'What I do say is that in law this creature can be regarded simply as an unfamiliar species of animal. I intend to report that in my professional opinion it is being confined in too small a cage, and clearly without proper opportunities for exercise. I am not able to judge whether it is being adequately nourished, but it is easy to perceive that it has needs that are not being met. Twice already when it has attempted to express them to us you have intimidated it.'

'Alfred,' I put in, 'don't you think that perhaps—' but I was cut short by the creature thrumming like a double bass.

'I think he's wonderful! The way his glass eyes flash! I want him!' It sighed in a kind of deep vibrato that ran along the floor. The sound certainly was extremely mournful, and Alfred's one-track mind pounced on it as additional evidence.

'If that is not the plaint of an unhappy creature,' he said, stepping closer to the cage, 'then I have never—'

'Look out!' shouted Dixon, jumping forward.

One of the creature's hands made a darting snatch through the bars. Simultaneously Dixon caught him by the shoulders, and pulled him back. There was a rending of cloth, and three buttons pattered on to the linoleum.

'Phew!' said Dixon.

For the first time, Alfred looked a little alarmed.

'What—?' he began.

A deep, threatening sound from the cage obliterated the rest of it.

'Give him to me! I want him!' rumbled the voice, angrily.

All four arms caught hold of the bars. Two of them rattled the gate violently. The two visible eyes were fixed unwaveringly on Alfred. He began to show signs of reorientating his outlook. His own eyes opened a little more widely behind his glasses.

'Er—it—it doesn't mean—?' he started, incredulously.

'Gimme!' bellowed Una, stamping from one foot to another, and shaking the building as she did so.

Dixon was regarding his achievement with some concern.

'I wonder—I wonder, could I have overdone the hormones a bit?' he speculated, thoughtfully.

Alfred had begun to get to grips with the idea now. He backed a little farther away from the cage. The move did not have a good effect on Una.

'Gimme!' she cried, like a kind of sepulchral public-address system. 'Gimme! Gimme!'

It was an intimidating sound.

'Mightn't it be better if we—?' I suggested.

'Perhaps, in the circumstances—' Dixon agreed.

'Yes!' said Alfred, quite decisively.

The pitch on which Una operated made it difficult to be certain of the finer shades of feelings; the window-rattling sound that occurred behind us as we moved off might have expressed anger, or anguish, or both. We increased our pace a little.

'Alfred!' called a voice like a disconsolate foghorn. 'I want Alfred!'

Alfred cast a backward glance, and stepped out a trifle more smartly.

There was a thump which rattled the bars and shook the building.

I looked round to see Una in the act of retiring to the back of her cage with the obvious intention of making another onslaught. We beat it for the door. Alfred was first through.

A thunderous crash sounded at the other end of the room. As Dixon was closing the door behind us I had a glimpse of Una carrying bars and furnishings before her like a runaway bus.

'I think we shall need some help with her,' Dixon said.

Small sparkles of perspiration were standing on Alfred's brow.

'You—you don't think it might be better if we were to—?' he began.

'No,' said Dixon. 'She'd see you through the windows.'

'Oh,' said Alfred, unhappily.

Dixon led the way into a large sitting-room, and made for the telephone. He gave urgent messages to the fire-brigade and the police.

'I don't think there's anything we can do till they get here,' he said, as he put the receiver down. 'The lab. wing will probably hold her all right if she isn't tantalised any more.'

'Tantalised! I like that—!' Alfred started to protest, but Dixon went on:

'Luckily, being where she is, she couldn't see the door; so the odds are that she can have no idea of the purpose or nature of doors. What's worrying me most is the damage she's doing in there. Just listen!'

We did listen for some moments to the muffled sounds of smashing, splintering and rending. Among it there was occasionally a mournful disyllabic boom which might, or might not, have been the word 'Alfred'.

Dixon's expression became more anguished as the noise continued unabated.

'All my records! All the work of years is in there,' he said, bitterly. 'Your Society's going to have to pay plenty for this, I warn you—but that won't give me back my records. She was always perfectly docile until your friend excited her—never a moment's trouble with her.'

Alfred began to protest again, but was interrupted by the sound of something massive being overturned with a thunderous crash, followed by a noise like a waterfall of broken glass.

'Gimme Alfred! I want Alfred!' demanded the stentorian voice.

Alfred half rose, and then sat down agitatedly on the edge of his chair. His eyes flicked nervously hither and thither. He displayed a tendency to bite his fingernails.

'Ah!' said Dixon, with a suddenness which started both of us. 'Ah, that must have been it! I must have calculated the hormone requirement on the overall weight—*including* the carapace. Of course! What a ridiculous slip to make! Tch-tch! I should've done much better to keep to the original parthenogen—Good heavens!'

The crash which caused his exclamation brought us all to our feet, and across to the door.

Una had discovered the way out of the wing, all right, and come through it like a bulldozer. Door, frame and part of the brickwork had come with her. At the moment she was stumbling about amid the resulting mess. Dixon didn't hesitate.

'Quick! Upstairs—that'll beat her,' he said.

At the same instant Una spotted us, and let out a boom. We sprinted across the hall for the staircase. Initial mobility was our advantage; a freight like Una's takes appreciable time to get under way. I fled up the flight with Dixon just ahead of me and, I imagined, Alfred just behind. However, I was not quite right there. I don't know whether Alfred had been momentarily transfixed, or had fumbled his takeoff, but when I was at the top I looked back to see him still only a few steps up, with Una thundering in pursuit like a rocket-assisted car of Juggernaut.

Alfred kept on coming, though. But so did Una. She may not have been familiar with stairs, nor designed to use them. But she tackled them, for all that. She even got about five or six steps up before they collapsed under her. Alfred, by then more than halfway up, felt them fell away beneath his feet. He gave a shout as he lost his balance. Then, clawing wildly at the air, he fell backwards.

Una put in as neat a four-armed catch as you could hope to see.

'What co-ordination!' Dixon, behind me, murmured admiringly.

'Help!' bleated Alfred. 'Help! Help!'

'Aah!' boomed Una, in a kind of deep diapason of satisfaction. She backed off a little, with a crunching of timbers.

'Keep calm!' Dixon advised Alfred. 'Don't do anything that might startle her.'

Alfred, embraced by three arms, and patted affectionately by the fourth, made no immediate reply.

There was a pause for assessment of the situation.

'Well,' I said, 'we ought to do something. Can't we entice her somehow?'

'It's difficult to know what will distract the triumphant female in her moment of success,' observed Dixon.

Una set up a sort of—of—well, if you can imagine an elephant contentedly crooning . . .

'Help!' Alfred bleated again. 'She's—*ow!*'

'Calm, calm!' repeated Dixon. 'There's probably no real danger. After all, she's a mammal—mostly, that is. Now if she were a quite different kind like, say, a female spider—'

'I don't think I'd let her overhear about female spiders just now,' I suggested. 'Isn't there a favourite food, or something, we could tempt her with?'

Una was swaying Alfred back and forth in three arms, and prodding him inquisitively with the forefinger of the fourth. Alfred struggled.

'Damn it. Can't you *do* something?' he demanded.

'Oh, Alfred! Alfred!' she reproved him, in a kind of besotted rumble.

'Well,' Dixon said, doubtfully, 'perhaps if we had some ice cream . . .'

There was a sound of brakes, and vehicles pulling up outside. Dixon ran swiftly along the landing, and I heard him trying to explain the situation through the window to the men outside. Presently he came back, accompanied by a fireman and his officer. When they looked down into the hall their eyes bulged.

'What we have to do is surround her without scaring her,' Dixon was explaining.

'Surround *that*?' said the officer dubiously. 'What in hell is it, anyway?'

'Never mind about that now,' Dixon told him, impatiently. 'If we can just get a few ropes on to her from different directions—'

'Help!' shouted Alfred again. He flailed about violently. Una clasped him more closely to her carapace, and chuckled dotingly. A peculiarly ghastly sound, I thought: it shook the firemen, too.

'For crysake—!' one of them began.

'Hurry up,' Dixon told him. 'We can drop the first rope over her from here.'

They both went back. The officer started shouting instructions to those below: he seemed to be having some difficulty in making himself clear. However, they both returned shortly with a coil of rope. And that fireman was good. He spun his noose gently, and dropped it as neatly as you like. When he pulled in, it was round the carapace, below the arms so that it could not slip up. He belayed to the newel-post at the top of the flight.

Una was still taken up with Alfred to the exclusion of everything else around her. If a hippopotamus could purr, with a kind of maudlin slant to it, I guess that's just about the sort of noise she'd make.

The front door opened quietly, and the faces of a number of assorted firemen and police appeared, all with their eyes popping and their jaws dropping. A moment later there was another bunch gaping into the hall from the sitting-room door, too. One fireman stepped forward nervously, and began to spin his rope. Unfortunately his cast touched a hanging light, and it fell short.

In that moment Una suddenly became aware of what went on.

'No!' she thundered. 'He's mine! I want him!'

The terrified ropeman hurled himself back through the door on top of his companions, and it shut behind him. Without turning, Una started off in the same direction. Our rope tightened, and we jumped aside. The newel-post was snapped away like a stick, and the rest of the rope went trailing after it. There was a forlorn cry from Alfred, still firmly clasped, but, luckily for him, on the side away from the line of progress. Una took the front door like a cruiser-tank. There was an almighty crash, a shower of wood and plaster and then a screen of dust through which came sounds of consternation, topped by a voice rumbling:

'He's mine! You shan't have him! He's mine!'

By the time we were able to reach the front windows Una was already clear of obstructions. We had an excellent view of her galloping down the drive at some ten miles an hour, towing, without apparent inconvenience, half a dozen or more firemen and police who clung grimly to the trailing rope.

Down at the lodge, the guardian had had the presence of mind to close the gates. He dived for personal cover into the bushes while she was still some yards away. Gates, however, meant nothing to Una; she kept on going. True, she staggered slightly at the impact, but they crumbled and went down before her. Alfred was waving his arms, and kicking out wildly; a faint wail for help floated back to us. The collection of police and firemen was towed into the jumbled ironwork, and tangled there. When Una passed out of sight round the corner there were only two dark figures left clinging heroically to the rope behind her.

There was a sound of engines starting up below. Dixon called to them to wait. We pelted down the back stairs, and were able to fling ourselves upon the fire-engine just as it moved off.

There was a pause to shift the obstructing ironwork in the gateway, then we were away down the lane in pursuit.

After a quarter-mile the trail led off down a steep, still narrower lane to one side. We had to abandon the fire-engine, and follow on foot.

At the bottom, there is—was—an old pack-horse bridge across the river. It sufficed, I believe, for several centuries of pack-horses, but nothing like Una at full gallop had entered into its builders' calculations. By the time we reached it, the central span was missing, and a fireman was helping a dripping policeman carry the limp form of Alfred up the bank.

'Where is she?' Dixon inquired, anxiously.

The fireman looked at him, and then pointed silently to the middle of the river.

'A crane. Send for a crane, at once!' Dixon demanded. But everyone was more interested in emptying the water out of Alfred, and getting to work on him.

The experience has, I'm afraid, permanently altered that air of bonhomie which used to exist between Alfred and all dumb friends. In the forth-coming welter of claims, counter-claims, cross-claims and civil and criminal charges in great variety, I shall be figuring only as a witness. But Alfred, who will, of course, appear in several capacities, says that when his charges of assault, abduction attempted—well, there are sev-eral more on the list; when they have been met, he intends to change his profession as he now finds it difficult to look a cow, or indeed, any female animal, in the eye without a bias that tends to impair his judgement.

A GOOD SHELLACKING

Stanislaw Lem
(translated from the Polish by Michael Kandel)

It was a mid-European writer who coined the term 'robot'—the Czech author Karel Capek in his play R.U.R. *(1921): the word derived from the Czech* robota, *meaning 'statute labour'—so it seems particularly apt that another writer from this part of the world, Polish-born Stanis-law Lem, should have created some of the best comic fantasies about man-like machines. Not that he is alone: the Americans Henry Kuttner* (Robots Have No Tales, *1952),* Ron Goulart *(The Robot in the Closet, 1981) and Isaac Asimov (who devised the famous 'Laws of Robotics') have all written stories about malfunctioning robots in comic situations; while the adventures of Douglas Adams's paranoid robot, Marvin, in his* Hitch Hiker's *Guide to the Galaxy* saga, *have earned the unpredictable machine a cult following.*

Stanislaw Lem (1921–) has been described as a 'mischievous mind-twister and leg-puller'. His robotic fables are a unique blend of comedy and philosophy. Born in Lwow in Poland, he originally planned a career in medicine, but after the turmoil of the Second World War when the country was overrun by the Nazis, he began to write sf in the Fifties and his books have since been translated into at least thirty languages and sold many millions of copies. The calibre of his work has earned him comparison with H. G. Wells; and Brian Ash in his Who's Who in Science Fiction *(1976) has called him 'The Titan of East European science fiction'. Among Lem's most popular works are* Solaris *(1961), which was filmed in 1971; the series of space operas about Pirx the pilot; and the Cyberiad cycle which focuses on his dual fascination with cybernetic technology and robot sociology. All of his work is infused with wild imagination and comic invention, and in Klapaucius the constructor, who features in 'A Good Shellacking' (1965), we have another character in the same mould as Dr Klopper, Captain Tichy, Professor Sadbottom and the rest of his extraordinary comic figures.*

*   *   *

Someone was knocking at the door of Klapaucius the constructor. He looked out and saw a potbellied machine on four short legs.

'Who are you and what do you want?' he asked.

'I'm a Machine to Grant Your Every Wish and have been sent here by your good friend and colleague, Trurl the Magnificent, as a gift.'

'A gift, eh?' replied Klapaucius, whose feelings for Trurl were mixed, to say the least. He was particularly irked by the phrase 'Trurl the Magnificent'. But after a little thought he said, 'All right, you can come in.'

He had it stand in the corner by the grandfather clock while he returned to his work, a squat machine on three short legs, which was almost completed—he was just putting on the finishing touches. After a while the Machine to Grant Your Every Wish cleared its throat and said:

'I'm still here.'

'I haven't forgotten you,' said Klapaucius, not looking up. After another while the machine cleared its throat again and asked:

'May I ask what you're making there?'

'Are you a Machine to Grant Wishes or a Machine to Ask Questions?' said Klapaucius, but added: 'I need some blue paint.'

'I hope it's the right shade,' said the machine, opening a door in its belly and pulling out a bucket of blue. Klapaucius dipped his brush in it without a word and began to paint. In the next few hours he needed sandpaper, some Carborundum, a brace and bit, white paint and one No. 5 screw, all of which the machine handed over on the spot. That evening he covered his work with a sheet of canvas, had dinner, then pulled up a chair opposite the machine and said:

'Now we'll see what you can do. So you say you can grant every wish . . .'

'Most every wish,' replied the machine modestly. 'The paint, sandpaper and No. 5 screw were satisfactory, I hope?'

'Quite, quite,' said Klapaucius. 'But now I have in mind something a bit more difficult. If you can't do it, I'll return you to your master with my kind thanks and a professional opinion.'

'All right, what is it?' asked the machine, fidgeting.

'A Trurl,' said Klapaucius. 'I want a Trurl, the spit and image of Trurl himself, so alike that no one could ever tell them apart.'

The machine muttered and hummed and finally said:

'Very well, I'll make you a Trurl. But please handle him with care— he is, after all, a truly magnificent constructor.'

'Oh but of course, you needn't worry about that,' said Klapaucius. 'Well, where is it?'

'What, right away?' said the machine. 'A Trurl isn't a No. 5 screw, you know. It'll take time.'

But it wasn't long at all before the door in the machine's belly opened and a Trurl climbed out. Klapaucius looked it up and down and around, touched it, tapped it, but there wasn't any doubt: here was a Trurl as much like the original Trurl as two peas in a pod. This Trurl squinted a little, unaccustomed to the light, but otherwise behaved in a perfectly normal fashion.

'Hello, Trurl!' said Klapaucius.

'Hello, Klapaucius! But wait, how did I get here?' Trurl answered, clearly bewildered.

'Oh, you just dropped in . . . You know, I haven't seen you in ages. How do you like my place?'

'Fine, fine . . . What do you have there under that canvas?'

'Nothing much. Won't you take a seat?'

'Well, I really ought to be going. It's getting dark . . .'

'Don't rush off, you just got here!' protested Klapaucius. 'And you haven't seen my cellar yet.'

'Your cellar?'

'Yes, you should find it most interesting. This way . . .'

And Klapaucius put an arm around Trurl and led him to the cellar, where he tripped him, pinned him down and quickly tied him up, then took out a big crowbar and began to wallop the daylights out of him. Trurl howled, called for help, cursed, begged for mercy, but Klapaucius didn't stop and the blows rang out and echoed in the dark and empty night.

'Ouch! Ouch!! Why are you beating me?!' yelled Trurl, cowering.

'It gives me pleasure,' explained Klapaucius, swinging back. 'You should try it sometime, Trurl!'

And he landed him one on the head, which boomed like a drum.

'If you don't let me go at once, I'll tell the King and he'll have you thrown in his deepest dungeon!!' screamed Trurl.

'Oh no he won't. And do you know why?' asked Klapaucius, sitting down for a moment to catch his breath.

'Tell me,' said Trurl, glad of the reprieve.

'Because you're not the real Trurl. Trurl, you see, built a Machine to Grant Your Every Wish and sent it here as a gift; to test it out, I had to make you! And now I'm going to knock off your head, put it at the foot of my bed and use it for a bootjack.'

'You monster! Why are you doing this to me?'

'I already told you: it gives me pleasure. But enough of this idle chatter!' And Klapaucius got up and this time picked up a huge bludgeon in both hands—but Trurl cried out:

'Wait! Stop! I have something to tell you!!'

'I wonder what you could possibly tell me to keep me from using your head as a bootjack,' replied Klapaucius.

Trurl quickly yelled:

'I'm not any Trurl from a machine! I'm the real Trurl—I only wanted to find out what you've been doing lately behind closed doors and drawn curtains, so I built a machine, hid in its belly and had it take me here, pretending to be a gift!'

'Come now, that's an obvious fabrication and not even clever!' said Klapaucius, hefting his bludgeon. 'Don't waste your breath, I can see right through you. You came out of a machine that grants wishes, and if it manufactures paint and sandpaper, a brace and bit, and a No. 5 screw, it can surely manufacture you!'

'I had all that prepared beforehand in its belly!' cried Trurl. 'It wasn't hard to anticipate what you'd need in your work! I swear I'm telling the truth!'

'Are you trying to tell me that my good friend and colleague, Trurl the Magnificent, is nothing but a common sneak? No, that I will never believe!' replied Klapaucius. 'Take *that!*'

And he let him have it.

'That's for slandering my good friend Trurl! And take *that!* And *that!*'

And he let him have it again, and again, clubbing and clobbering until his arm was too tired to club or clobber anymore.

'Now I'll have a little nap and rest up,' said Klapaucius, throwing aside the bludgeon. 'But don't you worry, I'll be back . . .' And he left, and soon was snoring so loud you could hear it even in the cellar. Trurl writhed and twisted until he loosened his bonds enough to slip off the knots, got up, crept back to the machine, climbed inside and took off for home at a gallop. Klapaucius meanwhile was watching the escape from his bedroom window, pressing a hand over his mouth to keep from laughing out loud. The next day he went to pay Trurl a visit. It was a gloomy and silent Trurl that let him in. The room was dark, but even so, Klapaucius could see that Trurl's person bore the marks of a good shellacking—though it was apparent that Trurl had gone to some trouble to touch up the scratches and hammer out the dents.

'Why so gloomy?' asked a cheerful Klapaucius. 'I came to thank you for the nice gift—what a shame, though, it ran off while I slept, and in such a hurry that it left the door open!'

'It seems to me,' snapped Trurl, 'that you somewhat misused, or should I say abused, my gift. Oh, you needn't bother to explain, the machine told me everything. You had it make me, *me*, then lured me, I mean the copy of me, to the cellar, where you beat it unmercifully! And after this great insult to my person, after this act of the blackest ingratitude, you dare show your face here as if nothing happened! What do you have to say for yourself?'

'I really don't understand why you're so angry,' said Klapaucius. 'It's true I had the machine make a copy of you, and I must say it was absolutely perfect, an amazing likeness. As far as the beating goes, well, your machine must have exaggerated a little—I did give the artificial Trurl a poke or two, but only to see if it was well made, and perhaps also to test its reflexes, which were quite good, by the way. It turned out to be very much on its toes, and even tried to argue that it was really you, can you imagine—? Of course I didn't believe it, but then it swore the gift wasn't a gift at all, but some sort of low and underhanded trick. Well, I had to defend the honour of my good friend, you understand, so I thrashed it some for slandering you so shamelessly. On the other hand I found it to be extremely intelligent; so you see, Trurl, it resembled you mentally as well as physically. You are indeed a great and magnificent constructor, which is precisely what I came to tell you so early in the morning!'

'Well, yes, in that case,' said Trurl, considerably appeased. 'Though your use of the Machine to Grant Your Every Wish was not, I would say, the most fortunate . . .'

'Oh yes, one other thing I wanted to ask,' said Klapaucius, all innocence. 'What did you do with the artificial Trurl? Could I see it?'

'It was beside itself with rage,' explained Trurl. 'It said it would ambush you by that mountain pass near your house and tear you limb from limb. I tried to reason with it, but it called me names, ran out into the night and started putting together all sorts of booby traps for you— and so, dear Klapaucius, though you had insulted me, I remembered our old friendship and decided to remove this threat to your life and limb. Hence I had to disassemble it . . .'

And he touched a few nuts and bolts on the floor with his shoe, and sighed.

Whereupon they exchanged kind words, shook hands and parted the best of friends.

From that time on, Trurl did nothing but tell everyone how he had given Klapaucius a Machine to Grant Your Every Wish, how then Klapaucius had insulted him by having it make an artificial Trurl, which he proceeded to beat black-and-blue; how then this excellently constructed copy of the great constructor made clever lies to save itself, and finally managed to escape while Klapaucius slept, and how Trurl himself, the real Trurl, eventually had to disassemble the artificial Trurl to protect his good friend and colleague from its vengeance. Trurl told this story so often and at such length, elaborating on his glorious achievement (and never failing to call on Klapaucius as a witness), that it reached the ears of the Royal Court at last, and now no one spoke of Trurl other than with the utmost respect, though not long ago he had been commonly called the Constructor of the World's Stupidest Computer. When Klapaucius heard, one day, that the King himself had rewarded Trurl handsomely and decorated him with the Order of the Great Parallax, he threw up his hands and cried:

'What? Here I was able to see through his little game and gave him so good a shellacking for it that he had to sneak home in the middle of the night and patch himself up, and even then he looked a sight! And for that they decorate him, praise him, shower him with riches? *O tempora, O mores!* . . .'

Furious, he went home, locked himself in and drew the blinds. He too had been working on a Machine to Grant Your Every Wish, only Trurl had beaten him to it.

FROM GUSTIBLE'S PLANET

Cordwainer Smith

The first alien invaders to appear in science fiction were the gigantic Martians who descended on the Earth in H. G. Wells's The War of the Worlds *(1898) and having set about exterminating mankind fell victim to the common cold germ. Despite the horror of these creatures, there was something almost comical about the manner of their demise, and although brutal conquerors from space have become almost a cliché in sf, they have also featured in a number of outstanding comic tales by writers like Fredric Brown ('Arena', 1944), John Wyndham ('Dumb Martian', 1952), Eric Frank Russell ('The Waitabits', 1955) and Philip K. Dick (in his novel,* Our Friends From Frolix-8, *1970). However, in my estimation 'From Gustible's Planet' (1963), with its aliens resembling oversize ducks who turn up not to destroy Earth but feed on its cuisine, takes the top award in this category.*

Cordwainer Smith (1913–1966) was the pen-name of Paul Myron Anthony Linebarger, who spent much of his early life in China before entering on a career as political scientist, military adviser and, finally, sf writer. He read a great deal of Chinese literature and, not surprisingly, many of the nation's traditions have a habit of finding their way into his stories—as the reader will notice in 'From Gustible's Planet'. Much of his sf falls into his 'Instrumentality of Mankind' universe, describing men and women in a far future where people live longer (400 years and more), can travel almost anywhere instantaneously, yet still find their ordered, aesthetic and baroque lives being interrupted by events of high comedy. The duck-like Apicians in this story are the ancestors of the inhabitants of Discworld and many of today's other comic fantasy kingdoms: but what lies in store for them on Earth—as Wells's Martians discovered—is equally full of surprises . . .

*   *   *

Shortly after the celebration of the four thousandth anniversary of the opening of space, Angary J. Gustible discovered Gustible's planet. The discovery turned out to be a tragic mistake.

Gustible's planet was inhabited by highly intelligent life forms. They had moderate telepathic powers. They immediately mind-read Angary J. Gustible's entire mind and life history, and embarrassed him very deeply by making up an opera concerning his recent divorce.

The climax of the opera portrayed his wife throwing a teacup at him. This created an unfavourable impression concerning Earth culture, and Angary J. Gustible, who held a reserve commission as a Subchief of the Instrumentality, was profoundly embarrassed to find that it was not the higher realities of Earth which he had conveyed to these people, but the unpleasant intimate facts.

As negotiations proceeded, other embarrassments developed.

In physical appearance the inhabitants of Gustible's planet, who called themselves Apicians, resembled nothing more than oversize ducks, ducks four feet to four feet six in height. At their wing tips, they had developed juxtaposed thumbs. They were paddle-shaped and sufficed to feed the Apicians.

Gustible's planet matched Earth in several respects: in the dishonesty of the inhabitants, in their enthusiasm for good food, in their instant capacity to understand the human mind. Before Gustible began to get ready to go back to Earth, he discovered that the Apicians had copied his ship. There was no use hiding this fact. They had copied it in such detail that the discovery of Gustible's planet meant the simultaneous discovery of Earth . . .

By the Apicians.

The implications of this tragic development did not show up until the Apicians followed him home. They had a planoforming ship capable of travelling in non-space just as readily as his.

The most important feature of Gustible's planet was its singularly close match to the biochemistry of Earth. The Apicians were the first intelligent life forms ever met by human beings who were at once capable of smelling and enjoying everything which human beings smelled and enjoyed, capable of following any human music with forthright pleasure and capable of eating and drinking everything in sight.

The very first Apicians on Earth were greeted by somewhat alarmed ambassadors who discovered that an appetite for Munich beer, Camembert cheese, tortillas and enchiladas, as well as the better grades of chow mein, far transcended any serious cultural, political or strategic interests which the new visitors might have.

Arthur Djohn, a Lord of the Instrumentality who was acting for this particular matter, delegated an Instrumentality agent named Calvin Dredd as the chief diplomatic officer of Earth to handle the matter.

Dredd approached one Schmeckst, who seemed to be the Apician leader. The interview was an unfortunate one.

Dredd began by saying, 'Your Exalted Highness, we are delighted to welcome you to Earth—'

Schmeckst said, 'Are those edible?' and proceeded to eat the plastic buttons from Calvin Dredd's formal coat, even before Dredd could say though not edible they were attractive. ╷

Schmeckst said, 'Don't try to eat those, they are really not very good.'

Dredd, looking at his coat sagging wide open, said, 'May I offer you some food?'

Schmeckst said, 'Indeed, yes.'

And while Schmeckst ate an Italian dinner, a Peking dinner, a red-hot peppery Szechuanese dinner, a Japanese sukiyaki dinner, two British breakfasts, a smorgasbord and four complete servings of diplomatic-level Russian zakouska, he listened to the propositions of the Instrumentality of Earth.

These did not impress him. Schmeckst was intelligent despite his gross and offensive eating habits. He pointed out: 'We two worlds are equal in weapons. We can't fight. Look,' said he to Calvin Dredd in a threatening tone.

Calvin Dredd braced himself, as he had learned to do. Schmeckst also braced him.

For an instant Dredd did not know what had happened. Then he realised that in putting his body into a rigid and controlled posture he had played along with the low-grade but manipulable telepathic powers of the visitors. He was frozen rigid till Schmeckst laughed and released him.

Schmeckst said, 'You see, we are well matched. I can freeze you. Nothing short of utter desperation could get you out of it. If you try to fight us, we'll lick you. We are going to move in here and live with you. We have enough room on our planet. You can come and live with us too. We would like to hire a lot of those cooks of yours. You'll simply have to divide space with us, and that's all there is to it.'

That really was all there was to it. Arthur Djohn reported back to the Lords of the Instrumentality that, for the time being, nothing could be done about the disgusting people from Gustible's planet.

They kept their greed within bounds—by their standards. A mere seventy-two thousand of them swept the Earth, hitting every wine shop, dining hall, snack bar, soda bar and pleasure centre in the world. They ate popcorn, alfalfa, raw fruit, live fish, birds on the wing, prepared foods, cooked and canned foods, food concentrates, and assorted medicines.

Outside of an enormous capacity to hold many times what the human body could tolerate in the way of food, they showed very much the same effects as persons. Thousands of them got various local diseases, sometimes called by such undignified names as the Yangtze rapids, Delhi belly, the Roman groanin', or the like. Other thousands became ill and had to relieve themselves in the fashion of ancient emperors. Still they came.

Nobody liked them. Nobody disliked them enough to wish a disastrous war.

Actual trade was minimal. They bought large quantities of foodstuffs, paying in rare metals. But their economy on their own planet produced very little which the world itself wanted. The cities of mankind had long since developed to a point of comfort and corruption where a relatively monocultural being, such as the citizens of Gustible's planet, could not make much impression. The word 'Apician' came to have unpleasant connotations of bad manners, greediness and prompt payment. Prompt payment was considered rude in a credit society, but after all it was better than not being paid at all.

The tragedy of the relationship of the two groups came from the unfortunate picnic of the lady Ch'ao, who prided herself on having ancient Chinesian blood. She decided that it would be possible to satiate Schmeckst and the other Apicians to a point at which they would be able to listen to reason. She arranged a feast which, for quality and quantity, had not been seen since previous historic times, long before the many interruptions of war, collapse, and rebuilding of culture. She searched the museums of the world for recipes.

The dinner was set forth on the telescreens of the entire world. It was held in a pavilion built in the old Chinesian style. A soaring dream of dry bamboo and paper walls, the festival building had a thatched roof in the true ancient fashion. Paper lanterns with real candles illuminated the scene. The fifty selected Apician guests gleamed like ancient idols. Their feathers shone in the light and they clicked their paddlelike thumbs readily as they spoke, telepathically and fluently, in any Earth language which they happened to pick out of the heads of their hearers.

The tragedy was fire. Fire struck the pavilion, wrecked the dinner.

The lady Ch'ao was rescued by Calvin Dredd. The Apicians fled. All of them escaped, all but one. Schmeckst himself. Schmeckst suffocated.

He let out a telepathic scream which was echoed in the living voices of all the human beings, other Apicians and animals within reach, so that the television viewers of the world caught a sudden cacophony of birds shrilling, dogs barking, cats yowling, otters screeching and one lone panda letting out a singularly high grunt. Then Schmeckst perished. The pity of it . . .

The Earth leaders stood about, wondering how to solve the tragedy. On the other side of the world, the Lords of the Instrumentality watched the scene. What they saw was amazing and horrible. Calvin Dredd, cold, disciplined agent that he was, approached the ruins of the pavilion. His face was twisted in an expression which they had difficulty in understanding. It was only after he licked his lips for the fourth time and they saw a ribbon of drool running down his chin that they realised he had gone mad with appetite. The lady Ch'ao followed close behind, drawn by some remorseless force.

She was out of her mind. Her eyes gleamed. She stalked like a cat. In her left hand she held a bowl and chopsticks.

The viewers all over the world watching the screen could not understand the scene. Two alarmed and dazed Apicians followed the humans, wondering what was going to happen.

Calvin Dredd made a sudden reach. He pulled out the body of Schmeckst.

The fire had finished Schmeckst. Not a feather remained on him. And then the flash fire, because of the peculiar dryness of the bamboo and the paper and the thousands upon thousands of candles, had baked him. The television operator had an inspiration. He turned on the smell-control.

Throughout the planet Earth, where people had gathered to watch this unexpected and singularly interesting tragedy, there swept a smell which mankind had forgotten. It was an essence of roast duck.

Beyond all imagining, it was the most delicious smell that any human being had ever smelled. Millions upon millions of human mouths watered. Throughout the world people looked away from their sets to see if there were any Apicians in the neighbourhood. Just as the Lords of the Instrumentality ordered the disgusting scene cut off, Calvin Dredd and the lady Ch'ao began eating the roast Apician, Schmeckst.

Within twenty-four hours most of the Apicians on Earth had been served, some with cranberry sauce, others baked, some fried Southern style. The serious leaders of Earth dreaded the consequences of such uncivilised conduct. Even as they wiped their lips and asked for one more duck sandwich, they felt that this behaviour was difficult beyond all imagination.

The blocks that the Apicians had been able to put on human action did not operate when they were applied to human beings who, looking at an Apician, went deep into the recesses of their personality and were animated by a mad hunger which transcended all civilisation.

The Lords of the Instrumentality managed to round up Schmeckst's deputy and a few other Apicians and to send them back to their ship.

The soldiers watching them licked their lips. The captain tried to see if he could contrive an accident as he escorted his state visitors. Unfortunately, tripping Apicians did not break their necks, and the Apicians kept throwing violent mind-blocks at human beings in an attempt to save themselves.

One of the Apicians was so undiplomatic as to ask for a chicken salad sandwich and almost lost a wing, raw and alive, to a soldier whose appetite had been re-stimulated by reference to food.

The Apicians went back, the few survivors. They liked Earth well enough and Earth food was delicious, but it was a horrible place when they considered the cannibalistic human beings who lived there—so cannibalistic that they ate ducks!

The Lords of the Instrumentality were relieved to note that when the Apicians left they closed the space lane behind them. No one quite knows how they closed it, or what defences they had. Mankind, salivating and ashamed, did not push the pursuit hotly. Instead, people tried to make up chicken, duck, goose, Cornish hen, pigeon, sea-gull, and other sandwiches to duplicate the incomparable taste of a genuine inhabitant of Gustible's planet. None were quite authentic and people, in their right minds, were not uncivilised enough to invade another world solely for getting the inhabitants as tidbits.

The Lords of the Instrumentality were happy to report to one another and to the rest of the world at their next meeting that the Apicians had managed to close Gustible's planet altogether, had had no further interest in dealing with Earth and appeared to possess just enough of a technological edge on human beings to stay concealed from the eyes and the appetites of men.

Save for that, the Apicians were almost forgotten. A confidential secretary of the Office of Interstellar Trade was astonished when the frozen intelligences of a methane planet ordered forty thousand cases of Munich beer. He suspected them of being jobbers, not consumers.

But on the instructions of his superiors he kept the matter confidential and allowed the beer to be shipped.

It undoubtedly went to Gustible's planet, but they did not offer any of their own citizens in exchange.

The matter was closed. The napkins were folded. Trade and diplomacy were at an end.

SPECIALIST

Robert Sheckley

Craft that can fly in space have challenged the imagination of science fiction writers ever since Jules Verne dispatched his travellers to the moon in a bullet-shaped projectile fired from a gun in From the Earth to the Moon *in 1865. When H. G. Wells plotted the same journey in 1901, his spaceship had the benefit of 'Cavorite', while it was in the pages of the sf pulp magazines of the Twenties and Thirties that the familiar atom-powered 'airship' type of spacecraft made its first appearance. Since then, genre writers have progressed from rockets to space shuttles and the vast, computerised juggernauts of* Star Trek *and* Star Wars. *The very diversity of these spaceships has been an encouragement to writers with a bent for humour, and there are some extraordinary craft to be found in the stories of Cordwainer Smith ('Three to a Given Star', 1965), Anne McCaffrey ('The Ship Who Sang', 1969), Stanislaw Lem ('The Invincible', 1973), and in the next item about a ship which is very much the sum of its parts—an 'Eye' that writes poetry, a 'Thinker' who stores everything 'good or bad, right or wrong', and the 'Walls' which get drunk at every opportunity!*

Robert Sheckley (1928–) has been referred to in the Encyclopedia of Science Fiction *(1995) as the 'James Thurber of sf' and the writer who has 'probably remained the most consistent and uproarious sf humorist of them all'. Born in New York, he became a favourite in the Fifties with his zany, satirical short stories that appeared in most of the leading sf magazines of the time. His first collection,* Untouched By Human Hands *(1954), was hailed as one of the finest debut works in the genre, and he has continued to write imaginative and amusing short tales plus the occasional novel ever since, including* The Tenth Victim *(1966), filmed with Marcello Mastroianni and Ursula Andress, and 'A Suppliant in Space', which won the Jupiter Award for the Best Short Story of 1973. In 'Specialist', written in 1953, Sheckley has created a unique spaceship made up of aliens who, after surviving a photon storm, set out to find a replacement for one of their number,*

*the 'Pusher', who has been destroyed. The interaction of the 'crew',
their language and moods—not to mention their ultimate solution to
the problem—is an example of Sheckley's rare comic talent at its very
best.*

*   *   *

The photon storm struck without warning, pouncing under the Ship
from behind a bank of giant red stars. Eye barely had time to flash a
last-second warning through Talker before it was upon them.

It was Talker's third journey into deep space, and his first light-
pressure storm. He felt a sudden pang of fear as the Ship yawed violently, caught the force of the wave-front and careened end for end.
Then the fear was gone, replaced by a strong pulse of excitement.

Why should he be afraid, he asked himself—hadn't he been trained
for just this sort of emergency?

He had been talking to Feeder when the storm hit, but he cut off the
conversation abruptly. He hoped Feeder would be all right. It was the
youngster's first deep-space trip.

The wire-like filaments that made up most of Talker's body were
extended throughout the Ship. Quickly he withdrew all except the ones
linking him to Eye, Engine, and the Walls. This was strictly their job
now. The rest of the Crew would have to shift for themselves until the
storm was over.

Eye had flattened his disc-like body against a Wall, and had one
seeing organ extended outside the Ship. For greater concentration, the
rest of his seeing organs were collapsed, clustered against his body.

Through Eye's seeing organ, Talker watched the storm. He translated
Eye's purely visual image into a direction for Engine, who shoved the
Ship around to meet the waves. At appreciably the same time, Talker
translated direction into velocity for the Walls who stiffened to meet
the shocks.

The co-ordination was swift and sure—Eye measuring the waves,
Talker relaying the messages to Engine and Walls, Engine driving the
Ship nose-first into the waves, and Walls bracing to meet the shock.

Talker forgot any fear he might have had in the swiftly functioning
teamwork. He had no time to think. As the Ship's communication
system, he had to translate and flash his messages at top speed, co-
ordinating information and directing action.

In a matter of minutes, the storm was over.

'All right,' Talker said. 'Let's see if there was any damage!' His filaments had become tangled during the storm, but he untwisted and extended them through the Ship, plugging everyone into circuit. 'Engine?'

'I'm fine,' Engine said. The tremendous old fellow had dampened his plates during the storm, easing down the atomic explosions in his stomach. No storm could catch an experienced spacer like Engine unaware.

'Walls?'

The Walls reported one by one, and this took a long time. There were almost a thousand of them, thin, rectangular fellows making up the entire skin of the Ship. Naturally, they had reinforced their edges during the storm, giving the whole Ship resiliency. But one or two were dented badly.

Doctor announced that he was all right. He removed Talker's filament from his head, taking himself out of circuit, and went to work on the dented Walls. Made mostly of hands, Doctor had clung to an Accumulator during the storm.

'Let's go a little faster now!' Talker said, remembering that there still was the problem of determining where they were. He opened the circuit of the four Accumulators. 'How are you?' he asked.

There was no answer. The Accumulators were asleep. They had had their receptors open during the storm and were bloated on energy. Talker twitched his filaments around them, but they didn't stir.

'Let me!' Feeder said. Feeder had taken quite a beating before planting his suction cups to a Wall, but his cockiness was intact. He was the only member of the Crew who never needed Doctor's attention; his body was quite capable of repairing itself.

He scuttled across the floor on a dozen or so tentacles, and booted the nearest Accumulator. The big, conical storage unit opened one eye, then closed it again. Feeder kicked him again, getting no response. He reached for the Accumulator's safety valve and drained off some energy.

'Stop that!' the Accumulator said.

'Then wake up and report!' Talker told him.

The Accumulators said testily that they were all right, as any fool could see. They had been anchored to the floor during the storm.

The rest of the inspection went quickly. Thinker was fine, and Eye was ecstatic over the beauty of the storm. There was only one casualty.

Pusher was dead. Bipedal, he didn't have the stability of the rest of the Crew. The storm had caught him in the middle of a floor, thrown him against a stiffened Wall, and broken several of his important bones. He was beyond Doctor's skill to repair.

They were silent for a while. It was always serious when a part of the Ship died. The Ship was a cooperative unit, composed entirely of the Crew. The loss of any member was a blow to all the rest.

It was especially serious now. They had just delivered a cargo to a port several thousand light-years from Galactic Centre. There was no telling where they might be.

Eye crawled to a Wall and extended a seeing organ outside. The Walls let it through, then sealed around it. Eye's organ pushed out, far enough from the Ship so he could view the entire sphere of stars. The picture travelled through Talker, who gave it to Thinker.

Thinker lay in one corner of the room, a great shapeless blob of protoplasm. Within him were all the memories of his space-going ancestors. He considered the picture, compared it rapidly with others stored in his cells, and said, 'No galactic planets within reach.'

Talker automatically translated for everyone. It was what they had feared.

Eye, with Thinker's help, calculated that they were several hundred light-years off their course, on the galactic periphery.

Every Crew member knew what that meant. Without a Pusher to boost the Ship to a multiple of the speed of light, they would never get home. The trip back, without a Pusher, would take longer than most of their lifetimes.

'What would you suggest?' Talker asked Thinker.

This was too vague a question for the literal-minded Thinker. He asked to have it rephrased.

'What would be our best line of action,' Talker asked, 'to get back to a galactic planet?'

Thinker needed several minutes to go through all the possibilities stored in his cells. In the meantime, Doctor had patched the Walls and was asking to be given something to eat.

'In a little while we'll all eat,' Talker said, twitching his tendrils nervously. Even though he was the second youngest Crew member— only Feeder was younger—the responsibility was largely on him. This was still an emergency; he had to co-ordinate information and direct action.

One of the Walls suggested that they get good and drunk. This unrealistic solution was vetoed at once. It was typical of the Walls' attitude, however. They were fine workers and good ship-mates, but happy-go-lucky fellows at best. When they returned to their home planets, they would probably blow all their wages on a spree.

'Loss of the Ship's Pusher cripples the Ship for sustained faster-than-light speeds,' Thinker began without preamble. 'The nearest galactic planet is four hundred and five light-years off.'

Talker translated all this instantly along his wave-packet body.

'Two courses of action are open. First, the Ship can proceed to the nearest galactic planet under atomic power from Engine. This will take approximately two hundred years. Engine might still be alive at this time, although no one else will.

'Second, locate a primitive planet in this region, upon which are latent Pushers. Find one and train him. Have him push the Ship back to galactic territory.'

Thinker was silent, having given all the possibilities he could find in the memories of his ancestors.

They held a quick vote and decided upon Thinker's second alternative. There was no choice, really. It was the only one which offered them any hope of getting back to their homes.

'All right,' Talker said. 'Let's eat! I think we all deserve it.'

The body of the dead Pusher was shoved into the mouth of Engine, who consumed it at once, breaking down the atoms to energy. Engine was the only member of the Crew who lived on atomic energy.

For the rest, Feeder dashed up and loaded himself from the nearest Accumulator. Then he transformed the food within him into the substances each member ate. His body chemistry changed, altered, adapted, making the different foods for the Crew.

Eye lived entirely on a complex chlorophyll chain. Feeder reproduced this for him, then went over to give Talker his hydrocarbons, and the Walls their chlorine compound. For Doctor he made a facsimile of a silicate fruit that grew on Doctor's native planet.

Finally, feeding was over and the Ship back in order. The Accumulators were stacked in a corner, blissfully sleeping again. Eye was extending his vision as far as he could, shaping his main seeing organ for high-powered telescopic reception. Even in this emergency, Eye couldn't resist making verses. He announced that he was at work on a new narrative poem, called *Peripheral Glow*. No one wanted to hear it, so Eye fed it to Thinker, who stored everything, good or bad, right or wrong.

Engine never slept. Filled to the brim on Pusher, he shoved the Ship along at several times the speed of light.

The Walls were arguing among themselves about who had been the drunkest during their last leave.

Talker decided to make himself comfortable. He released his hold on the Walls and swung in the air, his small round body suspended by his criss-crossed network of filaments.

He thought briefly about Pusher. It was strange. Pusher had been everyone's friend and now he was forgotten. That wasn't because of indifference; it was because the Ship was a unit. The loss of a member was regretted, but the important thing was for the unit to go on.

The Ship raced through the suns of the periphery.

Thinker laid out a search spiral, calculating their odds on finding a Pusher planet at roughly four to one. In a week they found a planet of primitive Walls. Dropping low, they could see the leathery, rectangular fellows basking in the sun, crawling over rocks, stretching themselves thin in order to float in the breeze.

All the Ship's Walls heaved a sigh of nostalgia. It was just like home.

These Walls on the planet hadn't been contacted by a galactic team yet, and were still unaware of their great destiny—to join in the vast Cooperation of the Galaxy.

There were plenty of dead worlds in the spiral, and worlds too young to bear life. They found a planet of Talkers. The Talkers had extended their spidery communication lines across half a continent.

Talker looked at them eagerly, through Eye. A wave of self-pity washed over him. He remembered home, his family, his friends. He thought of the tree he was going to buy when he got back.

For a moment, Talker wondered what he was doing here, part of a Ship in a far corner of the Galaxy.

He shrugged off the mood. They were bound to find a Pusher planet, if they looked long enough.

At least, he hoped so.

There was a long stretch of arid worlds as the Ship sped through the unexplored periphery. Then a planetful of primeval Engines, swimming in a radio-active ocean.

'This is rich territory,' Feeder said to Talker. 'Galactic should send a Contact party here.'

'They probably will, after we get back,' Talker said.

They were good friends, above and beyond the all-enveloping friendship of the Crew. It wasn't only because they were the youngest Crew members, although that had something to do with it. They both had the same kind of functions and that made for a certain rapport. Talker translated languages; Feeder transformed foods. Also, they looked somewhat alike. Talker was a central core with radiating filaments; Feeder was a central core with radiating tentacles.

Talker thought that Feeder was the next most aware being on the Ship. He was never really able to understand how some of the others carried on the processes of consciousness.

More suns, more planets! Engine started to overheat. Usually Engine was used only for taking off and landing, and for fine manoeuvring in a planetary group. Now he had been running continuously for weeks, both over and under the speed of light. The strain was telling on him.

Feeder, with Doctor's help, rigged a cooling system for him. It was crude, but it had to suffice. Feeder rearranged nitrogen, oxygen and hydrogen atoms to make a coolant for the system. Doctor diagnosed a long rest for Engine. He said that the gallant old fellow couldn't stand the strain for more than a week.

The search continued, with the Crew's spirits gradually dropping. They all realised that Pushers were rather rare in the Galaxy, as compared to the fertile Walls and Engines.

The Walls were getting pock-marked from interstellar dust. They complained that they would need a full beauty treatment when they got home. Talker assured them that the company would pay for it.

Even Eye was getting bloodshot from staring into space so continuously.

They dipped over another planet. Its characteristics were flashed to Thinker, who mulled over them.

Closer, and they could make out the forms.

Pushers! Primitive Pushers!

They zoomed back into space to make plans. Feeder produced twenty-three different kinds of intoxicants for a celebration.

The Ship wasn't fit to function for three days.

'Everyone ready now?' Talker asked, a bit fuzzily. He had a hangover that burned all along his nerve ends. What a drunk he had thrown! He had a vague recollection of embracing Engine, and inviting him to share his tree when they got home.

He shuddered at the idea.

The rest of the Crew were pretty shaky, too. The Walls were letting air leak into space; they were just too wobbly to seal their edges properly. Doctor had passed out.

But the worst off was Feeder. Since his system could adapt to any type of fuel except atomic, he had been sampling every batch he made, whether it was an unbalanced iodine, pure oxygen or a supercharged ester. He was really miserable. His tentacles, usually a healthy aqua, were shot through with orange streaks. His system was working furiously, purging itself of everything, and Feeder was suffering the effects of the purge.

The only sober ones were Thinker and Engine. Thinker didn't drink, which was unusual for a spacer, though typical of Thinker, and Engine couldn't.

They listened while Thinker reeled off some astounding facts. From Eye's pictures of the planet's surface, Thinker had detected the presence of metallic construction. He put forth the alarming suggestion that these Pushers had constructed a mechanical civilisation.

'That's impossible,' three of the Walls said flatly, and most of the Crew were inclined to agree with them. All the metal they had ever seen had been buried in the ground or lying around in worthless oxidised chunks.

'Do you mean that they make things out of metal?' Talker demanded. 'Out of just plain dead metal? What could they make?'

'They couldn't make anything,' Feeder said positively. 'It would break down constantly. I mean metal doesn't *know* when it's weakening.'

But it seemed to be true. Eye magnified his picture, and everyone could see that the Pushers had made vast shelters, vehicles, and other articles from inanimate material.

The reason for this was not readily apparent, but it wasn't a good sign. However, the really hard part was over. The Pusher planet had been found. All that remained was the relatively easy job of convincing a native Pusher.

That shouldn't be too difficult. Talker knew that cooperation was the keystone of the Galaxy, even among primitive peoples.

The Crew decided not to land in a populated region. Of course, there was no reason not to expect a friendly greeting, but it was the job of a Contact Team to get in touch with them as a race. All they wanted was an individual.

Accordingly, they picked out a sparsely populated landmass, drifting in while that side of the planet was dark.

They were able to locate a solitary Pusher almost at once.

Eye adapted his vision to see in the dark, and they followed the Pusher's movements. He lay down, after a while, beside a small fire. Thinker told them that this was a well-known resting habit of Pushers.

Just before dawn, the Walls opened, and Feeder, Talker and Doctor came out.

Feeder dashed forward and tapped the creature on the shoulder. Talker followed with a communication tendril.

The Pusher opened his seeing organs, blinked them, and made a movement with his eating organ. Then he leaped to his feet and started to run.

The three Crew members were amazed. The Pusher hadn't even waited to find out what the three of them wanted!

Talker extended a filament rapidly, and caught the Pusher, fifty feet away, by a limb. The Pusher fell.

'Treat him gently!' Feeder said. 'He might be startled by our appearance.' He twitched his tendrils at the idea of a Pusher—one of the strangest sights in the Galaxy, with his multiple organs—being startled at someone else's appearance.

Feeder and Doctor scurried to the fallen Pusher, picked him up and carried him back to the Ship.

The Walls sealed again. They released the Pusher and prepared to talk.

As soon as he was free, the Pusher sprang to his limbs and ran at the place where the Walls had sealed. He pounded against them frantically, his eating organ open and vibrating.

'Stop that!' the Wall said. He bulged, and the Pusher tumbled to the floor. Instantly, he jumped up and started to run forward.

'Stop him!' Talker said. 'He might hurt himself.'

One of the Accumulators woke up enough to roll into the Pusher's path. The Pusher fell, got up again, and ran on.

Talker had his filaments in the front of the Ship also, and he caught the Pusher in the bow. The Pusher started to tear at his tendrils, and Talker let go hastily.

'Plug him into the communication system!' Feeder shouted. 'Maybe we can reason with him.'

Talker advanced a filament towards the Pusher's head, waving it in the universal sign of communication. But the Pusher continued his amazing behaviour, jumping out of the way. He had a piece of metal in his hand and he was waving it frantically.

'What do you think he's going to do with that?' Feeder asked. The Pusher started to attack the side of the Ship, pounding at one of the Walls. The Wall stiffened instinctively and the metal snapped.

'Leave him alone,' Talker said. 'Give him a chance to calm down.'

Talker consulted with Thinker, but they couldn't decide what to do about the Pusher. He wouldn't accept communication. Every time Talker extended a filament, the Pusher showed all the signs of violent panic. Temporarily, it was an impasse.

Thinker vetoed the plan of finding another Pusher on the planet. He considered this Pusher's behaviour typical; nothing would be gained by approaching another. Also, a planet was supposed to be contacted only by a Contact Team.

If they couldn't communicate with this Pusher, they never would with another on the planet.

'I think I know what the trouble is,' Eye said. He crawled up on an Accumulator. 'These Pushers have evolved a mechanical civilisation. Consider for a minute how they went about it. They developed the use of their fingers, like Doctor, to shape metal. They utilised their seeing organs, like myself. And probably countless other organs.' He paused for effect.

'These Pushers have become unspecialised.'

They argued over it for several hours. The Walls maintained that no intelligent creature could be unspecialised. It was unknown in the Galaxy. But the evidence was before them—The Pusher cities, their vehicles—This Pusher, exemplifying the rest, seemed capable of a multitude of things.

He was able to do everything except Push.

Thinker supplied a partial explanation. 'This is not a primitive planet. It is relatively old and should have been in the Cooperation thousands of years ago. Since it was not, the Pushers upon it were robbed of their birthright. Their ability, their specialty was to Push, but there was nothing *to* Push. Naturally, they have developed a deviant culture.

'Exactly what this culture is, we can only guess. But on the basis of the evidence, there is reason to believe that these Pushers are—uncooperative.'

Thinker had a habit of uttering the most shattering statement in the quietest possible way.

'It is entirely possible,' Thinker went on inexorably, 'that these Pushers will have nothing to do with us. In which case, our chances are approximately two hundred and eighty-three to one against finding another Pusher planet.'

'We can't be sure he won't cooperate,' Talker said, 'until we get him into communication.' He found it almost impossible to believe that any intelligent creature would refuse to cooperate willingly.

'But how?' Feeder asked. They decided upon a course of action. Doctor walked slowly up to the Pusher, who backed away from him. In the meantime, Talker extended a filament outside the Ship, around, and in again, behind the Pusher.

The Pusher backed against a Wall—and Talker shoved the filament through the Pusher's head, into the communication socket in the centre of his brain.

The Pusher collapsed.

*   *   *

When he came to, Feeder and Doctor had to hold the Pusher's limbs, or he would have ripped out the communication line. Talker exercised his skill in learning the Pusher's language.

It wasn't too hard. All Pusher languages were of the same family, and this was no exception. Talker was able to catch enough surface thoughts to form a pattern.

He tried to communicate with the Pusher.

The Pusher was silent.

'I think he needs food,' Feeder said. They remembered that it had been almost two days since they had taken the Pusher on board. Feeder worked up some standard Pusher food and offered it.

'My God! A steak!' the Pusher said.

The Crew cheered along Talker's communication circuits. The Pusher had said his first words.

Talker examined the words and searched his memory. He knew about two hundred Pusher languages and many more simple variations. He found that this Pusher was speaking a cross between two Pusher tongues.

After the Pusher had eaten, he looked around. Talker caught his thoughts and broadcast them to the Crew.

The Pusher had a queer way of looking at the Ship. He saw it as a riot of colours. The walls undulated. In front of him was something resembling a gigantic spider, coloured black and green, with his web running all over the Ship and into the heads of all the creatures. He saw Eye as a strange, naked little animal, something between a skinned rabbit and an egg yolk—whatever those things were.

Talker was fascinated by the new perspective the Pusher's mind gave him. He had never seen things that way before. But now that the Pusher was pointing it out, Eye *was* a pretty funny-looking creature.

They settled down to communication.

'What in hell *are* you things?' the Pusher asked, much calmer now than he had been during the two days. 'Why did you grab me? Have I gone nuts?'

'No,' Talker said, 'you are not psychotic. We are a galactic trading ship. We were blown off our course by a storm and our Pusher was killed.'

'Well, what does that have to do with me?'

'We would like you to join our crew,' Talker said, 'to be our new Pusher.'

The Pusher thought it over after the situation was explained to him. Talker could catch the feeling of conflict in the Pusher's thoughts. He hadn't decided whether to accept this as a real situation or not. Finally, the Pusher decided that he wasn't crazy.

'Look, boys,' he said, 'I don't know what you are or how this makes sense. I have to get out of here. I'm on a furlough, and if I don't get back soon, the U.S. Army's going to be very interested.'

Talker asked the Pusher to give him more information about 'army', and he fed it to Thinker.

'These Pushers engage in personal combat,' was Thinker's conclusion.

'But *why*?' Talker asked. Sadly he admitted to himself that Thinker might have been right; the Pusher didn't show many signs of willingness to cooperate.

'I'd like to help you lads out,' Pusher said, 'but I don't know where you get the idea that I could push anything this size. You'd need a whole division of tanks just to budge it.'

'Do you approve of these wars?' Talker asked, getting a suggestion from Thinker.

'Nobody likes war—not those who have to do the dying at least.'

'Then why do you fight them?'

The Pusher made a gesture with his eating organ, which Eye picked up and sent to Thinker. 'It's kill or be killed. You guys know what war is, don't you?'

'We don't have any wars,' Talker said.

'You're lucky,' the Pusher said bitterly. 'We do. Plenty of them.'

'Of course,' Talker said. He had the full explanation from Thinker now. 'Would you like to end them?'

'Of course I would.'

'Then come with us! Be our Pusher!'

The Pusher stood up and walked up to an Accumulator. He sat down on it and doubled the ends of his upper limbs.

'How the hell can I stop all wars?' the Pusher demanded. 'Even if I went to the big shots and told them—'

'You won't have to,' Talker said. 'All you have to do is come with us. Push us to our base. Galactic will send a Contact Team to your planet. That will end your wars.'

'The hell you say,' the Pusher replied. 'You boys are stranded here, huh? Good enough! No monsters are going to take over Earth.'

Bewildered, Talker tried to understand the reasoning. Had he said something wrong? Was it possible that the Pusher didn't understand him?

'I thought you wanted to end wars,' Talker said.

'Sure I do. But I don't want anyone *making* us stop. I'm no traitor. I'd rather fight.'

'No one will make you stop. You will just stop because there will be no further need for fighting.'

'Do you know why we're fighting?'

'It's obvious.'

'Yeah? What's your explanation?'

'You Pushers have been separated from the main stream of the Galaxy,' Talker explained. 'You have your speciality—pushing—but nothing to push. Accordingly, you have no real jobs. You play with things—metal, inanimate objects—but find no real satisfaction. Robbed of your true vocation, you fight from sheer frustration.

'Once you find your place in the galactic Cooperation—and I assure you that it is an important place—your fighting will stop. Why should you fight, which is an unnatural occupation, when you can push? Also your mechanical civilisation will end, since there will be no need for it.'

The Pusher shook his head in what Talker guessed was a gesture of confusion. 'What is this pushing?'

Talker told him as best he could. Since the job was out of his scope he had only a general idea of what a Pusher did.

'You mean to say that *that* is what every Earthman should be doing?'

'Of course,' Talker said. 'It is your great speciality.'

The Pusher thought about it for several minutes. 'I think you want a physicist or a mentalist or something. I could never do anything like that. I'm a junior architect. And besides—well, it's difficult to explain.'

But Talker had already caught Pusher's objection. He saw a Pusher female in his thoughts. No, two, three. And he caught a feeling of loneliness, strangeness. The Pusher was filled with doubts. He was afraid.

'When we reach galactic,' Talker said, hoping it was the right thing, 'you can meet other Pushers. Pusher females, too. All you Pushers look alike, so you should become friends with them. As far as loneliness in the Ship goes—it just doesn't exist. You don't understand the Cooperation yet. No one is lonely in the Cooperation.'

The Pusher was still considering the idea of there being other Pushers. Talker couldn't understand why he was so startled at that. The Galaxy was filled with Pushers, Feeders, Talkers, and many other species, endlessly duplicated.

'I can't believe that anybody could end all war,' Pusher said. 'How do I know you're not lying?'

Talker felt as if he had been struck in the core. Thinker must have been right when he said these Pushers would be uncooperative. Was this going to be the end of Talker's career? Were he and the rest of the Crew going to spend the rest of their lives in space, because of the stupidity of a bunch of Pushers?

Even thinking this, Talker was able to feel sorry for the Pusher. It must be terrible, he thought. Doubting, uncertain, never trusting anyone. If these Pushers didn't find their place in the Galaxy, they would exterminate themselves. Their place in the Cooperation was long overdue.

'What can I do to convince you?' Talker asked.

In despair, he opened all the circuits to the Pusher. He let the Pusher see Engine's good-natured gruffness, the devil-may-care humour of the Walls; he showed him Eye's poetic attempts, and Feeder's cocky good nature. He opened his own mind and showed the Pusher a picture of his home planet, his family, the tree he was planning to buy when he got home.

The pictures told the story of all of them, from different planets, representing different ethics, united by a common bond—the galactic Cooperation.

The Pusher watched it all in silence.

After a while, he shook his head. The thought accompanying the gesture was uncertain, weak—but negative.

Talker told the Walls to open. They did, and the Pusher stared in amazement.

'You may leave,' Talker said. 'Just remove the communication line and go.'

'What will you do?'

'We will look for another Pusher planet.'

'Where? Mars? Venus?'

'We don't know. All we can do is hope there is another in this region.'

The Pusher looked at the opening, then back at the Crew. He hesitated and his face screwed up in a grimace of indecision.

'All that you showed me was true?'

No answer was necessary.

'All right,' the Pusher said suddenly. 'I'll go. I'm a damned fool, but I'll go. If this means what you say—it *must* mean what you say!'

Talker saw the agony of the Pusher's decision had forced him out of contact with reality. He believed that he was in a dream, where decisions are easy and unimportant.

'There's just one little trouble,' Pusher said with the lightness of hysteria. 'Boys, I'll be damned if I know how to push. You said something about faster-than-light? I can't even run the mile in an hour.'

'Of course you can push,' Talker assured him, hoping he was right. He knew what a Pusher's abilities were; but this one—

'Just try it.'

'Sure,' Pusher agreed. 'I'll probably wake up out of this, anyhow.'

They sealed the ship for takeoff while Pusher talked to himself.

'Funny,' Pusher said. 'I thought a camping trip would be a nice way to spend a furlough and all I do is get nightmares!'

Engine boosted the Ship into the air. The Walls were sealed and Eye was guiding them away from the planet.

'We're in open space now,' Talker said. Listening to Pusher, he hoped his mind hadn't cracked. 'Eye and Thinker will give a direction, I'll transmit it to you, and you push along it.'

'You're crazy,' Pusher mumbled. 'You must have the wrong planet. I wish you nightmares would go away.'

'You're in the Cooperation now,' Talker said desperately. 'There's the direction. Push!'

The Pusher didn't do anything for a moment. He was slowly emerging from his fantasy, realising that he wasn't in a dream, after all. He felt the Cooperation. Eye to Thinker, Thinker to Talker, Talker to Pusher, all inter-coordinated with Walls, and with each other.

'What is this?' Pusher asked. He felt the oneness of the Ship, the great warmth, the closeness achieved only in the Cooperation.

He pushed.

Nothing happened.

'Try again,' Talker begged.

Pusher searched his mind. He found a deep well of doubt and fear. Staring into it, he saw his own tortured face.

Thinker illuminated it for him.

Pushers had lived with this doubt and fear for centuries. Pushers had fought through fear, killed through doubt.

That was where the Pusher organ was!

Human—specialist—Pusher—he entered fully into the Crew, merged with them, threw mental arms around the shoulders of Thinker and Talker.

Suddenly, the Ship shot forward at eight times the speed of light. It continued to accelerate.

THE ADVENTURE OF THE
MARTIAN MOONS

William F. Nolan

Science fiction and crime might seem like an unlikely combination, but there have in fact been several classic sf mysteries and a number of important space detectives all endeavouring to maintain law and order throughout the galaxies. Take, for example, the 'Interstellar Patrol' series written by Edmond Hamilton during the Twenties, which featured the first interplanetary cops. They were followed by H. Beam Piper's 'Paratime Police' in the early Sixties, and later Ron Goulart's shape-changing 'Chameleon Corps', who have been turning up in magazines at regular intervals ever since The Sword Swallower *(1968). And among the galaxy's distinguished private detectives must be mentioned Lord D'Arcy, whose cases in an alternate Earth are recounted by Randall Garrett; Claudine St Cyr, in the Interplanetary Detective series written by Ian Wallace; and Sam Space, the hero of William F. Nolan's wildly funny capers, who has been called 'the best private eye on this or any other Earth'.*

William F. Nolan (1928–), born in Kansas City, and a racing driver and commercial artist before turning sf writer, is best known for Logan's Run *(1967), which he co-wrote with George Clayton Johnson, about a future where law enforcers are charged with putting to death everyone over the age of twenty-one in order to avoid overpopulation. The story was filmed in 1976—with the age of execution raised to thirty—and later inspired a TV series and two more novels which Nolan alone wrote:* Logan's World *(1977) and* Logan's Search *(1980). Nolan also has an abiding interest in crime fiction: he has written a biography of Dashiell Hammett and is currently engaged on a series of novels featuring Hammett, Raymond Chandler and Erle Stanley Gardner as private eyes solving cases rather than writing about them.*

The Sam Space stories are an amalgam of both of Nolan's interests. Writing about his character, who first appeared in Space For Hire *(1971), he explains: 'Sam is a hard-headed private detective deliberately cast in the Warner Brothers mould of the 1930s out of Bogart by Chandler, a Hammettised op thrown gun-first into the future.' In the course of his assignments, Sam has moved through space and time, changed shape, sex and age, been captured by mice, gunned down by hoods who refused to stay dead, worked for a man forever losing his body, bedded a robot, and even rescued a three-headed damsel in distress! In 'The Adventure of the Martian Moons'—which is appearing in print here for the first time—Sam is as cynical, cliché-cracking and ultra-tough as ever in a comic caper in which he joins in unlikely alliance with another legendary detective . . . the great Sherlock Holmes!*

*   *   *

I have never been a man given to petty complaints, but the inclement weather conditions in Bubble City on this particular morning had put me into something approaching a severe snit. Curtains of gritty red sand whirled and gusted around me as I exited the hoverkab. Unsnapping my nearleather coinpurse, I consulted the glowcard which told me the fare was an even ten solarcredits. I carefully counted out the required ten, added two more as a tip, and slipped the coins into the tummyslot of the gum-chewing robo kabbie.

'You call *that* a tip?' he growled. 'This is the Christmas season, bud. How much Christmas cheer can I buy with two lousy solarcreds?'

'I am well aware of the season,' I told him. 'And it seems to me, my dear fellow, that two solarcredits is an ample reward for your services in delivering me to this address. I shall not be badgered into giving you more.'

'Up yours,' snarled the kabbie, climbing back into his egg-shaped machine and whisking off through the sand.

Ungrateful clod! I gripped my cane in anger. Was it not enough that I had been forced to leave the comfortable lodgings at 221B to venture out on such a foul day upon the urgent request of my friend Sherlock Holmes? Must I also endure being insulted by a rude vulgarian? Indeed, the morning was ill begun.

I shook sand from my cape and adjusted my bowler as I approached the offices of the man I had been dispatched to find. The hallway of the building reeked of boiled cabbage, which I found indeed peculiar. Was cooking allowed in a commercial business establishment? Well, this was a most unsavoury section of town, and I supposed that the strictures of more civilised society did not apply here.

Ah, the correct door, proclaiming, in sputtering, begrimed neon letters:

SAMUEL T. SPACE
Investigations

On Earth, Mr Space would be referred to as a 'private orb'. An entire body of cheap literature had burgeoned around such individuals, replete with punchouts, explosions of hand weaponry, violent pursuits, and rapid exchanges of lurid street argot. One would hope that here on Mars such excesses might be greatly modified.

I opened the door and entered, expecting to encounter the usual secretary. Not so. The waiting room was unoccupied, although a desk and empty chair confronted me. At that moment the door to the inner office was opened by Mr Space himself. His timeworn zipcoat, rumpled trousers and scuffed brown shoes told me I had the right man. Holmes had described his unwholesome attire in some detail.

'Hello, pal,' said the shoddy detective. 'You'll have to excuse the fact that my robo secretary isn't here to buzz you in. Had to send her back to the shop to have her buttocks refurbished. Edna's a good kid. Keeps the bill collectors off my back—of which you're not one, eh?'

'No, I am most assuredly not.'

'I could tell from your fancy duds.' He stood aside and gestured me to a chipped nearchair. Then he settled into place behind an unsightly desk whose glowtubing had shorted out. I noted a brown fedora with a turn-down brim under a bell-jar on the desk, marked 'Classic Hat'. How colourfully eccentric!

'So . . . let's open your can of beans.'

'I am not carrying foodstuffs on my person,' I informed him.

'I meant . . . what's on your mind, fella? Just who are you?'

'John H. Watson, M.D.,' I replied, presenting my card. 'I came directly from the Hu Albin Amazing Automated Crime Clinic at Red Sands Avenue and 72nd Street here in Bubble City. I reside with my friend Mr Sherlock Holmes in an upper flat at 221B.'

'Sure, I know Albin's joint. Me and ole Hu go way back. He's been renting out those robo detectives of his since I was in knee pants. Last time I saw him he'd just added Bulldog Drummond and Miss Marple to his string. Already had Philo Vance, Boston Blackie, Charlie Chan and Nero Wolfe. Plus your pal, Sherlock. Who was a little wacko the day I was there.'

'Holmes . . . "wacko" . . . Surely you jest.'

'Nope, I'm feeding you the straight goods. Sherlock must have had a couple of screws loose because he pulled a horse pistol on me and insisted I was the infamous Professor Moriarty. Might have damn well shot me if Albin hadn't conked him with a champagne bottle. Hu apologised for the problem. Told me Holmes would be hunky-dory once he had his solenoids replaced.'

'Mr Holmes is perfectly sound now, I assure you.'

'That's good to hear. So . . . what brought you to my neck of the woods?'

'My conveyance was an egg-shaped hoverkab.'

'Don't take everything I say so damned literally,' Space protested, plainly vexed. 'Just tell me what you want.'

'Mr Holmes insisted that I come here straight away to fetch you. He is most anxious to be rented.'

Space made an unpleasant snorting sound. 'Forget it! The last time I rented one of Hu's robos, the damn machine squashed my mechanised cat.'

I bristled at his words. 'Sherlock Holmes is much more than a ''damn machine'', Mr Space. He possesses the most brilliant, supremely deductive mind in the entire solar system.'

'Yeah, well maybe he does—when his wires aren't crossed. But why should I rent him? I don't need extra help. My caseload is anything but fat right now.'

'You fail to understand the situation, sir,' I declared. 'Being a robot under the ownership of Mr Hubert Albin, my friend is not a free agent. He cannot rent himself. In order for him to work on a case he must be acquired by a legally qualified second party. You, Mr Space, are that second party.'

'You mean, he needs *me* to bail him out so he can go solve some case that's bugging him?'

'Precisely!' I nodded. 'It has come to Holmes's attention that his services are urgently required at Baskerville Hall. The family curse is once again exacting its fearful toll. Two of the male Baskervilles, in the direct line of descent, have, on the moor within these past months, been mauled and savaged in a most appalling manner. In each case, the unfortunate victim's head was completely ripped from his body.' My voice rose with the heat of emotion. 'Only Sherlock Holmes can save the final heir to the Baskerville fortune. Even as we speak the life of young Jonathan Baskerville hangs in the balance.' I stood up from the chair, waving my cane. 'I tell you, sir, the Hound of the Baskervilles once again stalks Grimpen Moor!'

Space was grinning at me. 'That's some speech, Doc. You remind me of a guy I worked for once on a Neptunian pig caper. Talked just the way you do. Lots of bluster and bombast. Even had a dinky little moustache like yours. He hired me to find out who was stealing all of his prize pigs from this farm he owned on Neptune. I disguised myself as a fat porker and rooted around in the pigpen—a nasty job, I can tell you—until these two pignappers showed up. Real mean characters. Frogboys from the Luani cluster. They have these super-long green tongues they catch bugs with and I—'

'Please, Mr Space, must you regale me with useless flummery from your past? I am here upon a vital mission regarding the House of Baskerville. There is simply no time for this pig twaddle!'

'Fine,' he said. 'You want to talk about the Baskervilles? I know all about 'em. Rich as sin. When they emigrated to Bubble City last year they had the family castle dismantled and shipped up here in a special rocket. Even imported their own moor. And, from what you've told me, they also brought along the family curse.'

'Indeed they did!' I declared.

Another unpleasant snort from the seedy detective. 'Tommyrot! There *is* no curse and never was. The Hound is pure flapdoodle, a fairy tale made up to scare witless idiots. I read about these two murders—and it's obvious that somebody is hot after the family. An old enemy maybe. Or a psycho who just hates their guts. I don't know who killed those poor schmucks out on that moor, but you can bet it sure wasn't any Hound from Hell.'

'You are a rigid, cynical man, Mr Space.'

'No, I'm a realist. I just don't happen to believe in fairy tales.'

I sighed. 'Believe what you must, but your intransigence has no bearing on the reason for my visit here. Will you, sir, in the name of justice, rent Mr Sherlock Holmes so that he may be permitted to save the life of Jonathan Baskerville?'

'Why me? Why can't the Baskervilles go rent your tin pal on their own?'

'Because they are not qualified to do so. A robot detective can be retained only by an officer of the law, a court official, or a licensed private investigator. Those are the rules.'

'Okey doke, let's say I agree to play in your ballpark. What's in it for me? I'm gonna need some heavy scratch.'

'That poses no problem. As you know, the Baskervilles are extremely well endowed financially. Holmes will see to it that you are reimbursed his rental fee and paid a very handsome sum for your cooperation in this matter.'

'*How* handsome?'

'He has named a figure of five thousand solarcredits.'

The rumpled detective stood up. 'Doc . . . you got yourself a deal.' He lifted the bell-jar to remove his classic hat, clapped it on his head, and accompanied me from the office.

The game, as my learned friend so often remarked, was truly afoot.

Mr Hubert Albin met us at the Crime Clinic and seemed genuinely pleased to encounter the grubby detective once again.

'Hey, Sam! Long time no see!' Albin pumped his friend's hand in a vigorous manner.

'Yeah, it's been a while.'

'You know, the other day I got to thinking about that pig guy from Neptune—the one who stiffed you out of your fee after you played porker for him in order to grab those two froggies.'

Space nodded. 'The creep really did a number on me. I had to pawn my electronic chimp to pay the office rent.' He shook his head sadly. 'I really loved that monkey.'

'Whatever happened to him?'

'The chimp?'

'No, the pig guy.'

'Well now, that's quite a story,' began Space.

'Come, come, gentlemen!' I protested. 'We are here to see Sherlock Holmes. Cannot these porcine recollections be explored at another more propitious time?'

Albin shot a smile at Space. 'So the good doc convinced you to rent out ole Sherlock, eh?'

'You got it, Hu. That's why I'm here.'

As we rode a jumplift to the upper level Space asked how things were going at the clinic.

'Well, crime is always good during the Christmas season,' said Albin, 'so I've been renting out some of the robos, but it's tough trying to keep them in shape. Miss Marple is always yapping about her chilblains and Philo Vance keeps wetting his bed. Then, last week, Travis McGee ran off to Florida with the robot maid.'

'Is Holmes functioning okay?' inquired Space. 'I don't want any more horse pistols pointed at me.'

'He's in great shape. Just finished rewiring his cortex.'

Albin opened the door to 221B and the rumpled detective whistled through his teeth. 'Wow! You've really done a job here!'

Hu Albin nodded proudly. 'Cost me a bundle, lemme tellya. It's an exact duplicate of the original London sitting room from Baker Street.'

He pointed out the bearskin rug and elephant's-foot umbrella stand, the deep armchair by the fireplace, the Persian slipper holding Sherlock's tobacco, the tall bookcase jammed with technical tomes and journals, the collection of antique pipes on the desk, and the research area in the corner, fully stocked with chemicals and scientific paraphernalia. Two alabaster lamps were reflected in the wide mirror above the mantel, and a crystal decanter of Napoleon brandy stood on the Indian coffee table.

I felt a warm glow suffuse me; I was very fond of this room.

'You've done yourself proud, Hu,' Space declared. 'But where's Sherlock?'

'In the sound-proof closet,' said Albin. 'I can't stand listening to him sawing away on his damn fiddle.'

'Yeah,' nodded Space. 'That kind of noise can drive you bats. Now, if he played a good jazz trumpet . . .'

Albin opened the closet door. 'Hey, Sherl, you got company.'

It was odious to hear Holmes referred to as 'Sherl', but the great man took it in his stride, smiling thinly and setting aside his violin. He extended a lean-fingered hand to the grinning detective.

'Ah, Mr Space, we meet again. I trust you have forgiven my somewhat aberrant behaviour when last you graced these humble lodgings.'

'Sure, sure. No sweat.'

Holmes broadened his smile. 'I am duly gratified to know that Dr Watson was able to prevail upon your good nature in having you come here at such short notice.'

'My good nature had nothing to do with it,' Space corrected him. 'It's the dough I'm after.'

'Ah, but of course. Personal remuneration is always a primary factor. I assume the good doctor named the amount I am prepared to have paid to you through the Baskerville auspices?'

'Yep. Five thou—plus what I'll be shelling out to rent you.'

'Then we are in mutual accord?'

'Definitely.'

Holmes withdrew his caped greatcoat and deerstalker from the clothes rack. 'We must make haste, Watson. Time is of the essence if I am to intervene in this dark business and save the last male Baskerville from a grisly and distressing death upon Grimpen Moor.'

Albin had already prepared the necessary rental forms, and once Mr Space had affixed his signature and turned over the proper sum of money the transaction was complete. The great man was free to go.

'You may return to your unkempt offices, Mr Space, while Watson and I pursue this most urgent affair,' Holmes told him. 'I shall, of course, see to it, my dear chap, that the agreed-upon sum is delivered to you upon my—'

'No dice, Sherlock!' Space cut in rudely. 'I'm sticking with you for the whole nine yards. If your skull gets ripped off out on that moor I don't get my fee, plus I lose my deposit, plus I have to pay for your new head. So, my "dear chap", we're together on this one all the way, whether you like it or not.'

'Very well,' nodded Holmes. 'So long as I am allowed to handle the case exactly as I see fit, without interference of any sort. Is this understood?'

'Yeah,' said Space. 'The caper's all yours.'

'Then let us repair at once to Baskerville Hall.' He turned to me. 'Watson, would you be so kind as to summon a kab?'

As I left to do so I heard Mr Albin chuckle: 'Good luck, Sam. I hope you and Sherlock come back in one piece.'

It was a sentiment I wholeheartedly endorsed.

Baskerville Hall was at the fringe of Bubble City, part of the new Martian Urbanisation Development Project sponsored by the mayor and city council. The Baskervilles had been given a large amount of tax-free land in return for their emigration to the Red Planet. As the richest family in Bubble City, they had brought prestige to the area. At least until the curse became public knowledge with the shocking deaths of Alexander and Reginald Baskerville. Now the family name was associated with madness and murder.

The house itself was massive, sprawling across a full acre, a castle-like assemblage of stone and wood and glass and brick, of crenellated towers, of turrets and battlements and courtyards and formal gardens.

Jonathan's aunt, Dame Agatha, a stout, rosy-cheeked woman in her mid-sixties who had initially phoned Holmes at the Crime Clinic, took us on a tour of the house. Holmes displayed particular interest in the library, with its vaulted Tudor ceiling and gracefully arched doorway, carefully examining several of the richly bound volumes contained therein.

Eventually, we were led to the west wing in which resided Sir Jonathan Rodney Baskerville, the last heir to the vast family estate. The lad was unmarried, and there were no other children to carry on the Baskerville name.

Sir Jonathan awaited us in his ornate bedroom, fitted out like a king's chamber; he was propped up with pillows in a high-backed gilt antique chair next to a crackling hearth fire. He gave each of us his bony, cold-fleshed hand to shake, seemed exhausted by the effort, and fell back into the pillows with a groan of pure anguish.

'Jonathan is terrified of the Beast,' Dame Agatha informed us. 'He is certain it will find a way to strike him down—although he seldom ventures beyond the confines of these four walls.'

The youth was fearfully unattractive. Small of stature, with bird-thin legs, frail arms, and a long reedy neck, his undersized head sat above his sloped shoulders like an egg on a stick. Although still in his early twenties, he was almost completely bald; a thin mist of hair did little to conceal the high dome of his forehead, and his eyes were pale and watery above a beaked nose and a thin, nearly lipless mouth. In all, a most unprepossessing individual.

After greeting the young heir, Holmes said very little, but had been poking about the room; now he walked to the high leaded windows, drawing back the thick brocade curtains. Below, spreading over a wide area, like a befouled grey blanket, lay Grimpen Moor. It was late afternoon and ominous black granite outcroppings threw long, jagged shadows across the moor's barren surface. It was a sere, desolate land-scape of bracken and bramble, of dripping moss, of stunted trees with gnarled roots, of lichen and gorse, green-scummed ponds, deep bog holes and cragged cairns.

'I beseech you, close the curtains!' Jonathan croaked. 'I cannot bear that awful view, It oppresses me mightily.'

'Why then, Sir Jonathan, remain in a room which overlooks the moor?' queried Holmes. 'You could easily occupy other quarters.'

Young Baskerville shook his balding head. 'No, no. I must face my enemy. The Hound is out there, and I cannot deny its foul presence.'

'Have you actually *seen* this creature?' I asked him.

'Yes! On two occasions—the nights my brothers met their fate. My first sighting of the Beast was when I was watching Alex across the moor from my windows. Suddenly, as if from nowhere, an immense hound, bathed in spectral fire with phospor-red eyes, leapt from a stand of boulders and struck out after my brother. It moved over the terrain with frightening speed. Alex heard it coming, and turned to face it, hands thrown protectively across his face. The creature sprang forward and . . . and . . .'

Baskerville closed his eyes against the dreadful image, lapsing into sobs, his body quivering with the horror of remembrance.

'And you witnessed Reginald's death in the same manner the follow-ing month?' asked Holmes.

'Yes! . . . God help me, yes.'

'And is it not true, Sir Jonathan, that on both of these fated nights, the twin moons of Mars were at the full?'

'Yes. On both nights. That's why I could see so clearly what was happening out there on the moor. I witnessed both murders from this very room!'

'Seems to me you could have opened the damn window and yelled a warning,' said Space, now directly facing Baskerville. 'When you saw that thing go after them, why didn't you yell?'

'I was frozen with fear,' said the pale young man. 'My throat was locked tight. And even if I *had* shouted a warning, what possible good would it have done? My brothers were doomed from the moment they set foot on Grimpen Moor.'

I posed a basic question. 'After Alexander's grisly death, why did Sir Reginald choose to traverse the moor after dark?'

'Reggie was a stubborn fool who mistakenly believed that he could defeat the creature who had struck down Alex. I did my best to warn him of the family curse, but he scoffed at the idea, and coldly ignored my fervent pleas not to walk Grimpen Moor once the sun had set.'

'Was Sir Reginald armed at the time of his encounter?' asked Holmes. 'The newspapers indicated that two weapons were found near the body.'

'That's correct,' said the youth. 'Reggie carried a brace of fully-loaded pistols with him that night. During the attack, I saw him fire point-blank at the Beast, unleashing a veritable hail of bullets, but they had absolutely no effect. I tell you, Mr Holmes, this creature is not of mortal flesh, it is of the Devil himself!'

Holmes folded his arms behind his back, a glint of determination in his shadowed eyes. I had seen him like this many times and I knew he was about to do something extraordinary.

'I intend to explore the moor tonight,' he told us. 'Both moons will again be at the full and conditions should be ideal.'

I was incredulous. 'Ideal? Ideal for *what*, in heaven's name? For the Hellhound's attack? Great Scott, Holmes, are you bent on achieving your own destruction at the jaws of this horror?'

'Not at all, my dear Watson,' he told me, a casual note to his tone. 'I have already formed a theory about the Hound, and I assure you I shall be in no great jeopardy if I am correct.'

'And what if you are *not* correct?'

Holmes smiled indulgently, tenting his long-fingered hands. 'When have I ever been wrong in matters of deduction?'

'What the doc here is saying makes a lot of sense to me,' argued

Space. 'If you insist on going out on that lousy moor tonight I'll have to go with you to protect my investment. And lemme tellya, it's the last frigging place I want to be!'

'Tush, my dear fellow,' said Holmes. 'Your highly emotional concern is wholly unfounded. I am sure no one will be at risk. Are you also planning to attend me, Watson?'

I nodded gravely. 'I shall be at your side whatever the cost. Although, in my view, such action is utter madness.'

Jonathan was leaning forward, his eyes wild. A frail hand gripped Holmes at the elbow. 'I beg of you, sir, as I beg of your two companions . . . do not set foot on Grimpen Moor this night! The Hound is out there, and he will most surely attack. Any weapons you might carry will be of no avail since, I swear to you, nothing can stop him. *Nothing!*'

Holmes gently extracted his arm from young Baskerville's bony fingers and moved to the door. 'I intend to indulge in a light repast, taken in my rooms, followed by a bit of reading in the library. Whereupon I shall nap until it is time for us to meet at the edge of Grimpen Moor.'

And he exited the bedroom, leaving us to stare in numbed shock at one another.

I knew enough about Sherlock Holmes to recognise his desire to ponder the case at hand, and I was careful not to disturb him, or in any way intrude upon his privacy, for the remainder of that long evening. After dinner, which I had served to me in the south wing, and to help calm my mounting sense of apprehension, I engaged in several spirited games of chess with Mr Space. His being able to play was something of a pleasant surprise, since I had not expected a person of his lower station to have mastered such a game. And master it he had, wresting victory from me three times out of five. In my own defence, however, I must point out that I was not myself, in terms of mental agility, with half my mind mulling over the dangers inherent in our imminent rendezvous with the spectral Beast.

During the course of these games, Mr Space expressed serious concern over the operation Hu Albin had performed on Holmes's cortex. Indeed, *had* my robot friend been properly wired? Perhaps not, given his 'nutso plan' (as Mr Space put it) to walk us straight into the jaws of doom.

And thus the hours passed . . .

Now we stood in the pitch of deep night at the dank edge of Grimpen Moor: Holmes, myself, and Samuel Space. A moaning wind had risen, increasing our discomfort, and the broken terrain stretching ahead seemed to promise unseen horrors.

It was reported to us by Dame Agatha that Jonathan was so distraught over our foolhardy expedition that he had locked himself inside his chambers and taken to bed. She herself was equally upset at the prospect of our journey, cautioning us in particular to watch out for quagmires and treacherous bog holes.

How clearly I recall the good woman's strained features as she delivered her dire warning: 'The moor can suck an entire horse and wagon under in less than a minute. I've seen it happen with my own eyes, and a most harrowing sight it is! Always keep to the solid paths, on firm ground, lest you be sucked into the bog. I pray you, hark well to my words!'

Thus, we had a troublesome new worry to add to the threat of the Hound itself. Holmes was, as always, imperturbable and staunchly resolute. Standing at his side by the moor's edge afforded me a modicum of courage on this night when courage was sorely needed.

Reaching into his greatcoat to consult his gold pocket watch, Holmes nodded to us. 'Time to embark, gentlemen. Onward! The game's afoot!'

We struck off on a narrow path over the great moor. Above us, the twin moons of Mars illumined the bowl of night sky. Carried by the wind, the miasmic odour of slimed plant life, rotting ferns and scummed ponds permeated my nostrils, a mephitic stench of mould and decay indigenous to such a foul arena.

Despite Sir Jonathan's protestations that weaponry would be useless, we were well armed. I had a loaded pistol within instant reach and Space carried a lethal .45-calibre Earth automatic in a shoulder holster. Holmes, too, was 'packing heat' (as Sam so colourfully phrased it). He had a Webley service revolver belted beneath his outer attire.

Surely no animal, however fierce, could stand against such potent firepower—yet the disquieting words of Sir Jonathan kept rising to the surface of my mind: 'I tell you . . . this creature is not of mortal flesh, it is of the Devil himself!'

We were a good mile into our journey, following a succession of grassy paths that zigzagged through the moor, and had just passed a high bank of mossed black granite when a truly blood-chilling howl split the night, a sound of such incredible menace that it stopped us full in our tracks.

The cry of the Hound!

'Ah,' said Holmes, scanning the sweep of moor with narrowed eyes, 'I see that our monstrous friend is indeed in the vicinity, just as I surmised he would be. I wager he will be paying us a personal visit in very short order.'

He spoke in a faintly musing tone, demonstrating no sign of the panic welling within me. Space, too, looked ashen in the silvered light of the double moons. We both had our guns out as we peered apprehensively into the shrouding gloom. Where was the Beast? How close?

'Come, gentlemen,' said Holmes. 'Let us proceed, but with a maximum of caution, maintaining a sharp watch for our redoubtable adversary.'

As we moved forward again, I kept darting my head around, striving to make out the phantom shape that stalked us. Jonathan was correct; only a fool would willingly venture here under such horrific conditions. At that fateful moment, in the wind-swept darkness of the moor, I could not help but believe the three of us fools. Perhaps Holmes's wiring *had* gone awry. It would explain his seemingly bland disregard for our personal safety.

Then . . . another blood-freezing howl, much closer.

It was coming for us now, and I could hear the drumming sound of its gigantic paws on the path behind us. Thump . . . thump . . . thump . . . Closer.

Very close now.

I had swung around, my eyes starting from my head in fear, a blade of ice running my spine. I raised my pistol, cocking it. Space swore under his breath, clutching the big .45 in both hands.

'Yes,' said Holmes, turning to face our onrushing enemy, 'it *is* time for weapons—although do not expect your bullets to deter this creature.'

'My God, Holmes!' I cried. 'You've brought us all out here to die!'

Holmes gripped my shoulder. 'Steady, Watson, steady!'

'You damn crazy robo!' shouted Space. 'We don't have a chance in hell against this thing.'

'Not in hell, perhaps,' replied Holmes, his service revolver poised, 'but there, on Grimpen Moor, the situation is quite different. Heads up, gentlemen, for the Beast is upon us!'

And then we saw it—loping rapidly towards us, snarling, with fanged teeth, covered with a bristling coat of ragged fur. Its eyes burned with an unholy fire in the moon-shafted night.

Space and I fired simultaneously, hitting our target full on, but our rounds passed through the charging monster like water through a sieve. All was lost; we were facing sure and certain extinction.

Then, with the slavering creature only scant feet away, Holmes brought up his revolver and fired a single shot. The giant howled in pain, falling back, slipping from the path into the sucking mire. Instantly, it began to sink as life ebbed from its body.

'Quick, Watson!' shouted Holmes. 'Help me free it. We cannot allow it to be lost!'

'But . . . but *why not*?' I sputtered. 'Isn't this what we came for?'

'Don't argue the point, man! Just *help* me!'

Sam also pitched in; working together, the three of us managed to drag the bog-slimed monster back to firm ground.

As I was later to realise, Holmes had precisely timed our adventure. A faint skein of light was beginning to stain the edge of the Martian sky. The sun would soon be above the horizon.

I stared down at our fearsome enemy. The animal was quite obviously dead, its fanged mouth hideously agape, its eyes wide and unblinking. A froth of crimson seeped from its open jaw and the rank fur covering its chest was matted with blood. Holmes's shot had proven fatal.

'That's sure one ugly-looking critter,' declared Space. He turned to my friend, a perplexed frown creasing his features. 'How could you be so certain of killing it? And with just one shot. Our bullets didn't *faze* the damn thing. There's a lot about this I don't understand.'

And then Sherlock Holmes explained the mystery . . .

'The first suspicious element I noted, within the scope of our conversation with Sir Jonathan at Baskerville Hall, was the degree of inner hostility he harboured for his two deceased siblings. I sensed his contempt for Alexander, and you will recall that he dubbed Sir Reginald a ''stubborn fool''. He showed no remorse whatever over their violent passing. What emotion he *did* display was sham.'

Holmes had always possessed an uncanny ability to probe beneath the surface of one's personality, to root out hidden truths in us all. Now he continued:

'You will, I am certain, also recall my curiosity as to why Sir Jonathan would wish to occupy chambers featuring a direct view of the area he pretended to fear and loathe. Why should he remain in a room facing the moor when he could so easily have availed himself of other quarters? When I questioned him, he gave no satisfactory answer. The truth is, gentlemen, the moor was his killing ground and he was out *here*, in this very area, on the two nights his brothers were so savagely butchered.'

'But Holmes,' I protested, 'Jonathan's aunt told me, upon hearing cries of despair from the moor on both of those fateful nights, that she had rushed upstairs and locked his door from the outside—to protect him from possible harm. She had the *only* key. When she unlocked the door to check on him later, he was in the bedroom with his horror story of what he had seen through the window. This happened on both occasions. Thus, if he were out here on the moor at the time of the murders, as you claim he was, how could he have left his room, let alone later re-entered it, having no key of his own?'

'Elementary, my dear chap,' said Holmes. 'While I was pottering about in Sir Jonathan's bedroom I came upon a small clod of hardened dirt wedged between the rug and the edge of the wall. From the distinctive colour and texture of the clod I ascertained that it had come from Grimpen Moor. I then discovered a hidden door, behind the closed drapery and set flush with the wall—extremely difficult to detect. I didn't have to open the door to know that the stairs behind it led directly down to the moor. Which is why Jonathan chose this particular room for his bedchamber. The clod of earth had dropped, unnoticed, from his shoe as he returned to the room after one of his nefarious excursions.'

'Amazing!' I whispered, in genuine awe of the man. 'Absolutely amazing.'

'Finally,' Holmes continued, 'I noted several volumes in the library dealing with the occult, each of them bearing the personal bookplate of Jonathan Rodney Baskerville. The lore in these books pertained directly to the twin Martian moons.'

'In what way?' asked Space.

'The fact that the moons were full on the night of each murder told me that our Hound was no ordinary animal. Under a full moon, certain tainted individuals revert to a primitive animalistic state. Their bodies attain great strength and agility—as we have witnessed in the case at hand.'

I stared down at the corpse. The wind had ceased and the sun was just edging the dun-coloured expanse of moor. 'Are you telling us,' I asked, 'that Sir Jonathan was *himself* the Hound of the Baskervilles?'

'Not a hound, Watson, but a wolf,' said Holmes. 'To be wholly accurate, a *were*wolf.'

Under the sun's rays, the features of the Beast began to shift and change. The matted fur seemed to melt back into the body; the fanged jaw became a thin-lipped mouth; the ferocious eyes softened, becoming the eyes of . . .

'Sir Jonathan!' Space said in a shocked tone.

'We couldn't kill him!' I said to Holmes. 'Our shots were totally ineffective. How could *you* have—'

'I used one of these,' said Holmes, freeing a round from his service revolver. He held it up and the cartridge glittered brightly. 'A silver bullet,' he said. 'The only sure way to kill a werewolf.'

'You mean, you brought silver bullets *with* you?' asked Space.

'I never discount any form of superstition,' said the great detective. 'And while I had not previously encountered a werewolf, I nevertheless took the precaution of keeping several silver bullets among my stock of ammunition. When I noted the fact, in news accounts, that there were full moons on the nights of each murder, I therefore decided it would be prudent to take these special rounds with me to Baskerville Hall.'

'Then Sir Jonathan's life was never in danger,' I stated. 'He killed his two brothers in order to inherit the family fortune. The curse regarding the spectral Hound of the Baskervilles was a hoax.'

'Not entirely,' said Holmes. 'Remember, Watson, there *was* a curse involved here—the dark curse of lycanthropy.'

I looked down at the slight pale body lying motionless in the early morning light. And I shuddered. Man into wolf, and now wolf into man.

The complex marvels of our universe can never truly be fathomed.

A final notation on this bizarre affair . . .

Of late, in the aftermath of our incredible adventure on Grimpen Moor, I find myself gripped with the unsettling conviction that my dear friend and companion, Mr Sherlock Holmes, is—in reality—the infamous master of crime, Professor Moriarty.

However, Hu Albin has assured me that I will be one hundred per cent 'hunky dory' again once my solenoids have been replaced. He will perform the operation on Christmas Day.

Which, for a troubled robot, will be a fine and welcome Yuletide gift.

THE GOLDEN YEARS OF THE STAINLESS STEEL RAT

Harry Harrison

Science fiction has also thrown up its share of double-dyed villains and criminal masterminds. The gang boss with the wonderfully sinister name, Blackie DuQuesne, was the Moriarty to Richard Seaton's Holmes in E. E. Smith's space opera series, 'The Skylark of Space', published in the pulps in the Forties and Fifties. A decade later, Philip José Farmer gave readers the renegade criminal John Carmody, who surprised everybody by reforming and becoming a priest. Roger Zelazny created the charismatic villain, Jack of Shadows. But of all the anti-heroes of sf, Slippery Jim diGriz, known throughout the galaxy as the Stainless Steel Rat, probably has the biggest following among contemporary readers. Introduced in The Stainless Steel Rat *(1961), he has since had his revenge, saved the world, got drafted and even run for president, in book after book of adventures which have seen him slip from one side of the law to the other with breathless comic audacity.*

Harry Harrison (1925–) was born in Connecticut and, like Bill Nolan, worked for some years as a commercial artist, before making his mark as an sf writer with Deathworld *(1960), a grim account of the colonisation of a planet overrun with hostile life forms. Harry has since written two sequels to this novel, as well as creating a stable-mate for diGriz in the person of Bill the Galactic Hero, whose more zany escapades include* Bill the Galactic Hero on the Planet of Bottled Brains *(1990),* Bill the Galactic Hero on the Planet of Ten Thousand Bars *(1991) and* Bill the Galactic Hero on the Planet of the Hippies from Hell *(1992). In a lot of his work, Harrison deliberately parodies the conventions of sf: especially with the stories of the Stainless Steel Rat, in which bureaucracy is one of his main targets. 'The Golden Years of the Stainless Steel Rat' (1993) finds diGriz in one of his usual tight*

*corners, and once again he has to resort to low cunning and high farce
to preserve his freedom . . .*

*   *   *

'Well if it isn't Dirty Old Jim diGriz!'

The man's ugly face broke into an evil grin when he saw me standing
there, handcuffed to the large policeman. He threw the door wide with
unconcealed pleasure, stepped out as the handcuffs were removed, and
took me firmly—a little too firmly—by the arm and hauled me forward.
I tottered but kept my balance, shuffled through the door, passed under
the verdigris-covered brass plate with its penetrating message:

THROUGH THIS GATE PASS THE
ANTIQUATED CRIMINAL
CROCKS OF THE GALAXY

Great stuff. That's the way with the police—always kick a man when
he's down. I had to shuffle faster as the sadistic attendant quickened
his pace.

'Got to sit—' I gasped, pulling feebly at his restricting hand as I
tried to sit on the bench against the wall.

'Plenty time to sit later, Pops—that's about all you will be doing.
You gotta see the warden first.'

I could only make feeble resistance as he hauled me down the corridor
to the heavy steel door. He knocked loudly. I staggered and gasped and
found myself facing a mirror on the wall with an admonitory warning
over it.

ARE YOU CLEAN?
ARE YOU NEAT?
WHEN'S THE LAST TIME
YOU WASHED YOUR FEET?

'Can't remember . . .' I quavered. Looking with trembling disgust at
my mirrored image. Wispy white hair tangled and matted. A white
string of drool on the pendent lower lip. Skin wattled and doughy, eyes
red and poochy. Not nice.

'In!' my keeper ordered as a green light flickered and the door clicked
open. He pushed me forward with a meaty hand; I stumbled and fought
to keep my balance. Behind me the door swung shut. Before me the
warden brooded over a thick file.

'Yours,' he said grimly, looking up at me. He had the face of an

VACANT SPACE

unshaven camel. 'The file of a criminal. James diGriz, a.k.a. The Stainless Steel Rat.' The rubbery lips twisted into a poor imitation of a smile. 'Stainless no more, rusty if anything.' He wheezed happily at his feeble joke, until smile turned to snarl.

'I get them all, Rusty Rat. In the end they all end up before Warden Sukks. They run and hide—but finally I get them. Even the smartest criminal grows old, grows dim, makes one mistake. That's all it takes to get caught and sent to Terminal Penitentiary. That's the official name. But do you know what they really call it . . . ?'

'Hell's Waiting Room!' Unwanted, the words slipped from my lips and dropped greasily to the floor.

'You got it. But that's what they call it on the outside. You come in but you don't go out. In here we don't use that fancy name. We have a better one. This is the Purgy. That's short for Purgatory if you don't know. Which is a word that means . . .'

'I gotta go to the toilet,' I wheezed, legs crossed tightly. His sneer deepened.

'That's all you old crocks ever do.' He thumbed a button and the door squeaked open behind me. 'Bogger will show you where the heads are. Then he'll take you for your medical. We shall see that you keep fit, diGriz—so that you can enjoy our hospitality for a nice long time.'

His sadistic laughter followed me down the corridor. I can't say that I was overly impressed with the reception.

Or the medical either. The burly, bored, and sadistic attendants stripped me naked, then slipped a flimsy grey smock over my scrawny bones. Then proceeded to drag me from one diagnostic machine to another, completely ignoring my mewling protests. Commenting offhandedly on the results.

'Pin in that hip. Looks kind of old.'

'Not as old as those plastic knee-joints. This ancient crock has had a lot of mileage.'

'The doc is really going to like this one. Spots on the lung. TB or black lung or something.'

'Done yet?' Bogger asked, popping up like a bad memory.

'Done. All yours, Bogger. Take him away.'

Clutching my clothes to my chest, barefooted on the cold floor, I was dragged to my cell and pushed through the door. Despite my feeble resistance Bogger pulled my clothes from me, shook the few personal objects from my pockets onto the floor, threw onto the bed an armload of coarse prison clothing and a pair of scuffs.

'Dinner at six. Door unlocks a minute before. If you're late you don't eat.' His sadistic chuckle was cut off by the closing door.

I sat tremblingly onto the bed, dropped my face into my hands. Shivered. A sorry sight for anyone watching from any concealed pickups. The end of a proud, though criminal, man. A doomed nonagenarian reaching the end of his tether.

What they could not see because my hands were over my face was the quick, happy and successful grin. I had done it!

When I raised my face the grin was gone and my lips were trembling again.

The transparent cover of my cheap plastic watch was so scratched that I could barely make out the numbers. I held it up to the light, twisted it and panted with the effort, finally made out the time.

'Dinner at six, oh deary me. Must get out when the door unlocks.' I shuffled up to it just when the door clicked open, pulled it wide, and stumbled through.

It was pretty obvious where the chow hall was, with the feeble horde of grey-clad geriatric figures all shuffling in the same direction. I joined the shuffle, took a tray at the entrance, held it out for dollops of institutional sludge. I could not tell what it was by looking at it, knew even less after I had tasted it. Well, hopefully it contained nourishment. I spooned it up with trembling hand.

'I never seen you before,' the octogenarian seated beside me said suspiciously. 'You a police spy?'

'I'm a convicted felon.'

'Welcome to Purgy, heh-hee,' he chuckled, cheered to see a newcomer. 'Ever hijack a spaceship?'

'Once or twice.'

'I did three. Third was a mistake. It was a decoy. But I ran out of credits, bad investments, nearing eighty and couldn't see so well . . .'

The reminiscences droned on like a babbling brook and were just about as interesting. I let them burble while I finished my muckburger and gunge. As I was choking down the last depressing morsel a familiar and detested voice cut through the clatter and slurp.

'Rusty Rat. You're finished with your dinner. So rattle your ancient bones to see the doc. Now!'

'How do I find him?'

'Follow the green arrows on the wall, numbnuts. The green ones with the little red cross. Go.'

I dragged to my feet and went. There were arrows of different colours pointing in both directions on the corridor walls. I blinked and leaned close and made out the ones I needed. Lurched off to the left.

'Come in, sit down, answer my questions, are you incontinent?' The doctor was young, in a hurry, impatient. I scratched my head and muttered.

'Don't rightly know . . .'

'You must know!'

'Not really. Don't know what the word means.'

'Bed-wetting! Do you wet the bed at night?'

'Only when I'm drunk.'

'Not much chance of that in here, diGriz. I've been looking at your charts. You're a wreck. Spots on the lung, pins in the hips, staples in the skull—'

'I led a rough life, Doc.'

'Without a doubt. And your electrolytes are all skewed. I'll give you a couple of shots now to slow the deterioration, then you take one of these pills three times a day.'

I took the jar and blinked at the bullet-sized tablets.

'Kind of big.'

'And you're kind of ill. Specially formulated for your multiple problems. Keep them with you at all times. A buzzer in the lid will tell you when to take one. Now—roll up your sleeve.'

He wielded a wicked needle. I swear the point hit bone a couple of times. With aching arms I stumbled around looking for my room, got lost, got put right by passing attendants, finally found it. The door locked when I closed it and a few minutes later the lights began to dim. I fumbled off my clothes, fumbled on the sickly orange pyjamas, dropped onto the bed, and was just pulling up the covers when the lights went out.

This was it. End of the line. Purgy. The purgatory before hell. Fed and healed to make the stay that much longer. The sentence with only one end.

Oh yeah! I said silently to myself, and permitted a wide grin to brush my lips under the cover of the blankets. My back itched under the transparent plastic patches and I scratched them happily. They were invisible to the eye, but coated with a lead-antimony alloy that blocked X rays. I had gambled on the fact that this place would not have expensive tomographs or such—and had won. On the two-dimensional X-ray plates the plastic patches on my legs looked like metal pins, on my skull dark staples. They had done their job, would dissolve and vanish the next time I washed.

I had done it! The first part of this operation was complete. Finding out about this hospital-prison had been the hardest part. It took a lot of risky work getting into planetary-government files before I managed to track it down. Risky but interesting. Guiding the twins in their successful semilegal careers had kept Angelina and me pretty busy. Now that they were successful, and rich I must add, we had been enjoying what might be called semiretirement. This suited Angelina quite well since she was happy with all those pleasure planets and luxury cruises. I, as you might very well imagine, loathed it. If I hadn't been able to polish off the occasional bank or lift a lucrative space yacht I might have gone around the twist. But it wasn't real work. Then this wonderful opportunity had revealed itself. A tiny item in the nightly news. I printed it out and brought it to Angelina. She read it swiftly, put it down in silence.

'We ought to do something,' I had said.

'No' was her quick response.

'I think we owe him something—or at least you do.'

'Nonsense. A grown man makes his own decisions.'

'Yes, of course. I still want to find out where they have sent him.'

When I had tracked him down and discovered the secret location of Terminal Penitentiary, I told Angelina of my plan. Her eyes narrowed as I spoke, her face grew grim. When I had finished speaking she nodded slowly.

'Do it, Jim. It is dangerous and looks suicidal—but you are probably the only man in the galaxy who could pull it off. With my help, of course.'

'Of course. Your first task will be to find a bent but professionally competent doctor.'

'Not a problem. Did you ever hear of a doctor—or a lawyer—bent or not, who could resist the continual flutter of bank notes onto a tabletop?'

'Now that you mention it—no. How is our expense account?'

'Running a little low. We could use a few million more. Why don't you knock off a really juicy bank while I line up the medic.'

'Music to my ears.'

But almost a year went by before the preparations were complete. There would be no rushing in, guessing or taking chances. Because if every detail were not worked out to the last decimal point I was going to be spending an awful lot of time behind bars.

Angelina came to pick me up at the clinic—and recoiled in horror.

'Jim—you look awful!'

'Thank you. It was quite an effort. Losing weight was easy enough, as well as skin ageing, hair dyeing, all the usual things. It's the muscles I miss the most.'

'Me too. Your gorgeous figure—'

'Wasted away with enzymes. No choice. If I am going to pass for an ancient crock I have to look like one. Don't worry, a few months of bodybuilding when this is over and I'll be as good as new.'

A tear glistened in her eyes and she gave me a warm hug. 'And you're doing this for me.'

'Of course. But for him as well—and for Jim diGriz so I can look at myself in the mirror. Not that I really want to just now.'

And that had been that. Pulling off an inept jewel robbery and getting nicked had been the easy part. I just made sure that the crime was committed on Heliotrope-2, the site of the original news report that had started this entire thing rolling.

It had rolled well. Here I was in Purgy and I had one week to acquaint myself with the layout, the alarms and videoscanners, before the operation went into phase two. It was time well spent. At breakfast next morning I looked around at all the bald heads and grey polls of my fellow inmates and found him at once. And stayed away. Time enough to renew an old acquaintance at the proper moment. As I spooned up the purple gruel I took everything in. And started with surprise.

Could it be him? Yes, it was. His hair was white now, his face tracked with countless wrinkles. But after two months together in an ice cave— well, there are things you just don't forget. I followed him after we had dumped our trays, sat down next to him in the morning room.

'Been here long, Burin?' I asked.

He turned his head and blinked at me nearsightedly—then his face lit up with a smile.

'Jimmy diGriz as I live and breathe!'

'And I'm most glad that you are living and breathing! Burin Bache, the best forger in the history of the galaxy.'

'Kind of you to say that, Jimmy. And it was true at one time. Not lately—' The smile faded and I quickly put my arm around him.

'Do you still get chilblains in your ankles?'

'You bet I do! You know—I still can't put ice into a drink. Hate the sight of it.'

'Yes, but the ice cave was only a hiccup . . .'

'Some hiccup! But you're right there, Jimmy me lad. After what we hauled down on that job I didn't have to work for ten years. You were young but you were a genius. Hate to see you ending up here like me. Never thought they would get you.'

'Happens to the best of us.'

As I spoke I had my stilo concealed in my cupped hands, printing a quick message on my palm. Then I rubbed my chin with the back of my hand and waited until Burin had looked at it, his eyes widening.

'Got to go now,' I said as I blurred the message with a saliva-dampened fingertip. 'See you around.'

He could only nod shocked and silent agreement as I left. I couldn't blame him. Since his incarceration I am sure he never thought he would ever read those words.

WE'RE GETTING OUT OF HERE.

The immense bribe that Angelina had paid to the city official had been well worth it. The building permission floorplans had not been complete—but they sufficed. I got close to the room we had selected on the second day, stuffed my stilo into the keyhole on the third. After being held in my armpit for an hour, the memory plastic of which it was made had softened to the consistency of clay. A moment after being pressed against the cold metal it had hardened into a perfect mirror image of the lock's innards.

We were permitted an hour in the garden every day and I had found a bench that was well away from any sites that might have held videoscanners. I sat there, apparently dozing over an open book. You would have to stand very close to see what I was doing.

That morning I had stripped off part of the plastic covering of my battered wallet. And chewed it well. It had not tasted as bad as some of the meals we had consumed. It had reacted with my saliva and had softened to a nice doughy consistency. And had remained that way in the darkness of my pocket. Now I pressed it against the mould of the lock's interior. It should be shaped to duplicate the key that would open it. When I was satisfied with the effort I held the plastic in the warm sunshine. The catalyst it contained reacted with the light and it hardened instantly.

Logically I should have waited for the right moment to try to open that door. But I had to make a dry run. Get any problems out of the way so I could move quickly and smoothly at the decided time.

Burin was more than happy to help. We synchronised watches and at the precise moment I reached the door he stumbled and fell onto the table where the card game was in progress. There was a great crashing, shouts of anger and dismay as I slipped the homemade key into the keyhole. Turned and pressed.

Nothing happened. I took a deep breath, held it—then used every iota of skill acquired during a lifetime of lockpicking.

It grated slightly—and the door opened.

I was through in an instant, closing and locking it behind me. Listening for footsteps, shouts of alarm.

Nothing. Only then did I look around me. I was in a small storeroom piled high with reams of paper and mounds of forms so dear to the bureaucratic heart. There was enough light from the small window to see clearly. I memorised the layout of the room, then moved one box that blocked a direct path. Enough. Time to go. I was too close to D Day, H Hour, M Minute to get into any trouble now. Silence in the hall. Through the door, lock it, stroll back to the morning room, where a sort of antique fistfight was going on. I was sorry we had to spoil their game. No, I really wasn't. Burin glanced in my direction and I flashed him a sort of conspiratorial wink, or tic, then passed on.

Angelina and I had agreed on absolutely minimum contact this first meeting. And the timing was crucial. It had to be after dark for concealment—but not so late that we had been packed off beddy-byes. On the selected evening I was first through the door after dinner, stumbling swiftly in the direction of the heads. Past that door and up the stairs. I had cut it too close, only seconds left. Lock and relock the door, tread quickly the few steps along the memorised path—my watch ready in my hand.

Grasped in both hands so I could draw the watch strap back and forth across the window lock with a quick sawing motion. This stripped away the surface plastic that covered the far harder plasteel of the flexible saw inside. It rasped noisily until there was a sharp click. I stuffed the watch into my pocket, seized the window, and pulled it open.

Angelina, all in black, black gloves and blackened face, was outside. She pushed the package into my hands. Despite our agreement she could not resist a softly hissed 'About time!' as I pushed the window shut.

I retired at once, the bundle concealed in my clothing, pushed under the pillow as I got into bed. I left it there after I had worked the detector out of it.

Soon after the lights were out I began to toss and turn.

'Can't sleep,' I moaned. 'Insomnia and arthritis got me down. Groan.'

I thrashed a bit longer, then rose and stumbled about the room rubbing my leg. Rubbing the controls on the detector as well with gratifying results. There was only a single detector over the door. Which left at least two blank spots in the room out of its field of view. A good night's sleep was now in order, because there was plenty to do on the morrow.

It was almost noon before I went looking for Burin Bache, sat down next to him in the sun porch. He raised his eyebrows quizzically but I did not respond until I had moved about a bit with the detector.

'Great,' I said. 'Just don't talk too loud. Contact has been made.'

'Then you have everything?' He was trembling with excitement.

'Everything. Most of it hidden where they can't find it. Let's go out into the garden in exactly twelve minutes.'

'Why?'

'Because concealed in my mouth is an optical laser communicator.' I opened my lips to reveal the lens. 'I can hear through my hard palate.'

'Hear what?' He was mystified.

'The dulcet tones of my dear Angelina, who even now is making her way to the upper floors of that office building that you can just see peeking over the wall in the distance. Untappable communication. Let's go.'

I leaned back in the deck chair and at the proper moment smiled in the direction of the distant building. My aim didn't have to be too precise since she would have opened up a two-metre receiving lens.

'Good morning, my love.'

'Jim, I'm sorry we ever got involved with this insane plan,' her voice said squeakily through my head bones.

'Only way out now is full steam ahead.'

'I know that. And I didn't enjoy climbing your building—even with molecular grappling gloves and boots.'

'But you did it, my love. You are strong and skilful—'

'If you dare add—for a woman of my age—I will skin you alive when you get out!'

'The farthest thought from my mind. What I wanted to ask is—do you think we can take out two instead of one? I have found an old acquaintance here who, truthfully, saved my life once. In an ice cave. I'll tell you about it one day. How about it?'

She hesitated a moment and I could imagine her sweet little frown of concentration. My Angelina does not speak until she is certain.

'Yes, of course. I'll just have to change transportation.'

'Good. If you are changing transportation make sure the vehicle is big enough.'

'For four?'

'Not really. What I had in mind was well, a figure a little closer to sixty-five ...'

'Message breaking up. Repeat last. It came through as sixty-five.'

'Right! Bang-on! That is correct!' I tried to sound cheerful and not smarmy. She was not fooled.

'Don't try it on, diGriz—I know you. Sixty-five—that must be every inmate there.'

'Correct, my love. Exact number. I would suggest a tourist bus. I did this kind of thing once before and it worked. Locate the bus and I'll get back to you same time tomorrow with more details. Must go— someone coming.' I clicked off. We were still unobserved but I wanted Angelina's justified wrath to have twenty-four hours to cool before I talked to her again.

'What happened?' Burin asked. 'I could hear you mumble a bit, that's all.'

'Gears meshing like clockwork. Couldn't be better. My dear wife is filled with wild enthusiasm for the plan. Particularly its new dimension.'

'What—?'

'Details later. Let's go in to lunch now. Don't drink the water.'

'Why not?'

'I tested it this morning. Laced with pacifiers, saltpetre and brain-scrambling drugs. That's why the inmates mumble and stagger around so much. I think almost all of them are in far better shape that what we see.'

Angelina's anger had cooled when we talked the next day. More than cooled. Her voice, even vibrating buzzily through my ear bones, had a positive chill that brought back memory of the ice cave.

'I have the bus. Bought legally. What else will I need?'

'A bus driver's uniform for yourself to explain your graceful presence behind the wheel. And, well—a few other items—'

'Like what?' Temperature of liquid nitrogen. When I had dictated the list her voice was approaching absolute zero.

'This is the most insane, harebrained, impossible plan that I have ever heard. I shall make every effort to see that it does not fail, that you are not injured and escape in one piece. So I can then personally kill you myself.'

'My love—you jest.'

'Try me.' She clicked off.

Maybe it wasn't such a great idea. But now that I had started down this path I had to go all the way. For the first time I was more depressed than excited. Too much of the drinking water maybe. Then I remembered the medicine I had put into the bundle for just such a moment as this.

Out of sight of the pickup above my door I opened the wall grate and removed the plastic bottle labelled DANGER —HIGH EXPLOSIVE.

In a way it was. One hundred and ten proof and twelve years in the barrel. My good humour returned in a surge.

For six more days Angelina and I had our daily chat by laser. Formal and brief no matter how I tried to be friendly and crack the occasional joke. All this was ignored. My darling was in a temper. With good reason, I sighed. Only thing to do was get on with it.

On the seventh day our conversation was most one-sided. She spoke a single word and disconnected. I turned off the transmitter with my tongue and turned to Burin—who looked much more alert now that he wasn't drinking water with his meals.

'The date is set.'

'When?'

'I'll tell you after dinner.'

He started to speak—then clamped his mouth shut. Appreciating the wisdom of my decision. The fewer that knew the less chance of any slipups. A maximum of one keeps a secret a secret.

That evening when the rattle of spoons on metal had slowed and the slurping of the jellied grey dessert had replaced it, I took my tray into the kitchen, came out without it, and closed the door. Was watched by some of the slurpers with bleary-eyed interest as I slipped a tiny metal packet over the cable to the pickup on the wall.

'May I have your attention,' I called out, hammering on the table with a spoon. I waited until the hum of voices had died down—then pointed to the side door.

'We are all going to leave now by that side door. The gentleman who is now opening it, Burin Bache, is your guide. You will follow him.' I had to raise my voice to be heard over the babble of voices. 'You will shut up now and ask no questions. All will be revealed later. But I can tell you now that the authorities will definitely *not* like what we are going to do.'

This drew nods of approval since every inmate was here because of flouting the law and thumbing the nose at authority. This, plus all the hypnotics in the drinking water, had them trooping out quietly following my orders. I stood by the door, smiling and patting an occasional shoulder as they went by, working hard not to show any impatience.

With each passing minute there was a growing chance that the mass escape might be discovered. The kitchen staff and two guards were sleeping quietly in the storeroom; the wall pickup was transmitting a recording of happy diners munching away. And the two other doors were locked. That was the weak spot in the plan. Normally no one came into the dining area during a meal. But there were exceptions. I crossed my fingers behind my back hoping that this wasn't one of the exceptional days.

As the bent shoulder moved by in front of me I sighed with relief, stepped through, and locked the door behind me. Following my shuffling colleagues down the stairs to the service corridor, closing and locking each door after going through it. I did the same thing as we passed through the cellar, to the boiler room at the far end. The fire door here was heavier and slid closed with a satisfactory thud.

I turned to look at my colleagues, wringing my hands with pleasure.

'What's happening?' one of them called out.

'We are leaving here,' I looked at my watch, 'in exactly seven minutes!'

As might very well be imagined that caused no little stir. I listened to the voices then shouted them to silence.

'No—I'm not mad. Nor am I as old as I look. I had myself arrested and incarcerated in this place for only one reason. To crack out. I will now pass through you, that's it, move aside, thank you, to the far wall. You may or may not know that this prison is built on a hillside. Which means that while the other end of the building is deep in the earth and rock—this end is level with the road outside. Will you all kindly move to the far side of the room, that's it. As you can see I am placing a shaped charge of macrothermite on the wall. When ignited this not only burns but penetrates and keeps on burning until it reaches the other side.'

They watched in tense silence as I patted into place a rough circle of the doughy substance, then sprayed it with sealant and pushed in an igniter.

'Push close together—get as far away as you can,' I ordered, looking at my watch. When there were five seconds to go I pushed the igniter button and hurried to join them.

It was most dramatic. The igniter flared and a ring of fire sprang out from the wall. It crackled and flamed and smoked; there was a lot of coughing as the smoke spread and then vent fans laboured to clear it. Then I pulled the hose from the reel and opened the valve to spray water on the wall. There were cries of fear and more serious coughing as clouds of steam added to the discomfort.

The hissing and crackling died down and I turned off the water, strode forward. I raised my foot and gave a good push against the circle of wall. It obliged me by falling outward with a rumbling crash.

'Lights out!' I ordered, and Burin threw the switches.

A streetlight lit up the ground outside, revealed the roll of carpeting.

This began to rotate and the flexpowered end crept in through the opening. The carpet was red as I had ordered.

'Let's get out of here! One at a time. No talking and don't touch the wall or the ground. Stay on the carpet, which is heatproof. Burin—over here.'

'It's working, Jim—it's actually working!'

'Your faith is touching. Make sure they are all out before you leave.'

'Will do!'

I joined the line of shambling figures, hurried along the carpet, and jumped off to join the neatly uniformed figure of my wife.

'My love—'

'Shut up,' she suggested. 'There's the bus. Get them aboard.'

There it was indeed. Engine idling, coachwork gleaming. A large banner on the side bore the message—

RETIREES MYSTERY TOUR

'This way,' I said and turned the nearest man in the right direction and led the way to the door. 'Go to the rear and find a seat. Put on the clothes that you will find on the seat—and the wig as well. Go.'

I repeated this until Burin appeared. He took over the message muttering while I herded the remainder aboard. Angelina climbed in as well and sat in silence in the driver's seat.

'That's the lot,' I said as cheerfully as I could.

'Door closed and we're away! I did this once before, years ago, only with bicycles.' I turned and nodded approval at the grey wigs and dresses, at what appeared to be a busload of old ladies.

'Well done,' I shouted. 'Very well done.'

And that was very well that. Other than my wife's cold silence everything was just about perfect. We rolled merrily into the night and were well out of the city before we saw a police checkpoint ahead. I struggled into a dress, popped on the wig, then led all the assembled ladies in a sing-song of 'Row, row, row your boat—'

The bus had barely rolled to a stop before we were told to move on. There was many a high-pitched shriek of joy and a flutter of waved handkerchiefs as we left.

It was almost midnight before the headlights lit up the sign BIDE-A-WEE RETIREMENT HOME FOR GENTEEL LADIES. I jumped out and opened the gate, then closed it behind the bus.

'Inside, ladies,' I called out. 'Tea and cakes waiting—as well as a self-service bar.'

The last drew shouts of hoarse pleasure as they streamed inside, dresses and wigs now cast aside. Angelina signalled me over and I hurried to her side.

'What do I say to him?'

'I thought you were angry with me?'

'That's long past. It's just . . .'

He stood aside from the others, saw us talking. Walked slowly over to join us.

'I must thank you both—for what you have done for all of us.'

'It just worked out that way, Pepe,' I said. 'The truth is we set the whole thing up to spring you out of that place. The operation sort of, well, grew a bit after that.'

'Then you still remember me, Angelina? I recognised you at once.' He smiled warmly and his eyes grew damp.

'It was my idea,' I said quickly, before things got out of hand. 'I saw this item in the news and felt obligated to do something. For old times' sake at least. Since I was the one who arrested you for stealing the battleship.'

'And I was the one who led you into a life of crime,' Angelina said firmly. 'We felt a certain—responsibility.'

'Particularly since we have been happily married for years and have two fine sons. If you two had not been partners I would have never met the light of my life,' I added to make sure all the ground rules were known. Pepe Nero nodded and knuckled his eye.

'I guess about all I can say is . . . thanks. So it all comes out even in the end. I think I was always suited for crime, Angelina. You just set my foot on the right road. Now I am going to have a really large drink.'

'That is a really great idea,' I agreed.

'A toast!' Burin called out. 'Jim and Angelina—our saviours. Thanks for life!'

Cups and glasses were raised—as well as a hoarse cheer from all present. I put my arm around her waist and this time it was I who had the tear in my eye.

NO MORNING AFTER

Arthur C. Clarke

And finally, to another of science fiction's enduring themes, the End of the World, about which one would imagine there is very little that could be said which is funny. *One of the earliest writers to explore the apocalypse idea was Mary Shelley, fresh from her triumph with* Frankenstein, *in a tale she called* The Last Man *(1826), and this was followed thirteen years later by Edgar Allan Poe with his short story about the world destroyed by a comet, 'The Conversation of Eiros and Charmion'. H. G. Wells, M. P. Shiel and R. H. Benson all brought their own bleak individual visions to bear on the topic, but it was not until the Fifties that any writers started to approach the idea with anything resembling satire. Among those tales which qualify are probably 'Not With a Bang' (1950), Damon Knight's account of the meeting of the last man and woman;* Dr Strangelove *by Peter George (1963), which was later filmed with a splendidly crazed performance by Peter Sellers; and the ironic 'When We Went to See the End of the World' by Robert Silverberg (1972). Arthur C. Clarke may just have made the most unique comic contribution to the field with 'No Morning After'.*

Arthur C. Clarke (1917–) the prophet of so many innovations in modern space technology and author of a string of worldwide best-sellers, was a young fan of sf in his native Somerset and has since risen to bestride the genre like a colossus. Although perhaps best known for his part in the creation of Stanley Kubrick's landmark movie, 2001— A Space Odyssey *(1968)—which was based on one of his stories, 'The Sentinel' (1951)—and his major novels including* The Sands of Mars *(1951),* Rendezvous with Rama *(1973) and* The Songs of Distant Earth *(1986), Clarke is a man with an infectious sense of humour. Indeed, his love of jokes is very evident in his collection of tall stories,* Tales from The White Hart *(1957), and individual short stories like 'Rescue Party' (1946), 'The Nine Billion Names of God' (1953) and 'No Morning After', which he wrote in 1954. His comments—and the story itself— provide an ideal finale to this collection: 'Tales of cosmic doom have long been a science fiction staple . . . but there is one with a difference: offhand, I can't remember another humorous story about the End of the World . . .'*

*   *   *

'But this is terrible!' said the Supreme Scientist. 'Surely there is *something* we can do!'

'Yes, Your Cognisance, but it will be extremely difficult. The planet is more than five hundred light-years away, and it is very hard to maintain contact. However, we believe we can establish a bridgehead. Unfortunately, that is not the only problem. So far, we have been quite unable to communicate with these beings. Their telepathic powers are exceedingly rudimentary—perhaps even non-existent. And if we cannot talk to them, there is no way in which we can help.'

There was a long mental silence while the Supreme Scientist analysed the situation and arrived, as he always did, at the correct answer.

'Any intelligent race must have *some* telepathic individuals,' he mused. 'We must send out hundreds of observers, tuned to catch the first hint of stray thought. When you find a single responsive mind, concentrate all your efforts upon it. We *must* get our message through.'

'Very good, Your Cognisance. It shall be done.'

Across the abyss, across the gulf which light itself took half a thousand years to span, the questing intellects of the planet Thaar sent out their tendrils of thought, searching desperately for a single human being whose mind could perceive their presence. And as luck would have it, they encountered William Cross.

At least, they thought it was luck at the time, though later they were not so sure. In any case, they had little choice. The combination of circumstances which opened Bill's mind to them lasted only for seconds, and was not likely to occur again this side of eternity.

There were three ingredients to the miracle: it is hard to say if one was more important than another. The first was the accident of position. A flask of water, when sunlight falls upon it, can act as a crude lens, concentrating the light into a small area. On an immeasurably larger scale, the dense core of the Earth was converging the waves that came from Thaar. In the ordinary way, the radiations of thought are unaffected by matter—they pass through it as effortlessly as light through glass. But there is rather a lot of matter in a planet, and the whole Earth was acting as a gigantic lens. As it turned, it was carrying Bill through its focus, where the feeble thought-impulses from Thaar were concentrated a hundredfold.

Yet millions of other men were equally well placed: they received no message. But they were not rocket-engineers: they had not spent years thinking and dreaming of space, until it had become part of their very being.

And they were not, as Bill was, blind drunk, teetering on the last knife-edge of consciousness, trying to escape from reality into the world of dreams, where there were no disappointments and setbacks.

Of course, he could see the Army's point of view. 'You are paid, Dr Cross,' General Potter had pointed out with unnecessary emphasis, 'to design missiles, *not*—ah—spaceships. What you do in your spare time is your own concern, but I must ask you not to use the facilities of the establishment for your hobby. From now on, all projects for the computing section will have to be cleared by me. That is all.'

They couldn't sack him, of course: he was too important. But he was not sure that he wanted to stay. He was not really sure of anything except that the job had backfired on him, and that Brenda had finally gone off with Johnny Gardner—putting events in their order of importance.

Wavering slightly, Bill cupped his chin in his hands and stared at the whitewashed brick wall on the other side of the table. The only attempt at ornamentation was a calendar from Lockheed and a glossy six by eight from Aerojet showing Li'l Abner Mark I making a boosted takeoff. Bill gazed morosely at a spot midway between the two pictures, and emptied his mind of thought. The barriers went down . . .

At that moment, the massed intellects of Thaar gave a soundless cry of triumph, and the wall in front of Bill slowly dissolved into a swirling mist. He appeared to be looking down a tunnel that stretched to infinity. As a matter of fact, he was.

Bill studied the phenomenon with mild interest. It had a certain novelty, but was not up to the standard of previous hallucinations. And when the voice started to speak in his mind, he let it ramble on for some time before he did anything about it. Even when drunk, he had an old-fashioned prejudice against starting conversations with himself.

'Bill,' the voice began. 'Listen carefully. We have had great difficulty in contacting you, and this is extremely important.'

Bill doubted this on general principles. *Nothing* was important any more.

'We are speaking to you from a very distant planet,' continued the voice in a tone of urgent friendliness. 'You are the only human being we have been able to contact, so you *must* understand what we are saying.'

Bill felt mildly worried, though in an impersonal sort of way, since it was now rather hard to focus onto his own problems. How serious was it, he wondered, when you started to hear voices? Well, it was best not to get excited. You can take it or leave it, Dr Cross, he told himself. Let's take it until it gets a nuisance.

'OK,' he answered with bored indifference. 'Go right ahead and talk to me. I won't mind as long as it's interesting.'

There was a pause. Then the voice continued, in a slightly worried fashion.

'We don't quite understand. Our message isn't merely *interesting*. It's vital to your entire race, and you must notify your government immediately.'

'I'm waiting,' said Bill. 'It helps to pass the time.'

Five hundred light years away, the Thaarns conferred hastily among themselves. Something seemed to be wrong, but they could not decide precisely what. There was no doubt that they had established contact, yet this was not the sort of reaction they had expected. Well, they could only proceed and hope for the best.

'Listen, Bill,' they continued. 'Our scientists have just discovered that your sun is about to explode. It will happen three days from now— seventy-four hours, to be exact. Nothing can stop it. But there's no need to be alarmed. We can save you, if you'll do what we say.'

'Go on,' said Bill. This hallucination was ingenious.

'We can create what we call a bridge—it's a kind of tunnel through space, like the one you're looking into now. The theory is far too complicated to explain, even to one of your mathematicians.'

'Hold on a minute!' protested Bill. 'I am a mathematician, and a darn good one, even when I'm sober. And I've read all about this kind of thing in the science fiction magazines. I presume you're talking about some kind of short cut through a higher dimension of space. That's old stuff—pre-Einstein.'

A sensation of distinct surprise seeped into Bill's mind.

'We had no idea you were so advanced scientifically,' said the Thaarns. 'But we haven't time to talk about the theory. All that matters is this—if you were to step into that opening in front of you, you'd find yourself instantly on another planet. It's a short cut, as you said— in this case, through the thirty-seventh dimension.'

'And it leads to your world?'

'Oh no—you couldn't live here. But there are plenty of planets like

Earth in the universe, and we've found one that will suit you. We'll
establish bridgeheads like this all over Earth, so your people will only
have to walk through them to be saved. Of course, they'll have to start
building up civilisation again when they reach their new homes but it's
their only hope. You have to pass on this message, and tell them what
to do.'

'I can just see them listening to me,' said Bill. 'Why don't you go
and talk to the President?'

'Because yours was the only mind we were able to contact. Others
seemed closed to us: we don't understand why.'

'I could tell you,' said Bill, looking at the nearly empty bottle in
front of him. He was certainly getting his money's worth. What a
remarkable thing the human mind was! Of course, there was nothing
at all original in this dialogue: it was easy to see where the ideas came
from. Only last week he'd been reading a story about the end of the
world, and all this wishful thinking about bridges and tunnels through
space was pretty obvious compensation for anyone who'd spent five
years wrestling with recalcitrant rockets.

'If the sun does blow up,' Bill asked abruptly—trying to catch his
hallucination unawares—'what would happen?'

'Why, your planet would be melted instantly. All the planets, in fact,
right out to Jupiter.'

Bill had to admit that this was quite a grandiose conception. He let
his mind play with the thought, and the more he considered it, the more
he liked it.

'My dear hallucination,' he remarked pityingly. 'If I believed you,
d'you know what I'd say?'

'But you *must* believe us!' came the despairing cry across the light--
years.

Bill ignored it. He was warming to his theme.

'I'd tell you this. *It would be the best thing that could possibly
happen.* Yes, it would save a whole lot of misery. No one would have
to worry about the Russians and the atom bomb and the high cost of
living. Oh, it would be wonderful! It's just what everybody really wants.
Nice of you to come along and tell us, but just you go back home and
pull your old bridge after you.'

There was consternation on Thaar. The Supreme Scientist's brain,
floating like a great mass of coral in its tank of nutrient solution, turned
slightly yellow about the edges—something it had not done since the
Xantil invasion, five thousand years ago. At least fifteen psychologists
had nervous breakdowns and were never the same again. The main

computer in the College of Cosmophysics started dividing every number in its memory circuits by zero, and promptly blew all its fuses.

And on Earth, Bill Cross was really hitting his stride.

'Look at *me*,' he said, pointing a wavering finger at his chest. 'I've spent years trying to make rockets do something useful, and they tell me I'm only allowed to build guided missiles, so that we can all blow each other up. The Sun will make a neater job of it, and if you did give us another planet we'd only start the whole damn thing all over again.'

He paused sadly, marshalling his morbid thoughts.

'And now Brenda heads out of town without even leaving a note. So you'll pardon my lack of enthusiasm for your Boy Scout act.'

He couldn't have said 'enthusiasm' aloud, Bill realised. But he could still think it, which was an interesting scientific discovery. As he got drunker and drunker, would his cogitation—whoops, *that* nearly threw him!—finally drop down to words of one syllable?

In a final despairing exertion, the Thaarns sent their thoughts along the tunnel between the stars.

'You can't really mean it, Bill! Are *all* human beings like you?'

Now that was an interesting philosophical question. Bill considered it carefully—or as carefully as he could in view of the warm, rosy glow that was now beginning to envelop him. After all, things might be worse. He could get another job, if only for the pleasure of telling General Porter what he could do with his three stars. And as for Brenda—well, women were like streetcars: there'd always be another along in a minute.

Best of all, there was a second bottle of whisky in the *top secret* file. Oh, frabjous day! He rose unsteadily to his feet and wavered across the room.

For the last time, Thaar spoke to Earth.

'Bill!' it repeated desperately. 'Surely all human beings can't be like you!'

Bill turned and looked into the swirling tunnel. Strange—it seemed to be lit with flecks of starlight, and was really rather pretty. He felt proud of himself: not many people could imagine *that*.

'Like me?' he said. 'No, they're not.' He smiled smugly across the light-years, as the rising tide of euphoria lifted him out of his despondency. 'Come to think of it,' he added, 'there are a lot of people much worse off than me. Yes, I guess I must be one of the lucky ones, after all.'

He blinked in mild surprise, for the tunnel had suddenly collapsed upon itself and the whitewashed wall was there again, exactly as it had always been. Thaar knew when it was beaten.

'So much for that hallucination,' thought Bill. 'Let's see what the next one's like.'

As it happened, there wasn't a next one, for five seconds later he passed out cold, just as he was setting the combination of the file cabinet.

The next two days were rather vague and bloodshot, and he forgot all about the interview.

On the third day something was nagging at the back of his mind: he might have remembered if Brenda hadn't turned up again and kept him busy being forgiving.

And there wasn't a fourth day, of course.

ACKNOWLEDGEMENTS

The editor would like to record his special thanks to Colin Smythe for suggesting a number of the stories which appear in this collection, as well as to Donn Albright, Bill Nolan and Steve Miller, who also made recommendations and helped in the tracking down of rare stories. He and the publishers are grateful to the following authors, their publishers and agents for permission to include copyright stories in the book: Colin Smythe Limited on behalf of Terry Pratchett for 'Turntables of the Night', Copyright © 1989 by Terry Pratchett; A. P. Watt Literary Agency for 'A Slice of Life' by P. G. Wodehouse; Mercury Press Inc. for 'The Better Mousetrap' by L. Sprague de Camp and Fletcher Pratt; Harper & Row Inc. for 'Sam Small's Better Half' by Eric Knight; The Estate of Mervyn Peake for 'Danse Macabre' by Mervyn Peake; The Estate of C. S. Lewis for 'The Shoddy Lands' by C. S. Lewis; Random Publishing Group and Jonathan Cape Ltd for 'Harrison Bergeron' by Kurt Vonnegut Jr; Ziff-Davis & Co, Inc. for 'Possible to Rue' by Piers Anthony; Peters, Fraser & Dunlop for 'The Right Side' by John Collier; Elizabeth C. Brown for 'Nasty' by Fredric Brown; Coward-McCann for 'The Gripes of Wraith' by Nelson Bond; Victor Gollancz Ltd for 'The Roaches' by Thomas M. Disch and 'The Lady of the House of Love' by Angela Carter; Orion Publishing Group for 'The Stone Thing' by Michael Moorcock; A. M. Heath Literary Agency for 'The Shrink and the Mink' by Robert Bloch; *Telegraph Newspapers Ltd* for 'Ah Sweet Mystery of Life' by Roald Dahl; Penguin Publishing Group for 'The Man in Asbestos' by Stephen Leacock and 'Female of the Species' by John Wyndham; Random House Publishing Group and Secker & Warburg for 'A Good Shellacking' by Stanislaw Lem; Scott Meredith Literary Agency for 'From Gustible's Planet' by Cordwainer Smith, 'Specialist' by Robert Sheckley and 'No Morning After' by Arthur C. Clarke; the author for 'The Adventure of the Martian Moons' by William F. Nolan; and Abner Stein Literary Agency for 'The Golden Years of the Stainless Steel Rat' by Harry Harrison. The illustrations in the